From bey..ay to the right, German infantry with mortars were relentlessly pounding the upper reaches of the beach.

Diamond seemed unaware of their existence. Following tracks left by other vehicles he gunned the jeep through the soft sand as if intent on reaching Rome by morning. The jeep's progress was marked by a series of accompanying explosions which left small craters of charred smoking earth. Sand spewed up in all directions and the air was filled with flying metal and grit as the jeep navigated in charmed fashion through these eruptions.

Several times Quilley was almost thrown bodily from his seat as the front wheels hit deep ruts. His stomach was a quivering jelly inside him when a particularly nasty lurch nearly put him through the windscreen, and his eyes saw the reason for the vehicle's sudden leap. The front wheel had hit an obstruction. It was a headless corpse . . .

Also in Arrow by Douglas Scott

ALBATROSS RUN
CHAINS
DIE FOR THE QUEEN
EAGLES BLOOD
THE HANGED MAN
IN THE FACE OF THE ENEMY
SHADOWS

The
Spoils of War

DOUGLAS SCOTT

ARROW BOOKS

Arrow Books Limited
62–65 Chandos Place, London WC2N 4NW

An imprint of Century Hutchinson Limited

London Melbourne Sydney Auckland
Johannesburg and agencies throughout
the world

First published in Great Britain by
Martin Secker and Warburg Ltd 1977
Arrow edition 1988

© 1977 by Douglas Scott

This book is sold subject to the condition that
it shall not, by way of trade or otherwise, be lent,
resold, hired out, or otherwise circulated without
the publisher's prior consent in any form of binding
or cover other than that in which it is published and
without a similar condition including this
condition being imposed on the subsequent
purchaser.

Printed and bound in Great Britain by
Anchor Brendon Limited, Tiptree, Essex

ISBN 0 09 955810 6

I

The Rogue

QUILLEY sat under the palm tree flicking tiny stones at the toes of his army boots. His back was against the trunk of the tree, his legs stretched out before him.

The stones bounced off the brown leather boots and landed with little puffs of dust in the red powdery earth. From where he sat, Quilley could see the city of Algiers. It lay like a white penny against the green patchwork of the hill on which it had been built.

A steady drone rose from the constant stream of traffic which coursed west along the coast road and round the curve of the bay into Algiers. Quilley's vantage-point was about half a mile from the busy road, at the end of a rutted earthen track which petered out in a dead-end overlooking the sea.

Quilley tired of throwing stones at his boots. He glanced impatiently at his watch and rose to his feet. He flexed the stiffness from his muscles in jerky movements which betrayed the kind of nervous tension an athlete feels as he waits for the big event.

He glanced frequently at the empty road, waiting. But nothing stirred along its length. Quilley strode nervously to his parked jeep and re-arranged the cushion on the driver's seat. The cushion covered a heavy-calibre service revolver.

Quilley inspected the weapon, rolling the chambers and checking that each was charged. He thumbed off the safety catch and carefully replaced the revolver under the cushion.

From a pocket in his denims, Quilley extracted a pack of Lucky Strikes. He lit a cigarette but the taste of tobacco was dry in his mouth. He ground out the half-smoked cigarette under his heel.

An impatient excitement gripped him as a black Citroen swung into sight from the main road and made its way towards him through a haze of dust thrown up by its wheels. It was Bouvard's car. Quilley, even at this eleventh hour, had not finally decided if he would kill Bouvard.

Humanity, conscience or respect for human life had nothing to do with Quilley's indecision on the matter of killing Bouvard. The act itself would cause him no more qualms than crushing a scorpion.

No, Quilley's one reservation on ridding the world of Bouvard depended entirely on the presentation of opportunity and the likelihood of success. There was no other consideration.

The Citroen eased to a halt a few yards from where Quilley was standing. The driver was an Arab, a red fez perched on top of the menacing pock-marked face. He had the bloodshot eyes of a hashish-smoker and wore an air of meanness which would have sat well on a cobra with neuralgia.

Wordlessly, the Arab slid from the car and opened the door for the passenger in the back.

Bouvard got out of the car gracelessly. He was a dumpy little man with podgy hands and wrists. His neck and forehead glistened with sweat. His once white suit was stained at the cuffs and armpits. He looked like a Hollywood caricature of a white-slaver, as played by Peter Lorre.

The disconcerting irony of Bouvard's appearance was not that he resembled something out of a B movie but that he was the living embodiment of the fictional creation.

He was a petty thief who had graduated to pimping by way of a succession of criminal practices which were as diverse as they were despicable. The trafficking of girls from his native Marseille to North Africa had made him rich enough to afford fine clothes and a shirt for every day of the month, but wealth had not educated him to the need to change a shirt more than once a fortnight.

Quilley hated Bouvard. This did not set Quilley apart. Everyone who came in contact with Bouvard hated him and, in Bouvard's circle of acquaintances – a segment of society which would be flattered to be called its garbage – this was considerable testimony to the Frenchman's capacity to turn strong stomachs.

Treachery came as second nature to him. Even the scum of the Casbah said of him: "Trust Allah if you can, the Devil if you must – but never trust Bouvard."

Quilley eyed him now, every muscle and nerve in his body at a state of alert.

"You're late, Bouvard. What kept you?"

The Frenchman allowed his lips to curve. It was not a smile.

"You Americans ... You have no patience."

"Patience is a virtue, Bouvard. I'm fresh out of virtues. Have you got the money?"

"I have had great difficulty."

"Have you got the money, Bouvard?"

"Ten thousand American dollars, Sergeant Quilley. No more."

Quilley's tanned face reddened with fury. Shedding his watchfulness and caution, he took a pace forward and seized the lapels of Bouvard's jacket in one pineapple-sized fist. The Frenchman was dragged forward and suspended against Quilley's chest, his heels off the ground. Quilley's words were spat at him rather than articulated:

"The price was twelve thousand dollars, Bouvard. Twelve goddamned thousand!"

Despite his ridiculous position and Quilley's grip, the tone of the Frenchman's voice did not change.

"Remove your hands, Sergeant," he said. "It would be regrettable if Achmed had to kill you because you chose to be unreasonable."

Quilley relaxed his hold on the jacket. A glance over Bouvard's shoulder showed him that Achmed, the driver, was holding what appeared to be a butcher's fleshing knife in his hand. The Arab's expression suggested that some pleasure would be derived from employing the weapon in a way which caused pain.

In his calm voice, Bouvard continued:

"That's better, Sergeant Quilley. Now, just let me remind you what our agreement was. You were to deliver eight thousand gallons of gasoline at a price of one hundred francs a gallon. That makes eight hundred thousand francs. And I will still pay you this amount in Algerian notes if you wish ..."

"You know I want dollars ... Not your crummy Algerian francs!" interrupted Quilley. "And my arithmetic says that, give or take a few cents, you owe me twelve grand in US currency. And you're gonna goddamn pay!"

"Our agreement was for francs, Sergeant Quilley, not dollars. The fact that you demanded payment in dollars has meant considerable risk for me and a loss in exchange which you will have to share."

"You're lying in your teeth, you little greaseball."

"Calling me names, Sergeant Quilley, will not change things. You can take the ten thousand or leave it. The alternative is much less profitable for you."

"What alternative?"

"Oblivion is the alternative, my good Sergeant. When Achmed has finished with you, your own mother would have difficulty telling whether you were her son or a parcel of dog meat. Please do not force me to employ the alternative, even if the financial reward for me has many temptations."

Quilley looked from Bouvard to the pock-marked Arab. In spite of himself, the big American felt a quiver of fear run up his spine. He was not a man who was easily cowed. Quilley had courage. But it was a courage which more readily made itself manifest when the odds were ten-to-one in favour of Quilley.

"Okay, Bouvard," he said at last. "I'll take the ten thousand. But don't think it's because your hatchet-man scares me. I've eaten his kind for breakfast and they just give me a pain in the gut."

"You and I ... We may want to do business again, Sergeant Quilley. It would not be wise to underestimate

Achmed. In a city like Algiers where people who kill for money are thicker than ants on a dung-heap, Achmed is an artist. And he loves his work ... Art for art's sake, you might say."

"I'll take your word for it. He's a real Michelangelo with that potato peeler. In the meantime, do I die of old age or do I get the money?"

Bouvard stared at the American insolently. Some other time, his look said. Right now, you can talk tough but I am patient. Some other time, your usefulness will be over and your quick tongue will sing another tune.

Quilley stared back, reading the other's mind like a tickertape. It helped him reach a decision.

Bouvard called back over his shoulder:

"Achmed, get the money from the car."

The Arab sheathed the knife with a grimace of disappointment and went to the Citroen. He returned with a canvas bag. He tossed it at Quilley who caught it neatly without taking his eyes off the Arab.

Quilley's stare was iced with challenge, not a flicker of fear. The Arab met it with equal intensity.

For a few moments, all the race hatred in the world was polarised in the two men.

Quilley: tall, blond, with piercing blue eyes; the pink-skinned Caucasian brimful of superiority and arrogance. The Arab: dark, swarthy, brown eyes flashing a lust for revenge for a millennium of real or imagined wrongs.

Quilley, with a swagger of bravado, turned his back and walked round the jeep, brushing his hand along the name painted in white tarbrush lettering, "Tillie the Toiler". He carefully placed the canvas bag on the open seat. While seeming to steady the bag upright with his left hand, the fingers of his right reached under the seat cushion until they closed over the butt of the heavy revolver. He made no move to use it until Achmed turned at a gesture from Bouvard to open the Citroen's door for his master.

As soon as the Arab's back was turned, Quilley raised the gun, levelled it on the crook of his left elbow against the jeep's hood, and fired twice. One bullet hit the Arab's spine about three inches below the neck. The other went through the body below the left shoulder, shattering the heart.

Bouvard, taken by surprise, half turned and threw up an arm as if to protect himself. There was a look of incredulity on his face as Quilley aimed and pressed the trigger a third time. Bouvard crashed backwards over the mudguard of the Citroen, the blood bursting over his face in a grotesque mask.

Quilley made certain that both men were quite dead before tucking the pistol in the waistband of his trousers. He then worked quickly.

He wrestled both bodies into the back seat of the Citroen. From the jeep he took a can of gasoline and emptied it over the car's interior.

The ground sloped gently down towards a crag which dropped vertically to rocky beach below. Quilley paused only long enough to light a cigarette, aware that he was running a risk in the fume-laden atmosphere. He leaned into the Citroen and released the handbrake. The vehicle began to run slowly forward.

Quilley tossed the glowing cigarette into the car and threw himself backwards in one fluid movement. For a sickening moment he thought the Citroen was going to stop. The conflagration he expected to erupt did not immediately occur.

Then, slowly, the car began to edge forward again towards the crag. From inside there came a burst of flame. There was a puff of sound as the first tongue licked over the leather upholstery, then it seemed to rush in all directions until the interior was enveloped. Oily smoke gushed from the open driver's window and blackened and cracked the glass of the others.

The lumbering inferno accelerated in its long slither towards the edge of the crag, where it teetered for a moment before somersaulting to the beach below. The Citroen stood crazily on its long black snout, flames leaping from it, then it disintegrated with a rush of sound.

Pieces of torn metal rained down, rattling and clanking an anti-climactic succession of discords to end the noisy requiem.

Quilley was already in the jeep, the engine revving fiercely. Dust rose in a cloud as he bumped the vehicle along the pitted track towards the main road. Some startled Arabs were running from the road junction towards him, obviously curious about the explosion they had heard. They scattered out of Quilley's way as he roared past them. He wove into the Algiers-bound traffic ahead of a lumbering British army truck. He put his foot hard down.

During that summer in Algiers, explosions rang out at many times of the day and night. Some were big – like one at the docks which was heard in faraway Oran and claimed three hundred lives – and others were small. The one which marked the end of Bouvard's Citroen went almost unnoticed. Quilley could not believe his luck. To him it had sounded like the last trump and the panic, which had frayed his nerve ends in his desperation to put distance between himself and the scene, subsided only slowly.

He had expected sirens, bells, whistles and an instant concurrence of police, fire engines, and trigger-happy military patrols. But there was none of that.

On the city outskirts, Quilley slowed the jeep and drove carefully in the heavy traffic. Most of the bigger army trucks on the road were taking the low road to the docks. Quilley filtered left to the south of the city then back towards the coast again, following the Oran signposts.

There were beads of sweat on his forehead and his blond hair was damp with the steady excretion from the pores of his scalp. But the racing of his pulse had slowed now. A smile flickered across his lips at the memory of Bouvard's dying look of incredulity. He had outfoxed the Frenchman.

Bouvard, he knew, would have killed him the moment he ceased to be of value. But Bouvard was the type who would milk the goat dry before killing it for meat. Not Quilley.

Quilley knew there were always other goats to be milked.

The bag of American dollars beside him gave him a comfortable feeling. He reckoned the loot put him further on the way to becoming the richest sergeant in the US army. Not that he intended to blow it. Quilley knew how to use money in the pursuit of power. With money, palms could be greased, mouths could be shut, blind eyes turned.

Quilley used money to gain power over weaker men. Then he used that power to obtain more money. It was a never-ending progression to which Quilley saw no end. Only that Quilley would possess money and power in ever-increasing quantities.

The fact that his country was at war was a nuisance – but the fact had also presented him with the opportunity of dishonesty on a scale which would have been impossible in any other circumstances. So he tolerated the fact of war.

In a similar way, he tolerated the army as an institution which could serve him profitably for as long as he had to be in it. Not the other way round. There was no question of the army using Quilley. He used it. And he used the people in it. True, he had only the rank of a sergeant, but a five-star general would not have been ashamed of Quilley's power and influence over officers and men throughout the North African theatre of operations.

Quilley was a fixer. At least three full colonels who had found him a magnificent organiser of nubile girls and the best Scotch whisky had wondered how on earth he did it when they should have been wondering *why*. They were now paying heavily for his silence concerning their indiscretions and, consequently, getting deeper and deeper into his power. He seldom extorted money from them. He simply asked favours, like a signed requisition for a three-ton truck loaded with PX supplies for a unit which didn't exist. Or a receipt for a consignment of tyres or gasoline which would never be delivered. The officers signed their names on slips of paper – and then lay awake at nights thinking of courts-martial and penitentiaries.

Yes, the money on the seat beside Quilley made him feel

good. It would help to make sure that his war was not only comfortable and safe but more profitable than ever before.

Quilley was aware that, today, there seemed even more traffic on the road than was normal. Several truck-loads of infantry in full combat kit passed heading east. They were probably shipping out from Algiers. Something big seemed afoot and Quilley was glad he wasn't involved.

Suckers, he thought. Those tense-faced foot-sloggers would be eating dirt and dodging lead sometime soon and they were welcome to it. He'd think about them with tears in his eyes as he got drunk on muscadel and rented his pleasures from some full-breasted Arab whose brains were all in her pelvis. But it was to be no Arab girl tonight. No, the confidence and security which were welling up in Quilley flashed a vision of white haughty flesh to his brain. Until now, that flesh had been remote, untouchable, beyond any price he could offer. But he had removed one barrier. Tonight, the others would fall.

Quilley turned the jeep off the Oran road. He was driving south now towards a white flat-roofed building, standing alone and surrounded on three sides by pleasant groves of trees. It had once been a private school for the daughters of rich French colonials. It was now headquarters of 1st Divisional Supply Company, 467 Ordnance & Transport Battalion.

Quilley had a better billet than the Company Commander. He had secured a first-floor room formerly tenanted by a comfort-loving principal teacher of languages. His commanding officer, on the other hand, bunked in what had been the Headmistress' quarters – and that lady must have been a member of a particularly ascetic holy order. His two-roomed suite was spacious enough but resembled a compromise between a prison cell and a religious shrine. With small narrow windows, it was sparse of comfort and light but rich in the spiritual inspiration afforded by sundry statues of saints set in high wall niches.

Quilley wasn't wild about saints. He had never met any. He drove the jeep past the main building and round to a yard at the rear. Here, three out-houses formed three sides of a square. A couple of GIs on fatigue duty were emptying trash cans into an open civilian truck of some antiquity.

The GIs didn't even look up as Quilley drove past them and nosed the jeep through the broad open doorway of what, in former days, had been a stable.

He closed the door of the stable and, by the light from two broad skylights in the roof, began to work on the rear floor of the jeep with a screwdriver. Lifting out a rubber floor-cover, he removed a metal panel to reveal a rectangular cavity which had been constructed below the false floor. It was packed with American currency. He took the ten thousand dollars obtained from Bouvard and neatly packed the money with the rest of his hoard. Then he replaced the floor panel, made fast the screws and covered it with the rubber mat. Next, he removed the rotor arm from the vehicle's engine, pocketed it and left the stable, locking the door from the outside.

As he passed the trash truck, he threw the canvas bag which had contained the money in amongst its load of rubbish. He was whistling tunelessly as he made his way towards the main building.

The biggest classroom in the former school had been converted into a main office, and this had been sub-divided into small cubicled departments by shoulder-height plaster-board partitions. Quilley made for his desk in one of these corner cubicles.

Corporal Garcia, a sallow-skinned Mexican from Santa Barbara, looked up from a sheaf of papers as Quilley passed. "The Old Man's been lookin' for you, Sergeant," he said. "Said he wanted to see you the moment you showed up."

Quilley halted, aware that the eyes of everyone in the office were on him. They all knew that Quilley was the real boss of this outfit, that he had the Old Man under his thumb, and they were as surprised and as curious as Quilley at this unexpected summons. They wondered if, at last,

Quilley had gone too far and if the Old Man was finally about to stand up to him.

Quilley grinned at the room at large. He knew precisely what the others were thinking and he had no intention of losing face.

"So the Captain wants to see me, does he, Mex? Well, ain't that a shame. He didn't make no appointment. Reckon he'll just have to wait until I'm good and ready."

He picked up a copy of *Stars and Stripes* from the Corporal's desk, put the newspaper under his arm, and walked unhurriedly to his desk. Then, lighting a cigarette with deliberation, he sat back in his chair, placed his feet on the desk, and began to read the paper. Corporal Garcia shrugged his shoulders, made a face at the GI standing across from him, and continued with his work.

Quilley idled away fifteen minutes then got to his feet. He reckoned he had allowed sufficient time to pass to make the desired impression. He felt a vague unease over the summons from Captain Honeyman.

Honeyman had a capacity for acting first and thinking later.

It had happened at Camp Pilling back in the States, when they had been waiting to go overseas. Honeyman was married, very much a family man – but Quilley had observed the Captain's struggle with himself to come to terms with enforced celibacy.

Thousands of miles from his family, on the eve of going to war overseas, Honeyman had wanted desperately to break out from the prison of his Baptist upbringing and small-town respectability. To kick over the traces. He wanted to enjoy women and booze with the same uncaring gaiety as the other men in uniform.

Quilley had made it easy for him.

He had taken an almost patronising interest in his captain's welfare. Quilley had always seemed to be around when Honeyman was at his loneliest, bowed down by his inhibitions, and missing the solace of his wife's bed.

"It must be hard for a married man to have his life turned

upside down by war," Quilley would sympathise. "What you need, sir, is a night on the town. You work yourself too hard and you never let your hair down like the other officers. The General wouldn't approve."

"The General?"

"Sure. General Ridge. Old Tiger-guts. I used to be his driver."

"Are you kidding me, Sergeant? The Base Commander has always struck me as being stuffy and straight-laced. He busted a major only last week for hitting the bottle."

"Begging your pardon, sir, but Major Lickley was busted for making a mess of the catering accounts. The General don't bother about a man getting drunk – if he ain't hittin' the sauce in army time."

"And you honestly think the General would sleep happier in his bed if his company commanders went on a binge every so often?"

"I know it, sir. He told me often enough. 'The best officers are hellers,' he used to say. 'They like their women soft and their liquor hard.' Old Tiger-guts sure likes his liquor and his women anyway."

"But his wife ... They seem so happy."

"They *are* happy, Captain. What she don't know about don't cause her no grief. The General was always discreet. What was it he always used to say? Oh, yeah ... 'A private generally goes drinking and whoring but a general goes whoring and drinking privately.'"

"I don't believe it, Quilley. Where did he get his women?"

"They're always available, Captain – on both sides of the tracks. I gave him a few addresses myself."

"*You* did?"

"Sure. I know where the good times are. Not that I tell everybody. Any time you want fixed up with a broad, sir, all you gotta do is say the word."

It had taken only two more lonely nights before Captain Honeyman had said the word.

Quilley had telephoned a number in Falls City.

"That you, Doreen? It's Frank here. Frank Quilley. I want you to do me a favour."

There had been a tinkle of sound from the other end of the line which had caused Quilley to smile.

"No, honey, that's not what I meant though I sure would like to take you up on it. Look, I've got a friend who's kinda lonely. I thought you might cheer him up, get yourselves a good time ..."

When, finally, Quilley had laid down the telephone, he had beamed at Captain Honeyman.

The Captain, who had scarcely so much as looked at another woman during six years of marriage, had flung himself into the forbidden delights of adultery with a prodigality which astounded even himself. With the bravado that sheep-stealing would earn as severe a penalty as lamb-stealing, he had plunged into extramarital adventure as if determined to become the last of the big-time bovine rustlers.

He had found in Doreen Roberts a woman whose carnal appetite matched his own. There was no depth to the relationship. Each had an animal body hunger which demanded appeasement. It had no thought or care for the morrow.

Tomorrow had come weeks later for Captain Honeyman when Quilley came to him and said, "Captain, will you do me a favour?"

When the nature of the favour had been revealed, Honeyman had categorically refused. Quilley, containing surprise and anger, had said he'd been in touch with Doreen Roberts. She had been wanting to know the Captain's home address. So far, he hadn't revealed it.

Honeyman had huffed and he'd puffed but, in the end, had given in to Quilley's blackmail. From that moment, Quilley was the master.

From time to time Honeyman had tried to break free from Quilley's stranglehold but, each time, his nerve had failed at the last moment. Honeyman's initial folly – his liaison with Doreen Roberts – was now the least of his worries. There were the "favours" he had done for Quilley:

falsification of army documents, misuse of army equipment, failure to notify transfer of vehicles, misappropriation of stores and funds.

Officers had been jailed for much less than some of the charges which could be thrown at Honeyman. He was like a man in a morass. And every time he had tried to get out, Quilley had been there to push him deeper in the mire, humiliating him in the process as a punishment for daring to challenge him.

Quilley, however, had an uneasy feeling about Honeyman. There was still in the Captain a damn-the-consequences streak. He was capable of doing something completely irrational, like resigning himself to the worst but making sure Quilley went down with him.

Quilley was afraid that he might have pushed Honeyman just too far. He was right.

2

The Reluctant Volunteer

SAMUEL HONEYMAN was acutely aware of the uncomfortable silence. Damn Quilley, he thought. Where the hell was the man?

The young Lieutenant sitting across from Honeyman in the latter's office sensed the Captain's agitation. They had run out of small talk.

There was a knock at the door.

"Come!" bellowed Honeyman.

Quilley came in. An insolent smile cloaked the strange uneasiness he was feeling.

"You wanted to see me, Captain?"

"Yes, Sergeant, I do. For a start, I want to know where the hell you've been?"

This angry, authoritative Honeyman was not the Honeyman that Quilley had come to expect. Was he putting on a show for this other officer?

"Sorry I wasn't around, Captain. I had to go to Transit Four and check out some radio trucks."

"Is that so? That'll be why Embarkation Control have just been on the phone asking me when the hell you're gonna show at Transit Four and let them move those radio trucks out!"

Quilley was taken by surprise.

"There must be some misunderstanding, sir. I don't understand it."

"Well, I understand it, Sergeant. You are a goddamned liar. You're just lucky that the foul-up at Transit Four isn't the foul-up I want to see you about right now."

Quilley reddened. Captain Sonofabitch Honeyman was going to pay for this little bit of mouth-shooting. But all in good time. Just what was the silly mothersucking upstart leading up to?

There was a determined almost desperate look in Honeyman's eyes.

"Yesterday, Sergeant, I gave you explicit orders about six vehicles in the service compound ..."

"Yeah. The four utility wagons and two jeeps."

"They were to be ready by fourteen hundred hours today," rasped Honeyman.

"Well ... ? Sir," Quilley added belatedly for the benefit of the watching Lieutenant. He was puzzled.

"One of the jeeps needs a new dynamo, the brakes are all to hell, the clutch slips, the radiator's full of holes ... It doesn't need servicing ... The goddamned thing needs to be rebuilt!"

"So, it's ready for the junk heap ... sir. That kind of thing happens. I don't know what you're getting at, sir."

"You said you had personally checked those vehicles, Sergeant, and that all of them would be serviced and ready to ship out at fourteen hundred hours today."

"We'll just have to get a replacement jeep. I'll phone Jensen at Division workshop ..."

"I've already phoned Jensen," said Honeyman. "I have also phoned every Vehicle Supply unit between here and Oran. There is not one single jeep going spare this afternoon in the whole of North Africa. It would be easier to lay hands on a twenty-ton bar of solid platinum. They are almost but not quite as scarce as jeeps."

Quilley grinned with relief. Honeyman was steamed up over a jeep. One lousy jeep. That was no problem.

"I could get a jeep, sir. All I need is a coupla hours. I'll have one back here quicker than ..."

"We don't have two hours," said Honeyman stonily. "And I don't want the British or the French on my neck because you stole one of their vehicles."

"I didn't say nothing about stealing, sir ..."

"You don't need to. I know you too well. No, Sergeant

Quilley, there is a simple solution to the problem – one you are not going to like, but it's expedient."

Quilley waited. Honeyman seemed to be enjoying the moment, aware of the other's apprehension.

"I've been looking at the servicing log, Sergeant," Honeyman paused, smiling. "You personally serviced a jeep this morning. The workshop sergeant says you always service this vehicle yourself, that you won't let anyone else near it. Perhaps you have the English crown jewels hidden under the seat?"

Quilley blanched. Honeyman's shot-in-the-dark remark was nearer the truth than bore thinking about.

Honeyman was grinning at him like an idiot.

"I am requisitioning *your* jeep, Sergeant Quilley," he announced as if it were an immense joke. "Lieutenant Holcroft here will give you a receipt for it. All you have to do is hand over the keys – and also the rotor arm, which I am told you always diligently remove."

Honeyman's smile vanished with the effect his words had on Quilley's face. There was such animosity in Quilley's look that he thought the Sergeant was about to attack him.

"You bastard, Honeyman! You can't get my jeep. You can't do this to me."

Lieutenant Holcroft sprang to his feet. He, too, thought Quilley was about to strike Honeyman although he couldn't understand the currents that were passing between the two men.

"Steady on, Sergeant," said Holcroft.

"You keep out of this, Lieutenant," spat Quilley. "This is between the Captain and me."

Honeyman made a steadying gesture to Holcroft, indicating that he didn't want him to rock the boat, that he could handle it.

"Remember that there's a witness present, Sergeant. I'm prepared to overlook what you just said because I know you have an unnatural attachment to that jeep. But it doesn't alter things. Lieutenant Holcroft is shipping out tonight. **His own jeep was damaged in an air raid two nights ago**

23

and the one he should have got is the one you said would be all ready and shipshape at two o'clock today. As it has to be loaded aboard the ship by six tonight, there isn't any time to waste."

"But Captain ..." Quilley was barely controlling himself. Desperately he was trying to work out how he could remove his money from the jeep or, alternatively, get the chance to sabotage the jeep so that they couldn't even move it out of its lock-up.

"No buts, Sergeant," Honeyman went on. "Just put the keys and the rotor arm on the table. Oh, and the key to that stable. I know how you like to keep that buggy under wraps."

"The Sergeant protects that old rattletrap like it was his own property," Honeyman said in an aside to Holcroft. To Quilley, he said: "I'm waiting, Sergeant."

"I'll go and get the vehicle out for the Lieutenant," volunteered Quilley. "I'll drive it round to the front and check that it's OK for gas. I seem to remember the tank was low."

"That won't be necessary, Sergeant. The keys, please."

Still Quilley hesitated. God, that stupid Captain! How could he be so dumb? I'm going to kill the bastard for this, he thought.

"Just five minutes, Captain. That's all I need ... To get some of my stuff out of it."

"The keys, Sergeant." Honeyman wasn't giving an inch. It was as if he *knew*.

Slowly, Quilley took the keys and the rotor arm from his pocket. He placed them on the table. His brain seemed paralysed. He was giving away a fortune in dollars and he couldn't see a way to prevent it.

Honeyman took the keys and rotor arm.

"Stay here, Sergeant. I haven't finished with you," he said. "Come with me, Lieutenant. We're gonna get you some wheels."

They went out. Quilley stood, swaying on his feet like a man lost in a deep trance. He felt like the wizard who turned himself into a toad and had only to say the magic word to turn himself back again. Only he couldn't remember the magic word.

The sound of a revving engine brought him back to life. Quilley rushed to the window in time to see Lieutenant Holcroft driving off in his jeep. He watched powerless as the young officer gunned the vehicle down towards the road. A terrible fury began to engulf Quilley.

When Captain Honeyman strode back into the room, the broad grin on his face was too much for Quilley. He threw himself at the Captain and had him on the floor throttling him when the mists began to clear. He released the officer and stood up.

"I ought to kill you, you sonofabitch," he said unemotionally, "but it wouldn't do me any good. Get up, you no-good bastard."

Honeymoon, taken competely by surprise and shocked by the ferocity from which he had just escaped, was shaking like a leaf.

"I'm going to have you busted right out of the army for this,' he muttered. "You're going to be so long in jail, Quilley, that you'll look like Rip Van Winkle when you come out. This time you've gone too damned far."

"Can it," said Quilley. "You're not going to do anything about me because if you do, you're going to be bunking in the next cell. So sit up and pay attention. I want some information and I want it fast. I think, Captain Honeyman, that it's time you and I parted company. You don't amuse me any more. To me you're just a fly on the wall and the more I see of you the more reasons I'm likely to think up for swatting you, so don't tempt me."

"What do you want?" said Honeyman wearily. He had used up his quota of courage for one day.

*　　*　　*

The clock above the American Bar in the Hotel Aletti showed six o'clock. Colonel Henry P. McGivern occupied a corner stool at the bar. His companion was a major who had flown in only that morning from England to join HQ staff. McGivern was initiating the younger man into drinking, North African style.

"If you want to get broke before you get drunk," he was saying, "then you drink spirits in a place like this. If, however, you want to drink well and cheaply, get a good glow on and yet still be able to walk downstairs or talk sensibly to a passing general, then I have the secret."

He called the barman over.

"Henri, deux bouteilles de Cap D'Or et limonade, s'il vous plaît."

"Oui, monsieur. You want two bottles of Cap D'Or and two of lemonade also?"

"That's what I want, Henri. Oh, and two glasses of course." McGivern laughed loudly, his leathery face creasing like a well-worn boot.

The order was delivered. Ceremoniously, McGivern awarded one of the bottles of wine and one of the bottles of lemonade to his companion.

"A whole bottle of wine?" said the Major apprehensively.

"The only way to drink it is by the bottle. It's not wine, it's vermouth, quite mild really and the lemonade takes away any harsh edges. It's really pleasant to drink. And it don't give you no hangover like some of the rotgut around here."

He splashed wine into a glass.

"Com – bee – yen, Henri?"

"Combien, Monsieur? Two hundred seventy, Monsieur."

The Colonel peeled off three hundred-franc notes and told Henri to keep the change.

"Not bad for four dollars, eh, Major?"

McGivern was letting his first drink of the evening slide down when a white-helmeted Marine came into the bar. He looked around and headed straight for McGivern.

The Marine saluted.

"Are you Colonel McGivern, sir?"

"Yes. What do you want?"

"There's a GI sergeant asking for you at reception, sir. We can't let him up because of the officers-only rule. He said it was mighty urgent. Would you come down, sir?"

"Did he give his name?" asked McGivern.

"Quilley, sir. Sergeant Quilley."

McGivern's jaw tightened.

"That's bad news for sure. Will you excuse me, Major?"

Quilley was standing in the foyer near the front door when McGivern, his leathery face expressionless, arrived and greeted him brusquely.

"At ease, Sergeant. Just tell me what this is all about. I warn you that it had better be good."

"I want your help, sir. It's one last favour – then I'll never trouble you again. I want to close the book."

McGivern looked around, making sure that the conversation could not be overheard.

"You have already made me pay pretty dearly for my indiscretions, Quilley. If it's money you want, you're out of luck."

"It's not that, Colonel. I want to ship out of Algiers ... tomorrow."

McGivern's face brightened.

"Now you really *are* interesting me, Quilley. Where do you want to go? The South Pacific? The Aleutians? I can send you just about anywhere you want to go ... except the USA."

"I don't know where the ship is going, Colonel. I just know it's going out of Algiers, possibly tomorrow – and I want to be on it."

"What's the name of this tub?"

"It's a British freighter called the *Fort Harrison*. There are GIs aboard already. We shipped some of their transport to the docks this week – mainly radio trucks for a signals outfit, but there's a light AA unit I know about, too."

McGivern's face was a study. It didn't make sense. Quilley was asking for a place on what was likely to be one of the most hazardous military operations of the war.

For weeks, McGivern had been at work directing and

27

redirecting the personnel who were to make up General Mark Clark's Fifth Army for the Allies' first sea/land strike on the mainland of Europe. And Quilley wanted a one-way ticket.

McGivern chose to ignore the reasons why Quilley wanted out of North Africa. Better if he didn't know. What he did know was that the gods had suddenly presented him with the opportunity of ridding North Africa of a more poisonous kind of scorpion than any born under an Algerian rock. The opportunity had to be grasped speedily and without any other considerations.

McGivern instructed Quilley to wait for him while he went and made excuses to his Major friend. The latter had already worked his way through half a bottle of Cap D'Or and was well on the way to acquiring a taste for it. He offered no protest when McGivern told him he would have to drink the other bottle as well.

With Quilley at his heels, McGivern walked through the warm night to the heavily guarded administration building which housed his suite of offices. A WAC secretary was pounding away on a typewriter in McGivern's outer office.

McGivern stopped briefly at her desk.

"No rest for the wicked, Shirley. Could you bring me the Transport and Deployment of Personnel folders for 'Avalanche', please? Oh, and the embarkation timetables, too."

If the girl was surprised at the Colonel's return, she didn't show it. A moment later, she backed into McGivern's office with a pile of cardboard folders which she carried on her forearms and kept from toppling with her chin.

Thirty minutes later, McGivern had sifted several documents from the mountain of Top Secret material. Quilley was sitting at the window, a bored expression on his face.

"*Fort Harrison*," McGivern said aloud. "Net registered tonnage, seven thousand three hundred and thirty-one tons. Built Vancouver, Canada. Registered London in January of this year and managed by the Northumbria Cargo Steam Company for HM Sea Transport ... Bla-bla-bla ... Ah, here we are. She's scheduled to carry five hundred and four US personnel, list of units attached. See sheets ten to twenty-seven and File AF stroke BLK sixty-three."

He fished around some more, then he exclaimed, "Quilley, I think you're in luck. There's a Supply Company already embarked on the *Fort Harrison* and it's short of personnel. Two men went AWOL from the transit camp the day they should have embarked and, how's this for coincidence, Top Sergeant A. G. Bronowski admitted to Ninety-Fourth hospital with suspected appendicitis."

Quilley got up and faced the Colonel across the desk.

"You can definitely get me on that ship?"

"It shouldn't be too difficult. Just a few phone-calls and some paperwork. Three replacements have been notified and are standing by for embarkation. I'll let the two enlisted men's orders stand and cancel Bronowski's replacement and arrange the posting in your name."

Quilley frowned.

"Where is this outfit shipping out to, Colonel? There's a mighty lot of Top Secret stamps over them papers."

"It's more than my job's worth to say exactly where you're going, Quilley, but the direction is a little further east."

"Sicily? They've driven the Krauts out now, haven't they?"

"That was a very shrewd guess, Quilley. And if you can put two and two together, what's the point in me denying it. Only you mustn't talk about it outside this room. It *is* Top Secret. My bet is that you'll find your destination a pleasant change from North Africa."

A smile flickered across Quilley's face. He was enjoying a mental picture of green hills and vineyards and smiling signorinas.

McGivern, too, allowed himself an ironic smile. He had not been entirely frank with Quilley. The chances were that he would indeed *see* Sicily, if only briefly, and the island could understandably hold a special appeal for Quilley. After all, it was the home of the Mafia.

*   *   *

Since the incident with Quilley during the afternoon, Captain Samuel Honeyman had remained in his room, hemmed in by the statued saints around the walls, drinking. He was on the third bottle of the cheap red wine which he had bought at the café down the road from the old school.

Although what he had consumed had cost him only a little over thirty-five American cents, he was well on the way to being drunk. The more he drank the more he despised himself. If he'd had any guts he would have settled Quilley's hash long ago. At least that is what he told himself.

There was a knock at his door.

Honeyman lurched across and opened it. He blinked stupidly at the figure of Corporal Garcia. If he observed the look of disgust which the Mexican momentarily displayed at the sight of his commanding officer, he made no sign.

"You're wanted on the telephone, sir. It's Staff Headquarters."

"It'll be Eisenhower," said Honeyman drunkenly. "He can't run the war without me."

He laughed raucously and put an arm on Garcia's shoulder.

"I'll come and get it, my little Mexican friend," he mumbled. "I'll come and see what the General wants."

It wasn't the General at the other end of the line. It was Colonel Henry P. McGivern.

"I've got some bad news for you, Captain," said McGivern. "Afraid I'm going to have to take one of your best men away from you."

"You can take the whole bloody lot," slurred Honeyman.

"I beg your pardon, Captain."

"Sorry, Colonel," said Honeyman, recovering himself. "I was talking to my office orderly."

"Oh, well, I know it's late. But this is an emergency. We have some personnel shipping out of Algiers this week and I need a good noncom in a hurry who knows something about transport supply and ordnance. You've got a sergeant, name of Quilley. He's the man we want. He'll replace a

Sergeant Bronowski of four-five-three Battalion who is in dock with appendicitis.

"Quilley has to report with full kit at ten hundred hours tomorrow morning to Captain Sanderson at the Docks Embarkation Office. Got that? Captain Sanderson, Docks Embarkation Office, ten hundred hours. You'll have the posting orders by breakfast tomorrow but I thought I should put you in the picture tonight. You'll have to arrange transport to get Quilley to the docks."

Honeyman could scarcely believe his ears.

"I'll be sorry to lose Quilley. He's a good soldier," he lied cheerfully.

"Yeah," said McGivern drily. "I've read your reports. He has lots of unexpected talents. However, his enterprise will be put to good use where he's going. C'est la guerre, Captain Honeyman."

"Yes," echoed Honeyman. "C'est la guerre."

"That's the name of the game," said McGivern. "Goodnight, Captain."

* * *

When Quilley had left McGivern's office, there was no shaking a deep-seated anger. It smouldered in his mind like a cigarette which had burned its way into the stuffing of a mattress.

He made his way up the rue D'Isly, stopping at three cafés to pour several glasses of fiery cognac down his throat. Each fed the flames of his anger. The principal object of his rage was Honeyman, whose interference and crass stupidity had separated Quilley from his jeep and the money he had so carefully accumulated.

Feeling frustratedly homicidal about Honeyman was not how Quilley had planned to spend his evening. Tonight had been mentally reserved for a special kind of triumph, one he had planned in his mind a thousand times ... Ever since he had first known Bouvard.

Now, this night was to be the last he would spend in

Algiers. From a pavement café, he watched a French family out for their evening promenade. Unmistakably, they were a father, mother and three daughters. The girls were nubile, bursting out of their gossamer-thin frocks; and the parents flanked them like anxious hens with chicks as they passed through the strolling throngs of servicemen in khaki and white.

Quilley gulped yet another cognac. Lust and envy mingled with his anger. For a moment, the eye of the tallest of the three girls caught Quilley's. She looked quickly away, aware of the frank outrage of her body concomitant in the soldier's stare. She shuddered.

Bitch, thought Quilley. She's starving for it but she knows damned well that Daddy will keep her under wraps until he finds her some pansy husband with the right education and a million francs in the family vaults.

Quilley left the café, contemptuously throwing what passed in Algeria for a wine glass into the gutter. It had started life as the bottom of a lemonade bottle but had long since been parted from the neck and top. Drinkers didn't have to worry about alcoholism in Algiers, thanks to these crude drinking vessels. Lacerated lips were a great deterrent to downing more than two or three glasses at any one sitting.

Leaving the main road, Quilley lurched drunkenly across a pleasant palm-surrounded square and climbed lanes of stone steps leading high into a pleasant residential area of the French city. As he climbed, the sounds of the rue D'Isly faded to a distant hum. Looking back, the lights of the port twinkled like fairy lanterns.

Quilley stopped at a wrought-iron gate set in a narrow archway. The garden beyond gave a glimpse of a paved terrace and trees with exotic spiky leaves. Quilley tried the gate. It was locked. He looked around. A short distance from the gate an ancient fig tree was growing in and through the stucco wall and was now part of it.

Using a gnarled branch as a support for his weight, Quilley pulled himself up on to the flat top of the wall. He lay for a moment getting breath. Then he dropped into the garden below. A light from a window ahead guided him to the terraced path. He walked silently past a polished black door with a huge brass handle and went to the lighted window. He looked in. There was one occupant in the room. Indeed, the absence of light from any other quarter suggested there was only one occupant in the house.

Jacqueline, Comtesse de Bernes-Fonteaux by birth but plain Madame Bouvard by marriage, was not only alone in the house, she was afraid. Her husband should have been home at six and it was unlike him to be more than an hour late. Particularly on the eve of one of his many trips — Oran this time — with an early start the following day.

At nine, Jacqueline Bouvard had told the two Arab house servants they could go home. She would serve the master's food when he returned.

Theirs was a strange marriage — that of the impoverished French noblewoman and the one-time Marseille pimp — but an oddly satisfactory one. Neither party had been under any illusions. Bouvard had wanted a decorative wife to provide a socially acceptable veneer to his black market activities. She had wanted the life of luxury and ease which he could provide. She had overcome an initial revulsion for Bouvard on discovery that he had no physical interest in her. He wanted her simply as other men sought priceless paintings, to give grace and elegance to his home.

And the arrangement had worked. He made no demands other than she be in his home. He brought men home to look at her and to admire her and be envious of him. They could look but not touch. And *he* did not touch. One does not acquire a rare work of art to play with like a toy. Possession is enough.

Quilley, who had met Madame Bouvard on three occasions, hated her as much as he hated Bouvard — but with a much more complicated hatred. It was easy to hate anyone as outwardly ugly and unsavoury as Bouvard. With Madame Bouvard it was different. She confronted you with a cold statuesque beauty and a body sculptured for delight.

Ivory skin and moist red lips invited passion, but icy blue eyes forbade even the thought of it.

Before her, Quilley felt inferior, unclean. And he hated her for it, wanting to brutalise that untouchable beauty, exult in the despoliation.

He watched her now through the window. She seemed on edge. She paced about the room like a caged cat. She lit a cigarette and then stubbed it out half-smoked. She sat on a long, low couch, flicking the pages of a magazine, then she threw the magazine aside impatiently.

Quilley left the window and went to the polished black door. He pulled twice on a wrought-iron bell pull. There was a faraway jangle.

Madame Bouvard opened the door. She showed no pleasure in recognising Quilley.

"What do you want? How did you get through the gate?" Quilley grinned.

"The gate's still locked. I just fell over the wall. Where's your husband, Countess?"

"He is not here."

"You expecting him?"

"Yes – and I do not think he would like to find you here uninvited. Goodnight."

She moved to close the door but Quilley moved more quickly. He jammed the door with his foot, then thrust it aside and moved into the hallway.

Angry lights danced in Jacqueline Bouvard's eyes.

"What is the meaning of this?"

"I'd like a drink," said Quilley. "Where's your hospitality? Ain't you gonna offer me a little something?"

"I want you to leave."

Quilley closed the door. He glanced at Madame Bouvard to make sure he was observed. Then, slowly, deliberately, he pushed home the heavy black iron bolt which secured the door from the inside.

"Why are you locking the door?"

"Because we're going to have a little drink, Countess," said Quilley. "We don't want nobody disturbing us, do we?"

34

"My husband will have you killed for this," said the woman.

"Will he?"

Something in the way Quilley spoke – his very calm – alarmed Bouvard's wife.

"Where is Emile? What has happened to him? Do you know something?"

Quilley grinned.

"I heard it on very good authority that he's run out on you. He's skipped town. I also have it on good authority that he ain't never coming back."

"That's a lie!"

Quilley shrugged.

"You don't need to take my word for it. Just sit around till you're old and wrinkled and grey and see if I'm a liar."

She leaned against a mahogany-topped hall table. Something terrible *had* happened to Bouvard. The American was lying but he knew something. Madame Bouvard's skin was cold with fear. The American was speaking again. She had to shake off a feeling of faintness to hear his words:

". . . come as a bit of a shock to you. Looks like we could both use that drink. What do you say, Countess?"

"All right. In here."

She led the way into the room where he had seen her from the window. The sound of his footsteps came and went as he trod first on a polished wooden floor and then on the soft, gaily coloured rugs scattered here and there.

He watched her as she poured generous measures of brandy into two goblets. She was dressed simply in a navy-coloured skirt with white piping and a white blouse with navy piping. Her long black hair cascaded over the white of the blouse in dramatic contrast. Her legs were bare.

The blouse was worn loosely, with the top buttons undone. As Jacqueline Bouvard bent over the drinks, Quilley's eyes were riveted on the pale flesh of throat which merged into bulging breast. If the Countess wore anything beneath her blouse, there was no sign of it.

Quilley moved behind her and circled an arm round her.

His hand closed on her right breast. She reacted as if she had been electrocuted. A goblet crashed from her hand and splintered in a hundred pieces. A pool of brandy trickled out from the centre of the occasional table and dripped over the side on to the polished floor.

She pulled herself free from Quilley and whirled, facing him, her eyes ablaze with fury.

"Bastard!" she said.

Quilley's smile had an ugly confidence.

"I just wanted to see if it was real," he said. "Now I know you're not made of ice-water."

"Please go," she said. "Leave me alone."

"No chance, baby. You're a tease, Countess, and sooner or later a tease gets what they shop for and never buy. Why don't you relax and just enjoy it?"

"Do not dare touch me."

He reached out an arm and held her slim wrist in a bruising grip.

"Please," she cried, "I'll give you money ... if you will just go away, leave me." She was shaking with fear.

With his free hand, Quilley seized the neck of her blouse and pulled. There was a rending of cloth as he ripped it from her shoulders. The garment came away leaving only the sleeve on her right arm. He ripped that away.

Still holding her wrist, he pushed her away from his body. His eyes feasted on the milky whiteness of her breasts. She was jibbering hysterically. He hit her twice across the face with the flat of his left hand.

"Shut up, you stupid whore or I'm going to get mad at you."

"Animal!" she cried.

He hit her again. Letting go her wrist, she crumpled on the floor.

The side of her face was an angry red mass.

"Get up!" he ordered. "And do as I say or I'll boot your goddamned face into the back of your head."

Sobbing softly and eyes wide with terror, she got to her feet.

"Take off your skirt," said Quilley. "I want to see if the rest of you is real."

She stood there, cowed, making no move.

Quilley took a handful of skirt and wrenched it from her body.

"Now the pants," he said.

Fearfully, she moved now, slipping her panties down over her knees and half stumbling as she stepped out of them. She stood before him naked.

"Now come here. Help me unbutton my shirt."

Dumbly, she obeyed. Then, seeing his eagerness and the trembling lust of him, she panicked and tried to get away from him. He caught her in two strides and began to beat her. Whichever way she squirmed, he slapped ... the white alabaster of her buttocks, the flat of her belly, her sides. The echoing sound of hand on flesh seemed to excite and delight him. Saliva ran from his lips as he slapped and punched until his arms grew weary.

Then he threw her on her back on the wooden floor and, straddling her, fused his thrashing body into hers. It elicited no response from her below neck level. Baring her teeth like a she-cat enduring labour, she mouthed one word over and over again.

"Cochon ... cochon ... cochon ... cochon .."

Quilley seemed to spend himself He twisted his body away from hers. She half-crouched, looking at him triumphantly. Her smile was the smile of a tigress.

"Cochon!" she said again, spitting the word at him. "You are no man."

Quilley did not speak. The speed with which he moved took her by surprise. He was across and standing over her, flaunting the towering pillar of his manhood in her face. He seized her long dark hair with his right hand, twisting the gathered strands in a windlass grip.

With a turn of his wrist he rotated her body as if she had been a doll. She sprawled before him on all fours with a cry of pain. He did not relax the grip on her hair.

Then she felt him against the nakedness of her hips. A

37

sob was wrung from her throat as he entered her from behind with a poker thrust that sent fire through her body. Another sob burst from her lips.

Her whole body began to tremble. She wanted to embrace the exploding pain that threatened to engulf her in ecstasy. Her body reached for and welcomed the violating invader. Every nerve and muscle pulsed to receive and hold that throbbing flesh, her body arching and falling with a frenzy of desire.

Finally, she collapsed, as a crescendo of animal cries escaped from her throat and spent themselves in the closed atmosphere of the room.

Quilley grunted triumphantly.

"I knew you weren't made of ice. Come on, you teasing bitch. I ain't near finished!"

He was still holding her hair. He twisted her over on to her back, spread her thighs with his knees and fiercely entered her again. Slowly and in spite of herself, she began to respond again. Then she subsided, drowning in the pleasure and the pain and humiliation. By the time he had violated her for the fourth time, she was lost in the depths of a black pool beyond the edge of consciousness.

He left her there, lying on the floor.

3
The Ship

THE SHIPS in Algiers harbour had been packed like sardines in a tin. They lay five and six deep against every available quay space or trussed side by side between mole and buoys. Others lay out in the anchorage where two guarding corvettes crept round like watchful collies. When a ship in the anchorage exchanged places with one in the harbour, there was so much rearrangement it was like a game of musical chairs.

Just after midnight, while Sergeant Quilley was busy packing his gear together for a morning departure, the duty officer of the *Fort Harrison* was sipping a well-earned mug of coffee. He had been constantly on the go since six in the morning.

Second Officer Andrew Fairweather Mitchell was not dismayed at the prospect of getting out of Algiers. He knew it wouldn't be long now.

Leaving his empty mug in the saloon pantry, Mitchell went forward. Beneath blazing arc-lights, Arab stevedores supervised by Royal Engineers dock-force sappers were bottle-screwing the last of the deck cargo in place – five-ton American army trucks with machine-gun mountings on the cabs and familiar white star markings on the doors.

Mitchell made his way up the port side to the fo'c'sle-head and returned on the starboard side, stopping only to check one of the army boys from lighting a cigarette. There were two thousand tons of case petrol in holds one, two and five. It would make a pretty mess if it went up.

There was a fair amount of ordnance in the number two hold, too. Eleven hundred tons of five-hundred-pound bombs – enough explosive to destroy a city, never mind one small cargo ship.

Mitchell made his way aft. Four hundred American troops had been squeezed into the tween-decks of holds four and five. They slept in hammocks above rudely erected mess tables. The air below was suffocating and Mitchell pitied the soldiery who had to endure it.

Quite a few of the Americans had decided that, in harbour, they didn't need to endure the conditions and were sleeping on the deck. Good luck to them, thought Mitchell. They'll get damned little sleep in this racket, though. The rattle of winches on fifty ships, the shouts of the stevedores, the clank of shunting railway wagons, made Algiers harbour as peaceful a resting place as the average blacksmith's yard.

Over the incessant din came another eerie and intruding sound. It started with the siren up near the naval barracks below the Casbah wall and spread as other air-raid sirens all over the city took up the wailing.

The harbour had been lit up like Blackpool Promenade but, before the notes of the sirens had died away, the lights were going out among the forest of masts until only flickers here and there defied the darkness.

The city, which had been hidden in darkness beyond the docks, could now be made out as a sprawling shape, seemingly illuminated by a scatter of stuttering candles. The civilian population of Algiers were much less blackout disciplined than the residents of the target area, the docks.

Mitchell ran to the bridge to trigger the ship's alarm system. Footsteps and curses intermingled on the night air as gunners stumbled and ran to their stations. Even before the bells on the *Fort Harrison* had stopped ringing, the heavy artillery of Algiers' AA barrage was throwing up its awesome box of fire into the sky.

A figure joined Mitchell on the bridge. The Second Officer recognised the craggy outline of Richard Lansing, the ship's Captain.

"Our gunners are wasting their time going to stations," observed the Old Man. "These long-range Jerry bombers fly far too high. Firing at them with Oerlikons is about as rewarding as peeing over the rail into a gale."

Both men heard the unmistakable whistle of falling bombs and crouched low into the flying-bridge. A series of lightning flashes was followed by a deafening rush of noise and shockwaves of hot air.

"Jesus Christ!" said the Old Man. "That was too bloody close."

"Over there," said Mitchell. He pointed over the roofs of the nearest cargo sheds to where tongues of fire were leaping in the air, already bathing their faces with crimson light.

"I'll run out our fire hoses on to the quay," said Mitchell, already moving quickly down the bridge ladder. "God knows what's in these sheds between us and that fire."

"Get the deck crowd on that, Mr Mate," shouted the Old Man. "I'll get the Chief to get up steam. We may have to move out in a hurry, although God knows how anything will ever be able to move in this bloody rugby scrum of a harbour. It'll be like Cowes Week with knobs on."

Within minutes, Mitchell had organised a gang of sleep-tousled seamen to run the ship's fire hoses from points on the deck waterpipe to the quay side. The operation was conducted quickly and without fuss although shrapnel from the anti-aircraft fire was raining down like hailstones.

Pendlebury, the Chief Officer – whom the crew had nick-named The Bishop – slouched down the companion ladder to where Mitchell was standing on the quay.

"Everything under control, Mr Mitchell?" he enquired.

There was no love lost between the two men. Pendlebury envied Mitchell his youth, his efficiency as a navigator and seaman, his popularity with the men and his firm but easy control of them. He was all the things that Pendlebury never would be.

Mitchell, on the other hand, disliked Pendlebury for the sheer negativeness of his personality. He, himself, was a positive kind of a man. He wanted to be good at anything he tackled. It was not in him to blame anyone or to hold it against a person for failing – but he had little time for people who gave up without trying.

Pendlebury was the worst kind of failure, both as a man and in a professional sense. He blamed everything and everyone for his own shortcomings, except himself. He could work up great emotion over trivialities and then, when faced with an issue of any importance, would display the resolution of a jellyfish.

"It's just a precaution, Mr Pendlebury," said Mitchell. "There's fire the other side of the cargo shed. It could come in our direction."

"If I were the Old Man, I'd take the ship to hell out of it," said Pendlebury.

Yes, you would, thought Mitchell. Aloud, he said:

"That wouldn't be too easy with all those ships moored alongside us. We're right at the bottom of the barrel and if they want to sit it out, we're stuck here."

"It's that jerrycanned petrol that bothers me, not to mention the bombs in number two. It only needs a spark to blow us all to Kingdom Come. Those other guys might want to sit things out but they're not sitting on a bloody great bomb like we are."

"Oh, I don't know about that," said Mitchell. "The outside ship from us, the *Empire Seadrift*, has four thousand tons of high octane aboard – and that's quite a lot of lighter fuel. They're creeping around the decks in rubber shoes and laying eggs if anyone so much as drops a teaspoon."

"You seem to find that amusing, Mr Mitchell."

"Not amusing. But I'm not giving myself a nervous breakdown over it. I bet there isn't a ship in the harbour that wouldn't go up like Vesuvius if it was hit and, if that happened, the rest would go up like a box of firecrackers one after the other. We're hemmed in. We can't run anywhere – and it wouldn't do any good if we could."

"In that case, your hoses are rather a waste of time," said Pendlebury.

"Very likely," agreed Mitchell, "but they could buy a little time for anybody who wants to take to the hills."

Pendlebury read something personal into Mitchell's last remark.

"What are you insinuating, Mr Mitchell?"

"I'm not insinuating anything."

"When you talked about taking to the hills, you were hinting that that's what I'd like to do. You think I'm scared, don't you?"

Mitchell sighed with exasperation.

"I don't really give a monkey's whether you're scared or not, sir. It didn't cross my mind. I only know that right now I wouldn't mind being about fifty miles inland."

He strode off.

"Just a minute, Mitchell. Where do you think you're going?"

The omission of the courtesy Mister, traditional in the Merchant Service, angered Andrew Mitchell. He stopped and swung round, eyes glinting.

"It's *Mister* Mitchell, if you please, sir. I'm not somebody's butler. As to where I'm going ... I'm going round the back of the cargo shed to see just how close that fire is ... And if it's spreading this way."

He turned on his heel and walked off. Pendlebury watched him go. He said nothing but his mouth was working as if the saliva level was in danger of immediate overflow.

When he reached the rear of the cargo shed, Mitchell saw at once that the *Fort Harrison* was in no immediate danger. Several hundred yards of vacant ground separated the shed and the long low building where the fire was raging.

Three appliances were pouring foam on to the shell of the building. Its roof had completely disappeared and only parts of the outer wall remained. The conflagration, which was still fierce enough, seemed to be confined to within the shell.

A team of denim-clad naval ratings withdrew from the scene hauling a big cart-wheeled foam pump which had expended its foam. They came towards Mitchell at a trot and brought the lumbering carriage to a halt only a few yards from where he stood.

"That'll do here," shouted one of the seamen with PO markings on his overalls. His sweating face was streaked black.

His companions threw down the shafts of the pump and sat down on the ground, resting aching muscles and drinking air into their lungs.

"What a bloody heat!" said the PO. "You don't have a fag do you, mate?" he said to Mitchell. "I reckon it's safe enough here in the open to have a gasper."

Mitchell flung a twenty pack of Senior Service to the PO, who caught it deftly.

"Looks as though you boys have earned it," he said, handing his lighter to the grinning navyman. "What was it that got hit?"

"Paint store. Bloody lucky really, considering the stuff that's lying around these docks. There was only one bomb did any damage. The rest all fell on the wide open spaces beyond berth forty-four – you know, where that Norwegian ship blew up two months ago and flattened everything within a mile."

"The fire seems to be going down a bit now," said Mitchell.

"We were just helping out until the docks mob got their engines here. We can leave it to the Frenchies now. There's nothing to be saved. All they can do is damp it down and make sure it don't spread."

The anti-aircraft guns were now silent. The blue fingers of searchlights still probed silently amongst the clouds. Then they, too, switched off one by one.

The steady note of the all clear erupted from high in the city. In the distance away to the east, there was still the steady clump-clump-clump of gunfire. Flashes lit the horizon.

"Some poor devil's still getting it," said the PO.

"That's a long way away," replied Mitchell. "Well, time I was getting back to the ship. Let's hope that's all the excitement for tonight."

He wished the navy firefighters a good night.

Returning to the *Fort Harrison*, the first face he saw when he set foot on the deck was that of the young American officer whose acquaintance he had made only the evening before. He had arrived at the ship driving a jeep emblazoned "Tillie the Toiler" – a jeep which, had anyone known it, had more currency under its floor than the *Fort Harrison* held in the ship's safe. Lieutenant Holcroft had come aboard just after six and Mitchell had taken an immediate liking to him.

Temporary cabins had been built for the army officers in the tween-decks of number three hold, but Mitchell had offered Holcroft the use of his own much more comfortable accommodation. The Lieutenant had been only too glad to use the Second Officer's settee as a bunk and forego the gloom and cramped quarters of the hold.

"Hello there, shipmate," Mitchell greeted him now. "What's the matter? Couldn't you sleep?"

"Something woke me. I was having the most beautiful dream and then all of a sudden ... Ker-runch! I woke up on the floor. I thought we'd been torpedoed at least!"

"The nearest bomb was half a mile away ... hit a paint store. The rest of the stick landed on waste ground. Close enough just the same."

"I won't be sorry to see the last of Algiers," said the American. "The sooner we're on the move the better."

"Can't wait to get on with the war, eh?"

"Hell, no," said Holcroft. "I just want a change of scenery!"

Mitchell laughed. "You're not the only one. Let's go and have a cup of coffee. We'll have a look at the tourist brochures and decide where we'll go next."

"The GI scuttlebutt has it that we're bound for Sardinia."

"They say it's very nice there at this time of year," said Mitchell. "But according to our galley wireless we're heading for Greece."

"And what do *you* think?" asked Holcroft.

"Well," said Mitchell, "it could be Sardinia and it could be Greece, but I'm the kind who just likes to wait and see.

One thing's sure. Sooner or later somebody is going to have to tell me where we're going."

"What makes you so sure?"

"It's only polite," said Mitchell. "I'm the navigator."

Holcroft smiled broadly. There was something about the Britisher's dry sense of humour which established a very real bond between the two men.

"OK," he said, "so you're the navigator. Show me how good you are. Navigate me to that cup of coffee you were talking about. I like mine strong and black."

"Strong and black, eh?" said Mitchell. "That, I'm told, is how Mr Pendlebury likes his women."

The last of the stevedoring gangs and shore labour left the *Fort Harrison* at six in the morning. By ten, the ship's crew had made the vessel ready for sea.

Just after eleven, Captain Richard Lansing returned from convoy conference ashore. He sent for his three deck officers.

"We're all battened down and ready to sail, sir," said Mr Pendlebury. "All the same, I must express my misgivings about keeping things shipshape with all those troops aboard. I'll never get the decks washed down if they're going to be allowed to sprawl all over the place."

Lansing fixed a withering eye on Pendlebury.

"Perhaps you want me to ask their commanding officer to order them over the side so that your deck-washing rites may be observed, Mr Pendlebury?" he said.

Pendlebury flushed. Andrew Mitchell remained neutrally poker-faced while Colin Durham, the tall beanpole Third Officer, chuckled audibly.

"Did I say something amusing, Mr Durham?" asked Lansing.

"No, sir. Excuse me, sir. Private joke."

He seemed in no way repentant and, as Lansing turned to extract some documents from his briefcase, he winked at Andrew Mitchell.

"Well, gentlemen," said Lansing, "I have our sailing

orders. We move out to the anchorage at noon and we'll be sailing just after dark."

Lansing held up a large manila envelope.

"These are our sealed orders," he said. "Your guess as to our final destination is as good as mine. These orders are not to be opened until we are at sea and receive a signal from the Commodore of the convoy instructing us when they may be opened. I shall put them in the safe."

"How about charts, sir?" said Mitchell.

"I've got the usual stuff about minefields and wrecks," said Lansing. "But you can look out the South Med charts from here to Cape Bon."

"That means we are going east?" volunteered Durham.

Lansing stared at the Third Officer.

"What a profound deduction, Mr Durham," he said drily.

Mitchell smiled. For the Third Mate's benefit, he said: "We have to go east if our destination's anywhere in the Med, Colin. They haven't loaded us up with Yanks to reinforce Gib or move them to a rest camp in Oran. We could be bound anywhere between the Gulf of Lions and Crete. Unless we're being given a holiday from the war, we have to go east."

"I don't know about that," said Pendlebury. "If we were to open a second front in the South of France, they would use the shortest possible communication lines. And that would mean striking due north from here."

"That's a good theory," observed Mitchell, "if you ignore the obvious snags."

"What snags?" said Pendlebury, bridling.

"Well, there are the geographical ones. Sail due north from Algiers and you'll have to go over or through the Balearics. Go anywhere within a hundred miles of them and Franco's men would be on the phone to the Jerries in no time saying there's an invasion fleet on the way. But that apart, there's the question of minefields. They have them stretched out to seaward from Barcelona to the Gulf of Leghorn. The only feasible approach would be from the south-east, and that's bloody near impossible."

"You're talking nonsense," said Pendlebury.

"No," said Captain Lansing, "the Second Mate's talking sense. Wherever we land, it will have to be within a range of our land-based fighter aircraft and along short sea routes from our main supply bases. It's only a guess but I'd say we'll be putting our guests ashore on mainland Italy, not too far away from our fighter bases in Sicily. France is out of the question unless they conjure up half a dozen aircraft carriers out of thin air. From here to Marseille is four hundred miles and that's a hell of a long line to go out on."

"But think of the surprise Jerry would get," said Pendlebury. "That's what counts in war, you know – surprise. Catch 'em with their pants down."

Lansing laughed humourlessly.

"Yes," he said. "All the better to urinate on us."

He offered his three officers cigarettes from a fifty tin. Only Pendlebury took one. Lansing gave him a light and then lit up himself.

"Gentlemen," he said gravely, "there are some things I *can* tell you about the forthcoming operation. It has been code-named 'Avalanche', and if you thought the landings in Sicily were lacking in excitement I have a feeling that you are going to get your money's worth this time."

"Sicily gave me enough excitement to last for another ten years," said Mitchell.

"I'll second that," said Lansing. "But this show could make it look like a picnic. For a start, I got the impression that it wasn't going to be the main show ... More of a diversion. And it's under American command. What gave me an uncomfortable feeling was meeting some of the military brass. They talked like death-or-glory boys getting ready to raid the Commanche. That makes me nervous.

"But I have a lot of bumpf I want you all to read. Instructions on what to do if E-boats and U-boats get through to the beach-heads or if the Italian fleet puts to sea and brings its combined might to bear against us. There is also some speculative stuff about a new German air weapon. Intelligence suggests that they are about to use it in this theatre but nobody seems to have any idea what it is."

"We got a lot of that kind of stuff when we got our orders for Sicily, sir," said Mitchell.

"I suppose we did," said Lansing. "But I also got quite different vibrations for the Sicily do. I got the impression that it was magnificently planned in detail right down to the last bullet or tube of toothpaste.

"This operation strikes me quite differently. I think it has been set up in an almighty hurry, that the whole thing is being played by ear. It could turn out to be the brightest bit of military ingenuity since Hannibal went over the Alps on an elephant. On the other hand it could be the biggest shambles in history."

He shook his head.

"However, gentlemen ... Ours is not to reason why."

Suddenly he grinned.

"By God, you do look solemn! Forgive me if I've been sounding like the voice of doom. It's just that I want you all to be ready for any eventuality because any one of you might find yourself in command of this ship."

"Surely not, sir," said Mitchell, strangely embarrassed by the Old Man's talk. It wasn't like him at all.

"Oh yes, Mr Mitchell," Lansing replied. "If we get to our destination safely – and there's no guarantee of that – you can bet on it that we shall be bombed, machine-gunned, even shelled from the shore. We got off lightly at Sicily. We only had a few casualties and none of them were serious. We may not get off quite so luckily this time."

Mr Pendlebury was a mixture of emotions. The thought of suddenly being thrust into command while Lansing lay mortally wounded filled him with great pleasure. It was an appealing dream. At the same time, the thought of the responsibility which would consequently be heaped upon his shoulders was enough to make his palms run with sweat and his whole body tremble.

He found it difficult to keep his mind on what Lansing was saying to him after that, when the Second and Third Mates had been dismissed and he had been asked to remain for instructions about manoeuvring away from the quay.

Mitchell and the Third Mate, Durham, blinked at the sunlight when they emerged on to the Captain's bridge-deck.

"That was creepy," said Mitchell.

"What was?" asked Durham.

"The way the Old Man was talking."

"Privilege of command," said Durham airily. "Invest everything with a little bit of melodrama. Play the mystic."

"But it's so unlike Lansing," persisted the Second Mate. "He's straight as a die, no side to him. I've never heard him talk like that before. Like he was putting his affairs in order ..."

"Well, you never know when you're going to buy it in this racket and he's had four ships sunk under him already. Probably just a touch of the glooms at all that talk of what's waiting for us. I hope to God nothing does happen to him. Can you imagine it?"

"Imagine what?"

"Pendlebury being in command."

"Oh my God," said Mitchell. "I see what you mean."

"Never mind, Andrew, old son. I'll see that it never comes to that. If anything ever happens to Lansing, that's when I put emergency plan A into operation."

"And *what* is emergency plan A?"

"Oh, nothing very subtle," said Durham with a laugh. "I tell Pendlebury I've lost a five-pound note on the deck and when he rushes out and goes scrabbling around the scuppers looking for it, I boot him over the side."

"That could be considered conduct unbecoming."

"Oh, nothing as serious as that," said Durham. "Just simple, straightforward assassination."

4
The Convoy

THE DARKENED convoy ploughed eastwards at a speed of six knots.

The *Fort Harrison* was in convoy station "21", that is, it was the leading ship of the second column. There were eight columns of ships with six ships in each column.

In ten minutes it would be midnight – the end of Durham's watch. But he was in no hurry to go below. There was an air of suppressed excitement permeating the ship and the lanky young Third Officer was far too keyed up to think of sleep.

Andrew Mitchell had the same feeling. It had brought him to the bridge fifteen minutes before he was officially due to relieve Durham.

Captain Lansing was also on the bridge, having shared Durham's watch with him since eleven.

The three men stood now on the starboard wing, sipping tea from enamel mugs. Lansing kept glancing at the luminous dial of his watch.

"Give me the chart-room time, will you, Mr Durham?" Lansing said.

The Third Officer went through the wheelhouse and let himself into the chart-room by groping his way through the double blackout curtains.

He checked his own watch with the clock on the wall, dowsed the light above the chart-table and slid the blackout screen from the open starboard port-hole.

"It's four minutes to eight bells," he sang out, waited for an acknowledgement and then began replacing the blackout screen.

On the bridge wing, Lansing turned to Mitchell.

"I'll go below now and open the sealed orders. I'll be back before we start the square-dance."

Mitchell grinned.

"We've got the easy part: we just hold our station. I just hope nobody makes an eightsome reel of it in the dark."

They were referring to the planned manoeuvre which the convoy was to make at 0030 hours, exactly thirty minutes after the hour appointed for the shipmasters to open their sealed orders. The signals indicating both events had been relayed to all ships shortly before sunset.

The signals had created a feeling of suspense and anticipation on every vessel in the tiny armada.

Durham rejoined Mitchell on the wing of the bridge.

"Old Man gone down below?"

"Yes. He'll be back when he's opened the orders."

"Why are we mucking about with the convoy formation in the dark? Bit dodgy, isn't it?"

"We're coming up for the Galita Channel. At least we'd be on it by daybreak," said Mitchell. "We can't go steaming through there eight abreast. It's only a mile wide."

"That means we'll be going south of Sicily?"

"Not necessarily," said Mitchell. "Your position at twenty-three hundred put us just west of Bizerta. That means we have four hours to play with before we alter course one way or the other. We could swing up due north towards Sardinia — where most of the Yanks seem to think we're going — or we could bear north and east to go round the top of Sicily ... Or south and east for the south of Sicily or Malta."

"So we've still got plenty of options open," said Durham. Then he added with feeling: "I just wish to hell someone would tell me where we're going."

"You'll know soon enough."

They turned simultaneously at the sound of footsteps on the bridge ladder.

Captain Lansing hauled himself on to the flying-bridge.

"Hold the fort for a minute, will you Mr Durham? I want the Second Mate in the chart-room."

Mitchell followed Lansing through the wheelhouse into the muted red glow of the chart-room.

"Find that position for me, Mr Mitchell, will you? You'll need the big Central Med chart I think."

Lansing put a piece of paper on the chart-table. On it in pencil had been scrawled a latitude and longitude.

Mitchell glanced at the paper and from the top drawer of the chart-table extracted a Central Mediterranean chart. With parallel rules and dividers he plotted the position from the figures given.

"There you are, sir," he said. "It's about twenty miles north of Palermo."

"That's what I thought," said Lansing bitterly. "Isn't it bloody marvellous!"

"That's our destination?"

"For the time being. It's a rendezvous. When we get there, the navy will be putting aboard further orders for all masters and military commanders."

"It's a bit of an anti-climax," said Mitchell.

"It's what I thought. They haven't made their minds up yet. The bloody generals are still arguing about it. They could have us running round in circles till we run out of fuel ... Yes, Sparks?"

A door behind them had opened and the head of the No. 2 Radio Officer was peering round it from the radio cabin.

"I just picked up the midnight communiqué from Algiers, sir. Interested?"

"What is it, Sparks? You're dying to tell us, so let's have it." Lansing's voice had an impatient edge.

"The Eighth Army has landed in Italy, sir. They've been pouring across the Straits of Messina all day and are penetrating deep. They've met hardly any opposition."

"So it has started," said Lansing.

"I thought you'd like to know, sir," said Sparks, and disappeared back inside the radio cabin.

Lansing studied the chart and frowned.

"Now, if we're bound for the Straits of Messina, why

should they have us traipsing around the Tyrrhenian Sea? It would make a lot more sense to make the southerly approach."

"Just what I was thinking," said Mitchell. "Isn't it more likely that our lot will be landing further north? Round about Sapri or somewhere along the Calabrian coast. Somewhere ahead of the Eighth Army, so that the troops coming up from the south can link up and join forces."

"You could be right," said Lansing. "Sparks said there was little opposition. That's encouraging. Maybe the Germans have pulled right out of Italy, or intend to."

Mitchell coughed expressively. Lansing looked at him with an acknowledging light in his eyes.

"Okay, Mr Mitchell, so the Old Man's a bloody optimist. Well, maybe it is wishful thinking on my part but you can't blame me for hoping we get things easy for a change."

"Believe me, sir, I hope we get our American friends ashore without a shot being fired but I can't help remembering the Sicily landings. Five miles inland by sunset on D-Day – remember the communiqués? Everything going according to plan. They made it sound like a picnic – yet I said my prayers more than once. And those poor bastards on the *Fort Pelly* ... blasted out of the water ... Remember what the news bulletin said?"

"Yes, I remember," said Lansing, and there was sadness and bitterness in his voice. Lansing had lost more than one good friend on the *Pelly*, most of them from Geordieland like himself. There had only been a passing mention in the radio news during the Sicily landings:

"*... Troops of the Eighth Army have encountered fierce German resistance in their drive towards Catania. Two enemy aircraft were shot down during attacks on our ships landing supplies in Port Augusta Bay. The raids caused some damage and casualties.*"

Some damage and casualties.

Lansing shivered involuntarily. In Algiers he had had a strange premonitory feeling about this trip, unlike anything he had ever known before. As if a time-limit had been set on his life.

Always before, even in very rough times, life had seemed to stretch before him like a path winding endlessly into distant hills.

But the vision had changed. Or rather – suddenly – it was no longer there. He had tried to think of the future, of the voyage after next, of the end of the war, of his next reunion with his wife ... But no image came.

It was as if there was nothing there. Nothing at all.

Some damage and casualties.

Would that be his epitaph? And Mitchell's? And young Durham's?

Some damage and casualties.

*   *   *

At precisely thirty minutes after midnight, the convoy began its pre-planned formation change. The four columns in the northern half of the convoy increased speed by two knots while the four columns in the southern half reduced speed.

As the faster columns pulled ahead the slow group altered course to port, increased speed, and fell in astern of them.

Now the convoy was four columns wide.

The same manoeuvre was repeated with the two columns on the port wing maintaining speed and position and the two starboard columns falling in behind them.

The ships were now two abreast and strung out over ten miles of ocean. The destroyer carrying the Senior Officer (Escort) criss-crossed ahead of the *Fort Harrison*. Six corvettes flanked the two files of transports, three to the north and three to the south. A second destroyer brought up the rear, zig-zagging in the convoy's wake.

When all the ships were in position, the snake-like procession slowed to six knots.

Every so often, blue-tinted Aldis lamps would start winking out from the Commodore ship, which was directly abeam of the *Fort Harrison*.

The messages were short. An alteration of course and the time it was to be executed required only the coded references from Mersigs (the Top Secret signalling manual). Course would be indicated by the appropriate alphabetical letter and three numerals. Time would be indicated by an alphabetical letter and four numerals.

Andrew Mitchell found that the four hours between midnight and 4 a.m. flashed past, so much was there to occupy his attention.

When Pendlebury relieved him at four there were, in addition to all the normal instructions, a sheaf of signals to pass on. These had all been entered in the Signal Log.

Pendlebury moaned and groaned at the prospect of a busy watch.

"There's a course alteration to zero-three-five at oh-six-hundred hours," said Mitchell. "And at oh-six-thirty, the convoy is regrouping in eight columns of six."

"Why do they always do these manoeuvres in my watch?" complained the older man.

"We all get our share," said Mitchell. "Not that it always makes sense. Since we're not going through the Galita Channel, there wasn't really any point in stringing the convoy out in two columns. But maybe the Commodore feels we need the practice."

"Bloody waste of time."

"It helps pass the watch," said Mitchell. "I must admit I quite enjoy all the activity."

'You would!" said Pendlebury acidly. Well, I'll get the Old Man out for the fun and games. Then, if we ram the Commodore, he'll have to do the explaining."

Mitchell pushed an open book across the chart-table to Pendlebury.

"This is the diagram for the formation alteration. We just go back to where we were before – or rather, the other ships do. We don't have to alter course or change position

... We just reduce speed to four knots and wait for everybody else to catch up and get in line."

Pendlebury scowled.

"I still think it's a lot of nonsense. The navy just loves playing admirals and it has us careering around all over the ocean just for the hell of it."

"Well, I'll get below," said Mitchell. "We're right on station and the speed seems dead right at forty-eight revs. But we can check when we get outside that we're not edging any nearer the Commodore than we should be."

The two men walked out to the port wing of the bridge and studied the rakish outline of the *Confidenza*, the Dutch liner in which the Convoy Commodore had chosen to house himself and his staff as the convoy's nerve-centre.

"She can do eighteen knots," said Mitchell conversationally. "It must be boring the pants off her engineers to dawdle along at six – like keeping a greyhound on a lead."

"We seem to be ahead of her," said Pendlebury with sudden anxiety. "I'm going to go down two revs."

Mitchell eyed the other ship. In his judgement the two vessels were in perfect line, bridge to bridge. He was about to say so but when he turned, Pendlebury was no longer there.

With short dumpy strides, the Chief Officer had entered the wheelhouse. He was now buzzing the engine-room on the direct line by furiously cranking the bell handle.

When it was answered by the Second Engineer, Pendlebury said:

"Down two revs."

"Aye, aye, Mr Mate," came the reply. "Down two it is."

Pendlebury chalked the change in revolutions on the little blackboard which was used for the purpose and also for noting the compass course.

Returning to the bridge wing, he studiously ignored Mitchell. Presenting his back to the Second Officer, he raised his binoculars and focused them on the *Confidenza*.

After an interval, he feigned surprise.

"Still here, Second Mate? You can go now. I'll get the ship back on station."

Mitchell could sense rather than see the supercilious smirk on Pendlebury's face. The Second Mate felt a tremble of anger transmit itself through his body. His two fists clenched involuntarily.

He controlled an impulse to smash one of his fists into Pendlebury's face.

"I'll say goodnight then," said Mitchell in an even voice.

"Goodnight, Second Mate."

Pendlebury's tone indicated dismissal. And it contrived to indicate a whole lot else. It indicated that the bridge was now in capable hands and no longer at the mercy of an incompetent. It also indicated that where, before, the ship had been off station, the situation would soon be under control.

Mitchell wondered at his own self-control as he left the bridge. One of these days, Pendlebury was going to provoke such an explosion of anger from him that it would be terrible to witness.

He reached deck level but did not enter the accommodation alleyway. Instead, he went to the rail and looked across at the *Confidenza*.

The *Fort Harrison*'s bridge was now almost in a line with the Dutch vessel's stern.

"Is that you, Andrew?" said a voice from the darkness.

Mitchell turned to see a figure in a white boiler-suit gingerly picking his way forward near the coaming of number three hatch.

"Yes, Charlie. Over here."

Charlie Bedford, the Third Engineer, crossed to where Mitchell stood at the ship's rail. He held a can of beer in each hand.

"Fancy a small refreshment before you turn in?" asked the Engineer. The two men kept the same watches – and a beer and a final smoke at 4 a.m. was a fairly routine event for them. Because both men had American army officers bunked on their cabin settees, they usually adjourned to the ship's saloon for their nightcap.

"I'd love a beer," said Mitchell.

"What are you doing out here?" asked Bedford. "I should have thought that four hours on the bridge would be plenty for counting stars."

"I was just cooling off. His Holiness, Mr Pendlebury, decided we were off station and took us down a couple of revs. I've just been looking at the result ... Oh, there goes the engine-room phone again."

The two men heard the grating vibrationary sound, like that of a chain being hauled through a deep subterranean pipe, which they knew was the hand-operated bell on the bridge being used to call the engine-room.

"That'll be Pendlebury asking the Second to go up four revs," said Bedford. "Are we supposed to be abeam of that ship over there? It's that Dutch liner isn't it?"

"Yes, the *Confidenza*."

"Well, let's leave it to the Mate and our Worthy Second Engineer. They'll be going 'Up two, down two, up four, down two' until breakfast time. Pendlebury has poor old McWilliams nearly round the twist."

"And me!" said Mitchell. "It's bad enough him taking the ship all over the ocean on his watch but when he arrives on the bridge and immediately insinuates that we're off station, it makes me mad as bloody hell."

"Forget it, Mitch. You know he doesn't fool anybody — only himself."

"That's what bothers me," said Mitchell. "Some day that clown is going to run us up on the beach or into a tanker ...And we'll all wake up in the water. But you're right, Charlie boy. I shouldn't let him get under my skin. Let's have that beer!"

On the bridge of the *Confidenza*, a sad-faced Dutch Chief Officer stared across at the *Fort Harrison* and made a solemn observation about his opposite number on the British ship's bridge.

Lieutenant Anthony Pennington-Greaves, RNVR, one of the Convoy Commodore's staff, said:

"I don't know what you said, old man – but am I correct in assuming it was a comment about the *Harrison*'s officer of the watch and his attempts to stay on station?"

A ghost of a smile crossed the Dutchman's sad face. He said in English:

"I merely said that he should never have left the farm where he was born."

5
The Allies

THERE WAS one officer aboard the *Fort Harrison* who did not offer the hospitality of his cabin to any of the American army personnel who were temporary guests on the ship.

Mr Pendlebury didn't see why he should. In the first place, he didn't like Americans. In the second, he saw no way in which he could possibly derive any benefit.

So, the strange intimacy he was to effect with one of the American soldiers was as unexpected as it was unnatural. More surprising, since Pendlebury was a snob, was the fact that the man was not even an officer. He was a sergeant, a noncom.

Since his arrival on the *Fort Harrison* and the ship's subsequent departure from Algiers, a growing horror had filled Sergeant Quilley at the enormity of his folly in arranging his own transfer. Admittedly, there remained the considerable incentive of regaining his hundred thousand or so dollars – but what became more and more apparent to Quilley was the realisation that the recovery of his ill-gotten wealth might be quickly followed by his own severe injury or even death.

The latter eventuality had figured in none of his plans. He quickly realised that Operation Avalanche was not going to be – as he had blissfully imagined – a peaceful milk-run to a comfortable billet in some pleasant Sicilian resort. No, something altogether much more dangerous was afoot – and it was made no more palatable by the fact that he had been stupid enough to have volunteered for it.

Nor had his humour improved when he had been recognised on encountering the same Lieutenant Holcroft who, unwittingly, had been the instrument of his present predicament. On that score alone, Quilley was prepared to hate Holcroft without reservation.

The two came face to face as the *Fort Harrison* moved out of Algiers harbour into the bay anchorage.

"I didn't expect to see you here," said the young officer. And his surprise was genuine. During their previous brief encounter, Quilley had struck him as insolent and insubordinate certainly – but there was a feeling that went deeper than that. Something about Quilley had registered with Holcroft as "wrong". The Sergeant was not the kind of man Holcroft would instinctively trust.

"You're looking at a volunteer, sir," said Quilley, enjoying the pose. "I didn't join this man's army to sit around on my butt in a pox-hole like Algiers."

"You sure didn't waste any time," said Holcroft.

"It was all done in six hours, Lieutenant. This other sergeant crapped out – appendicitis. When I heard, I got Captain Honeyman to pull a few strings and get me shipped out in his place."

If not entirely convinced of Quilley's integrity, Holcroft was at least impressed by his apparent enthusiasm.

"Good for you, Sergeant. I hope you don't live to regret it."

"I sure as hell just hope I live, sir," said Quilley.

He laughed at this seemingly brave sally. Holcroft grinned back at him. "See you around, Sergeant."

Quilley had gone about "casing" the *Fort Harrison* as if it had been the First National Bank and the object of a billion-dollar robbery.

He asked many questions, quickly finding that the British sailors – a friendly bunch – enjoyed airing their knowledge of shipboard functions. They would take pains to describe to him in detail the watchkeeping systems, the chain of command, the location of the various stores, living-quarters and so on.

One of the items of information gleaned by Quilley was that the Chief Officer kept all the cargo stowage plans. He alone could tell the exact location of any item of cargo – including the various army vehicles the transport was carrying and how they were identified.

So, Quilley reckoned that if he was to find the jeep which concealed his money hoard it would be a good idea to cultivate the Chief Officer.

From his conversations with crewmen, Quilley quickly learned that Pendlebury was an odd and unpopular figure. More than one seaman described him as "an old woman".

Quilley stalked Pendlebury for twenty-four hours before making a move.

He had discovered that Pendlebury was a pipe-smoker and favoured mild tobaccos. He had also formed the impression that Pendlebury was as tight-fisted as a Brooklyn pawnbroker.

A small investment seemed worth Quilley's time.

At a morning PX issue, he bought two twelve-ounce cartons of Raleigh pipe tobacco. Then he went in search of the Chief Officer's cabin. It was located at the forward end of the bridge accommodation on the port side.

Mr Pendlebury looked up in surprise from some papers when his "Come in" – in response to a knock at his door – produced the sight of the tall, fair-haired American sergeant.

"Are you the Chief Officer, sir? Mr Pendlebury?"

"That's right. I'm busy – what do you want?"

"Oh, I ain't aimin' to intrude, sir ... The guys told me you're real keen on American tobacco and I was wondering if I could make a little gesture of appreciation ... On account of how you ship's people have been so downright kind to us GIs. Well, sir, it's this tobacco ... It's a gift, sir."

Pendlebury's eyes lit up at the sight of the two big cartons.

"Raleigh," he said. "One of my favourite brands. I like a mild one, you know. I say, that's very decent of you ... Er ..."

"Quilley, sir. Sergeant Frank Quilley."

"I don't know what to say. What a very generous thought."

"No need to say anything, sir. We GIs are the ones who're grateful. You're looking after us real swell an' I thought that leastways I could kinda try to say thanks."

"Well, sit down, Sergeant. I was about to order some coffee from the pantry. Perhaps you'll join me in a cup."

"That's real civil of you, sir," said Quilley. "I'd count it a real honour to take coffee with you."

Over mugs of coffee, the two men continued to softsoap each other as if locked in a competition to see which could be the more ingratiating.

Quilley's performance was superb because, like most people, he found Pendlebury a pretty revolting specimen. A creep he most certainly was. An old woman! Indeed the thought crossed Quilley's mind that Pendlebury was in the wrong job. He should have been a brothel-keeper not a ship's officer.

Quilley did not allow his revulsion to show. He even began to enjoy manipulating the old fool.

Pendlebury, meantime, was revising all his opinions about the brashness and arrogance of Americans. What a fine young man, he thought. So courteous and generous and so respectful.

"There *is* one thing you could do for me, sir," Quilley was saying. "I sure would appreciate it if you could give me some schooling about ships. What I mean, sir, is that you're the most important guy on the ship – even more important than the Captain, some say, because you're the guy that's got to get things done. I sure would like to find out more about your job and how you run things."

Pendlebury was flattered. There was nothing he liked more than to air his authority and flex his muscles before a captive audience.

"I'd be delighted," he told Quilley. "If you want to know anything about ships and the way they're run, you've come to the right person."

The seeming friendship of the two men developed from that point.

Quilley, with his curious ability to detect the most

64

vulnerable areas of his fellow men, quickly realised that Pendlebury in addition to being grotesquely vain was a desperately lonely man. He lived in an isolation of his own making. He craved companionship but demanded from it a constant feeding of his own ego.

Quilley knew how to feed egos. He buttered Pendlebury's self-esteem with such diligence that the Chief Officer, questioned on the possibility of his own divinity, would not have denied it. More likely, he would have rebuked his questioner for the length of time it had taken to perceive the obvious.

Thus it came about that when Pendlebury made his daily perambulation of the ship to consider the work to be allotted to the bosun and day men, Quilley followed behind like a devoted disciple. The pair seemed almost inseparable.

It was only a matter of time before Quilley forsook the sweaty confines of number four tween-deck and, at Pendlebury's invitation, installed himself in the Chief Officer's cabin. It was only a matter of time, too, before Quilley had established the whereabouts of his long-lost jeep. It was at the foot of number three hold; that hold situated immediately abaft the bridge and forward of the engine-room and bunkers.

On the sixth night out from Algiers, Quilley decided to recover his money.

In spite of intentions to remain awake, Quilley was dozing when he heard a sailor shake the Chief Officer with the admonition that "it had gone seven bells". He was fully awake but feigning sleep when the man returned to tell Pendlebury that it was "almost one bell".

Using only his bunk-light, Pendlebury dressed hastily, making revolting throat-clearing noises in the process. He disappeared briefly to use the toilet at the after end of the alleyway. Then he came back to the cabin to pocket pipe and tobacco and don his uniform cap. Quilley heard his slow footsteps on the metal of the lower bridge ladder, then they passed overhead along the timbered deck of the lower bridge.

Quilley looked at his watch. The luminous dial showed it was 0355.

He dressed silently in the dark.

Everything was in readiness. From his pack, he took an empty first-aid haversack in which he placed some tools wrapped in a rag. He buckled on a web belt to which a commando knife in a sheath had already been clipped. He checked a heavy-duty rubber flashlight before slipping it into the thigh pocket of his denim trousers.

Leaving the cabin, Quilley paused momentarily outside the open door and fluttering curtain of the adjacent cabin, that of the Second Officer. From inside, came the even breathing of Lieutenant Holcroft. Quilley knew that Mitchell would not be down from the bridge for five or more minutes.

He moved soundlessly to the end of the inside alleyway. There, he paused again in the darkness between the double blackout curtains, so that his eyes would quickly attune when he emerged on deck.

He stretched a long leg over the high-weather step and stood on the deck. Overhead, the sky was studded with stars. Phosphorus glinted in the oily sea and, across a short stretch of it, Quilley could see the liner *Confidenza* pushing aside a wash of ghostly luminosity as it cleaved the ocean on the *Fort Harrison*'s beam.

Quilley padded on rubber-soled feet to the alleyway skirting the exterior of the officers' accommodation. Midway along it, the watertight door leading to number three hold was open, hooked securely to the bulkhead.

Quilley climbed inside on to the runged ladder which descended vertically into the bowels of the ship. He began the sixty-foot descent into the pitch darkness.

Twenty feet down, he passed the tween-deck opening where sleeping accommodation had been built for military officers. All was quiet there.

Fighting a terrifying claustrophobia, Quilley went lower into the darkness. The shaft was only about four feet wide and the tomb-like eeriness was strangely intensified by the gentle rolling and pitching motions of the ship.

Beads of sweat, not all the result of physical effort, stood out on the American's forehead when his feet finally touched the floor of the hold. Here, every sound was magnified to strange proportions. The surging slap and swish of sea against the ship's side served as a constant reminder that the water level was now far above Quilley's head and brought a vivid awareness of the sea's massive pressure against the hull and the thinness of the plates withstanding it.

Here, the symphony of the engines was amplified to a rhythmic thundering which failed to drown out a variety of creaks and groans as cargo strained against wire lashings and the very metals of the ship's frame complained of the stresses exerted upon them.

Quilley switched on the flashlight and took a single step away from the ladder. He was struck a rasping blow which lifted the skin of his temple and sent him reeling back to hang on to the ladder. Raising his flashlight instead of shining it down, he found he had collided with wires bottle-screwed to rigidity between the tail-frame of a three-ton truck and an eye-bolt in a rib of the ship.

Cautiously, he edged round the truck. He climbed up on the step of the cab and from this vantage point, swept the hold with his flashlight.

All the army vehicles of any size had been loaded as close as they would go against the ship's side. The centre of the hold housed smaller vehicles; jeeps and scout cars lashed nose to nose.

Quilley got down from his perch and began to pick his way to the centre of the hold. It was no easy task. The vehicles were packed like herring and secured by masses of wires and bottle-screws. Even at that, some of them had movement on them. Quilley almost fainted with fright when a three-tonner lurched forward eighteen inches with a roll of the ship. Quilley scrambled on to the hood of the lurching truck and then shone his flashlight down into the space where, a moment before, he had been standing.

The gap had vanished and the bumper of the three-tonner was grating against the tail of a radio truck.

Had his reflexes been slower, he would have been cut in half.

His hands were shaking uncontrollably but he delayed only a moment. It seemed as dangerous to move back as to move forward, so he went forward, finally clambering on to a jeep on the centre floor of the hold.

Sweat poured off him in the airless void. He played the light around him. His heart gave a lift as he recognised a familiar cushion-tear on the driving seat of the next jeep but one. And then he saw the emblazonment – "Tillie the Toiler".

He climbed over the intervening vehicle and allowed himself a moment of affectionate reunion with the jeep he still regarded as his personal property. The back had been stacked with reels of signal wire. He began to unload these unceremoniously, not caring where he threw them.

Fifteen minutes later he had cleared the jeep and was dismantling the false floor.

His heart thudding with excitement, he finally uncovered the neat stacks of dollar bills. Methodically, he began to fill the deep haversack with them. Soon, the bag was crammed to bursting point, but several bundles of notes remained unpacked.

He began to fill the pockets of his denim jacket until they, too, were bulging. What remained he stuffed inside his shirt.

Hastily now, he replaced the false floor and rubber mat. A surging sense of triumph filled him. But the glow died with heart-stopping shock when a strident sound pierced at him from the darkness immediately overhead. The ship's alarm bells were shrilling their dramatic warning, chilling men's hearts as it wrenched them from sleep into fear-filled consciousness.

One bell was situated in the tween-deck, only forty feet

above Quilley's head. Had it been only a few inches from his ear it could not have startled him with more penetrating ferocity.

The sound reverberated in his brain and made pulp of his emotions. The signal was a short ring followed by a long ring – the letter "a" in the Morse Code. It signified air attack.

He heard the movement of many feet overhead as the residents of the tween-deck accommodation made their way on deck. He felt trapped.

Sweat blinding his eyes, he began the nerve-racking journey back across and between the trucks towards the ladder leading from the hold. A gasp of relief exploded from him when he eventually reached the comparative security of the lowest steel rungs.

He was holding on, bracing himself for the ascent, when there occurred the most violent assault so far on his fully stretched nerves.

A low rumble of noise came vibrating towards him through ocean and steel plate. It was the warning tremor preceding a far greater eruption of sound which battered against the ear-drums and then died with a monstrous metallic crump. It was followed at five-second intervals by three more explosions.

The wall of the ship beside Quilley seemed to bend towards him then be sucked out again as each blast struck. Quilley was convinced in these moments that the plates were about to cave inwards and admit a gigantic wall of water which would smash flesh and bone to jelly and engulf him forever.

But nothing happened. He had no way of knowing that the lone German bomber had dropped its cargo of death just astern and beyond the *Confidenza*.

Quilley began climbing the ladder. For the moment, the money loaded about his person was not the over-riding consideration. The one thought uppermost in his mind was escape from that hold.

He knew there was little chance of him encountering any

69

of the residents of the tween-deck on this ladder. For them, a much easier means of entry and exit to their accommodation had been erected from the hatch top of the hold.

As Quilley neared the top of the ladder, however, he became aware that there were men milling about on deck where the watertight door opened on to the alleyway at the top of the ladder.

This made a complication.

He did not want to be seen emerging on to the deck and face the curiosity of anyone who might be there.

So, when he reached the top of the ladder, he climbed above deck level to where the ladder ended in a funnel-like ventilator. He perched there in the darkness debating his next move.

The alarm bells rang a second time, the shock of strident noise startling him afresh. But this time the signal was "all clear", letting all off-watch men know they could stand down from their stations.

Footsteps echoed on the steel deck as gunners trooped aft from the forward gun-nests and returned to quarters. GIs, roused from sleep a short time before, began to make their way below again, the excitement over.

Quilley was aware that the light was improving. It would soon be daylight. He would have to move.

There was no sound of movement now from the alleyway. He edged towards the open watertight door and glanced outside. The alleyway was empty.

He clambered through the opening on to the deck.

The blood froze in his veins as a voice said:

"Where the hell have you been, soldier?"

The man must have been there all the time, leaning back against the bulkhead, invisible in the shadow. He moved forward now and Quilley could see his face in the grey light.

It was a young face – the face of a boy. But he wore a man's uniform and there was a deep Texan timbre to the drawled voice. Its owner could have been no more than twenty years old.

He wore the insignia of a Lieutenant

Quilley stood stock still, uncertain.

A piece of paper fluttered down from the neck of his jacket. The young officer, moving forward, caught it neatly before it reached the deck. He examined it.

"Ten bucks! You been mining the stuff down there, Sergeant?"

"We had a poker school going. I got lucky," said Quilley. He put out a hand for the return of the note. As he did so, two more ten-dollar bills fluttered from his jacket. A flurry of wind caught them and carried them over the gunwale and out to sea.

"I think maybe you got some explaining to do, Sergeant," said the Lieutenant steadily, his eyes fixed in an unwinking stare at Quilley's chest. "You're loaded with green stuff. The way I read it, you've been down below pussy-footin' around Three Deck while that Kraut bomber was layin' its eggs. Now Three Deck is off limits to you. It is reserved strictly for US officer personnel – and it's my guess you've bin light-fingerin' our quarters and skimmin' off every greenback that wasn't nailed to the floor. I know where that ladder goes to, soldier. I use it."

Anger and sheer frustration, more than fear, made Quilley grab at the Lieutenant's throat. No two-bit boy officer was going to rob him now. Not after all he'd done to get the money.

The Lieutenant was taken by surprise by the fury of Quilley's attack. But he was neither weakling nor coward. Although Quilley was nearly a head taller than him and close on fifty pounds heavier, the officer forced Quilley's hands from his throat and tried to turn him by twisting Quilley's right wrist down and behind his back.

"Don't make things worse for yourself," he muttered through clenched teeth. "There's no place you can run, Sergeant."

Quilley's answer was to free his right arm and bring the heel of his tensed open hand round in a vicious chopping arc. It struck the officer just above the bridge of his nose and he staggered back.

The Lieutenant's arms went up and spread automatically to take his weight as he crashed against the bulkhead. But his back and shoulders, which would have taken most of the impact, encountered no bulkhead. For none was there.

They encountered only space as he fell back through the open watertight door from which Quilley had so recently emerged.

The man's wrists and outstretched hands cracked against the steel sides of the opening and he emitted a grunt of pain. In that same split moment he tottered in a half-sitting position in the doorway, then the momentum of his upper body took over again.

The back of his knees arrested the backward movement fractionally, then the weight of his trunk propelled him backwards into space. He folded, his knees coming up to meet his chest – and then he vanished from Quilley's sight.

Quilley stared in astonishment at the open doorway.

He heard the sickening crack of bone against metal, the rasp of tearing cloth, the whack of limb and leather boot against plating, as the young officer hurtled down sixty feet of steel shaft.

There was a final echoing thud – and then silence.

Quilley looked fearfully forward and aft in quick succession. He could not believe that the noise of the brief struggle and its outcome could have gone unnoticed. But if any had heard, they were paying no attention.

He wasted no more time. Hugging the shadows, he moved silently to the end of the alleyway, crept under the bridge ladder and into the curtained corridor of the ship's officers' quarters.

All was silent inside.

A few quick steps took him to the far end and the sanctuary of Pendlebury's cabin.

Once inside, he lit a cigarette and sat there in the darkness smoking it and willing his hands to stop trembling.

*   *   *

Captain Lansing very seldom drank at sea. But after the

sea burial of the young American officer – a lieutenant from
Dallas, Texas, with the unusual name of Selwyn Rainwater
– Lansing felt that, for once, he could relax that self-
imposed discipline.

He took a bottle of White Horse from his cabinet and
placed it with two glasses on his day-room table.

"You'll join me in a small one, will you, Colonel?" he said
to the other person in the room: a tall angular man with
short-clipped grey hair and steel-rimmed glasses.

Colonel Dwight J. Moss was senior American officer
aboard the *Fort Harrison*. He looked up at Lansing now.

"Thank you, Captain. I reckon maybe we both need a
little stiffener."

As Lansing poured the drinks, the Colonel continued to
study him gravely through pale blue eyes.

"Captain," he said, carefully considering his words before
delivering them in machine-gun-like bursts. "Captain ... I
want to express ... the sincere thanks and appreciation ...
of all the officers and enlisted men under my command
... for the moving and dignified way ... in which you carried
out the ceremony of Lieutenant Rainwater's funeral
service."

He drew a hand wearily over his forehead, then he fiddled
nervously with a shirt button as if trying to make up his
mind what to do with the hand. Finally, he pulled out a
large khaki handkerchief and blew his nose noisily. The
deed seemed to appease his restless nerviness and he continued in a more relaxed manner. His words still came in
short -sharp bursts but they were linked better, giving
continuity to his diction.

"I'll write to his folks in Dallas, of course ... I think
they'll be comforted to know that their son was given full
military honours when he was committed to the deep ...
And that his last resting place in the ocean was saluted by
men and ships of several Allied nations. I was very, very
impressed, Captain ... It was a deeply moving experience."

Lansing handed the Colonel a glass and raised his own.

"To the memory of your young officer, sir. And to all

73

those other brave young souls whose company he now keeps."

The formal, almost ceremonial tone of Lansing's toast might have sounded mawkish or stilted coming from any other lips. Colonel Moss was to remember its sentiment and the sincerity with which it was offered long after other memories of the war had faded from his mind.

A heavy sadness lay on Lansing. There was more to it than the young American's tragic death. It was born of an accumulation of deaths in war, of which Rainwater's was the latest.

He looked across the table at Colonel Moss.

"There will be a full inquiry into Lieutenant Rainwater's death when the ship returns to a United Kingdom port," he said. "However, under the circumstances, I don't think it will be more than a formality. More a case of going over the paperwork again."

"You have already given me a clear picture of the legal obligations," said Colonel Moss. "I'll have the necessary documents drawn up as soon as possible. We have a stenographer with us who'll give you a nice neat job."

"Thank you, Colonel. I'll attach them to my log book alongside my own entries about the discovery of the body and so forth. I'm truly sorry, Colonel, that you should lose a good man in this way. There seems no doubt that it was an accident."

"None at all," said Moss. "We took statements from every guy who could tell us the slightest thing about him."

"He was first missed about eight?"

"Yeah. He didn't show for breakfast. Collins – that's his buddy – said he didn't return to quarters after that air attack early this morning. Collins and Rainwater shared a cabin down in Three Deck with two Medic officers. Collins and Rainwater were Signals. When Rainwater didn't show for any chow at breakfast time and they couldn't find him, they reported to me."

"And that's when you came to me and suggested we search the ship?" said Lansing.

"That's correct, Captain. Some of the guys thought he must have gone overboard but it just didn't make much sense. It was one of your crewmen who found the body."

"The Bosun, yes. Somebody told him that Rainwater was in the habit of using the hold ladder rather than the companionway up through the hatch – so the first place the Bosun looked was at the foot of the hold. These ladders can be damned tricky to the uninitiated, especially if there's any roll on the ship."

"He probably missed his footing in the dark. Doc Griffith said that death must have been instantaneous."

"This Doc Griffith," said Lansing, "that's the Major who eats with us?"

"The same. In civilian life, he was one of the best-known pathologists on the West Coast. I reckon that what he says should carry a lot of weight with any inquiry."

"He made a detailed examination?"

"Nothing like a full post-mortem – but that wasn't necessary. Doc was able to tell the score pretty well from the injuries. I've asked him to make a full medical report in writing for my own records. I'll give you a copy for your log."

"I'm indebted," said Lansing. "I don't usually have that kind of expert help to call on."

"Doc says Rainwater's spine was broken in three places. The neck was snapped clean as a whistle."

"Poor young devil," said Lansing. "He comes all this way to fight a war and slips off a bloody ladder!"

Lansing stood up and held out the whisky bottle.

"Look, Colonel, this has been a very sad occasion. Why don't you take this bottle ... you may want to split it with some of your colleagues. I know that regulations don't allow you to carry your own hard stuff – so, please be my guest. I have to get up to the bridge shortly."

Colonel Moss grinned lopsidedly.

"Captain Lansing, you're one hell of a guy. I know a couple of my guys who wouldn't say no to a shot – strictly for medicinal purposes, of course. Thank you."

When Moss had gone, Lansing allowed himself the luxury of picturing the American commander in his natural habitat, a pillar of the business world back in California. He could see him in dark suit and spotless white collar ... A Moss with a matronly wife in the background and a hilltop home in his native San Francisco. There would be a patio, drinks with ice cubes and a big sedan parked under the car-port.

The picture seemed clear and defined – but it faded and was shut from his mind by the single awareness of the steady rhythmic throb of the *Fort Harrison*'s triple expansion engines. The sound was muted and yet it shut out all other impressions. That throbbing engine was here and now. Nothing else existed.

The convoy had been steaming slowly in the Tyrrhenian Sea for thirty-six hours. Its movements were seemingly purposeless, weaving patterns on the ocean and betraying no evident intent of destination – yet moving nevertheless towards the rendezvous which Mitchell had plotted on the chart when the ships had been off Tunisia.

The flock of ships moved forward like sheep grazing a hill. Going first one way then the next but following a predetermined course towards a distant fold.

The seasoned campaigners on board the ships had not been alarmed by the simple physical presence just before daybreak of a single Junkers 88, nor by the release of four bombs which had caused neither damage nor casualties – but a deeper significance made them apprehensive.

The convoy's presence in these waters was now known to the enemy. So, further hope that the convoy could proceed to its destination in secrecy could be abandoned forthwith.

The Luftwaffe would now watch the convoy's movements with interest. Very likely, too, they would summon sub-marines and E-boats to the area with the promise of rich pickings.

Perhaps – and this was the most chilling thought of all – the most significant conclusion to be reached was recognition of what German Military Intelligence would deduce from the convoy's presence. What construction would they place on the appearance of what was obviously an invasion fleet – or one of several invasion fleets – within striking distance of the coasts of Sardinia and mainland Italy?

The options on the location of a military landing in strength were not so many that the Germans could not make an intelligent guess as to the correct one.

The chances were now very much less than even money that when the ships of Operation Avalanche discharged their human cargoes, it would be to deliver them directly into the jaws of a waiting enemy.

The tactical niceties of Operation Avalanche meant nothing at all to Quilley. He gave little thought to anything more complex than the immediate needs of his own survival and the preservation of what he considered to be his hard-earned wealth.

Even now, as the *Fort Harrison* proceeded towards its rendezvous north of Palermo, he was considering the possibility of avoiding disembarkation with his military comrades and taking his chance on the ship and wherever it was ordered to go.

Better to be a live fugitive with a hundred thousand dollars, he reasoned, than a dead sergeant on some lousy shell-swept beach. That was his thinking. But there were far too many imponderables.

If he could be sure in advance that the *Fort Harrison* would be despatched immediately to some neutral country, then the chance of going AWOL *was* worth taking. But Quilley knew this to be a fanciful hope. The freighter was a war transport, specially fitted to carry men and guns and, as such, was likely to be operating in a war theatre indefinitely.

No, it looked like he would have to take his chance on the beach and pray for a swift and easy campaign.

Since his escape from the hold and his encounter with Lieutenant Rainwater, Quilley had spent hours of anxiety. The subsequent discovery of the body and the intensive inquiries which that event had initiated had not immediately dispelled his unease. Indeed, they had increased it.

It was only as the day passed and no accusing finger was pointed at him that Quilley's confidence began to return. The realisation grew and then was confirmed that not a single person on the ship suspected that Rainwater's death was anything other than a tragic accident.

The more Quilley thought about his good luck, the less apprehensive he became about the battles – if battles there were – which lay ahead.

The way his luck was running, Eisenhower could parachute him into Berlin and the Nazis would probably lay on for him a fast car to the coast and a boat ticket to Sweden.

He lay on Pendlebury's settee congratulating himself on his capacity to outwit the nastiest tricks Fate could devise for him. The source of his confidence lay a few inches below his supine body in the settee locker. With all that green stuff so close, the world held no fears for him.

6

Operation Avalanche

AT 0230 hours on 9 September 1943, the assault troops of the Anglo-American Fifth Army began their attack on mainland Italy. At four separate landing points in the Gulf of Salerno, troops poured ashore from five different army groups – each with a combined aim.

That aim was to control, by dusk, a land area from the Chiunzi Pass in the extreme north to the town of Agropoli in the south and containing within its four-to-seven-miles-deep perimeter: the port of Salerno, the towns of Battipaglia, Eboli, Ponte Sele, Altavilla, Albanella and Capaccio and – most important of all – the airfield at Montecorvino.

The British Tenth Corps formed the Northern Assault Force and included the US Rangers, who were to attack Maiori, the British Commandos, who were to attack Vietri, and the 46th and 56th Infantry Divisions, who were to spearhead the drive on Montecorvino airfield and Battipaglia.

The Southern Assault Force, landing just north of Agropoli, was composed of two American infantry divisions making up the US Sixth Corps. These were the 36th Infantry Division, going in first, and the 45th Infantry Division, in reserve. Their D-Day objective was to secure the high ground from the 3,500-foot summit of Monte Soprano in the south and extending north along the range of hills running parallel with the shore.

Only one of the five army groups took their objective on schedule.

This distinction fell to the US Rangers. They encountered no opposition and, agreeably surprised, proceeded in three hours to occupy the heights above the Chiunzi Pass and the ridges which commanded the main road and rail links between Salerno and Naples.

The Rangers were lucky. Everywhere else, the German army was waiting to welcome the invading troops ashore. It was not a friendly welcome.

Since they had made the rendezvous north of Palermo on the night of 6 September, the British and American officers on the *Fort Harrison* had been aware of the parts expected of them in Operation Avalanche.

Throughout the 7th and 8th, the army personnel on Lansing's ship – who were to disembark at Blue Beach in the US Sixth Corps sector – had been undergoing intense briefing sessions from their officers.

Quilley was no exception. With a small group of noncoms, he squatted on his haunches on the port boat-deck and listened with mounting dismay as the Transport and Ordnance Co-Ordinator, Captain Wilbur Diamond, outlined their duties for D-Day and immediately afterwards.

Diamond was a short wiry man with crew-cut grey hair and a leathery dried-up prune of a face. He was tough as an old boot and a startling contrast to Honeyman, Quilley's former CO. If one was lily, the other was spiky cactus.

Quilley and his companions were provided with crude maps of Blue Beach and its environs. On these in various kinds of dotted or broken lines had been marked the projected infantry objectives and their timetables.

Behind the projected lines of advance were rectangles shaded in various densities, marking "safe" areas. These were assembly points for vehicles.

Other shaded rectangles marked dumps for small ammunition, for K rations, for howitzer shells, for aerial bombs, for cased octane, for engine oil, for every nut and bolt and lubricant that went to equip and maintain the machine of war.

It was to be the job of Quilley's section to locate one of these vehicle assembly points in a "safe" area and to organise the movement of trucks to and from the dump areas on the beach and the forward units.

Fuelling and maintenance points were to be established.

Precautions were to be taken against air attack, ground attack and – as a companion of Quilley observed – everything from a wet weekend to an earthquake.

Having never before been nearer to the actual firing-line than a hundred miles, Quilley liked neither the sound nor complexity of the bewildering mass of paper orders.

The ironic thing was that the mountain of instructions, logistics, timetables and projected eventualities – in advance of the event – amounted to nothing more than theory.

The translation of that theory into practice was to be traumatic.

Two hours before H-Hour on 9 September found the *Fort Harrison* cruising slowly in the Tyrrhenian Sea some fifty miles from the Gulf of Salerno. It was a beautiful night.

The sky was ablaze with stars and the late summer air was warm. The sea was as smooth as glass and, across it, the columns of ships left gently cascading paths of sparkling white water.

Standing the middle watch, Andrew Mitchell felt no great sense of taking part in an historic event. Nature and the night conspired against it. So, too, had the surprise broadcast by General Eisenhower the day before announcing the surrender of Italy.

The men on the ships had been filled with a strange euphoria at the news. A great victory had been achieved before they had fired a shot and there were many who believed that their arrival in Italy would be greeted with garlands and flowers.

There had been no sign of the Germans since the lone aircraft had dropped its bombs and even the old campaigners interpreted this as a good sign. No U-boats had come near. No E-boats had attacked. And now, in the first hours of an historic day, all of nature lulled the senses with a velvet serenity.

The air was like sweet wine, and sky and ocean held such tranquil beauty that Mitchell was utterly beguiled by it.

Such nights were the sailor's joy. Compensation for a hundred storms ... for the monotony of endless pitching and rolling ... for the nights of cold and wet and winds that cut like a knife.

It was the kind of night which made up for the loneliness of many oceans. A night when the sea hid its cruel and angry face and wore the smile of a seductress, charming the very souls of men.

For Mitchell that middle watch was to be the least eventful since leaving Algiers. But towards its end, its mood was to change.

The serenity of the elements did not change. But a shiver crawled down Mitchell's spine when, ahead, he saw the first flashes of fire crimson the horizon. Vivid streaks of orange leapt and played along the meeting place of sea and the sky's velvet dome.

Relentlessly, the convoy moved across the glassy mirror of ocean towards the flashing sky. A low booming rumble of sound rolled to meet them.

That sound was to grow in intensity and assault the eardrums without pause or respite for numberless days ahead.

Although every man on the *Fort Harrison* had been ordered to get as much sleep as possible that night, there were few who were not wide awake and stirring by 0330. The gunfire was more than distant thunder now. It was a constant companion to every whispered word and an echo of every quickened heartbeat.

The decks began to fill with men as the troops deserted the claustrophobic confines of the tween-decks. They squatted on hatches, on boat-decks, in trucks lashed to the deck. They crowded the alleyways and bunker-tops, wherever a space could be found.

Lansing joined Mitchell for the last hour of his watch. He had not been to bed, preferring instead to catnap on the chart-room couch fully dressed in case he was wanted in a hurry.

Mitchell had called him at the first sight of gunflashes

ahead. From that moment Lansing had given no further thought to sleep.

Five minutes before four, Lansing ordered the Second Mate to sound "Gun Stations". Within minutes every gun crew was standing-to. Helmeted figures were strapped into the twelve Oerlikons, with loaders at their sides.

The two twin Brownings were manned, as were the twelve-pounder in the bows, the HA four-inch at the stern, and the multiple-rocket-firing "pillarbox".

Mitchell was ship's gunnery officer. In this capacity he telephoned the four-inch gun platform and checked with PO Donovan, a peacetime regular in the RN and now in charge of the mixed naval and army gunnery personnel on the *Fort Harrison*.

"We've got one up the spout and we're ready for anything," reported Donovan. "All guns are manned, sir."

"Don't open fire unless you make a positive identification of enemy aircraft," said Mitchell. "We've been warned that low-flying aicraft may be our own paratroops going over — so pass the word, PO. That instruction expires at oh-six-hundred hours. After that it's open day!"

"Aye, aye, sir. The boys all know what our fighters will look like."

"Spitfires and American Lightnings. Anything else gets fired at first and worried about later."

Mitchell then phoned the twelve-pounder in the bows and talked in similar vein to Bombardier Frogtree. "What's all them pretty lights up ahead, sir?"

"Well, I'm hoping like hell it's the Royal Navy softening up the opposition," said Mitchell. "But stick around and see for yourself. There's no extra charge for your seat in the front row. Got the smoke canisters ready?"

"Ready and waiting, sir."

Mitchell left the wheelhouse and climbed the ladder to the monkey-island, the topmost part of the bridge. There was an Oerlikon nest built over each wing of the flying-bridge and two twin-Browning pits cheek by jowl in the central rear area above the chart-room and radio cabin.

The 60 mm cannon were both manned by RA gunners with two MN officer apprentices acting as loaders.

The apprentices were first-trippers, boys of sixteen. Their names were Lovell and Hardy and, inevitably, they were to the rest of the ship's company "Laurel and Hardy".

There was a happy innocence and enthusiasm about the boys which endeared them to Mitchell. His own apprentice-ship in a starvation-diet tramp ship out of Hartlepool had been full of hardship — but he felt it had much to commend it in comparison with the hazards to which these kids were exposed.

Lovell straddled a leg over the port gun-pit and Hardy looked out from the starboard pit at the sound of Mitchell's arrival on the monkey-island.

"OK you two. Out here a minute. I want a word with the pair of you."

The two boys leapt nimbly from the armoured walls of their respective gun-nests and approached Mitchell with grins splitting their faces. Mitchell, leaning against the binnacle-housing, surveyed them tolerantly.

"You're improperly dressed, both of you. Where are your life-jackets and tin hats?"

"Mine's in the gun-nest," said Lovell.

"So is mine," said Hardy.

"Go and put them on. Now!"

Mitchell watched both boys tie on their big orange and blue life-jackets and don steel helmets.

"Do we really have to wear these things, sir?" said Lovell.

"They'll keep the sun out of your eyes," said Mitchell. "Of course you have to wear the bloody things!"

Lovell turned to face his friend, a woebegone look on his face.

"That's another fine mess you got me into, Olly," he said.

Laughingly, Mitchell aimed a kick at the mimic's pos-terior. Lovell had no difficulty in skipping out of range.

"Now, now, sir. Surely officers are not allowed to kick apprentices," he said.

"Anyone's allowed to kick apprentices," said Mitchell. "That's what apprentices are for."

His tone softened.

"You're in good spirits, lads, and that's fine – but I want you to promise me a couple of things."

"The good spirits are a bit of an act, sir," said Hardy. "The fact is that we're both terrified out of our wits and we fool about so that nobody can hear our knees knocking."

Mitchell solemnly took in every word until he realised that Hardy was grinning like a Cheshire cat.

"Why, you young devil! Are you trying to take the mickey out of me?"

"I'm sorry, sir," said Hardy. "It was just that you looked so serious ..."

Mitchell looked at them wide-eyed.

"You know, I do believe that neither of you is the least bit scared. We're sailing right into the middle of God-knows-what and it's just another bloody lark! And I have actually been *worrying* about the pair of you."

Hardy looked at Mitchell apologetically. Lovell shuffled his heels.

"We'll be all right, sir," said Hardy.

"And we really do appreciate the way you look out for us," said Lovell.

"You're really more like a brother than an officer ... Well you know what I mean," said Hardy. "Well, you've got a sense of humour. We feel we can come and go a bit with you. It's not disrespect."

A lump rose in Mitchell's throat. He was silent.

"What did you want us to promise you?" asked Lovell.

"Oh, that," said Mitchell. "I ... I reckon I just wanted to give you some advice ... in a big brotherly sort of a way. Routine stuff, you know. Like keeping your tin lids on because your hair isn't really much protection against shrapnel. And your life-jackets are handy things, too – they're useful for more things than keeping you afloat. The padding won't stop a bullet but they offer some protection if there *is* muck flying around.

"I want you to wear them until we see what things are going to be like. And if the going does get rough up near the beaches, for God's sake keep your heads down. Don't expose yourselves any more than you have to."

When he left the monkey island, Mitchell could hear the two boys chatting away to their respective gunners. War to them still held an element of adventure. Even the horrors and the realities of it which they had already experienced had not obliterated the novelty of their involvement.

Mitchell hoped their eventual disillusionment would not be over painful.

Shortly after four, the convoy regrouped into two columns. All the escorts retired to the flanks while, ahead, two minesweepers began a patterned sweep across the convoy's path.

The first streaks of daylight began to light the sky to the east. As the sky brightened, so the flashing of the guns ahead decreased in brilliance. Now wraiths of smoke were visible along the horizon and above this the dim shape of mountains could be discerned with the naked eye.

"Land ahead," droned a voice from the fo'c'sle-head.

"Aye, aye," responded Lansing from the bridge.

A blue Aldis lamp winked from the bridge of the *Confidenza*.

The Third Officer acknowledged, writing on a signal pad, as the brief message was relayed.

Laying the Aldis on an ammunition locker, he went into the wheelhouse. He addressed Lansing.

"From Commodore to all ships, sir. Stream battle colours."

"Thanks, Mr Durham. See to it, will you?"

Durham returned to the wing of the bridge and extracted a whistle from the pocket of his battledress top. He blew two short blasts.

Apprentice Lovell appeared down the ladder from the monkey-island like a shot.

"You summoned me, Master," he said to Durham with a bow.

86

"Yes, genie of the lamp," said Durham. "Go aft and hoist the battle ensign from the mainmast. Do you know where it was stowed after Sicily?"

"It's in the locker under the chart-room settee."

"Jump to it then."

He went back to the Aldis lamp and began to call the ship immediately astern. The message would be relayed right down the line of ships.

Lovell, meantime, had entered the chart-room. He emerged a moment later clutching what looked like a mountain of red bunting. Scarcely able to see for his burden, he picked his way down the two bridge ladders and negotiated a passage through the swarms of American soldiers towards the after-deck.

The Americans politely cleared a path for the boy, who was obviously about ship's business. They opened ranks to let him through. Except for one sergeant, whom Lovell recognised as the one who bunked in Pendlebury's cabin. From the moment Quilley had seen the flashing of guns, he had become very nervous about the things that could happen to him and his money. When Lovell had sought to pass him in the press of bodies beside number three hold, Quilley had angrily turned, shouldering the boy, and cursed him into the bargain.

Lovell ignored the reaction and pressed on aft.

Interested GIs gathered round when Lovell unhitched the halyard from cleets on the after end of the mast-house overlooking number five hold. He bent on the flag which he carried and slowly began to run it up to the gaff. A slight breeze created by the forward movement of the ship caught the bunting and the monster-sized red ensign fluttered out over the winches and flew out over the centre of the hatch.

Lovell wrestled the halyard until the ensign was hove close to the gaff. The GIs, impressed by the spectacular size of the ensign, gave Lovell a cheer. Lovell looked up at it proudly. The ensign was fifteen feet in length. Only very rarely were battle ensigns flown by twentieth-century merchant ships. Yet Lovell – who had only been a few months at sea – had seen it fly twice from the mainmast of the ship in which he served.

On the bridge, Lansing, too, felt a strange thrill of pride as he looked aft and saw the outsized ensign stream bravely in the morning air. Perfect timing, he thought, as he turned to look ahead again. From over the rim of the Italian mountains ahead, the first bright arc of sun rose golden from its bed.

Suddenly there was much to see. Ahead of the convoy and to port, a line of heavy naval ships emerged from a bank of smoke, their guns flaming orange as they launched salvo after salvo at the distant land. The convoy passed inside their range from the shore to be met by a destroyer approaching head on at speed.

A signal lamp flashed from the destroyer's bridge to the *Confidenza* and the *Fort Harrison* in turn. The message was short: "Follow me."

The destroyer turned in a surge of wash through 180 degrees and took up station ahead of the double file of ships. The two minesweepers exchanged signals with the destroyer and departed on a south-easterly course.

The flock of ships ploughed steadily shorewards. The mountains now seemed very close but the shoreline itself was invisible behind a pall of smoke. The noise of gunfire was now a continuous thunder in the ears.

What happened next caused every man on the bridge of the *Fort Harrison* to freeze in his shoes and stare dumbly ahead in paralysed surprise. The water all around the destroyer erupted in great thirty-foot spouts which plumed black smoke at their tips.

Sandy beach was momentarily visible ahead but curling clouds of smoke lay along the shoreline obscuring a clear view. The hills beyond the beach stood out in bold relief above this black-grey blanket.

Lansing raised binoculars to his eyes and scanned these hills. Even as he watched, fresh puffs of smoke rose just below the level of a 1,000-foot ridge and spread like a fast-burning fuse along its half-mile length.

This time the shells screamed their approach. A solid wall of water rose from the sea directly ahead of the *Fort Harrison* completely hiding the destroyers. All around the *Fort Harrison* and the *Confidenza* huge fountains of white water leapt up like geysers as the shells from the German hillside batteries saturated the leading ships with a rain of explosive.

Still the ships ploughed on.

Yet another barrage screamed through the morning air. GIs huddled for cover on the decks of the *Fort Harrison* as the shells whined overhead and threw up fresh mountains of water astern. From the midst of this new maelstrom of leaping water came a cataclysmic roar of noise and a Vesuvius of black smoke and orange flame. This volcanic cloud mushroomed to a thousand feet and was followed by a rain of debris which peppered the ocean in a mile-wide circle setting up steaming, hissing splashes. For a moment, the sea seemed to boil.

Horror etched the watching faces on the *Harrison* as they looked astern to where the following ship, the *Empire Dornoch*, had been. There was no sign of the ship, only a heaving mass of oily flaming water, floating wreckage and bodies.

Some of the bodies lived, making frantic swimming strokes to escape the curtain of fire and smoke. Other bodies bobbed in the water like grotesque corks, their only movements dictated by eddies of water rippling out from the centre of the smoking cauldron of death.

Above the sound of the guns and more exploding shells came the screams of the dying and the maimed.

Eyes grim and jaw tight, Lansing forced himself to turn his back on the scene and look ahead.

"Starboard a bit," he called to the helmsman. The *Fort Harrison* and the *Confidenza* had drifted perilously close to each other during the bombardment, which had by no means finished. Having got the range and tasted success, the German gunners now seemed to be firing at will as more and more ships came within range.

Away to port and astern, flames and smoke belched from the midships section of the *Ocean Flint* as another shell hit target. The miracle was, however, that ships weren't sinking all over the place. So concentrated was the rain of shells that it seemed impossible for any of the vessels to emerge unscathed.

The destroyer ahead was signalling furiously.

Durham called out the message to Lansing while acknowledging with the Aldis.

"To Commodore and twenty-one," he called out. "Alter course now. Steer one-eight-oh degrees for one mile then alter course to two-two-five degrees. Make speed four knots on second alteration. Shall make smoke."

The destroyer swung immediately on to a southerly course and began to belch great clouds of dense black smoke.

Lansing ran out to the port wing of the bridge to see if any sign would be forthcoming from the *Confidenza* to indicate that she had received the signal.

The ten-inch lamp on the wing of the *Confidenza*'s bridge blinked out the single letter "R". Then it repeated.

Lansing acknowledged with a wave of his arm. The ships were close enough to enable Lansing to see that three pairs of binoculars were trained on him from the other ship's bridge. He knew that the letter "R", meaning "received", indicated that the destroyer's message had been understood.

"Hard a-starboard," Lansing bawled to the helmsman without further delay. He wrenched on the whistle lanyard and sounded a single blast.

"Bring her round to one-eight-oh, helmsman," Lansing called out. "Mr Durham, ring dead slow ahead."

As the *Fort Harrison* wheeled and slowed, so the *Confidenza* increased speed and held course. Then the Dutch liner gave a single blast on its siren and began a ninety-degree turn to starboard. It rapidly began to overhaul the *Fort Harrison*.

Lansing allowed the other vessel to pull ahead. Exactly ten minutes after the first alteration of course, he ordered: "Starboard the helm. Bring her round to two-two-five."

Again, Lansing sounded a single blast on the *Fort Harrison*'s whistle. The water astern of the *Harrison* erupted in yet another pattern of shellbursts, almost simultaneously. The shore and even the mountains were now completely obliterated from view by the wall of smoke set up by the pilot destroyer well to their eastward.

The sonorous notes of ships' sirens punctuated the continuing roll of gunfire as other ships in the convoy altered course in the wakes of the two leaders. The two columns had, in fact, effected almost a complete U-turn and were now heading back out to sea.

The flag "K" and the pendant "4" were streaming from the Commodore's signal mast. Durham called down Lovell from the gun-nest and instructed him to fly the same signal.

Two miles to the north, a corvette was picking up survivors from the *Empire Dornoch*.

Although it was a magnificent day and the sun shone from a cloudless blue sky, visibility at sea level was reduced to a mere two miles because of the clouds of war. Grey, hazy smoke drifted on the ocean, at times in the denser patches obscuring the sun.

From beyond this constant haze, the noise of guns on shore continued their monotonous thunder. For the convoy, however, there was respite from the shore batteries, now that the ships had moved out of range. The ships now seemed to be plodding in an eerie acrid-smelling limbo.

After an hour, they were overtaken by the same destroyer which had led them into the shellfire.

It manoeuvred close to the *Confidenza*.

A bizarre conversation then took place by loud-hailer between the Commodore and the Captain of the destroyer.

The Commodore opened the conversation:

"What the bloody hell is going on, old man?"

"Sorry for the farting around, sir. Slight case of shambles up on the beach. Did you get any of it on the RT?"

"Not a bloody word. Can't make head nor tail of their mumbo-jumbo."

"They contacted us just in time. We nearly landed you right in the middle of a ruddy Panzer division or something of the sort. The place is simply crawling with Nasties. They shouldn't have been there, of course. Our chaps were supposed to have cleared the area before daybreak but things didn't quite go according to plan."

"What the hell do we do now? Stooge around here for the duration?"

"No such luck, sir. We've got to take you in again. Further south. Game for another go?"

"Lay on, Macduff. Ours is not to reason why."

"Very good, sir. Just play follow my leader. I'll try not to get lost."

It was almost noon by the time the ships regrouped and headed in towards the beaches south of the Sele River.

The projected plan for Avalanche had anticipated that by noon of D-Day, the British Tenth Corps would have established control of the area north of the Sele River and the US Sixth Corps would have won the area to the south. In fact, the two forces had been hard put to gain a meagre toe-hold in their immediate landing areas. They were contained in isolated pockets, miles apart, and with little immediate hope of a link-up.

Later, that gap between the two Allied forces was to become the focal point of a German counter-attack aimed at the isolation and annihilation of the invaders. For the time being, however, the gulf between them represented only a dangerous no-man's-land.

The retreat to seaward allowed the troops on the *Fort Harrison* to enjoy a mid-day meal in comparative peace. The hubbub of excited chatter on the decks slowly subsided when two alterations of course and great signalling activity on the bridge triggered the realisation that the ship was once more pointed towards the Italian shore. Once more, the *Confidenza* and the *Fort Harrison* led the two columns towards the angry guns.

They were still ten miles from shore when the port column reduced speed and allowed the starboard column to move ahead. The *Fort Harrison* now led the single file formation towards a planned pattern of anchorage positions.

The pilot destroyer took up position ahead of the *Harrison*.

Once more the mountains loomed out of the smoke. Then the smoke suddenly thinned and there were the beaches and a forest of masts. Landing-craft of every shape and size were buzzing about like pleasure boats in the Solent. Warships cruised majestically, seaborne artillery hammering at targets on land. Merchant vessels lay at anchor disgorging their cargoes.

Here and there masts rose from the water marking a casualty's grave.

Mitchell stood alongside Lansing in the wheelhouse of the *Fort Harrison*. He held a large sheet of stiff paper in his hand. It was one of several anchorage plans which had come with Lansing's sealed orders.

"Does it make sense to you, Mr Mitchell?" asked Lansing.

"It seems pretty straightforward," said Mitchell. "We take our bearings from the Control Ship and the two marker vessels. The pilot up ahead there will take us approximately to where we drop the hook and the ships astern will take their cue from us. The *Confidenza* will be taking her lot to port while we go to starboard – that's from the marker vessels."

"You'd better go topside then. Give me a shout down the tube when we're past the markers and should be turning to starboard. I'll just follow the pilot ship and turn when she turns. But just in case our navy friend thinks we can turn on a sixpence, I want you to give me the wink anyway. We'll need a little bit of water between us and anything else that's at anchor."

Mitchell climbed to the monkey-island and stationed himself on the binnacle platform. He uncovered the compass and peered through the azimuth mirror at two peaks which he took to be Monte Soprano and Monte Sottane.

Below the twin summits, which stood side by side, smoke covered the lower slopes and extended to the apron of golden beach which skirted the Gulf of Salerno. He focused his binoculars on the beach. Vehicles were moving there. One caught fire and exploded as he watched.

Here and there men moved. Some – whom he took to be beachmasters' staff – directed landing-craft on the beach like traffic policemen. They were nonchalant and unhurried in their movements.

Elsewhere, squads of thirty or more ran at the crouch. They moved up the beach and disappeared into the smoke. Others worked methodically in groups at the top of the beach, stacking supplies and ammo. Every so often, these men would hurl themselves flat.

Mitchell could see on these occasions that little puffs of smoke would whip up from the sand. Shell-bursts or mortar fire. The thought that the enemy was near enough the beach to fire mortar bombs on to it gave Mitchell a cold feeling in his stomach.

The *Fort Harrison* passed between the two marker vessels. Mitchell heard Lansing ring "Slow ahead" on the engine-room telegraph.

"Pilot vessel is turning to starboard now, sir," he called down the voice-tube.

"Aye, aye, Second Mate," came Lansing's reply. "She's giving us plenty of room. I'll begin nursing her round."

The *Fort Harrison* began a slow swing to starboard in the destroyer's wake.

Mitchell's voice-tube emitted a short high-pitched whistle like a singing kettle. He uncorked the whistle attachment. "Yes, sir?"

"Can you see the Control Ship?" came Lansing's voice.

"Yes, sir. Bearing about red forty-five. The one with all the radio gear. Looks like a Christmas tree."

"What should she be bearing when I drop the hook?"

"Oh-three-oh, sir," said Mitchell.

"Let me know when she's coming up to that. Say, oh-four-oh."

"Aye aye, sir."

Mitchell turned his binoculars on to the USS *Ancon*, the Control Ship. She bristled with radio and electronic equipment. As the *Fort Harrison* passed abeam, Mitchell heard a klaxon sound aboard the American ship and saw a rating hoist a large red flag to the top of the signal mast.

He blew air into the voice-tube to the wheelhouse.

"What is it, Second Mate?"

Lansing must have been standing close to the tube.

"Control Ship has just hoisted the red flag. That's air attack."

"I'll sound the alarm," said Lansing. "Not that I imagine any of our lads have dozed off."

A moment later the *Fort Harrison*'s bells rang out their strident warning—a short ring followed by a long. The notes had scarcely died away when the nasal tones of an American voice came booming across the water from loud-speakers on the USS *Ancon*:

"Aircraft bearing one-eight-zero. Focke-Wulf one-nineties."

Even as the loudspeaker warning was repeated, Mitchell heard the drone of engines. The sun glinted on white wings.

Mitchell, looking up, counted five specks at about ten thousand feet before the sun made him look away. The aircraft had swung out to sea.

"They're coming out of the sun," he yelled to the bridge gunners. "Green forty-five."

"I can't see a bloody thing!" shouted the army gunner on the starboard Oerlikon.

"Just sight towards green four-five," yelled Mitchell. "Can't you hear the bastards? Here they come!"

All hell broke loose as the armada of ships gathered off the beach began to pump shells and rockets into the sky as if at a given signal. Through the ear-battering, mind-tearing pounding of noise came the scream of diving aircraft.

The Focke-Wulfs came in from between south and south-west in line ahead formation. Then, peeling off one by one, they followed their leader down to a thousand feet before releasing their bombs. Down through a sky blackened with exploding steel they hurtled.

The third aircraft faltered and broke off to seaward trailing smoke. A parachute opened and hung. The smoking aircraft burned a fiery trail lower and lower towards the horizon and then exploded into the ocean.

Exploding bombs sent great mountains of foam leaping into the air on both sides of the *Fort Harrison*. Eight hundred yards to the north, the foredeck of a Liberty ship vomited great lumps of steel skyward in a convulsion of flame and oily smoke. A twenty-five-ton LCM approaching the stricken vessel disintegrated in a cloud of spray and shattered metal.

Mitchell, crouching low over the binnacle, shook himself out of a kind of numbed trance. The shock of noise on the senses and the visual assault which accompanied it – in which the world seemed to be blowing up before the eyes – had the power to suspend all thought.

He had to force himself to remember exactly where he was and what he should be doing. He sighted the *Ancon* through the sights of the compass mirror. The American ship was bearing 038 degrees.

He whistled Lansing.

"Eight degrees to go on the bearing," he reported. "Sorry I'm a bit late, sir."

"Something distract you, Mr Mitchell?" Lansing inquired drily.

"It's this balmy Italian weather," said Mitchell. "We're almost on the bearing now, sir."

Down in the wheelhouse, Lansing clanged "Stop engines" on the telegraph.

He hailed Pendlebury on the fo'c'sle-head.

"Stand by to let go, Mr Mate."

"Aye aye, sir."

Lansing rang "Full astern". The water under the *Fort Harrison*'s counter began to boil towards the midship section as the ship lost way.

"Let go, for'ard!"

The clang of the carpenter's sledge-hammer rang out from the fo'c'sle-head. The cable rumbled through the hawse-pipe as the weight of the anchor took command and went splashing into the water and down to the seabed.

A few moments later, Lansing rang "Finished with engines". Immediately then, he rang the telegraph to "Stand by".

The *Fort Harrison* was now riding at anchor. Three hundred yards away was Blue Beach. They had arrived.

7
Beach-head

WITHIN MINUTES of the *Fort Harrison* having dropped anchor, the first trucks of the deck cargo were being unloaded over the side into landing-craft. The first LCT to come alongside brought five gangs of men from an American docks battalion. They swarmed aboard and moved quickly into action.

The LCT was fully loaded in less than an hour. It was given an encouraging cheer by the men lining the deck rail as it cast off and headed for Blue Beach.

Three LCMs immediately moved into the space vacated by the bigger landing-craft along the *Fort Harrison*'s port side.

Satisfaction at the speed of the operation turned to dismay on the ship's deck as attention was drawn to the arrival on Blue Beach of the truck-laden LCT. It grounded and dropped its gate, but as the big trucks lumbered on to the beach they ran into withering fire from German eight-eights lining the hills.

Only two out of the twenty or so three-tonners reached the top of the beach and the trees and rock which provided screen.

Colonel Dwight J. Moss and Captain Wilbur Diamond immediately went into a shocked huddle. According to the plans with which they had been provided, most of the enemy guns within range of Blue Beach should have been silenced long before now.

Both officers were stunned by the terrible wastage of men and vehicles. They had to decide, and decide quickly, if such losses could be afforded.

Diamond was in no doubt that they could not. He saw no sense in emptying vehicles out of the *Fort Harrison* in order to provide target practice for an enemy whose strength was greatly in excess of all expectations.

He pressed the Colonel to let him take a jeep ashore so that he could assess the situation and establish if sufficient ground had been taken beyond the beach to set up "safe" areas.

Moss was reluctant to hold up the disembarkation – but he also had a responsibility to land the army's mobile power as near intact as possible.

"Have you got a jeep ready to go?" he asked Diamond.

"I'm next over the side. That's my jeep they're putting into the LCM aside of number two hold right now."

"All right," said Moss, "but maybe you'd be safer to land at Yellow Beach and work your way south."

"I'll take my chance on Blue Beach, sir," said Diamond. "If I don't make it then you can send Lieutenant Gomez by Yellow Beach."

"We'll have to set up our own radio control ashore anyway," Moss said. "So Gomez will be coming right behind you with the radio truck whether you make it or not. I can hold back the Divisional Transport trucks but we gotta get a radio truck ashore and operating whatever else we do."

Moss agreed, however, to wait thirty minutes before committing Gomez to the fray.

"You'd better take somebody with you," he advised Diamond. "Good luck, Captain."

Diamond strode off. His eyes searched the faces of the men thronging the deck. They settled on the broad frame of Quilley, who was leaning over the bulwark intent on what was taking place ashore.

Diamond tapped Quilley on the shoulder.

"I reckon a man might have to be an idiot to volunteer to take a jeep up that beach," he said softly. "What do you think, Sergeant?"

Quilley turned, startled, taken offguard by the question.

"Well ... Yessir – he'd have to be an idiot."

"*You* don't look like an idiot, Sergeant. Are you?"

"No, sir."

"And do I look like an idiot?"

"No, sir."

"Well, I just volunteered to take a jeep up that beach. Does that make me an idiot?"

"No, sir," said Quilley, floundering.

"Good," said Diamond. "I'm not an idiot — and you don't *look* like one. So the chances are you won't feel like one or act like one when you come with me. I sure as hell don't want an idiot riding shot-gun!"

"You ... you want me to go ashore with you? You mean right now? In a jeep?"

"Immediately. At once. Forthwith!" said Diamond with a hard smile. "No need to pack a week-end suitcase or grab a toothbrush. Just come as you are."

"But my stuff ..." Quilley began.

"Forget it," said Diamond. "We're just going on a little scouting mission and we'll be coming back later to collect all our bits and pieces. That is ... if *we* don't come back in bits and pieces."

Quilley failed to see the humour in Diamond's attempt at a joke. He saw nothing funny in the situation whatsoever. And the thought of being parted, even temporarily, from his money induced a feeling akin to physical illness.

* * *

The LCM grounded on Blue Beach and the ramp dropped with a splashing thud into wet sand. Captain Wilbur Diamond drove his jeep up on to dry ground. Quilley sat beside him, his face white with fear.

Diamond had a stub of an unlit cigar stuck in his mouth. He chewed it, his jaw set forward in a determined thrust. From beyond a grove of trees away to the right, German infantry with mortars were relentlessly pounding the upper reaches of the beach.

Diamond seemed unaware of their existence. Following tracks left by other vehicles he gunned the jeep through the soft sand as if intent on reaching Rome by morning. The jeep's progress was marked by a series of accompanying explosions which left small craters of charred smoking earth. Sand spewed up in all directions and the air was filled with flying metal and grit as the jeep navigated in charmed fashion through these eruptions.

Several times, Quilley was almost thrown bodily from his seat as the front wheels hit deep ruts. His stomach was a quivering jelly inside him when a particularly nasty lurch nearly put him through the windscreen, and his eyes saw the reason for the vehicle's sudden leap. The front wheel had hit an obstruction. It was a headless corpse.

Diamond finally ran the jeep off the rough track under a rock overhang. Further progress was impossible anyway. The burning wreck of an overturned truck blocked the way.

The two men got out of the jeep and Diamond led the way to where a platoon of infantry was resting, backs against rock, in various states of exhaustion.

A lieutenant with a dirt-smeared face looked up wearily at Diamond.

"You aiming to go some place, Captain?"

"We got three hundred trucks coming ashore tonight. I gotta find a place to put them," said Diamond.

"You see the Beachmaster?"

"On the beach?"

"Where else? That's all the territory we got."

"All I saw on the beach was asses stickin' out of fox-holes. There ain't much movement down there."

"There's a lot of dead men down there."

"Yeah, I know. It's been rough, eh?"

"We've been eatin' shit all day. It was like the Krauts were expecting us. They got all the high ground. They blast anything that moves. They've got eighty-eights dug in and well hidden all along the high ridges and they've got all the cover on the lower ground ... Keep movin' their mortar positions here, there and everywhere and knocking hell out of us. We need artillery, armour, air strikes ... We can't fight this goddamned war on our own!"

"Your guys look kinda wore out," said Diamond

"They're down and ready to be counted out. They don't know what's hit 'em. Christ, here comes the Major!"

The Major was a hollow-faced man whose head seemed to be sunken in the cavernous depths of his helmet. He came loping towards them at a crouching run, dodging the outstretched legs of the sprawling soldiers.

The expression on his face was almost demoniac as he stared first at Diamond and then at the Lieutenant. He finally fixed his eyes on the Lieutenant. His breath was coming in great gasps and it was a moment before he was able to speak.

"Get your men ready to move out, Skolski," he said. "Charlie Company has been almost wiped out over on the right. What's left of it is pinned down just below the road to Agropoli and somebody has got to take the pressure off them."

"But my men are bushed, sir," protested the Lieutenant.

"I don't give a goddamn if they gotta crawl out on their bellies, Lieutenant, but they're going to get up there and over that road and knock out some of those Kraut gun-nests low down on Monte Sottane. Otherwise, these Krauts are gonna hit us during the night and over-run the whole goddamned beach."

Skolski bit his lip. Whatever his feelings, he kept them to himself.

"I'll get the men moving, sir," he said. "How do we get up there?"

The Major pointed.

"Circle round to your right for about five hundred yards. Then there's not so much cover – some trees and scrub that's all dried up – but there's a kind of gully which takes you right up to the road. Follow that and try to get across the road. There's plenty of cover if you can get to the other side. Charlie Company is pinned down below the road about a quarter of a mile from the gully."

Lieutenant Skolski called his sergeant, who moved along the line of men, cursing them and encouraging them in turn. Sullenly, with Skolski leading, the platoon moved wearily off in single file.

The Major turned to face Diamond and Quilley.

"What outfit are you, Captain?"

"Supply and Transport ... Co-ordinator," said Diamond. "I want to stake out a 'safe' area for the vehicles I got coming ashore tonight."

The Major laughed humourlessly.

"You shoulda stayed in Bizerta," he said. "It's heavy artillery we need – to knock the Krauts off those goddamned hills. Trucks are no goddamned good unless they've got roads to run on. You see the Beachmaster?"

"Nope."

"Well I suggest you do, Captain. They've got more real estate up back of Red Beach. They've crossed the railway and the roads at Paestum and are movin' up on Cappaccio. There ain't gonna be any safe areas near Blue Beach until we get the Krauts off those hills."

Diamond remained poker-faced.

"I reckon this spot right here would do," he said. "We got all this rock to protect us from the hills. And those trees on the right make a good screen from higher up. I reckon we could get a tidy number of trucks on the lee side of these rocks."

"Well, it's none of my business," said the Major. "My job is killin' Krauts."

"Don't let me keep you from it, Major," said Diamond.

The Major flung Diamond a venomous look, turned, and went off without another word in the direction taken by Skolski and his platoon.

"OK, Sergeant Quilley," said Diamond, "we got work to do. First, I want you to get back to the beach and find that goddamned Beachmaster ..." He pulled a map from a cavernous pocket and unfolded it. After a moment's study, he thrust it in front of Quilley and went on:

"I reckon we're about here. And here's the road. Now, we'll eventually have to get traffic moving from here to the road but I want to make a recce and be sure there's some kind of access. We may need some help from the Seabees to track over any soft ground and bulldoze a way up. They'll have to move that wrecked truck for a start ... But I want you to find out from the Beachmaster where we can locate the Seabees, then go and get one of their guys to come up here and see me. Get him to bring a radio-man so that he can talk back to his own Control and bring up equipment. Got that?"

"Yes, sir," said Quilley, who was far from delighted at the prospect of returning to the fire-raked beach. "You want me to go on foot?"

"Well, there sure as hell ain't any taxis," said Diamond. He glanced at his watch. "Try to make it back here by eighteen hundred hours. We'll meet at the jeep. Oh, and when you're down there, see if there's any sign of Lieutenant Gomez and the radio truck. He was due to hit the beach about thirty minutes after us. I just hope he made it. Tell him where I am and to get here pronto."

The next hour was a nightmare for Quilley. The beach, particularly the southern end, continued to be pounded by eighty-eight shells. The peculiar whine of mortar fire continued, too, but the mortar-carrying German troops must have been pushed back – or had withdrawn – to higher ground and their targets were now the GIs in direct opposition to them rather than the beach itself.

By bearing to the north, Quilley worked his way back to the beach by a safer route than would have been the case had he chosen the more direct path. Even at that, shells burst uncomfortably near on a number of occasions. When they did fall close, he burrowed his way into the sand, clawing at it in fear and desperation as if total integration of his body with the ground represented immunity.

On one occasion he flung himself into a ready-dug fox-hole and lay there with his face pressed against its soft warm sandy wall. He clung there blindly for fully five minutes before daring to end the fear-filled embrace. When, finally, he did look around him, it was to find that he was not the only occupant of the hole.

Sitting opposite him, a waxen grin on his face, was a young soldier. The man just sat there, hands clasped across his stomach, like a faintly surprised Buddha. Horror and revulsion rose in Quilley as he realised that the clasped hands were barely holding back what remained of the soldier's intestines and that their owner was quite dead. The grin was the agony of his death frozen in his face.

Yellow Beach, Green Beach and Red Beach – the three beaches to the north of Blue Beach – were hives of activity compared with the most southerly flank. And for the very good reason that they were not quite so exposed to the deadly fire of the German gunners. So, it was quite a relief to Quilley – when he found himself on Yellow Beach – that he encountered Lieutenant Gomez and the radio truck. They had been landed there.

Gomez, from his brief acquaintance with Quilley on the *Fort Harrison*, had looked upon the Sergeant as a cocky, arrogant individual. So he was surprised now at Quilley's dazed, bewildered state.

He motioned Quilley away from the knot of men round the radio truck and spoke to him low-voiced and sternly.

"Pull yourself together, Sergeant. You look green in the face and you're gibbering like an idiot. What the hell are the men going to think? Now take a grip on yourself and tell me exactly what Captain Diamond said and what he wants done about the Beachmaster and the Seabees. What you've jabbered at me so far isn't making sense."

Anger replaced Quilley's befuddlement.

"You don't know what it's like back there, Lieutenant," he snarled. "You haven't had to crawl miles on your belly dodging shells and bullets every inch of the goddamned way. We came right up Blue Beach, goddamnit! We didn't get no easy ride up Yellow Beach!"

Gomez shrugged.

"Okay, okay. Maybe I shoulda made allowances – but you were acting like a panicky hen. I thought you'd cracked up. So let's forget it. Just give me the story from Captain Diamond."

With the help of one of the Beach Control officers, a captain of Seabees was located supervising the landing of some of his heavy equipment. This, too, should have come ashore at Blue Beach but conditions had been ruled too hazardous.

It was quickly agreed that Quilley, Gomez and the radio truck set out immediately for the rendezvous with Captain Diamond. The Seabee unit would follow behind under cover of a naval barrage that was due to start at any minute with the aim of taking some of the pressure off Blue Beach.

Indeed, Quilley was no sooner seated in the radio truck and giving the driver instructions on Diamond's location than a thunderous barrage commenced to the south. A line of heavy naval ships, coming closer inshore than might have been prudent, could be seen manoeuvring through the anchorage, their guns belching flame.

"Let's go!" shouted Gomez from the running-step of the radio truck. It moved off. Lumbering behind came two Seabee half-tracks, loaded with wire meshing and men and, behind them, an earth-mover and more loaded half-tracks.

Some Seabees building wire-mesh tracks up Yellow Beach from the water's edge shouted ribald comments as the convoy moved off.

"Hey, you're going the wrong way!" yelled one Seabee, sweating from his labours. "Naples is thataway!" he signalled, pointing north.

"That's why we is goin' thisaway, man!" replied a beaming Negro GI, high on the side of a half-track. "We is doin' the gran' scenic tour."

* * *

The naval barrage had been watched with some awe by the men on the *Fort Harrison*. As Andrew Mitchell had gone about the hundred and one tasks which demanded his attention, he had found it difficult not to be distracted by what was happening all around. A port-working routine had to be established in conditions which, to say the least, were abnormal.

Compared with the beach, the *Fort Harrison* seemed a secure and comfortable place to the Second Mate – even although, with the variety of explosives and highly combustible ordnance in her holds, the ship was an outsize floating bomb.

The officers and crew of the *Fort Harrison* had gone immediately on to a four-hours-on four-hours-off watch-keeping rota. It was to prove meaningless. So frequently was the anchorage to be attacked from the air – necessitating off-watch men to assemble at gun stations – that a more accurate description of the watchkeeping system turned out to be four-hours-on followed by four-hours-on.

Sleep was to become an unknown luxury. Gunners would nap between the incessant alarms, still strapped to their guns. Loaders sitting down in the pits, arms aching from hefting sixty-pound magazines on to cannons with red-hot barrels, would keel over in sheer fatigue.

Tanned faces would become grey and hollow as shock and utter weariness took their toll.

The cooks and stewards were to work throughout this time supplying food and endless brews of tea or coffee to men who could only pause where they stood and snatch some kind of sustenance. They were to make endless supplies of soup – for this was one food which could be gulped from a mug in one hand and still leave the other hand free to operate a winch-handle or a trigger or a signal lamp.

The knives and forks from the saloon were never to leave their sectioned drawers in the pantry cabinets. Anything requiring a knife and a fork to be eaten was to remain uneaten – because hands that might have held them were to have more important things to do and there was no time.

Survivors of the Battle of Salerno Bay were to have a good one-word answer to the lightly offered admonition, "Go to Hell!" It was:

"Again?"

Three times before dusk on that first day, the German

warplanes returned to wreak death and destruction on the anchored armada. They ran a ferocious gauntlet of fire from the assembled ships, not always successfully. A fiery arc in the sky would mark the end of an attacker but could pass almost without notice in that fire-streaked smoke-wraithed space.

Darkness brought no respite from the aerial assault. Phosphorous flares floated gently down bathing sea and ships in an orange glow and, from above, a now unseen enemy maintained the rain of bombs.

A Liberty ship close to Yellow Beach vomited flame from its molten belly and, for the rest of the night, burned like a torch thrust from the water. A big fat-beamed landing-ship, emptying guns and trucks and ammunition from its whale-like jaws on to the beach, exploded into the atmosphere with a blast which sent a tidal wave surging seawards with such ferocity – as if the law of gravity had been reversed – that two smaller landing-craft were swamped and sunk.

The ring of escorts patrolling the seaward perimeter of the anchorage escaped the bombing – but had distractions of their own. Three E-boats broke through the ring but were engaged in a running battle which produced its own spectacular pyrotechnics. Tracer from cannon and pom-pom curved in low arcs across the horizon as the attacks were temporarily thwarted with at least one blazing casualty.

And so the night wore on, with attacks coming from the air every hour, on the hour, and seeming to increase in frequency and intensity just before dawn.

On shore, Quilley hoped that the night would never end. Somehow or other the radio truck and most of the Seabee equipment had successfully run the gauntlet of exploding shells to reach the rendezvous with Diamond above Blue Beach. But there, a confusion of regrouping infantry units were still pinned down by Spandau fire from the near ridges and heavier enemy guns on the high ridges.

It was some time after dark that the weary and frustrated men above Blue Beach became aware that the fury of sound which had been exploding over and around them all day had diminished. It did not stop. It was more as if the thunderstorm had moved away.

In fact, what had happened was that the guns immediately opposite them had fallen temporarily silent and they were hearing the continuing battle taking place in the British sector a dozen miles to the north.

Men who, before, had had to shout at the tops of their voices to make the simplest communications, now found that they were talking in whispers. Occasionally a flurry of shells would straddle the area to remind the invaders that the respite wasn't permanent – but, even at that, there was no disguising that the Germans were taking some kind of breather.

In fact, they were taking advantage of the darkness to move an entire Panzer division north towards the British sector in the belief that a Panzer Grenadier division arriving from Southern Italy – where they had been in opposition to Montgomery's Eighth Army – would take their place against the invading Americans.

Quilley knew nothing of these tactical manoeuvres. He knew only that the coming of night brought with it some relief from a day of nightmare. With Gomez and Diamond both in the radio truck organising the disembarkation of vehicles, Quilley found an unoccupied hollow among the rocks where he could appease the hungry rumblings of his belly. He wolfed a large bar of black raisin-filled chocolate, swilling it down with a can of orange juice. Then he smoked a cigarette.

He felt tired. Never in his life had he felt so tired. His head lolled forward and he leapt awake as the smouldering cigarette between his fingers burnt into his flesh. He stamped the cigarette out and sucked his blackened fingers. He closed his eyes, wanting to shut out this place and its total unreality.

His head lolled forward again. He escaped into a merciful blackness of sleep. He was still sprawled in sleep two hours later when Lieutenant Gomez found him.

Gomez prodded Quilley awake.

"On your feet, Sergeant. I've been looking all over for you. Come on! Off your goddamned butt. We got work to do."

Quilley's eyes opened in astonishment. Out to sea, fountains of tracer shells were leaping skywards from the anchored ships. Orange flares cast a glow through which dark masts stood out like the skeletal shapes of a forest in winter. The chorus of a thousand guns hammered out an orchestrated accompaniment of battering sound. Another air raid was in progress.

Quilley abandoned the limbo of haunted dreaming for the more fearful nightmare of wakefulness. He was glad that the ships in the bay rather than he were the target of the bombers, and yet a part of him suffered agonies at the thought of what might be befalling his money.

When morning came, would the *Fort Harrison* still be out there riding at anchor, or would it be another burning hulk?

8

Death in the Morning

THERE WAS no cloud in the sky. By ten in the morning the glaring sun had lifted the temperature to the high eighties.

But the direct heat of the sun scarcely penetrated the acrid fog of smoke which lay over the cauldron that was Salerno Bay. It filled the lungs with a sulphurous taste and hung like a grey mantle on the clusters of ships, so that only the tips of their masts showed.

Every now and then, the light breeze from the shore would thin the drifting cloud and begin the process of dispersing it. But whenever this process of dispersal began, the metallic voice from the loudspeakers of the control vessels would begin their urgent warnings of approaching aircraft and canisters, emitting fresh smoke, would be cast into the sea. Drifting gently, dense clouds of sulphurous yellow-grey would billow up and outwards from the bobbing cone-topped cylinders until once more the vaporous blanket was renewed.

It was during a temporary clearing of this toxic cloud that Andrew Mitchell said his farewell to Lieutenant Holcroft.

Their friendship had been of short duration, yet it had matured to one of considerable depth in the few weeks of its existence. Born an ocean apart into differing cultures and social conditions, the two men had been thrust briefly into each other's lives by the tides of war. Each had glimpsed in the other a reflection of commonly held values and aspirations.

These were not displayed like price-tickets on merchandise. Love of justice, honesty, idealism based on reasonableness rather than violence, tolerance, the capacity for concern and for courage – these are not instantly visible qualities.

But their possessors can instinctively recognise them in their fellows in a way that confounds the barriers of language and race whether they meet initially as enemies or allies.

Mitchell and Lieutenant Holcroft were allies, if only by accident of birth. They became friends by instinct and established a mutuality of companionship which both recognised as enriching and, in an undefined way, profound.

If they had grown up in the same neighbourhood, they would have been bosom friends. If they had met as older men, they would have found in each other an identification of interest and outlook capable of enduring to the winter of their days.

But they met as pawns in a war, two individuals swept momentarily together in the same eddying current.

*   *   *

It had been the same with Mitchell and Laura. Individuals in the currents of war. Swept briefly together. Then parted. Had he known her only three days? Was it only one short month ago?

It had been at the RAF Docks EU unit dance in Algiers soon after they'd got back from Sicily. Dick Mason, the RAF Sergeant who seemed permanently stuck with his docks job at Algiers and had been a daily visitor to the *Fort Harrison* round about morning coffee time, had invited Mitchell to the dance.

It was a weekly affair. Attended by all ranks and all services – the RAF didn't seem as hidebound as the army and navy about segregating officers and men – and by French civilians, British nurses from the military hospital, some WAAFs, some Americans.

Mitchell had danced twice with Laura. They had laughed at the heroic but not too expert musicianship of the band, admired the multi-coloured lanterns festooning the open courtyard which was the dance-floor, and apologised to each other when their feet got caught in the crevices between the paving slabs.

Then Dick Mason had hauled Mitchell away to the Sergeants' bar for drinks and he had hesitated to abandon his host and go in search of the girl with the laughing voice and upswept tawny hair. He had not been good company for Mason; toying with his drink, thinking private thoughts: trying to decide if he liked the name, Laura, and concluding that he did. She was a lieutenant in the Queen Alexandra's Royal Army Nursing Corps.

She was nowhere to be seen when Mitchell finally excused himself from Mason and returned to the courtyard, now crowded with dancers. The band were murdering "Moonlight Serenade".

Then Mitchell saw her. She was shaking hands with an RAF officer and seemed to be about to leave. The evening suddenly fell flat. On an impulse, Mitchell decided he would leave, too.

He returned to the bar to let Mason know he was leaving, collected his uniform cap from the cloakroom, and hurried into the street.

Laura was walking alone down the cobbled road, about a hundred yards ahead, making towards the city centre. It was also the way Mitchell had to take to return to the ship. He walked quickly after the girl, rehearsing in his mind what he would say when he overtook her and offered to escort her. Algiers was no place for a man to venture out alone after dark. A woman was taking her life in her hands.

The thought had no sooner crossed Mitchell's mind than Laura was the centre of a tableau involving three figures which – from Mitchell's distance – seemed to be enacting a mime play in the arc of light thrown out by a stuttering street lamp.

Mitchell had expected trouble to come from the sullen groups of Arabs who roamed Algiers in search of unwary servicemen with more money than alcohol tolerance. But the two men who were pulling at and jostling the lone girl were in uniform. American soldiers.

Mitchell broke into a run.

Long before he reached the men he realised that they were very drunk.

"Gimme a kiss, Baby. Gimme a kiss, Baby," one of them kept saying as he tried to wrap Laura in a wine-polluted embrace.

Mitchell turned the man and hit him a clubbing blow full on the nose. The soldier went down and remained sitting, his hand clamped about his nose trying vainly to stem a gushing flow of blood. He was weeping with pain and outrage.

The other soldier lurched drunkenly at Mitchell, fists flying.

"We saw her first, sailor," he yelled. "You're gonna wish you minded your own goddamned business."

A blow landed painfully on Mitchell's ear. He moved inside another wild swing and hammered a straight right to the point of the drunken soldier's jaw. The man's knees crumpled, then he fell forward on his face as if dead.

"Are you all right?"

Mitchell's voice was hoarse as he took the girl's shoulders in his hands.

"I'm OK. They didn't actually hurt me. Just gave me the fright of my life. What do we do now? Run before they come round?"

To her surprise, Mitchell didn't answer. He released her and ran towards a white jeep which had appeared from a sidestreet and was about to turn downtown away from them.

It stopped when Mitchell shouted. A moment later he was back and the jeep was unloading four husky military policemen with white gaiters and white helmets.

"They're your boys," said Mitchell. "They attacked this young lady."

"You must pack quite a punch," said one of the MPs, who had turned over the second attacker. "This one's out cold. He's stinking of hooch, too. Phew!"

"Do you want we should take you to hospital, Ma'am?" asked the Sergeant in charge.

"I'll be all right," said Laura. "I got a scare but they

didn't hurt me. I'm going to the hospital anyway. It's just over there ... I was only a few hundred yards from the gate. I'm a nurse."

"Are you all right, sir?" the Sergeant asked Mitchell.

"Sure, sure. I'll see the young lady gets back safely if you like."

The Sergeant turned again to Laura.

"I have to ask you, Ma'am. Was the assault ... intended rape?"

"I ... I don't know. They're very drunk ... They were trying to be amorous. Can't you just lock them up for the night? Maybe they'll be feeling pretty ashamed in the morning."

"You leave 'em to us, Ma'am," said the Sergeant. "It maybe saves a bit of red tape if you don't want to make a federal case of it. You can take my word for it they'll be disciplined."

In the garden of the hospital, Laura thanked Mitchell.

"I didn't know there were any Galahads left," she said.

"I had an ulterior motive. The dance fell very flat when I saw you leave and I followed you out. I wanted to know you better. I was going to catch up with you and ask you for a date. I can't blame two drunken Yanks for wanting to kiss you ... I have the same kind of inclination ... But I didn't like the way they went about it."

She smiled up at him, mischievous lights in her eyes.

"How would you go about it?"

"Gently," he said, "like this." And his lips caressed hers. Then the caress demanded more. She arched her body into his and the gentle kiss became one of passionate oblivion and mutual giving.

In the breathless aftermath, she pulled away.

"Why now?" she whispered, desolately, "when we may never see each other again."

"What do you mean?"

"I'm being transferred to Palestine. I go on a short leave the day after tomorrow. I want to know you a whole lot better, too, Sir Galahad — but there's just no future for us. I don't even know your name."

"We have tomorrow," said Mitchell, and introduced himself, telling her that no one ever called him anything other than Mitch.

"Is tomorrow enough?"

"In a war, tomorrow can be the rest of your life. A few hours ago I didn't know you existed. Now you do. Very intensely at that. And I don't want it to stop until the minute or second when it has to. And I can't do anything about it."

"You make me feel very special."

"You are."

Mitchell kissed her again, but less gently this time. Their embrace left them clinging to each other wordlessly, almost disbelieving the reality of their emotions but unable to deny the sheer physical wonder of their feeling.

Mitchell released Laura and began to spin a plan to escape from his duties so that he and Laura could spend the next day together. At first she demurred, still concerned with the pointlessness of a single day of potential pleasure in the arid, endless months of war. But, partly out of a growing affection and partly out of gratitude for her rescuer and after a further, long, and much deeper kiss, she finally agreed that they should seize the day.

Tomorrow, when it did come, was a day out of time. Mitchell had borrowed a transit van from his RAF friend, Mason, and he and Laura had driven twenty miles along the coast to a secluded beach.

They had romped like children in the sand, revelling in the solitude of their sunny paradise. They had swum in the warm Mediterranean and dried their bodies in the sun. They had eaten grapes and oranges bought from street vendors in Algiers and washed the fruit down with sweet red wine.

Mitchell knew that if he lived to be an old man with snow-white hair and rheumy eyes, he would never forget the wonder of their loving that day. There was a sweetness, a naturalness and a rightness about the consummation of the joy they had found in each other.

They cavorted in the water like dolphins then, breathless, a gentleness had come into their game. Hands touched and held. Their lips met under water in a kiss. They surfaced like seals, water cascading from their sleek backs. He had smoothed her wet hair away from her forehead, cupped the oval of her head in his hands and pulled her towards him. Bodies and legs intertwined in an aquatic ballet of loving. They had tumbled in the shallows, rising and falling rhythmically with the tideless sea as its deep swell broke in bursting surf against the African shore.

Spent, like breakers on the sand, they had whispered love and promised their lives to one another.

"Mitch," said Laura suddenly, "let's spend the rest of the week together."

He sat up and looked at her, questioning, not daring to think.

"I thought you were going to some desert leave-centre ... and then straight on to Palestine?"

"I don't want to spend my leave with a bunch of nurses. I want to spend it with you. Could you get a few days off?"

Mitchell thought about it.

"The ship's not doing anything. We're moored stern to the mole waiting for a berth. I'm sure old Lansing would let me go if I asked him."

Lansing had been like a fellow-conspirator.

"A woman, is it?"

"Yes, a very special one."

"Then go ... You're only young once."

Mitchell and Laura had found a quaint little hotel not far from what they now considered "their" beach. An elderly French couple had made the lovers welcome with much winking and smiling and nudging of elbows. Their room overlooked the sea.

Mitchell had only to close his eyes to picture again how Laura looked when he had wakened one night and found her gone from his side. She was standing naked at the window gazing out to sea, her body silhouetted against a path of moonlight rippling silver across the ocean.

He had risen and stood behind her, his hands gently cupping her breasts. She had snuggled her hips against him, rousing him.

"I've been admiring your other mistress," she said.

"The sea?"

"Yes. Do you love her?"

"I just live with her – and I respect her ... But you're the one I love."

His fingers caressed her thighs, stroked the soft hair of the pubis. She turned and stretched up on tiptoe to kiss him, thrusting her body into his and gently undulating her hips in a caressing motion.

He lifted her up on to him, so that her legs were wound round his haunches. Laughing, kissing, he carried her to the bed, then slid down on top of her. Eagerly, her hands moved down his thighs, helping, guiding him into her.

"Oh, Mitch!" she cried. "Now! Now! Now!"

Later, he had lain with his head on her breasts.

"I want to marry you, Laura. You know that. I want it to be like this always, just the two of us."

"I want that, too, Mitch. I want your love and I want your children. I don't want to share you with your ship and the sea and this beastly war. I want you to come home safe to me and never, never leave."

He traced a finger across her cheek and found it was wet with tears.

"You're mine now," he whispered, "for ever and ever ... before God and before man ... you're mine! And I'm yours! Whatever happens ... in this world or the next. Nothing can separate us now, whether we die tomorrow or live to be a thousand ... You belong to me. I belong to you."

"Oh, Mitch ... Are we mad?"

"We are the only sane people on Earth ... It's the world that's mad. One day, maybe, it will come to its senses."

"And we'll live happily ever after," said Laura.

"We'll *love* happily ever after," corrected Mitchell, a glimmer of a smile on his lips in the moonlit room.

Her fingers were playing up and down his spine. He kissed

the soft peak of her breast and felt her nipple harden under his tongue. Now her hands were exploring the down of his belly, reaching for him, exciting him. Their bodies met and grooved and became one.

Beyond their room, the seas rose and fell with a surge on the beach, as they had done since the beginning of time. But, just as a life is only the flickering of an eye on the face of eternity, so were their days together no more than a heartbeat in their lives.

No sooner had he met and promised himself to Laura, committed himself to her and a future that might never be realised, than she was swept out of his life by the currents of war — to nurse the casualties of that war in a faraway Palestinian hospital.

And the currents of war had swept him to the Bay of Salerno. As they had swept Jim Holcroft.

As Laura had briefly brought into Mitchell's life the joys and preoccupations of a more normal world, where there is a time for loving, so Holcroft had brought the less intense, less demanding but equally rich friendship which men know.

* * *

Mitchell had watched silently as Holcroft and some other American soldiers had taken the last rites of their church from a Roman Catholic padre who had been touring the ships performing this service. The priest blessed Holcroft and the Lieutenant's eyes met Mitchell's as he rose from the kneeling position.

A grin broke across the American's face as he came to meet Mitchell.

"A slight change of custody," he said. "That little ceremony means that the Almighty can take over the job of looking after me instead of the British Merchant Marine."

He stuck out a hand.

"Thanks for everything, Mitch. It sure has been nice knowing you."

"You're off ashore, then?"

"Another ten minutes. You know, I didn't reckon that I'd actually be sorry to get off this old rustbucket."

Mitchell grinned.

"I'm going to miss you, Jim. I've kind of got used to seeing your ugly mug around – to say nothing of your cast-off socks all around the cabin."

"I'll leave a few pairs behind if you like – just for atmosphere."

A frown crossed Holcroft's face.

"I sure hope we meet up again, Mitch. I would love for you to meet Debbie. And baby Patrick. If you get to Boston before I do, you'll look them up? I gave you the address?"

"I have it," said Mitchell. "And I'm not forgetting what you said about all those pretty sisters-in-law you've got tucked away in Boston."

"Too bad for you I got in first and married the prettiest girl in the family," laughed Holcroft. "Oh-oh – looks like somebody's trying to catch my attention. Time for me to push off."

The two men shook hands again.

"Look after yourself. Get this old rustbucket safely home."

"Good luck, Jim. Remember we've got a date Stateside when all this nonsense is finished. You can show me your medals."

Mitchell watched the young American officer climb down the scrambling-net into the landing-craft. His jeep was right in the bows of the LCT, first off. Holcroft threw his kit into the jeep and climbed in after it.

He perched on top and waved to Mitchell on the deck. Mitchell waved back.

They kept their arms raised in greeting as the vessel made the short journey to the beach. Holcroft gave a final wave as the ramp fell and he prepared to drive ashore.

Mitchell hopped up the bridge-ladder, got his binoculars from the chart-room and went out to the bridge wing to watch his friend ot of sight. He saw the jeep emerge from the jaws of the landing-craft and make a left-hand turn along the sand just above the waterline. He saw the driver's head turn seawards for a last look at the *Fort Harrison*. There seemed to be a smile on Holcroft's face.

Five seconds later, Lieutenant James Holcroft was dead.

One moment, the jeep was there. The next, it had disappeared, as if snatched up into the air by a giant invisible hand and crushed to a powder.

Mitchell heard the crump of the explosion seconds after the jeep had disintegrated before his eyes. Small particles of the vehicle rained down briefly, pitting the sand where they fell. The largest single item of debris was one wheel which fell back to earth and then set off on a crazy run along the water's edge, finally coming to rest in wet sand with water gently lapping over it.

Mitchell heard a voice come up from the foredeck.

"Christ Almighty! Did you see that? Must have been a land-mine – and a bloody big one. There's bugger-all left of that jeep."

Mitchell's bowels were in a knot, as if a massive force was pulling and contracting them in a claw-like grip. Grief was like a burning fireball inside him. The emotion he felt was physical pain; frustration and rage mingling with his anguish.

He thought of Debbie, a young mother in faraway Boston, of a baby called Patrick, who had never seen his father – and, now, would never do so. And he thought of his friend Jim Holcroft whose warm hand had gripped his only minutes ago. Nothing remained of him. Not enough to be collected and buried in a marked grave.

His frame of flesh and bone and warm coursing blood had been shattered in a thousand directions. A life, eager and vital only moments before, had ceased to exist as if it had never been.

No emotion showed in Mitchell's face but his eyes were pools of inward agony and his soul wept tears. Now these eyes rounded as he glimpsed a sailor on board the *Ancon* stream a large red flag to the masthead.

Mitchell's brain registered the warning of yet another

air raid. Forcing movement into his limbs, he postponed the tears he wanted to shed for Holcroft and all of humanity and went to sound the alarm bells.

Then, coldly, without passion, he unclamped the bridge Lewis gun from its rack in the wheelhouse and carried it up to the top bridge. The two Junkers 88s which came swooping out of the sun served for the moment as the target for Mitchell's inner fury. Firing from the shoulder, he emptied the magazine in the direction of the diving planes. Huge spouts of water rose in two lines across the anchorage as first one plane then the next banked and climbed with full throttle towards the mountains leaving a trail of bursting bombs behind them.

As quickly as they had come, they were gone. The chattering anti-aircraft guns fell silent.

Andrew Mitchell stood with the emptied Lewis clenched in his hands. All colour had drained from his tanned face. Whatever the therapy contained in his blasting away with the gun, it had to some extent worked.

Take a grip, he commanded himself. Someone you liked died. He's not the first and he probably won't be the last. And no matter how you tie yourself in knots, nothing you do, nothing you say, nothing you think or feel, is going to bring him or any of them back. Ever.

OK, so every time it happens, you die a little inside yourself. And you ask yourself how often it can happen before there's nothing left inside at all. You think you can't take any more, but you can. You can take it and take it and take it – because you are alive and walking about and talking and thinking and getting hungry and getting thirsty. And you learn to forget. And you learn not to ask questions that have no answers. Like why do good Christian nice guys like Holcroft get killed and why do the likes of me survive? Why can't it be the creeps that get killed? Like that profane foul-mouthed sergeant that Pendlebury's so chummy with? Why not him instead of Holcroft? You've just got to shut it from your mind. You've got to try to forget.

It's not that you want to forget, it's just that too much

remembering hurts – and to stop it always hurting, you try not to keep remembering. And gradually, even when you remember, it doesn't hurt quite so much. Like a wound. First, there's the pain, then the open rawness, then the flesh begins to renew and the wound closes. Then it gets itchy and there's a scab and then the scab goes and leaves a mark. And after a while you look at the mark and some-times you can feel the pain all over again. But it's never so bad because you can cover the mark, hide the scar. You can look at something else. There may even be times when your forgetting is too complete. You forget even what the scar means, what it stands for. Then, it is sometimes good to look at the scar, to make yourself remember.

He climbed down to the navigating bridge and returned the Lewis gun to its rack in the wheelhouse. Glancing out of the window towards the foredeck, he became aware of a commotion down there. The winches at number two had stopped working and a group of the stevedoring GIs were gesticulating angrily at one of their officers.

He went down to investigate.

A lieutenant in his mid-twenties was in the middle of what seemed to be a very ugly situation. Whatever the argument with his men, it had reached the stage where the officer had half-drawn his revolver from the holster at his thigh.

"I am ordering you men to get back to work," were the first words Mitchell heard.

A mountain of a man in a khaki-green sweatshirt and with hair all over his shoulders and arms seemed to be spokesman for the stevedores.

"All we want is a guarantee, Lieutenant. We'll work till we drop – but not when the red flag is up. That's all we want – not to have to stay down in the hold when the red flag is up."

The Lieutenant's face reddened with anger.

"Might I remind you, Sergeant Danovich, that it is your job to uphold military discipline, not to challenge it? You know as well as I do that since we got here, the air-raid flag has been flying longer than it's been hauled down. And we gotta discharge these ships whether the Krauts are throwing bombs at us or not. Christ, man, don't you realise that you're in the army and you're supposed to be fighting a goddamned war?"

"You can't fight a war with dead men, Lieutenant, sir," said the big man with acid in his voice, his eyes scornful. "And dead men is all you'll have if that gasoline down there goes up with my guys trapped in the hold."

"If that gasoline goes up, Sergeant, it won't matter much whether your men are down the hold or on deck," said Andrew Mitchell, stepping between the two men. "If that gasoline goes up, the only safe place to be is about five miles away."

"Who asked you to butt in, Limey?" snapped the Sergeant. "Why don't you go sail a duck in your bath-tub."

"Watch your tongue, Danovich," warned the Lieutenant. "What the officer says is right and you know it! It doesn't matter a goddamn where your men are when the red flag is up. Anything hits this ship and the whole goddamned thing will go up so fast and so far that they'll be picking up the pieces all over the Mediterranean."

"I still say we gotta fighting chance if we get up on deck when the red flag goes up. My men are all behind me. Right, guys?"

There was a chorus of "yeahs" and "Sure, Sergeant".

The big Sergeant looked insolently at the officer: "So what are you gonna do about it, Lieutenant?"

The Lieutenant drew his revolver and pointed it at Danovich.

"I'm ordering you for the last time to get your men below and get back to work," he said.

"Maybe we ought to do like the man says, Danovich," said one of the men sheepishly.

Danovich turned and glared at the man.

"This outfit does what I say. And I say we ain't movin' until we get the guarantees we demanded."

"You ain't in Manhattan docks now, Danny," said a slim dark-haired GI. "The Longshoremen's Union doesn't cut no ice in this man's army. I say we do like the Lieutenant says."

"I got your number, Angelo," said Danovich. "I don't forget lousy scabs. One night you're gonna wake up with a broken back."

Somebody behind the man called Angelo struck him viciously in the kidneys and he sprawled forward. Mitchell helped him to his feet.

"Any more scabs?" asked Danovich. "The Lieutenant here ain't gonna pull that trigger. He has more sense. Don't you, Lieutenant?"

"Don't tempt me, Danovich. So help me, I'm beginning to think I would be doing the world a favour if I let you have it right between the eyes."

Danovich laughed. He nodded his head and, taking it as a signal, two men who had edged behind the officer, pinioned him from behind and took his revolver.

"That thing might have gone off, Lieutenant," said Danovich. "You can't go round threatening enlisted men with guns. You could get yourself court-martialled, you know."

"By God, I'll see you're court-martialled," shouted the Lieutenant. "Goddamn it, man, don't you know anything about the Articles of War. You'll finish up in front of a firing-squad before all this is over!"

Danovich laughed. His laughter was devoid of humour. He spat at the Lieutenant's feet.

"You officer crap make me sick," he said.

"What are we going to do, Danny?" said one of the men in a perplexed voice. He was no officer-lover but what had before been spontaneous airing of a grievance now seemed to be a situation out of control.

"I'll tell you what we'll do," said Danovich. "We'll all stick together. There's a damned sight more of us than there are officers and that gives us a lot of elbow. Now we made a legitimate complaint to the Lieutenant here about working down in the hold when the air-raid flag was up — but you all saw what he did. He pulled a goddamned gun on us and threatened to shoot us. Well that ain't the way to get things done in a democracy and that's supposed to be what this goddamned war is all about. So we either stick to our principles or we let this officer crap get away with pushing us around. I say we stand firm and tell 'em to go to hell."

He looked round at the cluster of men, their ranks now swollen by the GIs who had been working in number one hold. All but a handful of waverers seemed to be in complete agreement with him.

Mitchell was staring at Danovich in disbelief. He just couldn't believe that uniformed soldiers of any nationality and in a theatre of war would strike like Sydney wharfies over a dirty-money allowance because of the imagined consequences of a bomb hitting the ship. It was all so preposterous that he stood rooted to the spot, aware that any action he might take could quite easily aggravate rather than improve the situation. Worse, it might provoke unnecessary hostility between British and Americans.

"Well?" challenged Danovich. "If there's any guy wants to chicken out, now's the time. Any of you who aren't behind me had better get off the foredeck. You, Skinny—" he nodded to one of his henchmen—"get aft to the other holds and tell the guys who want to come in with us to get up here pronto."

The one called Skinny went aft to spread the gospel. He was followed by three Docks GIs, who muttered sheepishly to Danovich that they weren't going to take on the whole American army just for his sake.

"There go the rabbits," jeered Danovich. "Remember their names, guys. Remember the names of them sons of bitches."

"What about the Lieutenant?" asked Mitchell. "You'd better let him go."

The officer was still being held by the two men who had disarmed him.

"You can go, Limey," said Danovich. "But the Lieutenant stays."

"Danovich, come to your senses," reasoned the Lieutenant.

"You know you can have the whole book thrown at you for this. It's madness."

"Let him come with me," said Mitchell. "What he says is right. You could be in big trouble."

"Shut up, Limey – and get your ass outa here," spat Danovich.

Mitchell, who was facing aft over Danovich's shoulder, saw a movement on the lower bridge-deck and his eyes glinted.

"Maybe you'd better take a look behind you, Sergeant," he said. "It looks like the party's over."

He had no sooner spoken than the voice of Colonel Dwight J. Moss rang out from the lower bridge.

"Release those two officers and raise your hands in the air. Any man making a move which I consider hostile or provocative will be shot."

Danovich turned slowly to investigate the source of this ringing command. Armed with a carbine, Colonel Moss was standing on the lower bridge, one foot up on the rail and the weapon aimed at Danovich's head. Three officers flanked Moss on his left and three on his right. Two had tommy-guns and four had rifles. The men with the rifles had them aimed from their shoulders in the firing position.

The captive Lieutenant shook off the men who held him and walked towards the bridge. Mitchell followed. Both men clambered up from the end of the hatch-coaming and pulled themselves through the rail on to the lower bridge-deck.

"Thank you, sir," the Lieutenant said to Moss. "I'm afraid that we're going to need some help with this little lot."

"Help is coming," said Moss. "From where we were in the ship's saloon, it looked like some kind of mutiny. We spoke to the Control Ship by radio and they said they'd handle it if we could get the drop on the ringleaders. That Danovich – is he crazy?"

"Crazy, I don't know," said the Lieutenant. "Dangerous, yes."

"Are they your outfit, Lieutenant?"

"I'm sorry to say they are."

"What in hell's name has got into them. I've seen soldiers get scared but I've never seen any who called a strike-meeting when the going got rough."

"They've got uniforms but they're not really army," said the Lieutenant. "Two months ago, most of them were civilians – longshoremen, in draft-excused jobs. When the army asked for volunteers for docks operation work overseas, they all volunteered. Nobody told them they would be thrown right into the front line. They were told their role would be strictly in support – loading and discharging ships in army-occupied ports. They feel they've been tricked and they've been beefing about it since we left Algiers."

"But they *are* army," said Moss. "Surely they know something about army discipline?"

"They gave 'em uniforms and two weeks' drill in boot camp and shipped 'em straight overseas – if that makes them army," said the Lieutenant. "They made the foremen and overseers corporals and sergeants – but they couldn't spell the word discipline, far less tell you what it means. You don't put an insubordinate on report in this outfit, you tell the union boss to get him into line."

Moss shook his head in disbelief.

"How the hell do you clear up a mess like this?" he asked the world at large.

He was soon to find out.

An LCM had sped across the anchorage from the Control Ship bumped to a halt against the midships section of the *Fort Harrison*. A moment later, a platoon of white-helmeted US Marines under a granite-faced captain scrambled over the bulwark and swarmed over the foredeck.

The mutinous stevedoring men were herded at bayonet-point to the bows of the ship where the Marine Captain segregated them into groups of six and conducted what seemed to be lightning interviews.

Fifteen minutes later, the mass of the docks battalion men were clustered on the starboard side of the windlass while a knot of about a dozen had been isolated on the port side.

The twelve, who included the hulking Sergeant Danovich, now had their hands chained. Bracelets were snapped on their wrists, each cuff being connected to its mate by thin chains nearly three feet in length.

The prisoners were marched aft and escorted into the waiting landing-craft under the rifles of the Marines.

The Marine Captain returned to Colonel Moss and the interested knot of spectators, which now included Captain Lansing.

He saluted Lansing.

"I am extremely sorry and ashamed at what has happened, Captain," he said, "but discipline has now been restored and there should be no more trouble. I regret that I omitted the courtesy of asking your permission to come aboard when we did so, but I am sure you will understand that it was an emergency."

"I understand," said Lansing. "In any case, Colonel Moss invited you aboard with my approval."

The Marine officer now addressed himself to Colonel Moss.

"We have arrested the ringleaders, sir. They will be dealt with summarily but we may require one or two witnesses for the inquiry. Is the officer who was assaulted and disarmed here?"

The Docks Lieutenant stepped forward.

"It was me," he said.

"You will probably get a signal calling you to the inquiry. I don't know when that will be. But in the meantime, you'd better get things rolling again here. It's important that the landing operations aren't fouled up because of a bunch of hotheads. My instructions were that the unloading has priority over all other things."

"Thank you, sir," said the Lieutenant. He saluted smartly. "I take it that the rest of these men on the foredeck there are cleared to go back to work?"

"I reckon they're itching to go," said the Captain with a grim little smile. "You see I've told them that we are taking their twelve friends over to the beach to shoot them. If there's any more trouble, I've told them I'll come back for another twelve and I won't be fussy how I pick them."

"You're not really going to shoot them?" asked the Lieutenant, his eyes wide with shock.

"Not before the inquiry," said the Captain blandly. "Gentlemen, enough time has been wasted. I bid you good day."

He saluted, turned on his heel and strode off towards the waiting landing-craft. The small vessel had scarcely pulled away from the ship's side than the metallic voice from the Control Ship rang out once more.

"Attention. Six aircraft bearing one-eight-zero. Focke-Wulf one-nineties."

Red flags were already fluttering from signal masts all over the anchorage.

The Docks Lieutenant strode purposefully up the fore-deck to where most of his men were still hanging around in sullen groups.

"OK, you men, let's have some action around here. Let's have these winches manned and cargo gangs down below. Let's get on with the goddamned war."

9
Death in the Afternoon

IT WAS four in the afternoon when a group of six Focke-Wulf 190s made the eleventh attack since sun-up on the anchorage. They were using a new type of bomb.

The marauding aircraft circled at 15,000 feet, their wings white in the sunlight. There they were safe from the barrage of AA fire which, nevertheless, was pumped at them relentlessly from the ships below. The raiders would pick their moment. Turning until the full glare of the sun was directly behind their line of attack, they would peel off and dive in line-ahead at the ships.

This time, however, instead of plunging down almost to mast height, they would begin to straighten out at about ten thousand feet and release these new bombs which were, themselves, like small aircraft with wings and fins.

Down these strange new missiles would glide until the gunners on the ships could see that each had a red light in the tail section. Four of the first six released accounted for two merchantmen and two warships – a deadly success-rate.

After the second such attack, the signal lamps began to flash urgently from ship to ship. Soon, every captain and gunner knew exactly what the device was: it was the radio-controlled glider bomb. The aircraft could release the bomb at a comparatively safe height and, by watching the light in its tail, navigate it visually towards the target.

A quick answer had to be found to combat this new German weapon, and a naval officer on the command staff came up with what seemed a brainwave. All the glider-bombs seen so far had displayed red tail-lights. "Why," asked the naval officer, "don't we fill the sky with red lights so the fliers lose track of the ones they're trying to navigate?"

The consequence of this quick thinking was an immediate signal to all ships that, in the event of a glider-bomb attack, they were to fire off red-star rockets, red Very Lights, flares – anything, in fact, that would fill the sky with red lights to confuse the enemy pilots.

These tactics were immediately confounded when, in the first attack after the order had been issued, the glider-bombs were seen to be guided by not only red, but green, blue and in some cases white lights. The orders were quickly amended with the advice that multi-coloured lights and rockets were to be fired against the glider-bombs.

All these tactical refinements contributed in Salerno Bay to what was probably the most spectacular and prolonged display of pyrotechnics seen in any battle before or since.

*　　*　　*

The end for the *Fort Harrison* almost came at precisely three minutes after four. The smoke cover had thinned to a wispy haze and the land lay limp in the furnace heat of the afternoon sun.

Andrew Mitchell was supervising the berthing of an LCT alongside number two hold at the height of the air raid when a bomb narrowly missed the number four hold at the far side of the ship.

A string of three LCMs was moored against that far side, the starboard, awaiting loading berths to become vacant on the port side. The bomb missed the ship but struck the middle of the LCMs and exploded.

From where Mitchell stood on the foredeck, he was convinced the *Fort Harrison* had been hit just abaft the engine-room. There was the deafening roar of the explosion and an eruption of metal, smoke and debris from just beyond the funnel.

The *Fort Harrison* lifted from the water and rolled so steeply over to port that it seemed she must capsize. But the vessel heeled lazily back to starboard with a lurching movement before settling into a nervous but regular rolling through a ten-degree arc.

Mitchell felt the entire deck ripple under his feet, and in the wake of the explosion a great grinding groan sighed from the metal of the ship as if she had been mortally wounded.

The Second Officer ran aft as quickly as his legs would take him. Men were sprawled everywhere, thrown down and dazed by the violent movement of the ship. He thrust past them, apprehensive of the scene which might meet his eyes on the afterdeck.

He emerged from the port alleyway beneath the boat-deck to hear the blood-curdling cries of wounded and dying men. The worst carnage was on the starboard side of the ship. The number three lifeboat had been blown from its davits and a section of it driven into the coaming of the open number four hold. The gun-pit at the after end of the engine-room accommodation had impeded the life-boat's blasted flight and its supports had buckled so that the gun-nest now tilted crazily over the ship's side, almost upside down. A dead gunner hung there in a grotesque position, still attached to the pillar of his Oerlikon by the straps. There was no sign of his loader.

The starboard afterdeck was no longer flat. It was corrugated in waves like a tin roof. It was littered with bodies and shredded clothing.

Most of the bodies had been hurled against the hatch-coaming and caught by it. Some had gone over the coaming and into the hold. Others had been blown into and against the starboard number four winch.

A naked, blackened figure came towards Mitchell.

"Second Mate, where's the Captain? Can you see the Captain? I was talking to him just seconds before ... I was on my way aft ... He went for'd ..."

The voice, more than anything else, told Mitchell that the blackened apparition was the Bosun.

"Are you hurt anywhere, Bosun?" he asked hoarsely. "Are

you saying that the Captain was down here?"

"He must have walked right into it, Second Mate. I'm OK ... you must try to find him."

Mitchell found Captain Lansing under the winch. His left arm was a pulpy mess and the left side of his head was like a red sponge.

He was alive – but only just.

Mitchell untangled his body and pulled him clear on to the deck. Lansing looked up at him with the one eye which was still visible. But the eye was misty and seemed sightless. And Lansing's mind was far from Salerno Bay.

"Call me ..." the voice croaked, and brought bubbles of red foam to Lansing's lips. "Call me ..." it repeated. "Call ... when you sight ... Ushant."

The head sagged back on Mitchell's gently supporting arm. Mitchell lowered the head to the deck and stood up.

Ushant? The light the homeward-bounders looked for. An Englishman hadn't far to go when Ushant was in sight. Was Lansing homeward bound in death? Was that what death was ... going home?

Mitchell became aware that some of the deck crew were standing behind him. He straightened.

"The Old Man's gone, lads. Nothing more we can do for him. Let's get the other wounded out into the open. A couple of you had better go down into the hold and see if there's anything that can be done for those who went over the coaming."

White-faced GIs – few of them had heard a shot fired in anger before embarking on the *Fort Harrison* – came forward to offer help. Colonel Moss appeared with a team of medics and a doctor.

All three landing-craft on the starboard side had been sunk by the bomb but, miraculously, two American navy-men had survived the blast and were rescued from the water.

Leaving the treatment of the injured to the medics, Mitchell organised a damage-assessment team. Men were despatched to the engine-room and all living quarters in the after half of the ship and to each hold and storage space with orders to report back to him as quickly as possible. The carpenter was sent off with his sounding-rod to report on the water levels in tanks and bilges.

Much of the ship had been so buckled by the blast that many cabin doors were jammed fast and had to be broken down. In the living accommodation at tween-deck level, not a standing steel bunk was left in one piece. They lay twisted and collapsed amid a general shambles of broken mirrors, shattered crockery and strewn personal effects.

But that damage was of little consequence. The most serious was that breathlessly reported by an able seaman who had accompanied one of the engineers into the bowels of the ship to explore the shaft tunnel. The precipitous climb up the engine-room access ladder had left him gasping.

"There's water pouring into the shaft tunnel and it's flooding," he told Mitchell. "They've got the pumps on it but the Third Engineer thinks it's still coming in faster than we can pump it out."

"Where is the Third Engineer?" asked Mitchell.

"He's down the shaft tunnel trying to find out where the water's coming in. Up to his neck in water he is. He says he'll need help but reckons it's a job for volunteers. Volunteers who can swim!"

"How far up is the water?"

"The bottom of the propellor shaft is in water and the cat-walk's awash. I had to wade back to the ladder."

"Go back and tell him I'll get down there myself as soon as I can. But, first, see if you can get hold of Walsh and Davis – they're both big strong lads and good swimmers – and ask them to get down there. They'll go without being asked to volunteer. I want to see Mr Pendlebury first, and the Chief Engineer ..."

Mitchell broke off as he caught sight of Colin Durham helping to lift an injured man on to a stretcher on the far side of the deck. He picked his way swiftly through the winches towards him.

"Colin," he called.

The Third Officer gently lowered the man on to the stretcher and turned a dirt-streaked face to search for the voice.

"Second Mate. I've been looking for you. What a bloody shambles. Look, you'll need to talk to Pendlebury. Did you know the Old Man's been killed?"

"Yes, I know," said Mitchell. "It was me who found him – over there under the starboard winch. But never mind that – we've got other worries. The shaft tunnel's flooding and I'll have to go down and take a look at it. Will you tell Pendlebury the score and keep an eye on things on deck. You'd maybe better signal the Control Ship and ask if we can have the serious casualties taken off to one of the hospital ships in the other anchorage. We can do nothing for them here."

"OK – but you can forget Pendlebury. That's what I wanted to see you about."

"What do you mean?"

"He's in a blue funk. One of the stewards came along to tell him that the Old Man had cashed in his chips and he nearly had hysterics. He went on and on wanting to know what the Old Man was doing on the afterdeck and not on the bridge, that there was no reason why the Captain of a ship should be strolling around the decks, that he had no business to be there and that he wouldn't have got himself killed if he'd stayed where he belonged. You've never heard anything like it."

"Where is he now?"

"Well, we eventually got him calmed down. He just went quiet, like he was in a trance. Then he went into his cabin and sat down at his desk and he just sat there, staring. He's still there ... sitting there staring at the bulkhead and not saying a damned word. I'm telling you, Mitch – he's flipped his lid. He is clean off his bloody head."

"That's just what we need," said Mitchell grimly. "Well, we've no time to play nursemaid. He'll have to unscramble his own marbles. Look, take care of things topside, Colin.

I'll have to check out the damage in the shaft tunnel. For all I know we could be going down by the stern this very minute. I was going to try to get hold of the Chief Engineer and sort out a plan of action but there's no time ... Can you get a message to him and tell him where I'll be? He may want to have a look for himself but it might be better if he stays in the engine-room and waits till I ring through to him on the phone."

Mitchell hurried in past the engineers' cabins and across the cat-walk which crossed the top of the engine-room. He crawled through a narrow opening at the top of the great bulkhead which separated the engine-room from the after end of the ship.

He peered briefly down the vertical steel ladder which disappeared into converging lines in the depths of the narrow steel shaft beneath him. Then he hauled himself on to the ladder and went down swiftly with the practised skill of the seasoned seaman.

Reaching the bottom, his foot touched water. Groping with outstretched toes, he felt for the cat-walk. Finding solid steel just below the surface of the oil-slimed water, he allowed his weight to go on to his feet. The water barely covered the tops of his shoes and sloshed about them with the slight movement of the ship.

He was at one end of a narrow cylinder of a tunnel lit by half a dozen overhead lights spaced out along its length. On his right, looking aft, was the great length of the propellor shaft, which – driven by the triple expansion engines – rotated the single screw beyond its far end under the stern and provided the thrust which could move the ten thousand tons of the *Fort Harrison* through a moderate sea at a speed of ten knots.

The damage caused by the blast from the bomb was to the plating which housed the glands and bearings at that point where the shaft passed through the stern of the ship and connected to the now dormant propellor in the sea beyond.

As Mitchell walked aft along the sloping cat-walk, he

became aware that the water deepened perceptibly the nearer he got to the stern. He could hear, too, the inrush of water through the stern glands, which threatened to flood the tunnel, and also the sucked breathing of the pumps which were trying to fight that flooding.

"Is that you, Andrew?" called a familiar voice as Mitchell approached. A dripping figure hauled himself from the water in the well below the shaft and swung into an upright position with the help of the hand-rail which skirted the cat-walk.

Charlie Bedford, the Third Engineer, wiped his face with a sopping sweatrag and pushed his dripping oil-smeared hair out of his eyes. A second figure emerged from the water. Mitchell recognised Nicholson, one of the firemen on Charlie Bedford's watch.

"How bad is it?" asked Mitchell.

"Oh, we'll keep the old cow afloat," said Bedford. "There's still a damned sight more sea coming in than we're pumping out – but what is coming in shouldn't be uncontrollable. I reckon I could get enough packing into the leaky part to stop it to a trickle but it'll be dodgy if I have to perform the operation underwater without a diving suit. Trouble is that there's a hell of a lot of muck in the well and the suction boxes are all clogging up. Nick and I have been swimming about down there trying to clear one – but we'll need help to do the lot right along the tunnel."

"Two of the deck crowd are on their way down – Walsh and Davis – maybe the Chief could spare some of the stoke-hold mob. I'll give him a ring on the blower. It's not quite as bad as I thought it would be."

Two burly young seamen clad only in shorts and sandals splashed their way along the tunnel to join the group.

"We've been sent down for a bath," grinned the one called Walsh.

"Well, the water isn't cold," said Mitchell, returning the grin. "We want you to dive in the well there and grope around for the suction boxes. They're clogging up with cotton waste, grime, and God knows all what."

"We're dab hands we are at groping about boxes. Ain't we, boy-o?" said Davis in a sing-song Welsh voice.

"Aye, Taff," said Walsh, "especially if they got a bit of hair around them. Come on, then. Let's get started. I don't like the sound of all that water pouring in up there."

Mitchell climbed on to the ladder leading to the steering-system house to take a closer look at the inrush of water.

"You could maybe seal this off temporarily until we dry the tunnel out a bit," he shouted down to Charlie Bedford.

"I'm going to," the engineer answered. "But I'll need some gear from the engine-room. Now that we've got a bit of help down here, I'll get on with it."

"I'm going to phone the Chief from the steering-house. Want me to give him a message?"

"No," grinned Bedford, "you wouldn't know what I was talking about. I'll come up with you and speak to him myself."

The two men climbed up the ladder and through a steel trap-door into the steering-house. Mitchell opened a telephone box on a pillar beside the huge emergency steering-wheel, which was linked directly by cog and wheel to the huge rudder but only set in gear if the hydraulic steering system failed.

Mitchell lifted the phone, turned the pointer dial to "Engine-room" and whirled the call-handle. It was the Chief Engineer himself who answered.

"Terrible about the Old Man," said the Chief. "I haven't quite taken it in yet."

He went on to give a detailed analysis of the damage reported to him and what action he was taking. He had already organised two portable motor pumps to be brought to the stern peak to supplement the pumping from the shaft tunnel. Hoses would be fed down through the trap, from which Mitchell and Bedford had so recently emerged, and water pumped up through them to deck level and over the side.

Mitchell sought and got the assurance that more men would be despatched immediately to the shaft tunnel to assist Bedford. Then he handed the phone over to the Third Engineer so that he could tell the Chief exactly what equipment he would require.

'You've got it all under control, so I'll leave you to it, Charlie,' Mitchell mouthed to his friend, who was still on the phone. With a movement of his extended forefinger, he made a hand signal that he was going topside.

With a wave, Mitchell continued up the ladder to emerge on to the deck under the poop. He made his way forward to Mr Pendlebury's cabin.

The Chief Officer was still sitting in his cabin exactly as described to him by Colin Durham. Mitchell felt a surge of impatient fury but restrained it.

"You can't sit there all day, Mr Pendlebury."

He shook Pendlebury's shoulder, but he continued to stare blankly in front of him.

"Look, I'm going to get that Yankee doctor to come and have a look at you. Somebody's got to take command of this ship and it should be you. What's the matter with you, man?"

Mitchell started involuntarily as Pendlebury suddenly turned his head and stared at him. He blinked twice as if waking from a dream.

"Why wasn't I called?" he rasped suddenly.

"I beg your pardon?"

"Why wasn't I called?" Pendlebury repeated. "I gave strict instructions that I was to be called at a quarter to four and nobody has come near me. I haven't even had my afternoon tea."

Mitchell was bewildered. The man really was unhinged. He seemed to have no idea of time, place or anything else. He was now looking at his watch.

"Is that the time?"

His voice was shrill with surprise. He looked at Mitchell warily.

"I remember somebody trying to tell me that the Captain was dead. Did you ever hear such preposterous nonsense? Fancy telling me that old Lansing was dead!"

"The Captain *is* dead," said Mitchell evenly. "And several others. A bomb hit a landing-craft alongside us on the starboard side. The shaft tunnel has been flooding ..."

Pendlebury stared at Mitchell questioningly.

"Lansing is really dead?"

"Yes."

"You are sure?"

"Quite sure."

"Then ... Then I am in command?"

"Technically, yes."

"What do you mean technically?"

"Well you seem to have had a turn ... to have been unwell."

"There is nothing at all wrong with me. What are you daring to suggest? That I'm not fit to take over from that fool Lansing?"

"Captain Lansing was not a fool." Mitchell coloured with sudden anger. "And I'll not listen to you or anyone else talking about him in that way. Good God, he hasn't been dead an hour and you have the nerve to talk about him like ... like ..."

Mitchell couldn't find the words to express his disgust.

"You're not fit to lace his boots," he stormed on, his powers of articulation returning. "And if you want my opinion – which you probably don't but are getting anyway – I don't think you're fit to take command of this ship. You're not fit to command a coal barge in Cardiff dock. As a man you're a bloody apology for the word and, as a seaman, you've got about as much idea as my grandmother. You make me sick to my stomach."

Pendlebury's eyes narrowed to slits. Pure venom glinted from them. His voice was controlled and even.

"Are you quite finished, Mr Mitchell?"

"Oh, there's a lot more I could add but that'll have to do for the moment. I've been wanting to tell you to your face for some time."

"And I shall remember every word," said Pendlebury. "I look on your conduct as nothing short of mutinous and

I shall enter your remarks in the Captain's log book. Furthermore, I shall make a special report to the Company, to the Board of Trade and to the Ministry of Transport. I'll have you hauled before a civil court ..."

"For heaven's sake, don't talk so bloody wet," said Mitchell wearily. "Look, I don't take back a single word I said. I can't stand your guts and I've told you so. You have never liked me. Well, let's leave it at that and decide what's going to be done to this ship. If you *are* going to take over command – and after your performance in the last hour, I'm not convinced you should – you are going to need me. But we've got to get a few things straight. I want to be damned sure that you're not going to pull a Rip Van Winkle act every time there's a hint of pressure. You're going to have to assure me that you'll behave with a bit of backbone and responsibility before I put my weight behind you and give you the support you're going to need."

"A master can accept no conditions on how he conducts his command, especially at the dictates of a junior officer. Are you trying to bargain with me?" asked Pendlebury.

"I am and you had better pay attention. The Company, the Board of Trade, the Ministry of Transport, and that court you were threatening me with might be very curious to know precisely what your actions were when the Captain was killed and the ship's safety was put in peril by bomb damage. There is a steward and the Third Mate and possibly others who can testify that you ran screaming to your cabin and turned your head to the wall. They may conclude, as I did, that I had very good reasons for questioning your capability of commanding this ship. Now I don't want to provoke an incident that is going to finish your career or anybody else's if it's going to produce more trouble than we've already got at this beach-head. I want to see this ship discharged and get the hell out of here with no more casualties than we already have. That consideration and that alone is going to govern exactly what I do as the result of this conversation."

Pendlebury became very thoughtful. The assurance which he had momentarily displayed fell away from him. His eyes shifted from side to side as he weighed the meaning of Mitchell's words.

"I wasn't aware of becoming ... unwell ... when the steward told me about Lansing. It must have been shock. I've been under a great deal of strain."

"We all have," said Mitchell quietly.

"Then you understand ... that it was shock ... that it could have happened to anyone?"

"I am prepared to take that view."

"On what conditions?"

"That you forget any animosity you may feel towards me. We don't have to like each other to work together for the good of the ship. You back me up and I'll back you up. It's as simple as that."

"I see. Well, maybe I was hasty in what I said to you. But you said some unpleasant things yourself."

"It was maybe better to get them out of my system. I was very fond of Captain Lansing. When you called him a fool ..."

"I had no right to do that," said Pendlebury humbly. "I wasn't myself. I could bite my tongue off for having said it. Please try to forget that I ever said it. It was mean and unforgivable."

This reasonable and penitent Pendlebury was a revelation to Mitchell. He felt a sudden optimism at the way events had turned. If his confrontation with Pendlebury produced no other end result than the making of the man, then that would be miracle enough.

It did happen sometimes that the weak unlikely man grew in stature and worth to fill the mantle that destiny had thrust upon him. Was it too much to hope that, in Pendlebury's case, his succession to Lansing's command would awaken in him a new awareness and integrity?

The charity within Mitchell to see the virtues in men rather than their vices persuaded him to give Pendlebury the benefit of the doubt in that instant of decision when the Chief Officer's fate was in his hands. It was in his power to depose Pendlebury or to protect his kingship. He chose the more humane course.

And he was to regret it.

10

Counter-attack

QUILLEY was displeased. A raw scowling disgust ate at him. Two days and a night on the beaches of Salerno Bay had greatly sharpened his adeptness at survival. So much so that by the second nightfall, he was devoting slightly less time to thinking about the preservation of his skin and rather more about the preservation of his possessions.

He spared little sentiment for the bulk of his military kit still in Pendlebury's settee locker on the *Fort Harrison*. No, his growing preoccupation was with the cache of US currency safely hidden with that kit.

Several times during the day, he had suggested to Captain Wilbur Diamond that he should be allowed to return to the ship in order to collect his belongings. But Captain Diamond had shown a marked lack of interest in the idea. He seemed to be strangely obsessed with the prosecution of the war and he obviously considered Quilley's harping on about his personal possessions as downright unseemly.

Diamond was pleased with the way things were going. Control was beginning to take the place of yesterday's chaos. The worst of the action had passed elsewhere. The greatest concentration of artillery and mortar fire now seemed to be at the other end of Yellow Beach and inland from there.

Things were sufficiently calm around sundown for Diamond to pass the word that a chow-break could be arranged.

So it was that, as darkness fell, Quilley and a dozen or so men were sitting in the lee of some trucks breaking into fresh K-rations. Diamond and Gomez were a little distance away huddled over a map.

Quilley, quietly mourning his separation from his hoard

of money, was sitting scowling in the direction of Diamond when a hard-driven jeep arrived from the direction of the beach. It stopped abruptly a few yards from Diamond and Gomez. Two men got out.

A colonel and a lieutenant, Quilley observed. He wondered what the hell they wanted. He had a presentiment of bad news.

The Colonel was doing all the talking. Diamond was listening respectfully. Quilley seemed to detect surprise registering on Diamond's face at one point. The Colonel went on earnestly, emphasising a point by gesticulating with his hands. Diamond nodded. He pointed in the direction of the men, all of whom were now watching intently.

Gomez left the small group and came across.

"Sergeants Quilley and Selzman," he called out.

Quilley and the sergeant called Selzman got up slowly and looked at Gomez expectantly.

"Get the guys assembled over by the radio truck at the double. And I mean everybody – even those you've got on guard duty."

When they were gathered, it was Diamond who came forward to speak to them. He carried a sheet of paper on a clip-board, a roll-call list of the seventy or so men of the detachment so far disembarked.

"At ease, men," Diamond began. "I'm going to call out thirty-two names. If your name is called, fall out and assemble in marching kit over beside Colonel Messiter's jeep – that's it over there. You are being temporarily transferred to the Colonel's command and will form 'F' platoon under Lieutenant Stoker. He will brief you in due course about your duties."

Diamond paused and a murmur of speculation went buzzing around the assembled men.

"Silence, please. Now pay attention. I want to stress that this assignment is temporary. The order has come from Division. You may not want to go any more than I want to lose you but I got to take orders like everybody else in this man's army. I suggest you don't take any more gear with

146

you than you can easily carry. A blanket and a poncho you'll need. Anything else you can dump in the store truck and we'll look after it until you get back. You should be back with us in twenty-four hours.

"Now here are the names:

"Quilley, Sergeant. Martin, Corporal. Privates Cohen, Metcalfe, Kovacs, Sullivan, Ford, Fernbach, Dubrowski, Rimmer ..."

Quilley heard very little after the shock of hearing his own name right at the front of the list. He was seized by a sickening feeling of apprehension.

He wanted to laugh out loud at Diamond's advice about taking only a poncho and a blanket. Did that mean he could go back to the *Fort Harrison* and get his? The whole thing was like a comedy gone sour.

Quilley, however, did not discount the possibility that this strange assignment, whatever it was, might be to his advantage. It was consceivable that being under the command of Lieutenant Stoker might be less trying than being kept on the hop by a diehard like Diamond.

In his gut, however, he didn't really believe this. The accuracy of his abdominal instinct in this instance was soon to be dramatically confirmed.

The first sign of confirmation came when Quilley and the thirty-one others were lined up in three ranks by Lieutenant Stoker. There was something mean-looking about Stoker. He obviously didn't set himself forward as a candidate in any popularity contests. His face wore a perpetual scowl and there was a decided lack of grace in the way he communicated with the rest of humanity. He didn't speak so much as snarl.

When the three ranks of men were assembled in a resemblance of military array, Stoker – who did not reserve his surly manner for those of lesser rank – snarled something about their state of readiness to the tall, elegant, silver-moustached Colonel Messiter. In the Colonel's case, however, Stoker, softened the effect of his snarled words by punctuating them with the word "Sir".

"Thank you, Lieutenant," said Messiter gravely, "I reckon I'd better say a few words to the volunteers."

He used the word "volunteers" without the semblance of a smile but it provoked a glow of almost evil amusement to appear in Stoker's eyes.

Messiter cleared his throat and said:

"If you men are wondering what the hell this is all about, I'll tell you. We need you up back of Yellow Beach. I know some of you are drivers and some of you are mechanics ... But you are first and foremost soldiers. And a soldier's first job is to fight the enemy. Maybe some of you thought you might never get the chance — but you're gonna be given that chance tonight. You are going to be given the chance to defend ground that was taken with American blood. I know you will defend that ground with your own blood. Men, we stand poised between victory and defeat. On your courage rests the outcome of the battle. Stand fast and victory is ours. There can be no retreat. The enemy's aim will be to push us into the sea. Ours will be to stop him or die in the attempt. I know you will not fail. Good luck."

If Messiter was aware of the effect of his words on the listening men, he gave no outward sign of it. Not as much as a facial muscle moved as each sentence of his speech was greeted with barely audible comments such as: "Who is this crap-pusher?" and "In a pig's eye", and "Who does this joker think he's kidding?"

Other remarks were passed. None of them were complimentary to Messiter and nearly all of them were obscene. Stoker heard them clearly enough and he glared at their authors, memorising faces, but he did not interrupt the Colonel's rhetoric.

"A word with you, Lieutenant," said Messiter in an aside as he turned away towards his jeep. When Stoker hurried to his side, Messiter spoke to him in a bored voice which he made no attempt to lower:

"Herd this lot of ragtag and bobtail up the Company lines, Lieutenant. I'll take the jeep and try to find that Major Mulvey and his mobile kitchen. Division said he had about forty cooks and bottle-washers we could draft for more important work."

"Yessir!" said Stoker and threw a careless salute at the departing Colonel. He turned, eyes glinting, to face Quilley's squad.

"OK, you stinking apologies for infantrymen," he bawled, "get ready to move out. I wanna see you march like soldiers, not like something outa the Nuns' Chorus. And stop talking in the ranks. You, soldier, what's your name?"

He advanced on a frightened-looking fair-haired boy of nineteen in the front rank and thrust his face to within inches of his nose.

"Your name, soldier?" he snarled.

"Rimmer, sir."

"Well Rimmer, my name is Stoker. Lieutenant Stoker. I may forget your name but you are NEVER going to forget mine. You may wish you'd never heard it but you will never forget it as long as you live. And when I say jump, you're gonna goddamn jump. You will obey me like your life depended on it and, believe me, your life will depend on it."

He took a pace back and began to walk up and down slowly in front of the makeshift platoon.

"There is no time," he said, "to whip you grease-gun pushers and bus-drivers into a fighting platoon, so you'll just have to pretend that you are fighting men. I'll pretend you are, too, and that means that when I say to do something you do it. No questions, no hesitation, no looking to God Almighty for help – you just do it. Got that? That's the first thing you have to remember. The second is that you have two things to fear. One is the enemy ... The other is me! Now, you'd better believe that the enemy is a lot nicer than me. He will kill you if you give him the chance – but I will goddamn crucify you if you think your chances are any better with me. When you face the enemy, you will not run. I will not hesitate to blow the head off any man in this outfit who does."

Quilley could not believe his ears. It was all a grotesque comedy. He had the feeling that the whole world had become a vast insane asylum, that he was trapped in a lunatic fun-house where – no matter which door he opened – every outlet led to a situation more hideous and bizarre than the one from which he sought escape.

When Lieutenant Stoker marched the platoon off along Blue Beach, Quilley had ceased believing that what was happening to him was real. It was all a crazy dream from which, sooner or later, he would wake up.

Their immediate destination was a line of trucks at the top of Yellow Beach. From the rear of one of these trucks, a corporal was handing out carbines. Each man in the platoon who was not already armed was given one. From another truck, each was given a short trenching shovel.

Then ten men were detailed to carry between them five boxes of .303 ammunition, each containing three thousand rounds.

Stoker, like a dog snapping at the heels of a bunch of bewildered sheep, hustled the men into two columns and moved them off at a quick march that threatened to become a trot.

To the north-east, there was the continuous roll and bark of heavy firing. The platoon marched in sweating silence towards that intense hubbub of sound. Overhead, a million stars looked down from a cloudless sky. The men's faces glowed white in the quarter light, reflecting occasionally orange as they caught a glint from the eastern horizon which seemed to be on fire.

They passed an advanced field dressing-station which was a hive of activity. Stretcher-bearers hurried to and fro with bloody burdens. Doctors and medics in reddened overalls knelt among orderly rows of casualties, fixing drips, giving injections, dressing wounds. To one side, unattended, lay the closer ranks of two companies' strength of corpses.

Barking at the men to maintain their pace, Stoker urged the platoon past the lights of the dressing-station onto new terrain. No longer was the sand of the beach underfoot. Here, it was hard dusty scrub-land with dried-up spiky bushes, and grass bents which cut at the legs through the thin military trousers at knee-height.

After about a mile, Stoker slowed the pace. Then he halted the platoon.

"Wait here," he commanded, and glided on alone into the darkness towards a grove of trees. A figure came out of the gloom to meet him.

They held a brief consultation, then both men returned to where the platoon had thankfully thrown themselves on the ground.

"On your feet!" hissed Stoker. "Captain Barrett wants to talk to you."

The newcomer had a blood-stained bandage round his head. He wore no helmet. He had a sub-machine-gun couched in the crook of his right elbow.

"Good to see you guys," he greeted in a friendly voice. "We sure are glad to see you. I'm sorry you had to be shanghaied from whatever you were doing but things are a little desperate around here."

He invited them to gather closer and take the weight off their legs.

"Look guys," he said, "I don't believe in making orders too complicated and I don't believe in keeping men in the dark over what they're supposed to be doing in a battle – so I'll tell you just what the situation is and what's going to be expected of you.

"Over there," he pointed with his machine-gun, "is the mouth of the Sele River. Way up beyond it on the other side is the beach where the British landed. Now, we shoulda linked up yesterday with the British but they're kinda hemmed in and haven't got as far south as they expected. We've had it pretty rough ourselves and we haven't got as far north as we reckoned on.

"This means that instead of us having a solid front with the British against the Germans, we've got a big wedge of unclaimed territory between us. Well, the signs are that the Krauts are aiming to drive to the sea between us and the British and keep us apart. Then they'll tighten the net round both of us. They reckon that they'll finish us off easier if they put the squeeze on two small pockets instead of one big one."

He paused and looked at the cluster of faces, aware that his audience was giving him rapt attention.

"Our problem," he went on, "is that we don't have enough men to cover the whole perimeter and protect the beach. There are a lot of gaps all along our line – and we got to plug these gaps. That's where you guys come in. That's why the Colonel is high-tailing it all over the beach getting motor and supply men like yourself, and cooks, and engineers, and aircraft maintenance guys – any guy who can hold a rifle – so that there just ain't any holes in our defence line where the Krauts can sneak through.

"You guys are gonna be responsible for defending about quarter of a mile of our perimeter. That is, you'll be dug in one man for every dozen yards along our line. There will be guys dug in nearer to the enemy but they will be stretched out further apart and in bigger pockets. The shit is gonna hit the fan as far as you are concerned if these guys get over-run or the Krauts get through between them. You are the last line. And the order from the top is that there is no retreat from your positions. We stand there and if it comes to it, we die there. There ain't no point in running if the Krauts do get on top of us because there's nowhere to go. If they get past us, they get the whole beach and we'd be all gone anyway. Any questions?"

"Captain. I gotta admit I feel kinda – well, I don't like to use the word scared – but I can't think of a better one. Most of us are better with spanners in our hands than rifles – and this has all been kinda sudden. Whad'ya reckon our chances are of comin' outa this?"

Captain Barrett smiled.

"What's your name, soldier?"

"Cohen, sir. What else with a nose like mine and a Brooklyn accent?"

"Well, Cohen, if there's a man anywhere on this beach-head tonight who isn't shit-scared in his stomach, it's because he's pig-ignorant of what's going on or he's already dead. Just remember we're all in this goddamned mess together and none of us are gonna get out of it if we act half as scared as we feel. Just you think what the folks back home are gonna say when they hear that you and your fox-hole was all that stood between the German army and them winning the Battle of Salerno. Now that story's gonna sound a whole lot better if you say, sure, you were scared as hell but you damned well stood and fought 'em!"

Captain Barrett's words may have lacked the inspiring prose of the Declaration of Independence but they sent a glow of courage through the ranks of "F" platoon. He had a calm authority which he somehow managed to exercise in a human and humane way, baffling to Lieutenant Stoker and inspiring only his contempt.

Barrett exchanged a few words with Stoker and then watched as the Lieutenant led the platoon off in single file. They skirted the grove of trees. The land sloped downwards towards the sea and they hugged a contour of the hillside, working steadily north.

They moved silently, having been warned by Stoker to make no noise. Considering the din of firing which was coming from just beyond a wooded ridge less than a mile to their right, it seemed a pointless instruction.

Quilley loped along a few paces behind Stoker. The events of the night so far had done nothing to lift the daze of unreality which hung on him, blunting all his senses. His mouth was dry with the taste of fear but he kept thrusting one leg after the other like an automaton. He had almost given up all hope now of being reunited with his money.

The conviction was heavily embedded in his mind that no matter what action he took now it would be futile – that it no longer made any difference whether or not he ever got back to that ship. By the cruellest and most perverse stroke of luck, he had landed himself in what was going to be one of the greatest American military defeats of all time. He had no doubt that the beach-head was doomed. The Germans were going to sweep down from the hills, just like the Captain had said, and they were going to over-run the whole beach. Nobody was going to get out alive. Nobody.

A voice challenging from the darkness ahead made Quilley all but cry out in terror. He stifled the sound escaping from his throat.

"It's 'E' platoon, you dumb ox," whispered Stoker. "Stay here."

The Lieutenant answered the voice ahead and moved forward alone. He returned moments later.

"We dig in just the other side of 'E' platoon. I'll lead the way."

They came to a line of fox-holes which lay at right-angles to the route they had been following. They extended to the right to a ridge which lost itself in darkness, and to the left through gently sloping scrub-land.

Stoker motioned a left turn and led them down a gentle incline. They passed fox-holes spaced about twelve yards apart. Each was occupied by one man, crouched, rifle at the ready, staring into empty darkness.

These men glanced up at the newcomers but did not speak as they filed past.

Stoker turned to Quilley as they reached a point beyond which no fox-holes were visible.

"OK, Sergeant, this is where we start."

He measured off about a dozen paces.

"I want the first man to dig in here. You, Sergeant, detail off a man at each place I indicate. Tell them to dig deep."

Quilley did as he was told and, in this way, each man was given a position until the perimeter line stretched out for another quarter of a mile below "E" platoon's. Quilley himself was told to dig his fox-hole at the lower extremity of the line.

The flash and thunder of gunfire rolled at them from north and east and, now, the night echoed with the ring of metal against earth and stone as the men dug. They did not need to be told to dig deep. They knew that their lives might depend on the cover they could make for themselves. Fear lent urgency to their labours.

The sound of the nearer firing was more sporadic now. The continuous rumbling of heavy guns never halted but seemed to maintain its distance. The closer thwack and whine of mortar-fire and the stutter of small arms and machine-gun fire would suddenly flare and fall. Each time it restarted, it seemed to be much nearer than before.

Stoker disappeared up the slope towards "E" platoon's positions. He returned an hour later leading a straggle of men who commenced to dig in below Quilley's fox-hole extending the line even further towards the sea.

Stoker came back up the line inspecting the new fox-holes. He stopped before Quilley.

"I've got a lot of territory to cover, Sergeant," he said. "I'm going to hold you personally responsible for keeping the guys in this section on their toes. You just remember one thing – that no matter what happens, these holes are not to be abandoned. You *stay* here – you *fight* here. You see one man high-tailin' it outa his slit trench, you shoot him! You got that? You shoot the son of a bitch."

"Yeah, I got it," said Quilley, who was thinking that if he had to shoot anybody, it would give him a whole lot of pleasure to put a bullet in Lieutenant Stoker.

"You say 'sir' when you speak to me, Sergeant."

"Yes, sir," said Quilley.

"Have you distributed the ammunition?"

"What amm ... No, sir. I was waiting for you to give the order, sir."

"Do it now, damn you," rasped Stoker. "How the hell did you think you were gonna stop the Krauts if they came up outa that wood – throw stones at them? See that each man has at least five hundred rounds."

"Yes, sir."

As Quilley hastily organised a distribution of ammunition, Stoker visited each fox-hole to tell its occupant that he expected to find him there in the morning – dead or alive, but in that fox-hole.

Then he moved on up the line.

It was just before midnight when the wood about half a

155

mile in front of Quilley's position erupted into flame. It seemed to be the target of a massive bombardment from higher in the Sele valley, to the north-east. Flames licked up and over the dry trees as fires started in about twenty different places. Clouds of smoke drifted in the near-wind-less night, wisping and curling towards their line. The noise was deafening. Like a prairie fire, the tide of war was sweeping towards them.

Then they saw figures running and stumbling in the darkness towards them.

Rimmer, the frightened youth whom Stoker had singled out for attention up behind Blue Beach, was in the fox-hole nearest to Quilley's right. He began to fire rapidly into the figures looming out of the smoke.

In a moment, muzzle flashes lit the line as others opened fire.

Screams and falling bodies indicated that some of the bullets were finding targets. Others of the advancing men threw themselves flat at the first hail of bullets.

Quilley's men stopped firing when it was apparent that no targets were now in sight. Only shadows and wraiths of wispy smoke.

From out of the smoke, a voice was screaming: "They're all round us! We're trapped!"

"These are our own lines," screamed another voice. "Our own goddamn lines!"

Away to Quilley's right, another voice was trying to make itself heard. Quilley thought he recognised the New Orleans drawl of Martin, the Corporal from Lieutenant Gomez' outfit.

"Hold your fire!" he was shouting. "Hold your fire! These are our guys out there! You stupid sons of bitches are killing Americans!"

Quilley, who had frozen at the first burst of fire from Rimmer, had not fired a shot. He now found his voice.

"Hey, you out there. If you're Americans, come forward slowly with your hands in the air. We ain't taking no chances."

A new torrent of explosions over by the wood drowned his words.

The only answer was the repeated cry of "Stretcher-bearer! Stretcher-bearer!" from somewhere in the smoke-filled darkness.

Quilley repeated his call. This time there was response.

"OK, we're coming forward. But for Chrissake don't shoot. We're friends."

Then they came out of the smoke. Men with the legs of their trousers cut away and field dressings taped round their legs; men without shirts, their chests and arms swathed in bandages; men who hobbled on one foot and supported each other. Walking wounded — men with haunted haggard faces and wide fear-filled eyes.

Behind them came stretcher-bearers carrying the pitifully wounded.

One or two of these men made sullen comments about trigger-happy bums as they passed through the line.

Cohen, the little Jew from Brooklyn, murmured:

"Sorry fellas, we thought you were Krauts comin' at us.'

He himself had not fired a shot. Suspecting the truth of the situation and not wanting to fire indiscriminately at anything that moved, he had been waiting for the new-comers to be challenged.

Rimmer kept his head down in his fox-hole, trying to muffle the sobs that racked his body. He was crying like a child.

Fire continued to rain down on the wood in front of the position. When a second wave of figures came running out of the darkness towards the line, Corporal Martin averted a second tragedy by getting out of his fox-hole and advancing several yards into the open to challenge them.

"We're Americans — for God's sake let us through!" came the reply. These men were not wounded but they'd had more than they could take. They were running.

Some still carried rifles. Others had thrown theirs away. But they all had a single ambition — to put as much distance as they possibly could between themselves and the enemy.

"Stick around here," suggested Corporal Martin. "You could re-group, help us out. This line's stretched pretty thin."

The general tenor of the replies he received was unprintable, but one of the more polite rejoinders was: "Screw you, buddy. I ain't stickin' around for anybody!"

The effect on the men of the makeshift "F" platoon was to demoralise them intensely. The encounter with Captain Barrett had somehow lifted them and if they had not taken up their positions cheerfully, at least they had done so with a philosophic acceptance of their lot.

Now they began to question in their minds the justice of a situation in which they – a group of inexperienced supply men – had to face a highly skilled enemy, while men trained for combat were scuttling to the rear like frightened rabbits.

At the same time, Lieutenant Stoker's lashing tongue had lifted red weals in their minds and they had a genuine fear of what his retribution would be should they desert their posts.

So, they stayed at their posts. But their morale had dropped to zero.

About thirty minutes after midnight, the prairie fire of war rolled up and over them and engulfed them in all its hellish fury.

It had become almost quiet – one of those lulls when the small arms and machine-guns had fallen silent. Below them the wood seemed to be ablaze from end to end. It threw off a red-orange light that constantly moved and filled the scrub-land with leaping shadows.

Quilley watched these shadows and his brain began to tell his eyes that the shadows were growing in number and were not caused by bushes and the stumps of trees interposed between his line of vision and the jumping flames. They were caused by men, moving quickly and methodically and in teams.

He could not divine their purpose. Their movements were too stealthy and indistinct. They did not come nearer and that was a consolation. It occurred to him that American units were digging in front of them, making at least one buffer between "F" platoon and the enemy.

The thought had no sooner been born than it was killed.

A series of reverberating thumps and spine-chilling whines – like monster corks being popped from Champagne bottles – preceded by seconds what seemed to "F" platoon to be the obliteration of the world.

All around them the earth began to erupt and explode. Flashes seared the eyes. Wave after wave after wave of shattering sound burst on the ear-drums and the air was filled with blasts of scorching heat and white-hot metal.

On and on it went, the flashing and the hellish noise and the earth spewing itself into the atmosphere. Quilley found himself chewing earth from the floor of his slit trench, hands over his ears, aware that in addition to the exploding world beyond his hole, a banshee-like scream was drilling at his brain. It was not until he twisted his mouth away from the ground to spit out earth that he realised that the hideous high-pitched scream was coming from his own throat.

He sank back into a sitting position, his head held low over his chest, hands still clapped over his ears to shut out the mind-smashing sound from the deadly rain of mortar bombs. But there was no escape from it. Stones fell on his shoulders and legs in a steady downpour.

Time ceased to have all meaning. The barrage seemed to go on without end.

Quilley even began to long for death. Anything to release him from this fiendish torture of pulverising sound.

He had no idea when it stopped. But it did. As suddenly as it had begun.

Quilley realised it had stopped with the sudden awareness that the choking sobs coming from his chest were the only immediate sounds he could hear. He was sitting in the foetal position gently rocking himself back and forward as he sobbed.

He stopped rocking, ventured to let his eyes look to left

and then right, and lifted his eyes slightly. Then another terrible sound pierced right to his brain. It came from a little distance away.

The sound died. Then it came again – a blood-curdling scream.

Quilley raised himself and peered over the edge of his fox-hole. The scream came again. And it seemed to be coming from a pale oval shape on the ground only six or seven feet from Quilley.

He strained his eyes against the darkness. The oval shape jerked a few inches. It was a human face.

Another scream faded into spoken words that were barely coherent:

"Christ save me. Save me . . . Save me . . ."

"Rimmer? Is that you, Rimmer?"

Quilley's question was a throaty whisper.

The face only moaned.

Quilley hauled himself over the top of his trench and belly-crawled towards the face. It was Rimmer.

The boy was clawing at the earth with outstretched fingers.

"Are you hurt, Rimmer?"

Again a moan.

"Why did you get out of your hole, Rimmer? Ain't you got no sense? How bad are . . . ?"

Quilley didn't complete his question. His eyes had glanced to where Rimmer's fox-hole should have been. There were shallow craters and the ground was indented and pitted but the fox-hole had either caved in or been blasted open. It just didn't seem to be there.

Then the truth dawned on Quilley. Rimmer hadn't left his fox-hole. He had been blasted clean out of it.

It couldn't have been a direct hit, he reasoned, or there would have been nothing left of Rimmer. It must have been a near-hit, or even two or three blowing in against each other so that Rimmer had been sucked right out of the ground and tossed down again like a rag doll.

He crawled closer and turned Rimmer over on his back.

A whimpering sound came from the boy's swollen lips. His face was pitted with tiny stones and grains of earth, masking him with red oozing spots. His body seemed like rubber, the way it collapsed when Quilley rolled him on his back.

There was not a lot of blood. A spreading stickiness just above the right knee. A trickle from the nostrils and the sides of the mouth.

Then Quilley noticed the splay of the legs, the unnatural twist at the waist as if the top half of the body did not knit with the bottom half. And Quilley knew that there was probably not a bone below the rib cage left unbroken.

He was trying to decide what to do when Rimmer gave a small sigh and died.

Quilley stared down at the body. A succession of explosions, so close together that they seemed to ripple towards him, suddenly reminded him of his exposed position.

This time, the mortars seemed to be concentrating their saturation either on the "E" platoon section or beyond it. There was no guarantee that the Germans would keep directing their fire there, however, and Quilley had no desire to stay around and find out. The thought of his money back on that Limey ship haunted him even now.

He stared again at Rimmer and the idea came to him.

He tossed his carbine aside, stood erect, then he stooped and hoisted Rimmer's body over his shoulder. With one final glance towards the line of fox-holes, he turned away from them and began to half-run, half-stumble into the darkness.

Twice, he encountered files of infantrymen moving up towards the line. They seemed to be heading towards positions some way inland from the part of the perimeter Quilley had deserted. Both squads challenged Quilley, then waved him on with directions when he said he was trying to get a seriously wounded comrade to a dressing-station.

The journey seemed endless. He halted frequently to let his breath come in great heaving gasps. Then there it was ahead of him. The tents, the activity, the poles with the little Red Cross flags, and the lights being freely used in spite of the nearness to the battle – the advanced field dressing-station.

A medic, who was giving sips of water to a man lying on a stretcher, looked up at Quilley's approach. He stood up and stared in disbelief at the sight which met his eyes.

Quilley was covered in Rimmer's blood and his own sweat. He presented a grotesque picture. His staggering steps were no simulation of exhaustion. Bent under his bloody burden, he lurched forward with little will over the movement of his aching legs.

The medic ran to assist him and his shout for a stretcher was quickly answered. A doctor, washing his hands at a row of ablution bowls on a trestle, turned to see what was going on.

As the medic helped Quilley to lower Rimmer on to the ground, the doctor had already slipped his fingers round the slack wrist and was feeling for a pulse.

"The kid's been badly hit," gasped Quilley. "Are you a doctor?"

The doctor made no reply. He had gently placed Rimmer on the ground on his back and was staring into the lifeless eyes.

"There's nothing we can do," he said quietly. "You've been carrying a dead man."

Quilley covered his face with his hands.

"Oh, God, no," he groaned. He was so weary that acting the role he had planned was almost effortless.

The doctor put a sympathetic hand on Quilley's shoulder.

"You look all in, soldier. Was he a special buddy?"

"He was one of my men," said Quilley. "I couldn't just leave him out there screaming. I had to do something."

The doctor turned to the medic.

"Any chance of rustling up a cup of coffee for this man, Dusty? He could sure use it."

"I'll see what I can do," said the medic.

"You've earned a rest," the doctor told Quilley. "Take the weight off your legs and have a coffee and a smoke. Dusty, there, will be back in a minute with the best mug of coffee you ever tasted."

"I should be getting back," said Quilley. "I had to leave my guys to try and save the kid. I should get back right away."

"Half an hour isn't going to make all that difference," said the doctor. "How far have you come?"

"I've no idea," lied Quilley. "I was kinda stunned by the blast that got poor Rimmer. I just picked him up. He was screaming something terrible. I had to do something. I have a feeling I was maybe walking around in circles with him until I sorta came to. Some guys movin' up told me this station was quite near."

The doctor peered at Quilley.

"Are you hurt anywhere? You weren't hit?"

"I don't think so. My head aches like hell."

"Could be concussion. Look, I'm needed for surgery – I can't run the rule over you. But stick around, at least until the grogginess goes. Have that coffee. If I get a minute later on, I'll check on how you're feeling. OK?"

"I'm grateful, sir," said Quilley.

The medic returned with a mug of steaming coffee soon after the doctor had gone.

"Doc says you maybe got concussion," said the medic. "It sure must be rough up there tonight. The word is that the Krauts have staged a big counter-attack and we've had to pull back."

"Yeah, it's rough," said Quilley, enjoying the coffee. "God, I'm tired."

"Why don't you get yourself some shut-eye?" said the medic. "You'll never find your way back up there in the dark, will ya?"

"I don't know," said Quilley wearily. "Maybe I'll do like you said. Grab me an hour."

"There's a pile of blankets over there." The medic jerked a thumb over his shoulder to indicate. "Why not grab one and find yourself a place to stretch out?"

And that's what Quilley did. With a blanket under his arm, he moved away from the dressing-station on to the sand of the beach. Making himself comfortable beneath a bank of bent grass, he curled up and went to sleep.

He awoke with the piercing rays of the sun striking his eyeballs and a voice bellowing in his ear.

He opened his eyes wide and sat up, startled. He found himself gazing up the muzzle of a heavy-calibre service revolver. At the other end of the revolver was the angry twisted face of Lieutenant Stoker. Behind Stoker stood two white-helmeted MPs.

"You are under arrest, Sergeant," Stoker was snarling. "I warned you, you lily-livered skunk. The charge is cowardice – desertion in the face of the enemy ... You're getting the whole goddamned book thrown at you."

II

Temporary Master

THE HOLDS of the *Fort Harrison* were emptying. All the army vehicles had been unloaded. Discharging from number three and four holds had been completed and at numbers one, two and five all that now remained was the small crate cargo – boxes of ammunition, octane in jerry-cans, detonators and light bombs.

Pendlebury, Acting Master of the ship, was little aware of what was going on and had made no contribution whatsoever to this satisfactory state of affairs. He had moved his personal belongings up to the Captain's day-room and cabin on the bridge-deck, locked himself in, and left the entire running of the ship to Andrew Mitchell.

Pendlebury was in nominal command. Mitchell was the *de facto* commander.

Mitchell was gaunt and hollow-eyed from lack of sleep. He had perhaps snatched four or five naps of twenty minutes each in the course of the last week. He was not alone in this respect. Few members of the ship's company had fared any better.

The air raids on the anchorage had continued night and day and showed little sign of let-up. Throughout all this time, the engine-room staff had been working ceaselessly to repair the damage caused by the near-miss bomb. Indeed, another alarming indication of damage had been discovered. The *Fort Harrison* might well be starting to split in two.

A galley-boy dumping trash over the side had noticed a crack beginning to appear in the ship's side just beside the bunker hatch. It had grown. A fracture in the plating of the main deck had begun to appear. It was structural damage which they could not even begin to repair outside

165

a dry dock or ship-yard.

It could only be watched with the hope that it would not get too bad. But it worried Mitchell. He knew that in an open sea with the stresses and strains which that imposed upon a ship, the *Fort Harrison* could break apart and sink in minutes.

Mitchell was proud of the way the ship's company had behaved at the beach-head. It had not escaped him that many of the seamen, relieved of their gunnery or deck duties for their watch off, had volunteered their services to the American army stevedore officer and had been helping to discharge the ship when they could have been snatching well-earned sleep. The docks troops had been insufficient in number to man all the holds at once and, because this had become apparent when some of the docks men had collapsed with exhaustion, the crewmen had come forward without being asked.

In addition to four fatal casualties as a result of the bomb, two of the *Fort Harrison*'s men had cracked up under the strain of the constant bombing.

A forty-five-old steward had gone completely berserk. He had to be physically restrained in a straitjacket and had been transferred to a hospital ship for care. The man had been torpedoed five times in the previous four years — experiences which in themselves had left great scars on the mind. The nightmare of Salerno had been the last straw.

It had also been too much for an eighteen-year-old gunner. His mind had just snapped like a piece of over-extended elastic and the world for him had become a place of terrifying hallucinations and endless bad dreams. He, too, had been taken to the sanctuary of a hospital ship.

And, of course, there was Pendlebury.

Mitchell had no doubt at all in his mind now that Pendlebury should have been taken to a hospital ship, too. Admittedly, he had given no difficulty since Mitchell had allowed him to assume Lansing's mantle — but his behaviour had become almost child-like.

Pendlebury had become totally preoccupied with the

trappings of his new office but had shown no interest at all in the functions of it. He was content just to *be* Captain and live in the Captain's quarters and wear the Captain's hat and summon the Captain's steward – but the Captain's duties he happily delegated to Mitchell.

Mitchell accepted the responsibility with the knowledge that others depended on him to carry it, but he drew no satisfaction from the position in which he found himself. He was sure he had made a cardinal error of judgement in taking a soft line with Pendlebury. In paying homage to Pendlebury rather than destroying him, he had acted from pity and not for the good of the ship.

Pendlebury was agreeable for the moment but the man was so volatile that there was no telling when his personality might undergo another violent change and his latent paranoia re-assert itself.

What made Mitchell uneasy was his fear that if a second occasion arose when Pendlebury's authority might have to be challenged, lives and the safety of the ship might first have to be put at risk. The opportunity which might have been the more painless had been missed.

Mitchell was absently staring from the deck at the skilful way an American sailor was bringing an LCM alongside number two hold. Sitting on the ledge of the cockpit, he was changing the gear levers of the twin engines with his feet and steering with his hands. A voice spoke behind him.

"I've put some fresh coffee and sandwiches in your cabin, sir. Can you grab 'em now while the coffee's still hot?"

Mitchell turned to face one of the young stewards.

"Sure. Thanks, Whitey. What's in the sandwiches?"

"A change from spam this time, sir. Corned beef."

Mitchell made a face.

"Well, I suppose the folks at home would give away their pension-rights for a couple of slices of corned beef. Thanks, Whitey."

When he sat down at his desk chair and eyed his repast, Mitchell wondered if he could find the strength to reach out for the coffee cup. God, he was tired. It would be the easiest thing in the world just to lean back and sleep.

He made a conscious effort to reach out for the cup and drink some of the scalding coffee. Strangely, he had no appetite, but because eight hours had passed since his last meagre snack, Mitchell forced himself to eat the food. His stomach may not have wanted it but he reasoned that his system needed it.

Colin Durham's head appeared round the gently billowing door curtain.

"Scoffing again, eh?"

"I'm having last night's dinner, this morning's breakfast and today's lunch all in one go," said Mitchell. "And all off the same plate!"

"One of our Yankee friends shared his K rations with me this morning," said Durham. "I had one of those monstrously thick bars of nutty black chocolate. Made me sick as a dog. So damned rich I won't have my appetite back for Christmas."

"Have a corned-beef sandwich," said Mitchell heartily.

"No thank you."

"Did you get the motorboat in the water?"

"Yes indeed. What's more, it still floats and the engine starts first time."

"That's a relief," said Mitchell. "I thought the timbers would be so dry it would fill with water up to the gunwales. Is one of the apprentices manning it?"

"Yes. Young Lovell. He's ready to go when you are. What's it all about anyway?"

"I'll be on my way just as soon as I've had this coffee," said Mitchell. "Didn't you see the signal? Commodore to Acting Master? The Commodore wanted an officer to report to him personally on the *Confidenza* with full details of our damage, casualties, seaworthiness, et cetera. He also wanted to know estimated time for completion of discharge and readiness for sea."

"What did Pendlebury say?"

"What he's been saying about everything. Look after it, will you Mister Mitchell. You can take care of it, can't you?"

"You should have put the old goat over the side in a straitjacket along with old Hawthorne the steward," said Durham.

"That's easy enough to say, Colin."

"There isn't a man on the ship wouldn't have backed you right up to the hilt."

"Well, it's too late now. At least he hasn't been any trouble."

"Yeah – but how long do you think it'll last? Any minute now, it's going to dawn on him that he's the re-incarnation of Captain Bligh and he'll be keel-hauling deck-hands and hanging engineers from the yard arm!"

Mitchell grinned.

"That's what I like about you, Colin – your unbearable optimism."

"Just you mark my words, Mr Christian," said Durham in an excruciating imitation of a West Country accent. "Just you mark my words, Mr Christian."

Mitchell got to his feet and smiled at Durham. "Look after the shop for me while I'm gone, Colin. Time I was off to the *Confidenza*. Oh, and if you're going by the sick bay, look out another straitjacket, will you?"

"What for?"

"Yourself, you nut. Just in case being Acting Deputy Master goes to your head."

*　*　*

Mitchell sat at the tiller of the thirty-foot motor lifeboat and enjoyed the light breeze in his face. Lovell, the apprentice, was perched beside him, and he, too, was enjoying the cool air fanning him as the boat chugged across the anchorage.

Landing-craft speeding in all directions provided a succession of navigational hazards and the boat rose and fell at the bows as it cut through the furrows of waves created by these other vessels.

The *Confidenza* was anchored almost a mile away from

the *Fort Harrison*. A string of LCTs was moored in a line near the after half of the Dutch liner but a lowered companionway near the midships section was untenanted.

Mitchell guided the motorboat just ahead of the companionway, put the engine astern, and the starboard bow of the boat swung gently against the fender at the foot of the companionway. Lovell, in the bows, put a line round the stanchion. Mitchell put the gear into neutral.

"Take the boat out a short way and just lie off until I give you a shout," Mitchell told the apprentice as he swung himself up on to the companion ladder.

"Aye aye, sir. I'll keep an eye open for you."

Mitchell climbed to the deck. A uniformed quartermaster escorted him to Commodore Britten's quarters.

Mitchell was shown into a broad airy cabin with white-painted walls and a red-carpeted deck. At one end, a long table which could have seated twelve occupied the centre area. At the other were two doors leading – Mitchell assumed – to bedroom and bathroom. There were three plush red settees, a desk, several armchairs, a small bar and drinks cabinet, and a row of metal filing cabinets which were obviously "foreign" to the rest of the decor.

Papers were spread across the big table and, over them, was stooped a tall white-haired figure with craggy white eyebrows and a hawk-like nose. He came forward now to meet Mitchell, hand outstretched.

"Jolly nice of you to come, my boy," Commodore Britten said. "I cannot tell you how distressed I was to hear about Captain Lansing."

He indicated a chair.

"Sit down, Mr Mitchell. I just want to ask you a few things. Get clued up, as my Lieutenant would say. He'll be here in a minute, by the way."

He scratched furiously for a moment at his backside and then returned his attention to Mitchell.

"Where was I? Oh, yes. This damage that you have to the stern glands – how bad is it?"

"Well, we're making the best repairs we can and the

Chief Engineer is reasonably optimistic – but we're not really going to know how successful we've been until the ship gets under way. That's when the crunch is going to come, sir – when the shaft is turning."

"I see. Does the Chief Engineer have any idea what speed you're going to manage – assuming, that is, that the screw doesn't fall off the moment you start the engines?"

Mitchell smiled at the way the question was put.

"I think, sir, that the Chief is going to be highly delighted if we can muster five knots. He says there's a real danger that the after end of the shaft and the propellor mountings are twisted and that if we gave the thing full revs it would be really asking for trouble. We might be stuck here for the duration."

"We can't risk that kind of immobilisation. Better if you could crawl out of here at three knots than gum up the whole bloody works."

"No hope of a tow if the whole shooting-match went?"

"None at all, Mr Mitchell. None at all. You *would* be here for the duration."

Britten scratched himself again. It seemed to help his thought processes.

"The speed that your ship is able to make is a critical factor, Mr Mitchell. We were banking on the ships going out light at a much faster speed than we brought them in. We've been trying to put together a twelve-knot convoy. It's a question of getting the escorts to cover as many eventualities as possible. The faster we can get them from A to B, the faster they can get on to C to take another lot to D or back to A. Sounds bloody confusing doesn't it? Well it's a confusing business. We just don't have enough escorts to cover all our networks."

He gave a sigh of exasperation.

"It's like working out railway timetables and trying to protect all the services you're running. The nine-thirty from Paddington doesn't get any protection unless you can speed up the night train from Glasgow so that it gets in at eight o'clock instead of ten o'clock at Euston and still leaves you time to switch its escort across to Paddington before nine-thirty."

To Mitchell's relief, they were joined by a handsome fair-haired man with two wavy gold bands on his epaulettes. Lieutenant Anthony Pennington-Greaves, RNVR, had heard part of Britten's discourse. He was mildly reproachful to his superior.

"Now, now, sir. Not playing trains again are we?"

He nodded to Mitchell.

"Pennington-Greaves, Flag Lieutenant to Sir here – disrespectfully known to the lower deck as the Commodore's bumboy. I consider the title a gross slander, so would be obliged if you do not encourage it."

Mitchell shook hands and introduced himself less flamboyantly. Britten was snorting with impatience.

"Penners, I wish you wouldn't float in here as if you were the First Sea Lord. I was trying to explain to Mr Mitchell about convoy speeds and the shortage of escorts. He's from the *Harrison*. She got a bomb up the backside and her engineer doesn't think she'll manage more than five knots."

Pennington-Greaves shook his head gravely.

"That *is* serious. Means she'll have to do the return trip on her Todd Sloan?"

"Her what?" asked Britten.

"Her Todd Sloan. You know, cockney slang – alone. No convoy, no escorts – lonely as the cloud that floats on high."

"I wish you'd stop talking like a ha'penny joke book, Penners," said the Commodore.

"Sorry, sir. Force of habit." He raised an eyebrow at Mitchell. "Did Sir tell you that we were trying to put together a twelve-knot convoy for the light ships?"

"He was doing that when you came in," said Mitchell.

"We've just about got that sorted out," said Pennington-Greaves. "There will be a second convoy, slower, but it will have to make eight knots minimum. Anything that can't keep up with that is up the jolly old creek. They'll just have to go solo and chance their luck."

"I don't think we have a hope in hell of risking eight knots."

"Independent passage then for the *Fort Harrison*, sir?" asked Pennington-Greaves.

"Don't see how it can be avoided," said Britten. "Damned hard luck and all that but it's just as well to take a chance in the open sea as sit around here and get bombed twenty times a day."

"Wasn't the *Harrison* nominated as our Wormwood Scrubs, sir? Will her reduced automotive capacity make any difference?"

"We were going to use her for prisoners, Penners," said Britten.

"That's what I was saying, sir. Will it make any difference? Can we put prisoners aboard a lame duck?"

"Don't see that it should make any difference. There's nothing in the Geneva Convention says we have to give 'em privileges which our own men don't have. They'll just have to take the same chance as Mr Mitchell here."

"I hadn't heard about any prisoners," said Mitchell.

"Oh, there won't be many," said Britten. "A few Jerries — mostly fliers we picked out of the drink and some survivors from a couple of E-boats that were sunk. Oh, and some Americans."

"Americans?"

"Yes, Mr Mitchell. There's been quite a bit of trouble here as you possibly know. Troops deserting their posts, threatening mutiny, that sort of thing. There's been drum-head courts-martial, military tribunals, the lot. I'm sorry to say it wasn't confined to the Americans. About three hundred of our own troops refused to go into action. Sat on the beach and told their officers to go to hell. I suppose it will all be hushed up, so for God's sake don't repeat what I've told you."

Mitchell came away from his conference on the *Confidenza* with his head spinning. He let Lovell take the boat's tiller and sat himself on a midships thwart pondering possible trials ahead.

It was bad enough having the Pendlebury situation and the damaged propellor shaft and the crack that was appearing in the ship's deck. But now there were more problems: an unescorted passage across the Med, prey for any lurking U-boat or marauding bomber, and a load of mutinous prisoners who could conceivably cause all manner of troubles. What next?

Future problems faded from his mind as an immediate one demanded his full attention. The Luftwaffe chose that particular moment for yet another bombing run on the anchorage.

Mitchell and Lovell, feeling more naked and exposed than at any other time when the bombs had rained down, crouched low in their tiny wooden boat as the sky blackened with anti-aircraft fire and the sea began to explode and spout all round them.

Mitchell became aware amid all the sound that Lovell was trying to tell him something.

"What are you saying?" he bellowed. "I can't hear you."

The boy put his mouth close to Mitchell's ear.

"Nasty, sir, isn't it?" he said.

12

Prisoner

QUILLEY stared at the rivets of the grey-painted deckhead eighteen inches above his nose. His cell in the prison ship to which they'd brought him was about seven feet wide by six feet across. He occupied the top bunk of two which folded down from the bulkhead on chains.

The door, painted in the same dark grey as the rest of the cell, was a solid steel affair with a rectangular opening about two-thirds of the way up. Two bars were mounted in the opening.

Quilley was reliving in his mind the events of the previous afternoon. He had been marched from his cell by two Marines along endless alleyways in this gloomy dark-grey ship, then up several decks into bright sunlight. He had been kept standing on the deck, gazed at curiously by the US navymen who passed by in the course of their deck duties. He was acutely aware of the bracelets on his wrists with their absurdly long length of chain.

Eventually he had been marched into a long narrow room converted from its normal use of saloon or mess into a temporary court.

Quilley was made to stand before a long table, behind which five army officers were seated. All were wearing combat uniforms. Three of the officers had arms or heads bandaged, indicating recent injuries. They had, in fact, been enlisted to their present duties from a field hospital. They were ambulatory casualties, not yet fit enough to re-join their units but cleared for light administrative duties while undergoing further treatment.

At side tables sat two stenographers and half a dozen other uniformed men whose function Quilley could only guess at. One of these uniformed men, a major, now rose as Quilley was left facing the table. The two guards retreated to take up positions by the door.

General Warren J. Slack, the central of the seated officers, spoke:

"All right, Major Bartholomew, you may explain to the prisoner the nature and functions of this court."

The Major read from a book of regulations the articles under which the court was constituted and the definition of its function and power.

He concluded by naming the five officers of the court, General Warren J. Slack presiding. Then the name and rank of the accused was read out and the charges against him listed.

General Slack faced Quilley.

"You have been charged, among other things, with cowardice and deserting your post in the face of the enemy. These are the most despicable charges that can be brought against any soldier in a time of war. Under a differently constituted court-martial they could bring you a sentence of death — because death by firing-squad is still the penalty of dishonour in the United States army. This court believes it would be exceeding its authority by awarding such a sentence in a situation where neither prosecution nor defence can be presented by qualified attorneys and where key witnesses cannot present their testimony in person. The latter are required for duties which must take priority — fighting a skilled and implacable enemy.

"You have the consolation, therefore, of knowing at the outset that if you are found guilty you will not suffer the maximum penalty which the charges against you allow. It does not follow that this court views these charges and their need to be heard with anything other than the deepest shame and regret and a determination to punish them, if necessary, with the utmost severity. Do you understand?"

"Yes, sir," whispered Quilley. And his spirits soared. A live coward could still find a way back to that money!

Major Bartholomew stood up once more.

"The first deposition, sir, is from Lieutenant Herbert

Langley Stoker of the Thirty-Sixth Infantry Division."

"Read it out to the Court, please, Major."

Bartholomew read Stoker's account of the hurried recruitment of several makeshift infantry platoons from other units and of his orders to position them along the perimeter of Yellow Beach.

He told of conveying to Quilley orders which had come to him from Division that the positions were to be defended to the death. He told how, after several mortar attacks, some German infantry had broken through the lines of "F" platoon – the section where Quilley had been left in charge. The enemy had almost encircled "E" platoon, and two fresh squads arriving from the beach hadn't driven the Germans back after fierce hand-to-hand fighting.

By morning, re-inforcements from the 45th Infantry Division had come through Stoker's part of the line and pushed the Germans back up the Sele valley. This had taken the pressure off his men.

It was then he investigated the German intrusion of "F" platoon. He found that, apart from three men killed in the first mortar attack just after midnight, "F" platoon had abandoned their positions. Two men had been found hiding a little to the rear. They said they had quit their positions when they saw Quilley abandon his fox-hole and throw away his carbine.

He had consequently instigated a search for Quilley as the man mainly responsible for a situation which could have cost the loss of the beach-head.

There were further depositions from six men from "F" platoon, all of whom were under close arrest awaiting disciplinary charges to be brought against them. All of them testified to Quilley's disappearance from his fox-hole position soon after the first mortar attack.

Two men had actually seen him throw his carbine away – it had not been fired – and had seen him carry someone or something away in the general direction of the beach. The four others said that, alarmed at the drift away from their position by their comrades, they assumed that an order to evacuate the line had been given but had not reached them.

They had sought the advice of Corporal Martin, whose leadership they apparently respected, but they found that Corporal Martin was dead. They had then tried to locate Sergeant Quilley but he could not be found.

Quilley was asked then to explain his actions.

He described the mortar attack and repeated the story he had told to the doctor at the field dressing-station – that he had been stunned by the blast which had wounded Rimmer. He said he didn't know rightly what he was doing but had come to his senses some distance from the line carrying a screaming Rimmer on his shoulder. He had no recollection of leaving his position nor of throwing away his carbine.

His first consideration had been for his wounded comrade, and some GIs had directed him to a nearby dressing-station. There, a doctor had told him that Rimmer was dead and that he himself was suffering from concussion. The doctor had told him to rest and that he would treat him later. A medic had given him a blanket and he had fallen asleep. The next thing he knew he was being arrested by Lieutenant Stoker.

"Was any effort made to find this doctor to substantiate the accused's story?" asked General Slack.

"Yes, sir," said Bartholomew. "It was established that the accused did, in fact, bring in a casualty – this Private Rimmer – but the man was found to be dead on arrival. The doctor in question was a Captain Edward Pascoe. I have a deposition from him, sir."

"You had better read it out," said General Slack.

Major Bartholomew cleared his throat when he had found the paper and read Pascoe's words:

" 'I remember the soldier coming in. He was carrying the other man across his shoulder and was staggering. He was in a state of near exhaustion. I remember thinking that the wounded man was very far gone if not already dead, just by the look of him. I then examined the casualty and it was obvious not only that he was dead but that he had been dead for at least an hour, possibly longer. I then ascertained that the man who had been carrying him was not wounded. He was not – but he did complain of headache and being previously stunned. I said I would have a look at him later, but he was not to be found and I assumed that he had returned to his unit. He had stated this was his intention.'"

Major Bartholomew paused and looked up.

"The following questions were put to Captain Pascoe by the investigating officer. One: 'Did you think it strange that a dead man should be carried a considerable distance without the man who was carrying him being aware that he was dead?'

"Captain Pascoe answered: 'Yes, strange inasmuch that it is unlikely. But I suppose it could happen as a result of fatigue or shock, or a combination of both these things.'

"Captain Pascoe was then asked: 'Have you experienced similar instances of dead men being brought in long after they are beyond aid?'

"He replied: 'Oh, yes. Usually, it is used as a subterfuge by the so-called rescuer. He believes that by pretending to try to save his buddy he has sufficient reason for removing himself from a situation of great danger to himself.'

"Captain Pascoe was then asked: 'What is your reaction to this?' His reply was: 'As a doctor, one of compassion. I have found that these soldiers do not go round looking for corpses to carry out of the line. Usually, the dead man is their closest friend. They are unable to accept the fact of his death and they become very afraid for their own lives. They therefore seek medical assistance for two reasons. They bring the dead buddy to a field hospital in the deluded hope that a doctor will perform a miracle and bring the friend back to life – but they are also motivated by the idea that they themselves will find safety at the hospital. As often as not, the man who seeks this form of escape is in need of medical treatment. Invariably, he has a proven battle record and has been involved with his friend in many life-or-death situations. Before, he and his buddy have always survived. It is when his buddy does not survive that the one who is left loses control and behaves in the way I've described. Call it battle fatigue, or what you like, but the survivor is as much a casualty as the man who stops a bullet. He has just had too many bullets fired at him.'

"Captain Pascoe was then asked if the case in question corresponded in detail with cases he had experienced in the past. He replied: 'No, this one was different. At least as far as my own observations are concerned and in light of the information which you have provided. Firstly, the man concerned is a sergeant and it turns out that he scarcely knew the boy who was killed. If there was a long record of the Sergeant harbouring paternal feelings for the boy, or even latent homosexual feelings, it could be much more easily explained. From the way he spoke to me it could be interpreted that he had feelings of responsibility for his entire squad – he said he had to get back to them – but then it has to be asked why he left them in the first place. And the strange thing is that the Sergeant does not appear to have experienced constant danger in a way that would normally induce battle fatigue. His behaviour is more compatible with that of a very raw recruit who goes into battle for the first time and the shock is such that he just loses his nerve.'

"That is all, sir," said Major Bartholomew.

General Slack looked round at his colleagues.

"Are there any questions you would like to ask the accused in the light of that deposition, gentlemen?"

A major, whose left arm was in a sling and who had been pencilling notes with his right hand, said:

"I have a question, sir."

He pointed the pencil at Quilley.

"Was Private Rimmer dead when you put him on your shoulder?"

Quilley averted his eyes from the Major's and stared straight ahead.

"No, sir."

"How do you know he was alive?"

"He was screaming, sir."

"You said before that you were stunned and that when you came to you were staggering around carrying this soldier. So how do you know he was screaming when you picked him up?"

"I knew he was alive because he was screaming. I don't remember picking him up."

"Were you very fond of Rimmer?"

"He was only a kid. I always felt ... Well ... sorry for him."

"Did you – you've been a sergeant for some time – always harbour paternal feelings for youngsters who came under your wing?"

Quilley hesitated, not quite seeing the point of the question but knowing after what that doctor had said that he would have to answer it carefully.

"I've always tried to look out for the guys in my squad."

"But you ran out on your squad."

"Not deliberately. I don't remember a thing between the whole place going up around our ears and me realising I was carrying the kid on my back."

"Are you satisfied, Major?" asked General Slack.

"Not quite," said the other officer. "I'm curious to know why the accused doesn't look me in the face when I'm asking him a question, but I have one final point."

Quilley forced himself to look at the Major. The bright blue eyes seemed to bore right through him; to be totally undeceived by what Quilley's exterior revealed.

"I want to be entirely fair to the accused," the Major said. "Circumstances and the evidence we've heard have not cast him in a pretty light. I should like to know if there's anyone who is prepared to say something good about him. We have seen the investigating officer's entire report, the accused hasn't. It is only right that he should be told that his own commanding officer declined the opportunity to speak on his behalf and that not a single serving man, commissioned or otherwise, could be found to make a character deposition on his behalf. Everyone who was approached – and I can understand many difficulties in the present situation – everyone approached said that they did not really know the man well enough. He seems to be the most anonymous soldier in the United States army ..."

"I volunteered for this operation," flamed Quilley. "I took the place of a sick guy. How well can you get to know other guys in three weeks?"

"Silence!" rapped General Slack. "Had you finished, Major?"

"No, sir. I was just going to ask the accused in his own interest if he could nominate *anyone* who could furnish us with character testimony of a nature favourable to himself."

"Well?" asked General Slack, staring at Quilley.

Quilley looked around desperately. His brain was numb. He was realising with a growing feeling of despair that there was not one man in the world he could call friend, that there was no one to whom he could turn for an iota of support, even a kind word. He felt he had to break this silence which was going on and on.

"I can't think of anybody," he snapped, his voice almost a screech. "They're all in Algiers. Anybody who knows me is in Algiers."

"Very well," said General Slack. "Give us a name."

Quilley felt his panic quicken. What could they do? Radio to Algiers for a character reference? Surely not. He could give them Honeyman's name. And he knew what Honeyman would say. He'd put the knife right in and twist it. Then there was McGivern. Quilley knew what McGivern would do, too. He'd roll Quilley's name around in his mouth and spit it out. Never heard of him. Suddenly he thought: Pendlebury. But no, they would never accept what that old woman had to say.

The court was still waiting.

"Well?" repeated General Slack.

"There's nobody!" shouted Quilley.

The five officers at the table exchanged looks. Here was an accused man who had been given the opportunity to name one person, one friend or comrade who was ready to come to his defence and say he was no coward, to say any thing good about him — and he couldn't produce a single name.

General Slack spoke:

"This court will now adjourn to consider the evidence that has been brought before it. Guards, you may remove the prisoner."

Quilley was marched from the room. Then the waiting began. It had still not ended by the following day.

He lay, looking up at the dark grey rivets, playing and replaying in his mind all that had been said in the court. At least they wouldn't shoot him. That had been a very real fear from the moment Stoker had surprised him on the beach.

But what would they do?

From part of what the doctor had said, Quilley entertained hopes that they might treat him as a medical case and let him off. From other parts of his statement, however, the court might have no difficulty in finding him guilty.

One thing was sure. He would never see his money again. He might get away with his life, might even be sent to a safe area to serve a sentence in the pokey, but he could say goodbye to his money.

He abandoned further speculation at the sound of footsteps outside his cell. Once again, flanked by two Marines, he was marched along the corridors and up to the temporary court-room. Once again, he was left facing the long table at which the five officers sat.

General Slack spoke:

"You have been brought here to hear the findings of this court."

He turned to his colleagues.

"This is case number twenty-three on the list, gentlemen — Sergeant Francis Quilley." He looked across to Major Bartholomew. "That is correct, isn't it, Major Bartholomew?"

Major Bartholomew rose, the inevitable sheaf of papers in his hand.

"That is correct, sir. Case number twenty-three."

The General stared coldly at Quilley.

"Stand up straight, Sergeant. You're supposed to be at attention."

Quilley straightened.

"The findings of this court," General Slack went on, "are that you – a man to whom less experienced soldiers might look for leadership – did desert in the face of the enemy from a position which you had been ordered to defend with your life. The court considers it a mitigating factor that you had not previously experienced combat duty but the court does not consider that this in any large part absolves you of having acted dishonourably and in contradiction to the traditions of your rank and the United States army.

"Your orders were plain – to defend your line or die where you stood. You wilfully disobeyed these orders. It is not uncommon in war that a soldier sees his comrades suffer and die. Indeed, all his training equips him to expect this eventuality and not to let it sway him from his own duty.

"You have said in your own defence that you were stunned by explosions and were not wholly responsible for your own actions. The court has used its discretion not to rule out the possibility of this being true. What the court cannot accept is that, having recovered from your alleged disorientation, you had still made no attempt to resume your duties ten hours after you had absented yourself from the line. The court feels that this casts some doubt on the veracity of your account of how you came to be absent from the line in the first instance.

"The court has not seen fit to consider your guilt or innocence in connection with the several minor charges which were laid against you but has concentrated instead on the most serious charges – that of desertion in the face of the enemy and the associated charge of cowardice.

"The court finds you guilty on both counts. It is the sentence of this court that you lose all rank and privilege and serve a period of not less than five years' penal detention."

Quilley was stunned. Five years. It seemed a lifetime. The two guards came forward.

As he was being marched from the room, Quilley heard General Slack say:

"Well, gentlemen, we have five minutes for a smoke before we deal with case twenty-four."

At four in the afternoon, they brought Quilley a mug of coffee and two biscuits. They were handed in from a trolley in the passage-way.

The dispenser of this repast was a swarthy navyman with a white apron tied to his waist.

"You're getting company," he told Quilley. "Lucky you."

"What do you mean?"

"I mean sooner you than me, buddy. He's a real mean one. He's up right now getting some time added to his sentence for clocking an officer. He packs quite a punch — broke the poor guy's jaw."

"They're putting him in with me?" asked Quilley.

"That's the scuttle-butt," said the seaman.

"What are they gonna do with us?" asked Quilley. "How long they gonna keep us cooped up in this old tub?"

"Hey, you're speaking of the ship I love. Old tub! Believe me, soldier, it's a dreamboat compared to the one you're being shipped out on."

"They're shippin' us out?"

"Sure they are. We're an operational ship and the US navy can't afford to keep you bad boys on board permanently. Not that I blame you guys for misbehavin'. It's one way of getting outa this war. Yeah, scuttle-butt says you guys are going back to Africa on some limey freighter."

"There's one limey freighter I'd like to be on," said Quilley sadly.

"You're joking," said the navyman.

Quilley became a little more guarded.

"I came over on a limey freighter," he said. "It wasn't too bad. The *Fort Harrison*."

"Hey, that's the tub. You just said its name. The *Fort Harrison*. That's the one they're puttin' you guys aboard."

Quilley looked at him in disbelief.

"You're sure of that?"

"I ain't never sure of anything in this man's navy. But that's the name the two-ringer said. He was wanting a boat's crew for ten tomorrow morning ... to go to this *Fort Harrison*."

But Quilley wasn't listening. He was laughing. Laughing so hard that a pain came in his side. It was the final irony. The *Fort Harrison*. Oh, it was a joke, a mistake. It couldn't be true.

The navyman shook his head and pushed the trolley along the corridor to the next cell. Quilley was still laughing.

Fifteen minutes later, Quilley's cell door was opened. A mountain of a man was pushed unceremoniously inside. He had been brought down by what seemed like a whole squad of Marines. The big man's wrists and ankles were manacled.

"Hey, ain't you gonna take these goddamn chains off?"

"Later, baby," said a husky Marine sergeant. "When you promise to be a good boy."

The big man's reply was very obscene.

The cell door clanged shut. The big man glowered at Quilley.

"What the hell are you staring at?" he said.

"Somebody who looks like he's badly in need of a friend," said Quilley.

"I don't feel very friendly. I don't even like your face much."

"You ain't exactly Rita Hayworth. But then I didn't choose you as my den-buddy," said Quilley.

The big man laughed.

"Rita Hayworth I am not. And you ain't Betty Grable. You gotta cigarette?"

Quilley took a pack of Luckies from under his pillow and gave the man one.

"Thanks," the man said. "They took mine away after I banjoed that prissy-mouthed officer."

"I heard about it. The word was they were gonna make you do more time for it."

"They doubled my sentence. The bastards doubled my sentence. They gave me two years for standing up for my rights and they've doubled it to four years for busting that sonofabitch's jaw. I shoulda broken his goddamn neck."

He looked at Quilley through a curl of smoke.

"What did you get?"

"Five years," said Quilley.

The big man gave a whistle and looked at Quilley with dawning respect.

"Hey, a celebrity! What did you do — shoot an officer?"

"I was tempted," said Quilley. "But, no, I didn't shoot nobody. You could say that's part of the reason I'm here. No, this pig of an infantry Lieutenant threatened to blow my head off if I didn't stay in my little fox-hole and let the Krauts blow it off. So I said screw all lieutenants and screw the whole bloody war. This kid beside me got wounded and I carried him over two miles to a field hospital. That's where they caught up with me and put the chains on me. I just hope I meet up with that lieutenant some day. I'll make him wish the Krauts had got him first!"

"They try to nail the cowardice thing on you?" asked the big man.

"They not only tried, they did."

"Me, too," said the big man. "Said I was inciting mutiny. Just because I didn't see the sense in getting roasted in a gasoline fire while the goddamned officers stayed in the fresh air where they could make a jump for it. We was workin' the transports, docks division. What's your name, soldier?"

"Quilley. Frank Quilley."

"Pleased to meetya, Frank. You seem all right to me. I'm Danovich. You can call me Danny."

13

Make Ready For Sea

"I THINK it's an imposition," said Pendlebury.

He stared across the day-room of the Captain's quarters at Andrew Mitchell. They were discussing the sealed orders which had just come aboard from the Commodore on the *Confidenza*.

"How are we going to accommodate these prisoners?" Pendlebury went on. "We can't lock them in the fore-peak or keep them chained in the tween-decks. They'll need to be exercised and guarded day and night. And how many men are they giving us to guard them? Does it say?"

Mitchell sifted through the sheaf of papers on the table and extracted a sheet.

"Here it is. It gives their names and regulations on guard rotas, etcetera. They are all US army personnel. The man in charge is Sergeant Millard O'Keefe. He will have ten men for guard duty. It says here that there must be two men on guard at all times over the military prisoners with another on stand-by. And it's the same for the prisoners of war – two men on guard at all times, with one on stand-by. That means they'll have to work a watch-and-watch rota with, presumably, the stand-by man doing a double watch so that the whole thing keeps moving."

"I don't follow."

"Well," said Mitchell, "they'll need to have four men on duty at any given time – two for the military prisoners and two for the Jerries. At the same time, there will be four guards off duty and two on stand-by – making a total of ten all told."

"That's something we can leave them to work out for themselves. I still don't think there's enough of them. How many prisoners are there?"

Mitchell fished out another sheet of paper.

"Here are the names for the passenger manifest — that's a bit of a joke isn't it? ... Passenger manifest!" He counted names. "Eighteen ... twenty ... twenty-four ... twenty-eight American military prisoners. And let's see now ... ten ... twelve ... thirteen prisoners of war. That makes the total number of prisoners forty-one — so there is one armed guard for every four prisoners, not counting Sergeant Millard O'Keefe. I don't suppose we could hope for more. After all, they can't run away once they're on the ship — unless they're very good long-distance swimmers."

"Any ideas where we put them?"

"Well, we could stow all the Jerries in that extra gunners' mess in number five port side. There are sixteen bunks in there. There are too many Yanks to go anywhere but in number four tween-deck. No bunks for them there — it'll have to be hammocks — but they'll have plenty of room at least."

"Can I leave you to look after all that?"

"No trouble. I'll put Mr Durham in the picture anyway. I'll need to look out charts and plot a course to Bizerta. They've routed us down through the Straits of Messina with the hope we may pick up an escort at Port Augusta. We won't need to do any zig-zagging on account of our estimated maximum speed being only five knots. A zig-zag pattern at that speed would mean that we'd not get to Bizerta until about five years after the end of the war!"

Pendlebury frowned.

"I hardly think it's a subject for levity, Mr Mitchell. Frankly, I find it all very worrying. I don't mind telling you that I've been finding the added responsibility a great strain. It's almost impossible to get any sleep. If it's not the noise of the guns, it's the rattle of winches. I can't remember when I last had a decent rest."

Mitchell refrained from telling Pendlebury that he had done nothing but "rest" since Lansing's death while every other man on the ship had worked to the very edge of complete mental and physical exhaustion. You great old hen, he thought. The boilers could fall through the bottom of the ship and you'd probably phone up the engine-room and ask them to make less noise.

It was always a relief to get out of Pendlebury's presence and into the fresh air. On deck, the *Fort Harrison*'s crew were preparing the vessel for sea. The last of the cargo had been discharged.

On shore, the Allied armies were making better progress. The beach-head, which at one time was in danger of becoming another Dunkirk, was for the moment safe. But the Germans had been counter-attacking in considerable strength and had been making the Allied thrusts into the coastal hills and uplands both bloody and costly.

The constant rumble of gunfire rolled outwards from the uplands across the Bay of Salerno and Mitchell contemplated it grimly as he made his round of the decks. It had been such a constant companion that he found it difficult to remember a time when it had not existed.

An American navy tender stood off from the *Fort Harrison* and a sailor in the bows hailed the deck.

Mitchell acknowledged the call.

"Got some passengers for you. Where can we come alongside?" asked the navyman.

Mitchell indicated the Jacob's ladder under the port bridge structure.

"Throw me your painter," he yelled.

He made fast the forward line himself and was waiting on the deck to welcome aboard Sergeant Millard O'Keefe and his ten men.

O'Keefe was a man of about forty-five, with a worn face. He was saved from looking ugly by two mischievous blue eyes and the fact that the lines on his face seemed to be permanently cast into a cheerfully benign expression.

"You Sergeant O'Keefe?" asked Mitchell with outstretched hand.

"What's left of that old reprobate," said O'Keefe with a grin. "Glad to be aboard, sir."

"I'm Mitchell, Second Mate. We've been expecting you,

Sergeant."

"I bet they didn't warn you guys about us though. Want to hear some of the names they've been giving us?"

"Names?"

"Sure – like O'Keefe's Coughdrops, the Sorry Squad and the Dysentry Detachment ... And those are only the ones I'd mention in polite company."

Mitchell smiled.

"You're not regular on guard duty, then?"

"Regular, Mr Second Mate. Hell, we're the original sick detail. Unfit for combat but if you can prop us up with a rifle in one hand and somethin' to lean on with the other, we'll keep an eye on your prisoners."

He grinned widely.

"Well, you look in good shape, Sergeant," said Mitchell.

O'Keefe lowered his pack to the deck, unbuckled his belt and opened his shirt front to reveal a dressing taped across his waist. He pushed the dressing to one side to show a raw criss-cross wound on his lower abdomen.

"When we went ashore on D-Day they had to carry me outa the landing-boat. You'll never guess what – appendix! The doc took it out right there on the beach, stretched me out on a wooden door that'd been washed up from some wreck. 'O'Keefe,' says he, 'you just weren't meant to see Naples and die. If I hadn't caught ye, ye'd never have seen Naples at all.' And says he: 'I don't want you to go straining and exerting yourself chasing after them nasty Germans with that stitched belly of yours. What you need is a nice restful sea voyage to get your strength back.' And that's why I'm here. Me and the other ten invalids."

The Sergeant's men were arriving on the deck one at a time. Now, their kit at their feet, they stood in a semi-circle discussing his appendix scar.

"They say that when they opened him up it was his brains they found down there," said one.

"And what was left of two rookies he'd chewed up at boot camp," said another. Yet another suggested: "The doc's supposed to have bust five scalpels on him. And that was just getting through his skin."

O'Keefe took it all good-humouredly.

"Mr Second Mate," he said, "maybe you'd show me where I could bed down these mindless malingerers. Any old bilge will do – just so long as there's plenty of rats and cockroaches and things to keep their empty heads occupied."

"They can go in the four-berth messes in number three tween-decks. That's the way down over there. Through that hatch. But Sergeant ..."

"Sure."

"For yourself – that's if you feel it might be more comfortable, and I reckon it is – you're welcome to share my cabin ... Use the settee."

O'Keefe was surprised and delighted at Mitchell's offer but declined. His place was with his men. Mitchell left the Sergeant to settle in and went up to the chart-room to prepare the charts for the run to Bizerta.

Colin Durham found him there an hour later and told him that a landing-craft with thirteen German prisoners of war was alongside number four hold. They went together to watch the Germans embark. O'Keefe and two of his men armed with carbines were already on the scene waiting to escort the prisoners below.

Four Germans were already on deck. A fifth was having considerable difficulty climbing the scrambling-net. His left arm was heavily bandaged and he seemed to be unable to grip the manila with his left hand.

On the landing-craft, which kept sheering off at the bows from the ship's side, a white-helmeted Marine was shouting exhortations to the prisoner.

Mitchell caught a look of intense pain on the man's face as he looked upwards in the instant that he realised he could not hang on. He fell into the sea between the landing-craft's bow and the ship's side.

Mitchell was the first, indeed the only man to move. He kicked off his shoes, poised momentarily on the rail and dived into the water ahead of the landing-craft.

When he surfaced, several quick strokes took him to

the floundering man. Pain-filled eyes flashed Mitchell a look of gratitude as he put an arm round his chest and under his chin and supported them both by paddling the other arm.

Someone threw a line from the deck and Mitchell secured it with a bowline round the prisoner's chest, then he manoeuvred the man to the scrambling-net. As those on deck took the weight of the prisoner, Mitchell shouldered the man from behind and helped him up the net towards the ship's rail.

Once there, Mitchell addressed himself to Sergeant O'Keefe.

"I hate spreading your responsibilities, Sergeant," he said, "but this man is hurt and I'd like him moved temporarily to the ship's hospital. You may want to put a guard outside the door, if only for your own peace of mind."

"No problem, Mr Second Mate. I'll detail a man. Where is the ship's hospital?"

"Mr Durham, the Third Mate, will show you when you've got your other prisoners below decks. In the meantime, I don't think this man's going to run away."

The prisoner who had fallen in the water was half-bent against the rail of the ship, holding on for dear life with his good arm. He looked very ill.

"Give me a hand with this man, Walsh," said Mitchell. The seaman, who had been an interested spectator, went to Mitchell's assistance.

Between them, they carried the prisoner to the ship's hospital, which was located in the after end of the bridge accommodation. The door – which opened directly on to the deck – was locked.

Mitchell swore.

"Hang on to him a minute," he told Walsh. "I'll need to get the key."

He returned with the key, having collected a couple of large bath towels and a tin of cigarettes on the way.

They stripped the man and placed him in the hospital's single bed, wrapped in the two towels. His skin was ice-cold and he was shivering.

Mitchell lit a cigarette and placed it between the blue lips. There was a nod of thanks and, for the second time, the eyes flashed unspoken gratitude.

"We'll need some hot coffee. Nip along to the pantry, Walsh, and see what you can manage. Tell them I want three mugs – that's one for yourself as well. I know you never refuse."

The seaman grinned and left.

Mitchell looked down at the man on the bed.

"I'm going to take that bandage off your arm. I'll try not to hurt."

The man managed a wan smile.

"Thank you, Herr Second Officer," he said.

Mitchell picked up a pair of scissors from the sterile tray. "You speak English, then?"

The man winced as Mitchell began to cut away the sodden bandages.

"I, too, was Second Officer. Bremen South America Line ... Before war. Since war, navy called me."

The man's arm had been burned from wrist to arm-pit. Some of the raw flesh was festering and Mitchell wrinkled his nose at the odour it gave off. He made an antiseptic solution and cleaned away pus oozing from infected areas with a lint pad.

The German flinched each time the pad touched the sensitive flesh but he made no sound.

"There was an American military doctor on board but he has gone ashore now," said Mitchell conversationally to divert his patient. "That means I'm the ship's doctor again – on the strength of a two-week medical course I attended when I sat my ticket."

Again the wan smile.

"I, too, used to be ship's doctor. Same college. For me it was giving men black medicine – what you call TNT, eh? Keep stomach movements open. You understand?"

Mitchell smiled.

"That's more my style. Black draught. Cure anything

from a hangover to sleeping sickness. What's your name?"

"Klemper — Willi Klemper. You want also my rank and number?"

The question was asked with the nearest the weary eyes could approach to a twinkle.

"Nope. We don't have much time for ceremony in our mob. I'll just call you Willi. Same as I would any other patient. Unless I should be calling you Kapitan or something like that."

"Leutnant, although I was Captain. Just a torpedo boat, you know. Maybe I should not say it, but I was very fond of my ship. These waters are made for cruising. In peacetime would be very nice."

"You do not like the war?" asked Mitchell.

"Only fools *like* war," said Klemper. "But a man must do his duty. When your country calls and says: fight ... you obey. You fight. It is just harder for us who are men of the sea. In peace, we are a brotherhood of all nations and our enemy is the sea. In war, we must fight our brothers and this is very sad."

Mitchell was strangely moved by his enemy's words. This is a murdering Nazi bastard you're doctoring, he tried to tell himself — but the thought had no conviction. Klemper was just another seafarer like himself, not wanting war but caught in it up to his neck.

What was that bit in the Bible? Love your enemies. Well, that was something that didn't come too easy if he was firing torpedoes at you or plastering you with bombs or machinegun bullets. But if he was weak and hurt and in your power and needed your help, it wasn't quite so hard.

Mitchell dressed and put clean bandages on Klemper's arm. He was just completing the task when Walsh arrived with three cups of steaming coffee.

"Sorry I was so long, sir. Had to go to the galley and boil the water myself. Hey, that's a neat job you've made of that bandage, sir."

"I'm good at tying up Christmas parcels, too.

He handed Klemper a mug of coffee. He surveyed himself

as he stood sipping his own coffee. He realised that his clothes were still wringing wet and that little pools had formed on the deck wherever he'd been. He stripped off his shirt.

"Looks like I'll have to put on some clean clobber whether I've got a clean shirt to my name or not."

"You'd better get yourself dried up, sir. You could catch pneumonia," said Walsh.

"I will, I will. That little swim freshened me up. Will you keep an eye on our patient until they get a guard posted. I'll leave that tin of fags for him."

Klemper raised himself on the bed.

"Herr Second Officer."

"Yes?"

"Thank you for saving me – and for your kindness."

"Forget it," said Mitchell. "I reckon you'd have done the same for me. I'll look back later and see how you are."

14
Departure

QUILLEY — who during his court appearance had been unable to think of a single friend to speak in his defence — rejoiced in the companionship of ex-Sergeant Danovich. They had sprung from similar backgrounds: Danovich from a tenement housing a hive of polyglot nationalities near New York's East River; Quilley from an Illinois jungle slum amid the stockyards and slaughter-houses of Chicago.

The time of their coming together occurred at a moment when both men considered themselves victims of a hostile and unjust world. Neither man was of a character to accept his misfortune with philosophical docility. And each recognised his personal need for an ally, just one other kindred spirit who could help him overturn the odds.

Danovich, for all his talk of principles and the rights of workers, adhered only to these principles as a means of achieving his own ends. The principles which he used today to topple an obstacle would be used tomorrow to defend his excesses when *he* was the obstacle. He expressed principles for all men but lived only by those which coincided with his own immediate interests.

If it was good for Danovich, it was good for the world.

Quilley and Danovich had known each other less than two hours when they were debating ways of defeating the bleak prospects of their present circumstances.

The irony of being returned to the *Fort Harrison* for transport to a detention camp in North Africa had been much on Quilley's mind. His personal kit must still be neatly stowed away in the recess under Chief Officer Pendlebury's settee — or surely discovery of his money hoard would have created shockwaves right back to him.

He had mentioned his kit to no one since he had exchanged words on the subject with Diamond. He had allowed his present captors to believe that most of his gear had been blown up in a baggage truck which had received a direct hit.

They had given him some clothing and basic toilet equipment.

Now, the more he thought about the *Fort Harrison* and his money, the more he thought about how both might facilitate *escape*.

He didn't tell Danovich about the money but he did tell him of his acquaintance with the *Fort Harrison*. It was a surprise to learn from Danovich that he was no stranger to the ship. Danovich had arrived at the beach-head in a landing-craft, with the rest of his docks battalion, and had been sent on board the *Fort Harrison* to unload its cargo. Indeed, it had been as a result of an incident on the *Fort Harrison* that he was now in his present predicament.

It was Danovich, in a moment of imaginative Slav enthusiasm, who mooted the impossible idea.

"Hey!" he exclaimed. "Why don't we steal the goddamned ship? We could sail it to a neutral country like Spain and sit out the rest of the war."

He was only half serious and Quilley's first reaction was to dismiss the idea as impossible. But the idea wouldn't go away. They began to talk about it.

"The old Chief Officer was a good friend of mine," said Quilley. "If they lock us up below decks, I could always get word to him that I wanted to see him, spin him a real sob story about a miscarriage of justice, get him on our side."

"Where would that get you?"

"You never know. The old guy really liked me. Once we were at sea, I could maybe con him into seeing me in his cabin or something. He had a gun in his desk — a forty-five ... I could get hold of that. Or if I could get up on the bridge during his watch. They got a Lewis gun on a rack in the wheelhouse and six Lee-Enfields."

"Now you're talking," said Danovich. "Look, there's gonna be other jailbirds on that ship besides us. None of them are gonna be happy about serving out four or five years in some lousy sweat-camp. We could organise them. There might be more of us on the goddamned ship than guards or anybody else. If you could get weapons and spring us, we could take over the ship and make 'em take us where we wanna go. If they don't wanna co-operate we could roast the Captain real slow over the galley fire or toss the Chief Engineer in one of the furnaces just to show we mean business."

"There's just one big snag," said Quilley. "One bigger'n God Almighty snag!"

He punched a fist into the open palm of his other hand.

"What snag?" asked Danovich. "I can see it happening. It could be perfect."

"But what about the other ships in the convoy? How do we stop them from knowing or radioing a message or making some coded signal with flags? And there'll be navy ships, destroyers. They could put aboard a landing-party with machine-guns – or just shell the ship and sink the goddamned thing rather than get it stolen from under their goddamn noses."

"When we make our move, the first thing would be to smash the radio before they have time to send out a message."

"No," said Quilley. "It wouldn't work. If only I could see a way of fooling those other ships. We just can't sail along with the convoy. We gotta lose it."

"We could get a signal put out. You know, by lamp. Sayin' we got an engine breakdown. I seen it happen when we come over. This ship just dropped away behind the convoy. We didn't see it no more for another week."

Quilley acknowledged that Danovich maybe had something there.

They talked long into the night.

*　　*　　*

None of the military prisoners ever learned the name of the ship on which they had been held and tried. She was known simply as the PX Ship, because of her role as a supply tender for the fleet. She carried everything from fresh paint to torpedoes and candybars, and vessels requiring replenishing simply tied up alongside her and had their stores transferred aboard. Her cell accommodation was something of a bonus, and rumour had it that a regular pre-war run had been from Pearl Harbor to San Diego with long-term prisoners from Hawaiian military establishments.

It was a varied assortment of villains who were transferred by motor tender from the PX Ship to the *Fort Harrison* late on that September afternoon of 1943. In addition to Quilley and Danovich, there were two equally colourful miscreants.

There was Mike Cordoba, former infantry private, due for dishonourable discharge and ten years in a penitentiary. He had disfigured his platoon sergeant hideously with a knife. He was no stranger to the inside of a jail. His last brief spell in the cooler had occurred in Algiers after he and a friend had tried to press their attention on a nurse walking alone in the street. The unexpected intervention of what he took to be a British naval officer had left Cordoba with a broken nose. He hoped fervently that he would meet that officer again.

Hooky Pritchard also had a distinctive nose. It had earned him the nickname "Hooky". But Hooky's nose was a natural disaster, not man-made. Florida had been his stamping-ground. A man on the fringe of the big-time rackets, his career as a muscle-man for a gambling syndicate had become a trifle too warm to pursue when the law had broken up the ring.

Pritchard had hastily decided on a vacation in New Mexico, where he had bummed around for two miserable months before enlisting with no other purpose than to get three square meals a day. By the time he reached Salerno, Pritchard had had his fill of military life.

The army, with a mistaken idea about his capacity for honesty, had appointed him driver of a truck destined to rendezvous in the mountains with a cloak and dagger group. On the truck was a large quantity of money which the cloak and dagger boys were to smuggle by devious routes to Milan to finance partisan activities.

With more initiative than intelligence Pritchard had made off with the truck during a chow stop, much to the bewilderment of his companions who included two majors, a corporal and three GIs like himself. His idea was to strike south, find some quiet little village by-passed by the war and buy himself anonymity and the rich life.

Two minutes' serious thought about the project would have deterred any other person but Pritchard.

The consequence was that he drove his truck almost head-on into a German Panzer division. It was hard to tell whether Pritchard or the outriders for the German column experienced the greater surprise. Pritchard had been the first to recover.

He had U-turned off the road, round a tree, and taken off back the way he had come in a cloud of dust. The Germans, not suspecting any American troops to be within twenty miles of the area, had investigated with caution, allowing him to get clean away.

Pritchard, of course, had run slap bang into his own people. One of the two majors had wanted to shoot the driver out of hand but had been prevailed upon by the other that a court-martial was a more acceptable solution.

His escapade had earned Pritchard five years.

The rest of the prisoners bound for the *Fort Harrison* had performed less spectacular misdemeanours. Most had been sentenced for taking to their heels under enemy attack without waiting for orders or a bugler to sound retreat. Many felt they had been made scapegoats and were bitter. At the same time, the bitterness of some was tinged with relief they had been reprieved from re-entering the holocaust of war.

Quilley felt a glow, almost of homecoming, when he saw the *Fort Harrison* again. The tender circled the vessel before being directed alongside and Quilley saw the damage to the ship where the bomb had exploded. One of the starboard gunpits had disappeared and only the twisted metal of its stilt supports remained. The lifeboat which had been slung in davits beside the gun-pit was no longer there.

The *Fort Harrison*'s crewmen watched in curiosity as the prisoners were herded aboard by US Marines and handed over to Sergeant Millard O'Keefe and his small posse of men.

One of the American prisoners who came aboard took a long hard look at Mitchell. The Second Officer was unaware of the scrutiny, although he did intercept an intense stare in his direction from a prisoner with a misshapen nose. He did not connect the man with a short sharp bout of fisticuffs in an Algiers street.

While O'Keefe talked to the Marine officer in charge of the transfer, Quilley observed a great deal of activity in the anchorage. Several empty transports were weighing anchor or actually on the move. Numeral pendants flying from signal-masts indicated that they were taking up convoy positions. Quilley did not appreciate the significance of the pendants but guessed that a convoy was assembling for departure. He fully expected the *Fort Harrison* to get under way, too, and become part of it.

It puzzled him, therefore, after two hours in the uncomfortable heat of number four tween-deck, that the *Fort Harrison*'s engines were still silent.

He and Danovich sat apart from the other prisoners and there was plenty of space for them to do so. The tween-deck had previously accommodated four hundred men, if not in comfort, certainly without difficulty. The prisoners, after the cramped cells of the PX Ship, luxuriated in the comparative freedom.

Already, Quilley and Danovich were observing and noting everything concerning their new whereabouts.

There were no guards at all in the hold. Two men with carbines did, however, guard the sole entrance and exit hatchway leading out over the hatch-coaming. Quilley knew that a hold ladder, similar to the one in which Lieutenant Rainwater had died, must also be present.

He found it. It led up to the after mast-house. But there was no exit there for them. The watertight door inside the mast-house had been screwed shut.

The shaft housing this ladder carried up through the mast-house into a big ventilator – and this did represent a means of escape from the hold. The only snag was the big metal grille covering the mouth of the ventilator. It was big enough for a man to pass through without trouble – but silently removing the grille from inside the ventilator represented a near impossible task without the aid of heavy cutters.

Having reconnoitred the premises as far as they could, Quilley and Danovich sat debating possibilities and surveying the other prisoners, who would make able recruits for any plan they conceived.

An hour after dark and after the barrage from a dusk air raid had long since ceased, the two men became aware of sudden activity on the deck above. Then from a distance they heard the clank of the windlass on the fo'c'sle-head as the *Fort Harrison* began to pull in her anchor.

A new sound came from beyond the great bulkhead just forward of them. It was the slow hissing clank and deep pulverising thud of the ship's triple expansion engines as they began to turn.

The sound quickened slightly, stopped for a moment, then began again. This pattern was repeated twice more before the tempo increased to a slow measured thumping. This slow but rhythmic pulsing was maintained and the frame of the ship settled into a groaning accompaniment.

The *Fort Harrison* was undeniably on the move out of Salerno Bay.

The prisoners below decks were blissfully unaware of a constant communication between bridge, engine-room and shaft tunnel as the ship moved slowly out beyond the escort screen and headed south alone on the sea at a painfully slow pace.

The first turn of the engine had caused water to stream into the shaft tunnel from the damaged stern glands, but the flow was not massive. Third Engineer Bedford observed that the emergency packing was holding well and that the intake of seawater was constant and of a quantity which the pumps could handle.

The ship was no sooner underway than the prisoners in number four received an issue of life-jackets and a ration of steaming coffee and hard biscuits. Then the hatch doors were closed and they were locked in for the night.

The air in the hold soon became suffocating, a situation which was not improved by the odour from the makeshift toilets: nothing more than a long cubicle housing a row of buckets which required daily emptying and disinfecting.

The prisoners lay in their hammocks strung above the mess tables and agonised in their own sweat. Some found the energy to climb up the steep stair and beat on the hatch doors and shout for more air to be admitted. But their cries went unheeded.

Sergeant Millard O'Keefe acknowledged to himself that conditions in the tween-deck must be damned near unbearable. But, first night out and with as few men as he had, there was no way he was going to relax his security before the position had been re-assessed in daylight.

At first light, he allowed the hatch doors to be opened – a move that earned cheers and a variety of comment from the men below. Then they were allowed out on deck two at a time so that they could go to the midships ablution sections and wash – a procedure which was to be followed so that they could collect breakfasts from the galleys.

Quilley and Danovich came up into the blinding sunlight, having paired together. They stood blinking around them. They were seized simultaneously with disbelief – disbelief which changed quickly into barely suppressed excitement.

They turned their heads slowly, looking all around. No matter in which direction they looked, the ocean was empty.

Neither man spoke as they walked ahead of the guard to the timber ablution sheds which had been built on the *Fort Harrison*'s deck parallel with the ship's galley. The guard did not follow them into the shed but waited at the door while they sluiced themselves at separate taps jointed in to the long fresh-water pipe stretched over a trough of similar length.

Water running from their faces, they beamed at one another, scarcely able to contain their delight.

"No convoy!" said Quilley, his eyes laughing.

"Not a goddamned ship for miles!" said Danovich, his expression matching Quilley's. "We can do it! You said it was the only snag!"

"We'll do it clever. No mistakes. I reckon we gotta day — maybe two at the outside — to work it out proper."

"Then we hit 'em!"

"Then we hit 'em so goddamned fast, they won't even know what happened!"

15

The Steal

"WHAT THE hell is going on, Mr Durham?"

Pendlebury's squeaky voice piped up the voice-tube at the Third Mate.

The *Fort Harrison* was making three and a half knots in a southerly direction some twelve hours out of Salerno Bay. It was mid-morning.

The noise which had provoked Pendlebury's querulous question was also puzzling Colin Durham.

"I don't know what the disturbance is, sir, but it's coming from the afterdeck. Perhaps if you could relieve me up here for a minute, I could go aft and find out what's happening."

"Very well," said Pendlebury. "I'll be right up."

With Pendlebury on the bridge, Durham made his way aft. What sounded like a clanking of tins and men's voices raised in a chant was coming from number four hold, where the American military prisoners were quartered.

Sergeant Millard O'Keefe, flanked by two guards with raised carbines, was facing a crowd of prisoners spilling from the hatchway to the tween-deck. The men were banging mugs on tin plates in rhythmic concert and shouting: "We want air. We want air."

"What's the trouble, Sergeant?" asked Durham.

"They're bitching about the heat in the hold," said O'Keefe. "It was pretty bad down there last night. They want to send a delegation to the Captain."

"That's very civilised of them," said Durham lightly. "What do you think?"

"I think to hell with them. I don't have enough men to have them roaming all over the deck. Better they stay down below where they won't get up to no mischief."

"Well, Sergeant, our acting Captain doesn't go a great bundle on this infernal racket. Perhaps if we let them have a parley they'll stop their bloody noise. Tell them I'll go and ask the Captain if he'll see a spokesman. One spokesman — not a bloody delegation."

"Okay," bellowed O'Keefe, "maybe you heard what the officer said. You stop your shenanigans and go quietly below and maybe the Captain will listen to your complaints. One guy can speak for you, hear that? One guy."

The noise subsided.

"We gotta guy right here who'll talk for us," said the big man in the middle of the hatchway. The speaker was Danovich. He pushed Quilley forward.

"You'll talk for us, won't you Frank?" he said.

Quilley had been pushed almost hard against the barrels of the carbines held by the two rather nervous guards. He raised his hands in a placatory gesture.

"Easy fellas. The guys don't mean no trouble. It's just that it's worse than the Black Hole of Calcutta down there. All we want is an even break. It ain't human to keep men in conditions like that."

"I'll go and see the Captain," said Colin Durham. "You stay right where you are." He eyed Quilley.

"Haven't I seen you somewhere before?"

"Sure, Mr Durham," said Quilley. "You remember me — Sergeant Quilley. I bunked on Mr Pendlebury's settee on the way over."

"I thought I knew you. How come you're under guard? What the hell did you do?"

Quilley shrugged.

"It's a long story, Mr Durham. I tried to save a guy's life. A mean-minded lieutenant thought I was trying to desert. They wouldn't listen to my side of it."

"You're breaking my heart," put in O'Keefe.

Durham shook his head. How the American army conducted its affairs was its business. God knew what they'd do next.

He reported to Pendlebury, telling him that the American prisoners were protesting at being kept in inhumane conditions.

"They want you to at least hear what their spokesman has to say. And this is the bit that's going to floor you. The spokesman is an old friend of yours – that Sergeant who bunked in your cabin on the way over."

"Sergeant Quilley?"

"None other," said Durham. "Seems he fell foul of some lieutenant and got charged with desertion. Says he was only trying to save somebody's life. Sounds mighty peculiar to me."

"I can't believe it," said Pendlebury. "Sergeant Quilley was a perfect gentleman. Go back and tell him I'll see him right away."

Ten minutes later, Quilley was seated in the Captain's day-room with a coffee at his elbow and a very large smile on his face. He had been unable to believe his luck. His idiot friend, Pendlebury, was now – by some remarkable stroke of fortune – in command of the *Fort Harrison*. It was too good to be true. Adding to his excited well-being was the almost certain knowledge that, very close, in Pendlebury's old cabin on the deck below was his treasure trove of dollar bills, still undisturbed.

Gravely, Quilley told Pendlebury of the terrible injustice that had been perpetrated against him by the US army.

"My crime," he said, "was to be placed temporarily under a man who hated my guts. I acted as any other decent human being would have done in the same circumstances. A friend of mine was terribly wounded and I was knocked unconscious by the blast that gave him these wounds. I have only a hazy idea of what actually happened. All I know was that when I sort of came to my senses, I was staggering around in circles with this friend on my shoulders and shouting for a medic. I had no idea where I was but some infantry guys tried to help. They said I was near a field-hospital and to take my buddy there. Well, I got there with him and collapsed ... A doc saw me and said he'd come back and fix me up because I was in a pretty bad way – but I flaked out again. The next time I came round, this mad lieutenant was waving a gun in my face and accusing me of deserting. And it just wasn't true."

Pendlebury was horrified.

"My poor fellow. How could they possibly accuse you of deserting? They surely didn't believe this maniac?"

"They put me in front of a lot of officers and they all took the Lieutenant's side. They just wouldn't believe the God's own gospel truth I was telling them. They sentenced me to five years! Can you believe that? Five years!"

Pendlebury was outraged. He had no doubt at all that Quilley was telling the truth. It simply wasn't the kind of story a man would make up. It also confirmed for Pendlebury the private view he had always held of America and the Americans, of whom Quilley was the single exception he'd ever encountered. They were a nation of brash and ignorant barbarians.

Quilley went on to tell him that most of the prisoners now being transported back to North Africa were, like himself, scapegoats of military stupidity. They were simple good-hearted men who had laid their lives on the line for their country and this was the savage reward of their patriotism.

Quilley pleaded that something be done to alleviate the hellish conditions in the hold.

"You are a British officer, sir, said Quilley. "You British are noted for your traditions of fair play and your kindness to animals. All I ask is that you treat the men in that hold as human beings. Our own officers have treated us worse than you would treat a dog. Please don't let their shame become your shame. That's all I ask. We can't escape anywhere – unless we jump into the sea. Let us up on deck ... even if you have to keep us in chains."

Pendlebury was deeply moved. He felt a righteous anger against the entire American military system. And, he concluded, there was one place where the American military system didn't count for a damn – under the British flag on the high seas. On the *Fort Harrison*, he commanded. And he would enforce that command in a civilised and merciful way.

He rang for the steward.

"I want the American Sergeant who is in charge of the guards to come and see me," he told the steward, aware that Millard O'Keefe had not moved from outside the wire-screen door to the Captain's quarters since he had delivered Quilley there a short time before.

O'Keefe was brought in. He did not hide his surprise at seeing Quilley comfortably ensconced in one of the Captain's armchairs.

"You wanted to see me, sir," he said to Pendlebury.

"Yes, I do," said Pendlebury. He stared at O'Keefe through narrowed eyes.

"As Acting Master of this vessel, Sergeant, I want you to understand that I, and I alone, hold responsibility for every person on this ship. No matter what orders you may have been given by your superiors, these orders are secondary to mine aboard this ship."

"I'm sure I'd be the last person on Earth to disagree with that, Captain," said O'Keefe. "My orders relate only to the prisoners and their security."

"I'm talking about the prisoners and their security," said Pendlebury. "You have weapons to guard them and you can carry out these duties without subjecting them to conditions which no human being should be made to endure. It is clear to me from what I've been told that conditions in number four hold are quite intolerable. Ventilation has been closed off to aid your so-called security. Well, men are not to be battened down like cargo in my ship. There are laws which prevent us from transporting cattle in this manner and I am not going to have men treated as inferior to cattle under the British flag. Do you understand me?"

"I understand you, sir. I just don't rightly understand what we can do about it. I know it's grim in that hold when all the doors and that are shut — but I only got two men at a time to guard these guys."

"If weather conditions allow it, you can take some of the hatch covers off. These men aren't going to run anywhere. There's no real reason why you can't let them stay on deck. Surely you can guard them just as well in the fresh air as down below."

"If you're ordering me that that's the way it's gotta be, there's not a lot I can do about it, Captain. It's your ship. But I'd like it to go on the record that I was over-ruled. My orders were that the prisoners were to be kept under confinement and not to be released for exercise or anything else more than two at a time."

"Well, I *am* over-ruling you, Sergeant – and you can complain to . Eisenhower or the President of the United States or anybody else you like. They are not in command of this ship – I am! And if you want a reason, the reason is simple humanity."

"Very well, sir. Can I now return this prisoner back to where he belongs?"

"No, you may not," said Pendlebury, to both Quilley's and O'Keefe's surprise. "This man was recently injured by blast. Did you know that, Sergeant? If he is prepared to give me his parole, and I'm sure he shall, I want to keep him in the ship's hospital for – er – observation."

"I didn't hear of him having any injury, sir. It would be ... irregular."

"I shall accept full responsibility."

O'Keefe shook his head.

"I just don't rightly know."

Pendlebury turned to Quilley.

"Will you give me your parole, Sergeant Quilley?"

"You know it, sir. But I ain't asking for any special favours. If it's gonna cause trouble between you and the Sergeant here, I'd just as soon go back with the other guys."

"Good grief, man," said Pendlebury. "I allowed you to use my cabin all the way from Algiers. I wouldn't have done that if I hadn't thought you were a man worthy of my trust. I haven't changed my opinion of you just because some stupid lieutenant victimised you."

"You know each other?" said O'Keefe.

"Of course I know him," snapped Pendlebury. "I also think he has been the victim of a gross miscarriage of justice. And don't think I won't make strenuous representations on his behalf just as soon as we get to port – because that is exactly what I intend to do."

"I'm afraid I'm a little out of my depth," said O'Keefe honestly. "I don't know nothin' about nothin'. Like I said, it's your ship, Captain. If you're gonna call the shots, I'll just have to go along with them."

"Too damned right you will!" said Pendlebury.

* * *

On Pendlebury's orders, the German prisoner in the sick bay was unceremoniously returned to the company of his comrades in number five hold – a fact which infuriated Andrew Mitchell when he went to change Klemper's dressings. Nor was his humour improved when examination of the new "patient" revealed one recently demoted sergeant in robust health.

Quilley told Mitchell that he had recurring blinding headaches as a result of being blown out of a fox-hole – but his eyes were so clear and his manner so free from care that Mitchell did not believe him. He said as much without too much beating about the bush.

"I don't know what your game is, soldier, but you don't con me as easily as you seem to have conned Mr Pendlebury. If it's just a comfortable berth you're after, it's no skin off my nose ... but you ought to know that a sick man had to be moved out of here to make room for you."

Quilley grinned insolently at Mitchell.

"I told the Captain I'd just as soon be with the guys but he wouldn't listen. Anyway, it was just a Kraut."

Mitchell's eyes flashed.

"Maybe you didn't notice the big red cross on the door. That means that nationalities stay outside."

"Maybe *you* shoulda stayed outside. You gonna do something about it?"

"Maybe. I'll have a word with the Acting Captain. He may just change his mind."

"I'll go along with anything he says," said Quilley confidently.

Mitchell had cooled down by the time he had searched out Klemper and treated his wounds. Oddly enough, it was the German who sensed his upset and cautioned him about making too much of it.

"They did not tell you that your patient had flown, eh? Is it this that makes you angry?"

"What makes you think I'm angry?" said Mitchell sharply. "Now hold still, will you, while I get this dressing off."

The German was not put off.

"Your eyes are full of angry lights. I flattered myself that it was because of me. You do not seem pleased to treat me down here in this hot place instead of in the sick cabin where there is much equipment."

Mitchell smiled.

"I was angry because the man who is now in the sick bay is not ill. He is just a friend of the Captain's – a soldier."

"Remember I am the enemy," said Klemper. "Do not make trouble for yourself because of me. I am all right down here – with my own people."

"I have no reason to love you or your people," said Mitchell, a little needled that a German prisoner should be concerned with his welfare. "A lot of good friends would be alive today but for you and your people."

"I am sorry," said Klemper. "I did not mean to patronise. No matter that we are enemies ... there is no personal animosity. I did not wish to offend you."

"Forget it," said Mitchell.

They were interrupted by a tall blond Aryan with a cropped head and wide ingenious blue eyes.

He clicked his heels, bowed briefly and addressed Mitchell.

"Herr officer, we are grateful for what you have done for our comrade. We saw you save him from the sea and he has told us of your kindness in caring for his wounds.

We salute you."

He bowed again sharply. He had spoken with a thick halting accent and seemed slightly embarrassed to be offering the short but laboriously composed little speech. The other Germans were nodding their heads gravely in approval.

Mitchell felt a wave of compassion for them. They didn't look like rapists or Jew-killers or men who had to answer for crimes against humanity. He realised that his incapacity to sustain hatred was probably a terrible defect in anyone engaged in war. He obviously wasn't cut out for the business. He kept looking at his enemies and seeing himself or replicas of his dead friend, Lieutenant Holcroft – men who weren't particularly political or religious or good or evil or hate-filled, but men whose lives had been interrupted and changed by principalities and powers over which they had no control.

Mitchell reached in his pocket and pulled out a recently opened tin of Marcovich Black and White.

He thrust the cigarettes into the hand of the young man standing before him.

"Share these around," he said and turned on his heel. He paused at the door. "I'll look back in the morning," he called to Klemper.

*   *   *

Quilley waited for morning. A feeling of well-being had continued to build up inside him from the moment early in the day when he had discovered that the *Fort Harrison* was alone on the ocean. It had risen sharply at his discovery that Pendlebury was now in command of the ship and, throughout every incident of the day, it had notched a little higher.

Only days before, Quilley had cursed the fate which seemed to be sweeping him along in every hostile current. Now the currents were all miraculously favourable as if destiny had singled him out to triumph over unbeatable odds. He felt he could conquer the world.

The only minor irritant of the day had been his rub with the Second Officer. Well, tomorrow would settle that account. Mr Mitchell wouldn't be so high and mighty then!

Danovich had nearly collapsed with gleeful mirth when Quilley had been allowed to return to number four hold and proclaim the outcome of his parley with the Captain.

O'Keefe had not followed Quilley down into the tween-deck. He had allowed him his moment of glory alone while he had fought a deep resentful anger at deck level.

Quilley had enjoyed his success.

The other prisoners had cheered each pronouncement of terms won.

During daylight hours, they were to be allowed on deck on condition that they stayed within a roped area of the afterdeck. The privilege would be withdrawn at the first sign of trouble.

At night in good weather, the hatches of number four hold would be opened as much as possible and ventilators leading to the hold were no longer to be covered.

Quilley had time for a private discussion with Danovich after the other prisoners had tired of congratulating him. He told Danovich of his parole and his new quarters in the ship's hospital. Danovich was astonished that Quilley wasn't even going to be under special guard while enjoying the comforts of the sick bay.

He, too, had been making progress. Two men, Cordoba and Pritchard, were both amenable to his guarded suggestions of an enterprise and would make useful lieutenants. The others, with maybe a couple of exceptions, would go along with the majority. Most of the men felt they now had little to lose.

"Be ready to move about four in the morning," Quilley had told Danovich. And these had been his last words to him before collecting his things and transferring to the hospital to finalise the plans formulating in his mind.

Shortly after eight in the evening, Pendlebury had called on Quilley and presented him with a tin of Churchman cigarettes. He had gone on at length for about half an hour telling how he intended to make representations to the highest possible authority as soon as the ship docked in an effort to clear Quilley's name. He had ranted on about injustice and victimisation until it began to bore even Quilley. It was difficult to humour him and still keep a straight face.

Impatiently, Quilley waited for an opening to turn the conversation to a matter close to his heart: the fate of his belongings which had been left in the First Officer's cabin.

Pendlebury saved him the necessity of raising this delicate topic by suddenly saying:

"Oh, by the way, did you know you left some stuff in my settee locker? The steward drew my attention to it the day he moved my stuff upstairs and I promised to do something about it ... But it went clean out of my head until this moment."

Quilley assured Pendlebury that, if it was okay, he'd leave the kit where it was for the time being. Simultaneously, his well-being took another soar upwards.

Left alone again after Pendlebury had gone, Quilley systematically examined his new quarters. In addition to the aft-facing door as a means of exit and entry, there were two large port-holes leading to the starboard alleyway. They were big enough for even a very large man to climb through if the need arose.

The medical kit produced two useful items – a surgical knife and a long silver-handled scalpel with a razor-sharp blade.

Quilley lay back on the bed and waited for morning. In his mind's eye he held a plan of the ship and he mentally checked off the positions where crew and gunners would be on duty. Eyes closed, he rehearsed in his brain the precise actions he would take and their timing.

He modified and altered these actions until he felt sure that the blueprint was right and nothing could go wrong. Then he waited. He could not have slept even if he'd wanted to. The adrenalin was flowing much too fast. A tense excitement gripped him, not one of fear but of eager anticipation.

This time, he would be calling the shots – and that was the way he liked it.

Around four in the morning, he heard the watches changing. His friend Pendlebury would now be on the bridge. He had said that he was keeping his old watch rather than throw the whole load on Durham and Mitchell.

Quilley allowed ten minutes to pass by wrapping the scalpel and the surgical knife in a towel. Then he switched off the light and raised the deadlight over one of the portholes. He opened the port by unscrewing the three clamps. He could hear no sound from outside.

Silently, he swung himself up and manoeuvred himself feet first through the open port. He landed soundlessly on the deck of the alleyway.

He looked forward and aft – but nothing moved. He climbed up on the bulwark and looked down for a moment at the phosphorescent foam whirling along the waterline below. Above him, the jolly-boat was swung out in davits from the bridge-deck. He grasped the belly wires slung below it, holding it fast against the protective boom, and swung his feet, then his body, on to the lower bridge above. He lay for a moment in the boat's shadow.

His luck was in. The flying-bridge, on the next level, seemed deserted. Pendlebury was either having his mug of tea in the wheelhouse or he was patrolling the port wing of the bridge.

With stealthy steps, Quilley crossed the short area of wooden decking to the housing of the Captain's day-room. A port was open, curtains fluttering in the light breeze. Another stroke of luck.

Risking the possibility of being seen from one of the fore-deck gun-pits, Quilley clambered on the handrail which skirted the outside of the housing and pulled himself through the open port-hole.

Once inside, he allowed his eyes to get accustomed to the darkness and took his bearings. The other ports were all blacked out, which meant Pendlebury must have only opened one for ventilation before going on watch.

The clamps on the open port were well greased. Quilley closed the port, gently lowered the deadlight, and screwed up the clamps. Then he checked each other port and the two doors to make sure all were closed and would not reveal light.

He groped for the light switch and found it near the outer door. He switched on the light.

His eyes took in the room quickly. He moved towards the big bureau varnished in oak and opened the top right-hand drawer. Good guess. There, side by side, lay two .45 calibre revolvers and several cartons of shells.

Quilley had known that, in the Chief Officer's cabin, Pendlebury had kept a revolver in the top right drawer of his desk. He obviously hadn't changed the location since moving into Lansing's quarters. The second revolver presumably belonged to the late Master of the *Fort Harrison*.

Quilley took both guns, carefully loaded them, and secured them in his waistband. Now he had two knives and two guns. The odds in his favour were getting better all the time.

Making sure that the bedroom was blacked out, he entered and switched on the light. In a wardrobe, he found a dark navy battle-dress jacket. He tried it on. It was made for a man with a much smaller chest but he left it on, swinging open.

He also found a peaked Merchant Navy officer's cap. He placed it on his head. Not too bad a fit. He grinned at his new image in the mirror.

Switching the lights off behind him, Quilley left the Captain's quarters by the interior stair. All was quiet down below in the vicinity of the pantry and saloon.

Avoiding the cabins on the port side, where the watch-keeping officers were quartered, Quilley took the starboard alleyway and emerged on deck at the side of the number three hatch.

He moved silently aft, knowing that he might be seen, but having to take that chance. He passed the galley, the door to the fiddley and stokehold, the carpenter's shop, and reached the shadows of the alleyway skirting the midships accommodation.

Now he moved with greater care. At the far end of the alleyway he paused and peered aft. One guard with a carbine was sitting on some hatch boards guarding the open hatch down to the tween-deck where Danovich and the others would be waiting. Where then was the second guard?

Quilley reasoned that since the top of the hold itself had been opened to allow better ventilation, O'Keefe must have posted the other guard somewhere on the port side.

In addition, there must be two other guards somewhere keeping an eye on the German POWs whom he knew were aboard. The grapevine had said that the Germans were somewhere in number five hold and locked in one big dormitory cabin down there. This probably meant that their guards were down in the tween-deck, too, sitting outside the locked doors. There certainly seemed to be no sign of them on deck.

Minutes ticked by. Quilley knew he would have to act. But he was worried by the fact that he had no idea where that second guard was.

He unwrapped the towel holding his two knives. To his horror, the surgical knife slipped out of his grasp and clanged on the steel deck at his feet. He had been so intent on not slicing off a finger with the scalpel, which had to be very carefully handled, that the other knife had slipped from a fold in the towel.

The guard beside the hatch turned at the sound. He saw a shadowy figure in peaked cap and bluejacket. He walked leisurely across in the hope of unexpected company.

Quilley, on hands and knees searching for the knife, realised that the man was presenting him with just the opportunity he wanted. He moved further into the alleyway, still in a half-bent searching position.

"You lost something?" asked the GI behind him.

Quilley worked his hand over the cool metal handle of the scalpel and tighened his grip over it. The towel was draped over his wrist and concealed all but the point of the finely honed steel blade.

He turned and rose in one movement. The soldier's wide ingenuous eyes opened wider in surprise as Quilley thrust upwards into the rib-cage just below the heart. The blade sliced through rib bone as if it were soft margarine and the man died with the briefest gasped cough and no other sound. He fell limp in Quilley's arms as he withdrew the blade.

Quilley transferred the weight of the body from himself to the bulwark and quickly removed the helmet from the dead man's head. He caught the carbine which slipped from the man's still warm grasp, just in time to prevent it clattering on the deck.

Next, Quilley stripped off the ill-fitting blue battle-dress jacket and tossed it over the side. The peaked cap quickly followed. He donned the man's helmet. Then, lifting the body by the legs, he tipped the dead man into the sea. The splash was scarcely audible above the surge and slap of water against the ship's side.

Lifting the carbine, Quilley strode aft across the open area beside number four hold.

"What you been doing over there, Sam?" came a voice from the far coaming.

It was the second guard.

"Thought I saw a rat," said Quilley. "You okay?"

"I gotta thirst like nobody's business. What time do you make?"

"Four twenty-five."

"Good. That means Hank should be along with the coffee in five minutes."

Quilley moved on a few paces, slowly forward, nearing a point where the timber hatchway would obscure him from the other man.

He waited in the shadow of the hatch, listening. From the far side of the deck came the soft footfalls of the other guard. He was promenading. Twelve paces forward, pause, turn, twelve paces aft.

Quilley let him do this two or three times to be sure that there was a pattern to the man's movements. Then he entered the hatch and moved silently down the timber stairs, his hand on the rail.

It was dark in the tween-deck but a figure loomed out of the shadows to meet him.

"That you, Danovich?"

"Yeah. Quilley?"

"We've not much time to jaw," said Quilley. "There's a guard due along with coffee for his buddies in about three minutes."

"What about the two on deck?"

"There's one on the port side. The other went for a swim."

"You killed him?"

"What the hell do you think?"

More men joined them from the shadows.

Quilley handed one of the revolvers to Danovich, nodded briefly in acknowledgement as Danovich introduced Cordoba and Pritchard, then outlined his plans. He parried the questions thrust at him.

"Just do exactly as I say. You gotta make no noise and you gotta move fast. We take the two guards first, then we take the bridge. Once we've got the Lewis and the Lee-Enfields, they can't stop us. But we gotta get those guns."

Quilley cut short another flood of questions.

"I'll take that first guard ... But I have to do it now."

Leaving Danovich and the others clustered on the stair out of the hatch, Quilley emerged on the deck. He made no move to conceal himself but walked boldly round the coaming. The guard heard him and spoke without looking up.

"Hey, Sam, come and look at them dolphins."

The guard, his carbine slung on his shoulder, was leaning on the rail watching a school of porpoise frolic in the phosphorescent water just off the port side.

Quilley stabbed him from behind.

"Sam ..."

The one questioning word gurgled from the man's throat

as he fell back in Quilley's arms. Quilley glanced back at the after Oerlikon-nests to see if his action had been observed – but the gunners were out of sight behind the high armoured walls of their pits.

He slipped off the man's helmet, took his carbine, and pushed the body through the rail. The splash coincided with several others made by the playful porpoise leaping and falling close to the ship's side.

Quilley returned quickly to the other side of the deck. In the hatchway, he handed helmet and carbine to Cordoba.

"Get that lid on and make like a guard. A guy called Hank is gonna be along with coffee any minute."

"What about the guy who had these?" asked Cordoba.

"He was interested in marine life ... dolphins and the like ... He joined 'em."

Cordoba was looking intensely at Quilley.

"You're a pretty cool cuss," he said. "You play for keeps, don't you?"

"It's us or them. Come on, that guy'll be right along."

"There he is now," whispered Danovich.

"You stay here," Quilley said to Cordoba. "Pretend you're looking down the hatch. Leave the rest to me."

Quilley strolled forward from the hatch.

"That you, Hank?" he called across.

"Yeah. Got a cuppa coffee for you, Sam. Where's Bowler?"

"Over here," said Quilley. "One of the guys down below is sick."

He turned and called towards the hatch:

"Coffee, Bowler."

Cordoba held up a thumb and nodded.

"I'm coming," he said. "Thought Hank had got lost."

The man called Hank, clutching a mug of coffee in each hand, negotiated the steampipe casing outside the Engineer's quarters and crossed the deck at the forward end of the hold.

He was helmeted and carried a carbine at the slung position.

Quilley turned his back as the man approached and allowed himself to be overtaken at the outside steps to the tween-deck hatchway.

"Put the coffee on the steps," said Quilley.

The man called Hank laid the mugs on the top of the four steps.

As he stooped, his view of Cordoba's feet provided him with his first and last inkling that something was wrong.

"Hey, Bowler, where's your gaiters?" he said. As he rose, Quilley arm-locked him round the neck from behind and half-pushed, half-lifted him over the four steps into the hatchway. Again the scalpel did its silent work.

Quilley let the body slither down the steps inside the hatchway.

"Take his helmet and his gun, somebody," said Quilley tersely.

The men clustered on the stair were looking at Quilley with a mixture of horror and admiration, possibly realising for the first time the truly desperate nature of the enterprise to which they were now committed.

"You didn't say there was going to be killing," one of the men said to Danovich.

"You're either with us or against us," said Danovich. "You'd better make your choice right now."

The man looked at the lifeless body of the guard called Hank.

"I'm with you," he said. "You pack a powerful argument."

"Okay," said Quilley, "we move out one at a time. Make for the starboard alleyway. Take your boots off until you get there. I don't want anybody fouling this up. Remember they got guys keeping lookout in every gun-nest. They're the ones you got to watch out for. If they spot us, they can phone the bridge and tell 'em somethin's up. Just watch for your moment and move quickly."

He detailed a dozen men.

"The rest of you stay here until we give you the word. We could probably take the bridge with six men, twelve will copper our bets. More could foul things up – make the deck look like Times Square on a Saturday night."

The hour between three and four in the morning is supposed to be the hour when man is at his lowest ebb. It was partly for this reason that Quilley had chosen it to steal the *Fort Harrison.*

Certainly, the element of surprise and the disarming quality of the hour before dawn were very much on Quilley's side.

Pendlebury's first suspicion of anything untoward was the hard stab of a carbine barrel being thrust in his back and Cordoba's admonition that one word or squeak would be his last. Quilley and Danovich had simultaneously entered the wheelhouse.

While Danovich warned and covered the helmsman, Quilley moved past him through the chart-room to the radio cabin.

The Chief Radio Officer looked up more in curiosity than surprise when the door was flung open and he was confronted by Quilley. He was going on with the action of lighting a cigarette as Quilley hit him hard on the head with the butt of the forty-five.

The man slipped from his swivel chair and lay prone on the deck, blood pouring from a temple wound.

Ignoring the man on the floor, Quilley stepped over and round him as he systematically began to rip wires from the equipment which surrounded him. He surveyed the results and, not quite satisfied, he retired briefly to the chart-room and returned with a fire-axe taken from a bracket on the wall.

He began to smash the radio cabinets with heavy blows. This done, he went out to the wheelhouse.

Pendlebury was cowering under Cordoba's carbine, whimpering like a child.

"You can't do this. I just don't understand," he was muttering fearfully.

His eyes lit up when he recognised Quilley.

"Sergeant Quilley," he cried in relief.

"Shut up," said Quilley. "Tie him up," he added to

Cordoba. "Gag him if he doesn't stay quiet."

Pendlebury's eyes popped in disbelief. This was the ultimate betrayal. The man whose cause he'd promised to take up, the one American he had ever liked, the man he had treated almost like a son ... was doing this to him!

"Sergeant Quilley ... I'm your friend."

Before Cordoba could move, Pendlebury slipped through the door into the chart-room. Quilley followed him, still holding the fire-axe.

Pendlebury stopped short when he saw the destruction inside the radio cabin and the slumped body of the radio officer.

He turned to face Quilley, ablaze with a righteous fury.

"What have you been doing to *my* ship?" he screamed, his voice a high-pitched whine of protest. He advanced a step towards Quilley as if intending to tear his eyes out, his hands raised like talons.

Quilley hit him with the fire-axe.

The older man fell, his face smothered in blood. He lay there, hiccuping muted sobs, choking in his own blood. Then the sobbing noises stopped and he lay quite still.

"The old fool asked for it," said Quilley when he returned to the wheelhouse and Cordoba asked what had happened. "We'll get rid of the body later."

All twelve of Quilley's men were now in the wheelhouse. Danovich was handing those nearest him the Lee-Enfield rifles from their rack. He had already taken the Lewis from its stand and had lain it on the deck at his feet.

"There's ammunition in that magazine box over there," said Quilley. "Help yourself," he told the men.

"What's our next move, Frank?" asked Danovich. "So far, you've done better than a five-star general."

"Next, we phone every gun-pit on the ship and tell the guy on lookout there that the Captain wants him on the bridge. Can any of you guys steer a ship? Better if we get a Limey voice to talk on the phone."

He waved a hand at the helmsman.

"You," he said. "You do the talking. And no tricks or

we'll kill you out of hand. Do exactly as I tell you."

"I can take the wheel for a coupla minutes," said Danovich. "What course you steering, buddy?"

"One-eight-five," said the helmsman. He was white with fear.

Danovich pushed him out of the way and took the wheel.

"I always wanted to do this," said Danovich.

"She's taking about half a turn to starboard," said the helmsman.

"Thanks buddy boy," said Danovich. "Steady as she goes."

"A coupla guys had better go up on the top bridge and persuade the two guys up there to come down and join us," said Quilley. "There should be a gunner in each of the wing-nests."

"I'll go," said Cordoba.

He nudged a weasel-faced individual whose name was Lomax. The man was clipping a magazine into one of the Lee-Enfields.

"You take one side. I'll take the other," said Cordoba.

"What do you want me to do?" asked Lomax.

"Just point that thing at the guy in the gun-nest up top. You take the left. I'll look after the right. Tell him to come down here nice and quiet. If he argues, hit him over the head. That right, Quilley?"

"Yeah, we don't want any firing. Not until we got all the gunners outa their pits and away from their guns."

He turned to the helmsman.

"Okay you, pick up the phone. The one on the right — that's the gun-nest blower, ain't it? Dial each nest in turn and say to whoever speaks that the Captain wants to see him on the bridge as fast as they can move their butts along here."

He pointed the forty-five at the helmsman.

"Make it sound good," he warned.

One after the other, the gunners on duty received the rather strange summons from the bridge. Puzzled but unsuspecting, each presented himself to the bridge to have a rifle poked in his face as he reached the top of the ladder to the bridge wing. Each was bound with signal halyard rope found in a chart-room locker and made to lie on the wheelhouse floor.

"It's gettin' a kinda cluttered in here," said Danovich from the wheel as the last man was bundled down.

"We'll put 'em down below later," said Quilley. "We still got two guys to account for and the deck is ours."

"Take the wheel again, sonny," he said to the helmsman, "and tell me where I'll find the other two guys on your watch. You always work in threes, don't you?"

"One's on lookout on the fo'c'sle-head. The other's probably down in the galley," said the helmsman. "He's the stand-by man."

"Right," said Quilley, "I want one guy to go up to the sharp end of this scow and take the lookout and another to take care of the guy in the galley. You, Danovich, take half a dozen guys and go down number three to take care of that sergeant and the other guards. I want Cordoba to look after the guys down number five who are watching the Krauts. He can collect some muscle on the way from the guys we left chewing their knuckles down number four."

Quilley himself stayed on the bridge.

He was, give or take a few little chores still to be done, in command of the *Fort Harrison*. Once the chores were out of the way, a pleasant reunion was in prospect down in the First Officer's cabin. Quilley was looking forward to touching with his fingers the cache of money in the settee locker. He was impatient to confirm that the banknotes were as crisp as he remembered them.

16
Change of Orders

ANDREW MITCHELL woke from a deep dreamless sleep with a cold hard metallic object sticking in his neck. He blinked his eyes open and found himself squinting up a carbine barrel. At the other end of it, two brown eyes beneath a thatch of thick black hair smiled down at him. It was the soldier with the broken nose.

"Easy does it, Mr Second Officer. This stick I got in my hand goes bang and kills people if I move my finger – and I'm a highly nervous guy. In addition to that I don't like you. So don't do anything to upset me, eh?"

"Who the hell are you?"

"The name's Cordoba. If we haven't met socially before now, it's because you've got a nasty habit of punching people before they're introduced and because I've been travelling tourist in that sweat-box of a hold. But now you know all about me, how about telling me all about you. They say that besides packing a wicked right, you're the guy that navigates this old rustbucket?"

"You could say so – but what's this all about? And would you please point that thing away from me." He glanced at his watch. "Hell's bells, it isn't six yet! What's going on?"

"While you were sleeping your head off, my Limey friend, this ole mudscow has had a change of ownership. So get up, buddy. You've been hijacked."

"You're one of the prisoners?"

"Right, buddy boy. Now get up nice and slowly and put some clothes on. The new Captain wants to see you on the bridge and discuss a slight change of destination."

"New Captain?"

"Yep. Name of Quilley. I believe you've already met. He don't seem to like you much – but he says you're a whizz-kid at navigating and you can thank your lucky stars about that. Seems he had a notion to burn you on the galley fire but not while you're still useful to us."

"You'll never get away with this," said Mitchell. "You must be out of your minds."

"We've got away with it so far," said Cordoba good-humouredly. "We've taken over the ship – like taking candy from a kid. Once we had the bridge, it was easy. We didn't have to go chasing your guys. We just phoned them up from the bridge and said the Captain wanted to see 'em immediately. Up they came, gentle as lambs, one after the other until they were all trussed up like chickens. Not one put up a fight. They didn't know what the hell was happening to them. Surprise, you see. Like you're surprised."

There was no doubting Mitchell's surprise. It was so damned impossible in his eyes that he couldn't quite believe it had happened.

He dressed in a daze. Then, with Cordoba coming along behind him with the carbine, he made his way to the bridge.

"Well, well, if it ain't the uppity Mr Second Officer Mitchell," Quilley greeted him. "Did he come quietly, Cordoba?"

"Like a little lamb," said Cordoba with a grin.

"I thought you mighta hit him with those two gold bands of yours, Mr Second Officer Mitchell, sir," said Quilley, his eyes teasing. "You didn't put up even the teeniest bit of a struggle?"

"He has a very persuasive line of argument," said Mitchell – "a loaded gun and an itchy finger. I thought it best to humour the gentleman."

Cordoba laughed.

"Hey, get that! He called me a gentleman."

"Just as long as he doesn't think I'm one," said Quilley.

"That's one mistake nobody could make," said Mitchell.

With a vicious back-swing of the arm, Quilley struck Mitchell hard in the face.

"Watch your whoring tongue!" he spat.

229

The blow took Mitchell by surprise. The force of it swung his head to one side but he stood his ground. He lifted his head slowly and stared hard at Quilley without any move to retaliate. A trickle of blood ran from his lip.

He spoke then, slowly and evenly.

"Hasn't the game gone on long enough, Quilley? You've proved you can take over a ship. God knows how you managed it – but you have. Don't you think it's time you backed down now? Have you any idea what to do next? Do you honestly think you've got a hope in hell of getting away with it?"

Quilley grinned.

"You're going to help us get away with it, Mr Second Officer Mitchell. You are going to take this ship to Spain."

Mitchell laughed in spite of himself.

"That proves you're out of your bloody minds. D'you think you're going to be better off rotting in one of Franco's jails than in one of your own? D'you think they're going to welcome you with open bloody arms?"

"They might do a deal. They might just like to lay their hands on a freighter that's worth maybe half a million dollars. They might just like to do a trade for all the secret papers and codebooks you got tucked away in the safe."

"And how the hell do you think this ship will ever reach Spain crawling along at three and a half knots and ready to split in two if we hit bad weather? How do we get through the minefields? How do we avoid the U-boats and the Jerry bombers between here and Gib? And what do our own lot do if they spot us swanning all over the ocean? Wish us a happy trip? Damn it, if they think this ship has been hijacked they'll sink it rather than lose it. They'll blow us out of the water so fast you'll wish like hell you stayed on the beach at Salerno."

"You make it sound like it might not be too easy," said Quilley. "Well, there's something you'd better understand. We're all washed up with the US of A. There ain't no going back for us. Not now. It's Spain for us or curtains. We're gonna goddamn get there or die trying. We've found our-

230

selves something to fight for, Mr Mitchell — US! OURSELVES! Wars are about freedom, Mr Mitchell ... Well that's something we really care about ... And we aim to fight for it ... Freedom! Our goddamned freedom!"

"You'll get no help from me," said Mitchell.

"Oh no?" asked Quilley. "Would you care to take a look at the foredeck through the binoculars? Cordoba, give the Second Officer here them big eye-glasses from off that hook."

Cordoba handed Mitchell the glasses.

"Take a look up front, Mr Mitchell," said Quilley. "Tell me what you see."

Mitchell studied the fo'c'sle-head through the binoculars. He stiffened with horror at the sight which met him.

The two apprentices, Lovell and Hardy, had been roped by the arms and shoulders to the port anchor cable.

Two of the American prisoners lounged nearby.

"Why have you got those boys up there?" asked Mitchell hoarsely.

"Insurance," said Quilley. "Insurance for good behaviour from every man on this ship that isn't one of us. And that goes for you in particular, Mr Mitchell. One wrong move from you and I give a little signal to my guys up front. They let go the anchor whether we're steaming along or not and, presto, your guys are minced dogmeat in five seconds flat. It won't be very pretty. These nice young kids being hauled through that chain pipe along with the chain. Very messy."

"You bastard," said Mitchell.

"Do you co-operate, Mr Mitchell?"

"Yes, damn you. You know it."

"I thought you would see reason," said Quilley.

With Quilley's forty-five never far from his spine, Mitchell was forced into the chart-room and made to produce a big Mediterranean chart.

"Now show me where we are and how we get to Spain," said Quilley.

"I still say it's impossible," said Mitchell. "Look, we're here. We're steering a little west of south to pass west of

Stromboli – that's a big volcanic island – so that when we get down to about here, we'd head east for the Messina Straits and down to Port Augusta, there ..."

"Never mind where you were supposed to go," interrupted Quilley. "Just show me how we'd have to go to get from where we are now to Spain."

He studied the Western Mediterranean area of the chart which showed the Spanish coast.

"Look, there's a place with an interesting sounding name and it seems almost in a straight line from us. Let's say we go there ... Alicante."

He rolled the name round on his tongue.

"Yeah, let's go to Alicante."

Mitchell shrugged.

"If we take the nearest route, there's all sorts of trouble. It would mean passing close to Sardinia and you'd be asking for it in two ways. First, the Germans have big minefields south of Cagliari. Second, they have planes and warships on the island and they'd blast us out of the water if we go anywhere near it."

"So what would you do?" asked Quilley.

Mitchell remembered Lovell and Hardy lashed to the anchor cable and sighed.

"I'd keep well south, to maybe forty or so miles off the North African coast and keep going west at about this latitude here. You're still liable to run into minefields and you're still likely to be spotted by German planes and our own from North Africa, but it's the only way. Your chances of getting halfway to Spain without being seen are about a thousand to one."

"Long odds don't frighten me no more," said Quilley. "What would you have said they were against us taking this ship over – maybe five hundred to one?"

"That was the easy part," said Mitchell. "I still don't think you have any idea how hard it's going to be to get this ship anywhere at all. Have you any idea just what kind of shape it's in?"

"What do you mean?"

"I mean that the damned thing's near crippled. Why do you think we're limping along at three knots without any convoy or escort? You weren't with us, were you, when that bomb nearly blew the starboard side in?"

For the first time, a suspicion of anxiety appeared in Quilley's eyes.

"I knew something had happened. You lost a boat and a gun-nest. Was there more damage?"

"Haven't you seen the split amidships?" said Mitchell, sensing that he suddenly had a psychological initiative. "Don't you know that if a sea gets up there's an excellent chance that this ship will split clean in two and sink like a bloody stone. Did nobody tell you about the damage in the shaft tunnel? We've got water coming in steadily through the stern glands and only some makeshift packing is preventing it becoming a bloody great flood."

Quilley grinned.

"You cunning bastard," he said. "You're trying to bullshit me."

"I wish to God I was," said Mitchell vehemently.

The grin vanished from Quilley's face.

"It don't alter nothing! We still take our chances on getting to Spain."

With the forty-five being waved at him, Mitchell spent the next half-hour drawing up courses which would take the *Fort Harrison* to Alicante. He consoled himself by thinking it was a hell of a long way to go and much could happen in the intervening time.

Already, the back of his mind was seething with ideas – admittedly some of them wild and improbable – on how to turn the tables on Quilley. One thought recurred again and again. He was sure that, like most landlubbers, Quilley and his men would have the landsman's almost pathological fear of sinking in mid-ocean miles from land. Give sea-going passengers a confidence in their ship and the sea held no terrors. But sow in their minds the idea that their ship was unsafe and might sink if hit by a twenty-foot comber and their fear could become almost psychotic.

233

Mitchell felt an almost grudging admiration for the thoroughness with which Quilley approached the running of the ship. Obviously, the time he had spent with Pendlebury when they were outward from Algiers had been well spent in assessing the everyday functions.

Every man not actively engaged in a normal watchkeeping function was herded into the tween-deck of number four hold – until recently the quarters of the American prisoners. Those on watch, from firemen in the stokehold to helmsmen on the bridge, were made to perform their duties under the guns of former prisoners working a rota which Quilley himself had drawn up. Even the German POWs, bewildered by what was happening, were herded into number four tween-deck and found themselves living cheek by jowl with the British crewmen, gunners, and the survivors of O'Keefe's guard squad.

As Pendlebury was dead, Quilley had decided that Mitchell would be the man through whom he would conduct the running of the ship. He had spelled out how this would be done.

"The ship is gonna be run as if everything was quite normal. Every four hours, the hostages roped to the anchor cable are gonna be changed. You can work out a rota yourself. Just see that two guys are ready every four hours to be taken up front and spend their share of time thinking about being minced through that hawse-pipe. Then the guys who have done their four hours can go back to the hold to rest.

"Everybody – and I mean every goddamn man on this ship – has got to get it firmly in their heads that one silly move, one trick, one step outa line ... and the guys roped to the anchor chain die a very nasty death. Got that?

"You, Mr Second Officer Mitchell, will personally tell all your guys just how well they gotta behave. You, personally, will see that not one of them steps outa line. Keep remembering what happened to dear old Mr Pendlebury."

"Yes, I will remember what you do to your friends," interrupted Mitchell.

"Just shut up and listen. Now, everybody stays down that hold. And it ain't gonna be nice. You guys are getting no chance to escape. Everything will be battened down so that there's only one way in and one way out. I hope it don't get too sweaty down there.

"You're gonna keep your watches just like normal. And I'll have some of my guys hanging around with artillery to see you do. I'll want one officer and one seaman on the bridge at one time. You'll have to split the time with your friend Durham. The seaman will take the wheel. One of my guys will always be on lookout for you – just like one of your sailors.

"We'll work the engine-room in the same way – an officer on the platform, three guys shovelling coal in the furnaces and another to do the trimming. Then there'll be an oiler like usual.

"The cooks will work the galley as usual – but under guard. If they need stores, they'll be allowed to get them but my guys will go along with them. The food ain't gonna be fancy but it'll be handed down the hold to your guys twice a day ..."

So Quilley had gone on, missing nothing.

Mitchell then had to go down to number four tween-deck and tell it all to the assembled crew. He did so with an anxiety to impress them that there must be no unilateral attempts to win back control of the ship.

"We just can't let them get away with it," complained Walsh, the able seaman:

"Nothing happens without my say-so," said Mitchell angrily. "You've all got to understand this. There has been enough loss of life and we've a hell of a long way to go. There is absolutely no percentage in going off at half-cock. You have to trust me. OK?"

Meanwhile, the *Fort Harrison* continued to limp slowly southwards.

Twice during Durham's morning watch aircraft flew overhead. Quilley, who had taken up residence on the bridge, nervously lit a cigarette and watched the planes out

235

of sight, but otherwise showed no sign of anxiety.

Quilley left the bridge only twice, on both occasions to go below to take his hoard of money from its hiding place – not to count it but simply to touch it and make sure that it still existed.

At two in the afternoon, Mitchell altered the ship's course more to the south-west while Quilley fluttered about asking questions and asking for every detail to be explained. Mitchell showed him on the chart how the course would take the ship towards the north-west tip of Sicily.

"We stay out of sight of land," warned Quilley. "That way it's safer."

Mitchell reassured him. "Our next alteration will be here ..." He pointed to the chart. "That's twenty-five miles from the nearest land. From there, we head west ... to Alicante. And at the speed we're making, we should get there for Christmas."

"Why can't we go faster?" said Quilley. "What's to stop the engineers shaking a few more knots outa this floating bath-tub?"

"Go any faster and one of several things could happen," said Mitchell patiently. "One, the propellor could fall off. We just don't know how much damage that bomb did to it. Second, it might just stop ... because of buckling. Third, turning the shaft at the present revolutions reduces the risk of shaking all our temporary packing out of the stern glands. Increase the revs and the vibration and you could shake the whole bloody thing to bits."

"And what would happen?"

"The sea would come pouring in – that's what would happen. That's maybe one thing you should start thinking about, Quilley – what's your plan if we start to sink and have to abandon ship?"

"No problem," said Quilley with an evil smile. "I see we got three lifeboats. If the ship sinks, me and my guys will be in them. You and your buddies stay with the ship."

"We'd better keep her afloat then," said Mitchell, returning the smile.

17

Change in the Weather

IT WAS just after seven in the evening. In a corner of number four tween-deck, the officers of the *Fort Harrison* held a council of war. Mitchell, whose leadership none disputed, presided.

Present were the Chief Engineer, John Loxton; Charlie Bedford, the Third Engineer; Roberts, the Fourth Engineer; McDonald, the Chief Radio Officer; and Llewellyn, the Second Radio Officer.

Durham and McWilliams, the Second Engineer, were on watch on the bridge and in the engine-room respectively.

"I don't think we should lift a finger," said the Chief Engineer. "I don't think there's anything we can do that's going to be effective. All that will happen is that some more people will be killed and they'll still be giving the orders."

"We've got to do something, Chief," said Charlie Bedford. "You heard what Mitch said about the minefields between here and Spain and north of the convoy routes. Our chances of getting through them are almost nil and these bloody madmen just don't realise it."

"The chances of being spotted by the Luftwaffe or a U-boat before we're as far west as Philippeville are just as high as hitting a mine," said McDonald, the Chief Sparks. His head was bandaged where Quilley had hit him. "Don't they know we haven't a hope in hell of reaching Spain?"

"They haven't done the Malta–Gib run as often as you, Mac," said Mitchell. "They have no idea of the risks, the distance, the time it's going to take at three and a half knots . . . or anything else. The point is that whatever crimes they committed in Italy, their lives aren't worth a damn now if they're caught. They killed three of O'Keefe's soldiers last night. They are right in over our heads."

"They won't be fussy about killing again either!" said Chief Engineer Loxton. "That's why I say we must go very easy."

"The longer we put off, the more risks we have to face," said Charlie Bedford. "I say we act!"

"But what the hell do we do against men with guns? We can't fight them with our bare hands," said Loxton.

"We persuade them to abandon ship," said Mitchell.

The others stared at him. Loxton snorted derisively.

"Just like that," he said. "We go up to them and say: 'Please give us back our ship. You sail away in one of our lifeboats and we'll take our ship back.' For God's sake, Second Mate, it was bad enough having poor old Pendlebury half out of his mind without you taking leave of your senses."

"I mean it," said Mitchell. "Something Quilley said gave me the germ of an idea ... And I think I know how we can do it. He said that if the ship starts to sink, he and his men will take all the boats while we take our chances with the ship."

Charlie Bedford looked up, his eyes alight.

"Is your mind working the same way as mine, Mitch? We've got to kid them on that the ship is sinking?"

"You're catching on fast," said Mitchell. "If we impress on them that *we* consider the ship so unhealthy that *we* want to abandon her, they might just decide to beat us to it."

"There's only one snag," said Loxton. "How do we make them think the ship's sinking? If we wait for a bit of weather to blow up, the chances are that the bloody thing will sink anyway."

"Say we developed a rather spectacular list to starboard," suggested Mitchell. "That can be quite unnerving if you're a country boy from the Kansas wheat-belt or a city slicker from Manhattan."

"It's great!" said Charlie Bedford. "The trick is heeling over as far as we can go without actually making the bloody ship capsize."

"It could be dangerous," said Loxton. "I don't think they'll be all that easily scared. It would only take a small error of judgement and you really would hazard the ship."

"The ship's light," replied Mitchell, "like a great oil drum on the water. We could damn near roll her on her side if we have to."

"How are you proposing to do this?" asked Loxton.

"Well, you know we filled both deep tanks with fresh water before we left Algiers. We've nursed the levels down equally because, as you know, it needs only a little difference port or starboard to start us listing ... Well, instead of pumping from both of the fresh-water tanks or even over the side, let's just pump out of the port deep tank into the starboard deep tank. I haven't worked it out but I reckon that a shift of about twenty-five tons from port to starboard would put us over between twelve and fifteen degrees."

"Maybe not as much as that. But it does kind of have a double effect. Move twenty-five tons and in effect it's like moving fifty tons. One side's that much lighter and the other side's that much heavier. How many tons are there in each tank?" asked Loxton.

"I make it about two hundred and fifty tons in each tank," said Mitchell.

Charlie Bedford grinned.

"Move that lot and we'll be dipping the masts in the water! When do we start pumping?"

"About an hour from now. When I'm on the bridge. By the time it's dark, our passengers could be getting a little nervous," said Mitchell. He looked across at Roberts, the Fourth Engineer. "You'll be on watch, Jim, so that means you're landed with the actual dirty work of getting the lines right and starting the pumping. Will you be able to do that OK with a couple of Quilley's goons breathing down your neck?"

Roberts smiled.

"The last two I had down the engine-room were like kids in a dentist's waiting-room, shaking in their boots. They don't like it down there below the waterline. They've no idea what the hell we're doing and all the noise and the heat really gets at them. We kept telling one of them that we've no chance down there if a torpedo hits and he was walking about shitting himself the whole watch. You leave it to me."

"I'll keep in touch by telephone. I won't be able to say directly to stop pumping or to keep it going so we'll need to have some kind of code."

"No problem," said Roberts. "If you want me to keep pumping, call me Jim. If you want me to stop pumping, be a little more formal and call me Mr Roberts. If you ring for any other reason, don't mention names at all. Just say Fourth. I'll get the message."

"That's simple enough," said Mitchell. "Jim for 'keep pumping', Mr Roberts for 'stop pumping'. For anything else, I talk to the Fourth Engineer. Well, Chief, you're the cautious one. Do we give it a try?"

Loxton smiled a tired kind of smile.

"Cautious maybe," he said, "but game, too. It might just work, laddie. I'm with you all the way." He paused. "Do we tell the others?"

"I don't think we should let anyone else in on what's happening except Durham and Mr McWilliams. Not yet anyway."

"I agree," said Loxton.

The council of war broke up and Sergeant O'Keefe, who had been studying the group from the far side of the tween-deck, sought out Mitchell.

The American was burning with anger and frustration.

Mitchell was alarmed to discover that the Sergeant and the seven survivors of his guard squad were planning to break out of the hold.

"Please, Sergeant O'Keefe, you mustn't try it," he pleaded. "Quilley and his crew have a Lewis gun covering the hatch door. They would shoot you down before you got five paces over the coaming. Believe me, we're as anxious to get out of this mess as you are. All I ask is that you give us a few more hours."

"You don't understand," said O'Keefe. "Me and my guys feel responsible for what happened. These prisoners were our responsibility. They're American – and if there's going to be a fight, it's me and my guys who have to do the fighting. Can't you see it makes us sick to our guts that these yellow-bellied murderers are our people, not yours? How are we going to raise our heads up like men if we're not the ones who take 'em on?"

"You lost three men," said Mitchell. "There's no point in losing more just because you want to make a gesture."

"You're not the one who's been shamed," said O'Keefe. "Yours isn't the country that's been betrayed."

"Your chance will come, Sergeant. And don't forget you were over-ruled by the Acting Master of this ship when this trouble started. You wanted to keep the prisoners all locked up and secured and you said your piece about it. Quilley himself told me all about it because he thought I would find it amusing. Well, I didn't – because it means that these prisoners got out because of the stupidity of our late Acting Captain. And he, poor devil, wouldn't have been our Acting Captain if it hadn't been for my stupidity back at Salerno. I knew he was out of his mind and I passed up the opportunity to do what should have been done about it. So, all this mess is my responsibility and I intend to do something about it – but not by getting you and your men killed off."

The Sergeant shook his head.

"There's no way you can blame yourself," he said.

"Oh, there is, Sergeant, there is – but right now I've got to think of everybody on this ship, and the ship itself. Give me that few hours, eh? That's all I ask."

"I'll talk to the guys," said O'Keefe, "but they're fightin' mad and getting madder. They've got a score to settle with these renegades and they reckon any one of them's as good as any ten of them yellow bellies."

241

"I bet they are, too," said Mitchell. "Just ask them to wait until I give them the nod. I'd love to see O'Keefe's Coughdrops go into action – but the important thing is that they come out on top."

"Okay, Mr Mitchell – but don't keep 'em waiting too long."

"I won't. All I want to do is change the odds a little."

"Can I ask what you have in mind?"

"I'd rather you didn't. It would spoil the surprise."

"Then I won't ask," said O'Keefe.

Two of Quilley's men, armed with carbines, called Mitchell to the hatch top at precisely five minutes to eight. They escorted him up to the bridge to relieve Colin Durham. The two officers were allowed a minimum of conversation before Durham was in turn escorted down to the tween-deck quarters.

The Third Mate imparted one significant piece of information before he left:

"The glass is falling."

Mitchell studied the sky. There was a building-up of cloud to the north-west and a freshening breeze was causing white crests to appear on wave tops. The *Fort Harrison* rolled gently as she laboured along at the agonisingly slow speed she had been maintaining.

Mitchell did his best to pretend that the two men with carbines were not there as he went about his duties. He checked the compass error – a routine task through which his personal armed shadow followed him to the monkey-island then back down the ladder to the chart-room.

At about twenty past eight, Quilley lumbered up the inside stair from the Captain's quarters. The smell of his breath revealed that he had located Lansing's whisky supply. But he was not drunk.

By then the wind had freshened considerably and a beam swell had risen and widened, making the *Fort Harrison* roll in a stomach-turning staggering motion. The roll to starboard was much more pronounced than that to port – as much as ten degrees. The transfer of water from the port deep tank to the starboard deep tank was already beginning to make the ship list.

Mitchell paced the wheelhouse anxiously, giving an excellent impression of a deeply worried man. Quilley watched him with amusement.

"Something on your mind, Mr Second Officer Mitchell?" he drawled lazily.

"No ... No ... Nothing," said Mitchell, still seemingly pre-occupied with some private torment.

He kept pacing nervously.

"For Chrissake, stand still," said Quilley eventually. "What the hell's into you?"

"The weather's getting up," said Mitchell. He started pacing again.

The ship gave a bigger than ever roll to starboard and began to lurch back.

"DID YOU HEAR THAT?"

Quilley nearly fell over, startled by the way Mitchell whirled and almost shouted the question.

"Hear what? I didn't hear anything."

"It was a loud crack, from amidships ... Like that split in the side had gone a bit further."

Before Quilley's startled eyes, Mitchell seemed to leap across the wheelhouse to the telephone. He whirled the call handle.

"Fourth Engineer?" he shouted into the mouthpiece. There was a pause and Mitchell had to work hard to keep his face straight as Roberts' voice said:

"This is your friendly neighbourhood engine-room, Fourth Engineer speaking."

"Did you hear it?" asked Mitchell, "a bloody great cracking sound from midships? You did! Then it must be that split. What about the shaft tunnel? Are we taking more water? I think we're taking a bit of a starboard list. There must be water getting in somewhere."

The words poured out of him.

Roberts, at the other end, was saying:

"Well, there's a bit of a knock coming from the sludge

filter valve and the boiler compressor sprocket is leaking a bit. Yes, I had one of these too and the wheel came off."

"You'd better take readings every five minutes and let me know if it gets any worse," said Mitchell.

"Is it supposed to?" said Roberts.

"Progressively," said Mitchell. "Just keep telling me the position."

"Roger and out," said Roberts.

Mitchell moved quickly towards the wheelhouse door and the bridge wing. He acted as if Quilley no longer existed. Quilley jerked him back by the shoulder.

"Just what the hell was that all about?"

Mitchell feigned anger without much difficulty.

"I'll tell you what it's all about," he said with feeling. "This weather is what it is all about. We're in for a storm — and I'm not the least bit optimistic that this ship is going to survive it. Can't you feel the way she's going over much more to starboard than to port? There's water getting in somewhere — probably the shaft tunnel, where the bomb damage was ..."

"What did the Engineer say?"

"He doesn't know if the shaft tunnel's flooding or not. He can't without going down and taking a look ... He can't leave the platform anyway — his job's in the engine-room. All they can do is keep pumping the wells and hope it doesn't get worse."

Quilley was perplexed. He hadn't a clue what Mitchell was talking about. His eyes lit suspiciously.

"You bastard, you're trying to scare me."

"That's where you're wrong," said Mitchell. "I'm the one who's scared. You may not have been in a shipwreck at sea before, Quilley, but I have and I didn't like it very much. I need men on deck. How the hell do you think we're going to get through this storm if I have only one man on watch and he has to steer the bloody ship."

"You're not getting any more men out of the hold. You're trying to pull something."

The *Fort Harrison* suddenly yawed wildly.

The helmsman was a young ordinary seaman called Blake. He called out now to Mitchell.

"She's not steering, sir. I've got the helm almost full to port and she's still running away to starboard."

Mitchell was not surprised. The sluggish speed, the balloon-like emptiness of the ship riding high out of the water, the increasing list, the rising sea on the starboard quarter ... all were creating conditions which made it a scientific impossibility for the direction of the ship to be controlled by the rudder. But that was knowledge which Quilley was unlikely to share.

Mitchell could have blessed Blake for his timing. The Second Officer turned back to Quilley, doing his best to look defeated while inwardly he had a taste of possible victory.

"That's all we need," he said. "That bomb must have done a damned sight more damage than we thought. The steering's gone!"

"You guy's are trying to trick me."

Quilley was confused and angry.

"Sure," said Mitchell, "we ordered this weather specially. Why don't you try steering the ship yourself? Go on, try it. Blake'll give you the wheel if you don't believe him."

Quilley edged over towards the wheel, unsure.

"Okay, sonny, let's have it. I'll see for myself."

Blake stepped down from the opposite side of the four-inch-high steering platform. Thinking Quilley had the wheel, he let it go prematurely. It was carrying nearly full port helm and the instant he relaxed his grip the wheel spun furiously, rapping and bruising Quilley's knuckles in the process.

Quilley cursed and seized the whirling spokes.

Mitchell looked at the compass.

"Try to keep her on two hundred," he said. She was on a heading of 205 degrees as he spoke.

Quilley turned the wheel to port until it could go no further. The ship's head continued to slide away to starboard. She swung to nearly 225 degrees and steadied. Then she edged back to 218 degrees. She refused to come any closer to a course of 200, although Quilley kept the wheel hard to port.

After a few minutes, he indicated to Blake.

"Here, take it back."

He stepped away from the steering platform, his face set in a heavy frown.

"What do you want me to do?" he said to Mitchell.

Mitchell hesitated. He knew he had to be careful not to overplay his hand.

"We'll just have to try to ride it out. If we bring her round head on to the wind, we've got just about enough way to hold our own. She'll maybe answer the rudder better, too."

"Do it then," said Quilley.

"Bring her hard a-starboard," Mitchell ordered Blake. "Try to steady her at about three-one-oh."

The ship began to pitch as she came head on to the wind and sea. She also maintained a staggering roll through an arc from ten degrees to port to nearly thirty-five degrees to starboard.

"She's steadier now, sir," sang out Blake. "I think I can hold her."

"Good," said Mitchell. "She's riding easier now but she's still heeling a long way to starboard. I don't like it."

There was a cry from the fo'c'sle-head.

"Those men in the bows are getting wet," Mitchell said to Quilley. "Surely you can dispense with that nonsense of keeping two men roped to the anchor cable now?"

Quilley turned to one of the two men with carbines, lounging nervously beside the port door of the wheelhouse.

"Go up front and tell our two guys to bring the hostages up here. Tell them to keep 'em tied. We'll keep them in the chart-room. One wrong move out of anybody and they still get a bullet in the head. Okay, Mr Mitchell?"

"You're still the boss, Quilley."

"And just don't you forget it!"

Twice during the next hour, Roberts telephoned from the engine-room and entertained Mitchell with delightful gibberish about discumknockerator tubes and alcohol intake

246

gauges. To all of this, Mitchell interjected the occasional "yes" and "I see". It was obvious that Roberts' watchdogs were not within eavesdropping distance at the other end.

Quilley, of course, questioned Mitchell on each occasion, far from re-assured by the lengthening frown on the Second Officer's face.

"One of the pumps has seized up," reported Mitchell the first time. "The Engineer's sure that the level of water in the shaft tunnel must be very high. He's worried about it."

On the second occasion, Mitchell said:

"There's a lot of water in the starboard bilges. The Engineer thinks it's getting up through into holds four and five and into the sand ballast beneath the floors that were built for your people's army trucks. It's soaking into the ballast and they can't pump it away because the sand has got down into the bilges and it's choking the suction points."

There was sweat on Quilley's brow.

"How bad is it?"

"You can see for yourself can't you? We're heeling over all the time."

Quilley could see all right. The *Fort Harrison* was now permanently heeled to starboard and the arc of her roll was between ten degrees to port and nearly fifty to starboard. She no longer returned to the upright position when she began to roll back from her deepest swings to starboard.

Mitchell was standing on the bridge wing peering into the dark when the bulky figure of Danovich arrived on the bridge via the outside ladder.

"Where's Quilley?" he grunted.

"He's in the wheelhouse," said Mitchell.

Danovich went inside and their voices came out to Mitchell.

"The guys are getting jumpy," said Danovich. "They don't like the way the ship's leaning over. They're scared she's going to turn turtle. I don't know how long I'm going to be able to keep 'em in line. They think we should maybe head for the nearest land."

"This storm will blow out by morning," said Quilley.

"What if it doesn't?"

"Then we ride it out."

"Maybe if we made it to Sicily, we could hide out in the hills."

"How do we get to Sicily – swim?"

"We could take the lifeboats. They say these things are unsinkable."

"Do you know how to sail a boat?"

"No, but we might stand a better chance than on this rustbucket. Even if we got picked up who's to know what happened if there's only us to tell about it?"

"And how do we make sure that there ain't any survivors besides us?" asked Quilley.

"We make them swim for it," said Danovich. "Without lifejackets."

Listening just outside the wheelhouse door, Mitchell's blood ran cold.

The eventuality that Quilley and his gang might kill off everyone on the ship before abandoning it had not crossed his mind. This was not necessarily to his discredit – because it takes a considerable depth of obscenely vile imagination to anticipate homicide on such a massive scale. Nevertheless, Mitchell could not escape from the awesome responsibility that he believed was his and his alone.

He had conceived and put into execution the bluff which, until this point, had seemed to be working remarkably well. Now he saw it all as a massive miscalculation.

He asked himself if Quilley could possibly have the ruthless, cold-blooded brutality required to take the lives of fifty or more human beings in order to ensure their silence. And the answer was inescapable. If any man had the capacity to do just that ... that man was Quilley.

Mitchell decided at that moment that the bluff had gone far enough.

He marched into the wheelhouse and crossed to the wall telephone.

Roberts' voice came up to him from the engine-room.

"That you, Mitch? What can I do you for?"

"Mr Roberts." said Mitchell deliberately. "I just want to check things with you. What's the latest?"

Roberts seemed disappointed at receiving the pre-arranged signal to stop transferring the fresh water from the port deep tank to the starboard.

"You want to call a halt?" he queried. "We could go a long way yet, Mitch. I don't know what reaction it's having up topside but it's working like a dream with the two goons down here. One is just about paralysed with fright and the other's been spewing his guts up for the last half hour. He's greener than the hills of Donegal."

"Thank you, Mr Roberts," said Mitchell and hung up.

Quilley and Danovich stared at him in silence.

"Well?" said Quilley. "Spill it. What did your engineer friend say."

"They're making headway," said Mitchell. "They've stopped the list to starboard. It shouldn't get any worse now."

"It doesn't matter all that much now," said Quilley. "Danny and me don't trust this old tin can of yours, Sailor Boy. We're thinking of leaving it. We don't think the old cow can make it to Spain."

18
Nothing To Lose

FOR AN HOUR, the temptation had been building up in Jim Roberts. The two American deserters whom Quilley had charged to control the engine-room and stokehold watch had become less and less attentive to their task since the weather had started to deteriorate.

Walking from one side of the engine-room to the other was like walking up or down a steep hill which kept dipping and plunging. The list to starboard was now very pronounced. The violent uneven movements of the ship had a disconcerting unpredictability which made control of human equilibrium difficult, to say the least. It made legs behave like rubber and stomachs heave with nausea.

One of the guards had been constantly sick. He was stretched out under a ventilator surrounded by his own vomit, his carbine at his side. The other guard kept continually on the move between the engine-room platform and the stokehold, prowling like a highly strung kitten in search of its maternal parent. He was not sick like his companion from the movements of the ship. But he was sick with fear.

The heat and the claustrophobic effect of being hemmed in beneath the clanking arms and big ends of the massive machinery had slowly but surely unnerved the man.

The temptation which ate at Jim Roberts was the certainty that both men could be easily disarmed and the engine-room restored to rightful ownership. The Fourth Engineer was acutely aware, however, that such a move could be answered by the sudden and violent deaths of two shipmates doing their stint as hostages lashed to the anchor cable.

He reasoned to himself that with two carbines, he could

then surprise the custodians of the Lewis gun on the after-deck, liberate the crew in the hold and, further armed, wrest back control of the ship. But he hesitated.

He was not afraid for himself. He feared that, in the event of anything going wrong, his actions would result in the deaths of those he was most anxious to save.

* * *

In number four tween-deck, Sergeant O'Keefe was wrestling with a similar dilemma.

Brad Colman, a quietly spoken ex-ranch-hand from Wyoming, was the most eager of his men to take on the renegades. Colman was motivated not entirely by patriotism or a need to restore American honour, although both honour and a love of his country ran deep in him. They were there in the man although he could not have articulated easily about them.

No, the prime source of his motivation was more elemental. A man used to wide open spaces, to the freedom and self-sufficiency of wilderness life, his whole being was in rebellion at the indignity of being enclosed against his will in the dank, airless hold. This represented an assault against the most natural and most basic of his instincts. It had aroused in him all the ferocity of a caged eagle. There was just no way he could learn to accept it.

Consequently, sensing the shame and frustration which ate at O'Keefe, he had maintained a flow of constant argument aimed at persuading his superior to take action.

O'Keefe found it strange that the one man in his squad to whom he would have credited limitless patience was the most eager to engage in precipitate action, regardless of consequence.

Yet, Colman gave the clue by offering a folksy nugget of his philosophy, rich enough in illogical content, to have been an Irishism mouthed by one of O'Keefe's Gaelic ancestors. Colman had said in justification of his own intolerance of the situation:

"There ain't but one box anybody's gonna lock me up in while I'm alive and kickin' — and that's my coffin after I'm dead."

The fact was that like a flower that needs the sun and the rain, Colman began to die a little the moment he was shut in and deprived of both. Hence, he was prepared to die quickly fighting a way into the open rather than endure incarceration.

After O'Keefe had told Mitchell that he and his men would bide their time, Colman had kept up a steady argument on why the Second Officer's wishes should be ignored.

"There's no way we're gonna get outa this without somebody bein' hurt," Colman had argued, "and we're the guys who're obligated. Them sailors have no part in it. They're just civilians and it ain't their fight."

"But we can't just rush these guys up there," said O'Keefe. "They got a Lewis gun covering the hatch. We'd get cut down before we could get near them. There's only eight of us."

"Ain't you never read the Good Book, Sarge? Ain't you never read how Gideon took on thirty thousand enemies of the Lord and whipped them?"

"The way I remember it," said O'Keefe, "that Gideon was a five-star general and craftier than a one-eyed she-wolf. He didn't go rushing at the enemy with his bare hands and a holler."

"No, I grant you that. But my ole paw used to say that Gideon had the best weapons a man can have in a fight. He was in the right, he believed he was gonna win, and he had more grit than the other guy. Just you think about them skunks who got that Lewis gun. They ain't got the grit of an egg-timer between them. Most of them took off like skinned cats the first time they saw a Kraut. Most of them ain't never killed a man before and would crap out if you stared 'em straight in the eye."

O'Keefe smiled at Colman's imagery. It was possibly true. It was his own reckoning that, apart from the ringleaders, most of the prisoners from Salerno had gone along like sheep with Quilley and perhaps one or two others.

And it was a fair bet that the ringleaders were busying themselves with nothing so commonplace as guard detail.

Boldness could pay off.

* * *

On the bridge of the *Fort Harrison*, Mitchell was trying to clear a fog of helplessness from his tired mind. He was overwhelmed by the thought that time was running out fast not only for himself but all those others on the ship for whom he felt a burdening responsibility.

It had all gone wrong.

Quilley and his ugly henchman, Danovich, were now – it seemed – intent on abandoning the *Fort Harrison*. And when they went, it was plain they intended to leave no one behind to live and tell the world about their crimes. They discussed the problem openly, in front of both Mitchell and the helmsman who had relieved young Blake at ten o'clock.

Quilley and Danovich seemed to be untroubled by any moral dilemma or scruples about killing more than fifty people. That solution just happened to be the only logical one in their minds. The people left on the *Fort Harrison* were going to drown anyway. Quilley's and Danovich's only concern was to make absolutely sure they did.

They felt they had no choice in the matter. It did not even occur to Quilley that anyone else might see it any differently or form a different conclusion. It did not even occur to him, so sure was he of the power he held in the situation, that discussing their imminent demise before two of the prospective victims would in any way alter the situation.

If he had reasoned it out, he might have defended this apparent arrogance by saying that if Mitchell or the helmsman cared to try anything because they now knew they no longer had anything to lose but the lives they were going to lose anyway, then they could try. They would be shot

253

down out of hand.

In fact, it was Quilley's contempt for his helplessless to combat the inevitable which was the decisive factor in propelling Mitchell into desperate action. Mitchell's conclusion from the situation was the sure knowledge that some loss of life – his own or the hostages or anyone else's – was no longer a brake on his own actions. Restraint and diplomacy and caution were now meaningless.

If they were all going to die, all previous bets were cancelled. All the cards were face up on the table now – and no one had any doubts about the stakes.

Having made up his mind on what he had to do, Mitchell tensed himself for action. He needed to arm himself and that meant getting his hands on one of the carbines. With surprise on his side and no qualms about shooting to kill, he could account for Quilley and Danovich for a start. The octopus without its head would be a much less dangerous proposition for the others.

Hanging up his night-glasses, Mitchell edged towards the guard who had stationed himself near the port door of the wheelhouse. He was sitting on one of the navigator stools, carbine resting on his knees.

The carbine was now less than three feet away from Mitchell's hands. He waited. His palms were wet with sweat. He dried them on his handkerchief.

He poised on the balls of his feet. The next roll of the ship ... He cast an eye in the direction of Quilley and Danovich.

To his dismay, both men moved in that moment towards the far door. Quilley stepped outside. He was saying:

"I've got some gear I want to collect from down below. Get some guys along to the boat-deck, Danny. I'll meet you there and take a look at that boat. I'd just like to be sure we can launch the goddamn thing. It might be easier to take the smaller one on this side rather than the one with the motor."

Mitchell held back, cursing silently. His chance to get Quilley and Danovich was lost.

The man on the stool was eyeing him. He took a firm grip on his carbine.

"I'll have to go topside," Mitchell said on the spur of the moment.

"I'll be right behind you," said the man. "Okay, Moose?" he said to the other guard.

"Okay," said the other, who was lounged against the far wall.

Mitchell climbed the ladder to the monkey-island. The guard was less nimble and hung on for dear life half way up as the ship rolled steeply. In the seconds available, Mitchell moved quickly to the side of the starboard Oerlikon-pit. On the deck beside it was a cylindrical tin from which wire led. It was attached to a rocket mounted in a stand.

The contraption was known as the PAC – parachute and cable. It was an anti-aircraft device. The rocket was fired by triggering a 303 cartridge from a wire-pull in the wheelhouse.

The rocket carried two hundred feet of wire cable and a parachute. In theory, the weapon was a device for fouling up the propellors of enemy planes making sea-level or low attacks – but Mitchell had never seen one used in anger. At that moment, however, he was not concerned with low-flying planes.

He unhooked the heavy-headed rocket and freed a length of wire, so that he could carry it like a club. He stood in shadow as his watchdog guard clambered from the top of the ladder on to the top bridge. The man paused a moment in the stooped position trying to make out where Mitchell had gone.

Mitchell took one swift step and brought the heavy rocket-head down on the man's head. He fell forward like a pole-axed steer.

Mitchell hauled him over to the binnacle-house and bound the man's arms and legs with wire which he continued to pull from the canister beside the rocket stand. He took the man's carbine and made sure it was cocked.

Silently, he climbed down the ladder to the flying-bridge. He cupped his hands to his mouth and called softly: "Moose."

A moment later, a head appeared tentatively from the open door of the wheelhouse.

"Are you okay, Johnnie?"

Mitchell brought the butt of the carbine down heavily on the exposed head. The man called Moose fell out on to the deck of the flying-bridge and lay still. Mitchell did not bother to tie him. He slipped into the wheelhouse. He now had two carbines.

Able Seaman Walsh, Blake's successor at the wheel, gaped as he recognised the figure with the two guns.

A finger over his lips in a keep-quiet gesture, Mitchell tip-toed towards the helmsman on his side away from the chart-room door.

In a low whisper, he spoke to Walsh, pressing one of the carbines into the AB's hands as he spoke.

"There are two goons in the chart-room with the Chippy and the Third Sparks ... It was their turn as hostages. Are you game for a bit of action?"

"Just try to stop me," said Walsh.

"Good. Here's what we'll do. Give me exactly two minutes – count up to a hundred and twenty or something – long enough for me to get down to the Old Man's door and up into the chart-room from the inside stairs. Then, come in from the wheelhouse and be ready to fire that thing or crack a skull with it."

"This, I am going to enjoy," said Walsh through clenched teeth. "When do I start counting?"

"Now," said Mitchell, already gliding towards the star-board door.

He was quickly on to the lower bridge and through the wire-screen door to the Captain's quarters. He crept quietly up the inside stair to the chart-room. Taking a deep breath, he flung open the door, the carbine thrust out before him at hip level.

Four startled faces looked up at him.

The Third Radio Officer and the Carpenter were sitting on the deck, bound hand and foot. The two men guarding them were sitting on the settee. One was in the act of holding out a match to light the other's cigarette. An unlit cigarette hung from his own mouth.

The two faces stared until the match burned down and burnt the finger of the man who was holding it.

"Make one sound and you're dead," said Mitchell. Neither man wanted to argue with the look in his eyes.

At that moment Walsh arrived from the wheelhouse. His disappointment at not having to crack a skull or fire a shot was made quickly apparent.

"You were hell of a quick," he said reproachfully to Mitchell.

In a short space of time, the two renegade soldiers were trussed and gagged on the chart-room deck and their two former captives were flexing their stiffened muscles and taking possession of their guns.

Mitchell led the three others into the wheelhouse.

"We'll let the ship drift," said Mitchell. "I'll ring Jim Roberts and tell him to stop engines. I'll put him in the picture, too. Watch the ladders and see nobody comes."

He found it hard to keep the excitement from his voice as he spoke to Roberts over the telephone.

"We've got back the bridge, Jim. They're planning to abandon ship just like we wanted them to – but they weren't going to let us live to talk about it. Do you think you can take the two goons in the engine-room?"

"Christ, am I relieved to hear that!" came Roberts' voice. "The fact is that I took a hell of a chance, Mitch. I relieved the seasick sod of his rifle while his mate was taking a walk in the stokehold. Then I went to tackle the other one. When he saw me with the rifle, he didn't know whether to shoot me or run a mile. While he was making up his mind, one of the lads bloody near knocked his head into his boots with a shovel. But, boy, am I relieved to hear you. I didn't know what the hell to do next. Any ideas?"

"First off, stop the engines," said Mitchell. "Then get

your two rifles and somebody who can use them on to the after gun-deck. It'll mean going aft via the shaft tunnel. But if we get a couple of guns aft and we've got four here, that means that Quilley and his mob are in the middle. They'll have to watch front and back. But Jim, don't waste bullets. You can't have many to play with. Don't give the show away and fire unless you have to. Shoot if you see any of the bastards trying to get at our people in the tween-deck or if you think we're getting into trouble but, otherwise, wait. Okay?"

"Leave it to us," said Roberts. "Ten minutes from now, we'll have somebody on the poop. I'll go along myself. I'll ring you when we're in position."

Walsh re-entered the wheelhouse as Mitchell was hanging up the telephone.

"The goons have half-lowered the motorboat," he announced. "There's a shower of them on the boat-deck. They've got it just about down to deck level. I think they aim to try to keep it there until they're ready to load up and push off. But they'll have a hell of a job getting it into the water the way we're listing to starboard."

Mitchell went to have a look.

"Hand out the binoculars, Walshie. They seem to be having a rare old howdie-do."

Mitchell focused the night-glasses on the port boat-deck. He had been puzzled that neither Quilley nor Danovich had returned to the bridge. Now he could see why they hadn't.

So anxious were some of the ex-prisoners to get off the *Fort Harrison* that Quilley's authority as leader was now facing something of a challenge.

Some men were already clambering into the partly lowered boat and it was patently clear that Quilley did not want them there. He was striding about the boat-deck, two large canvas haversacks slung around his shoulders, and brandishing a forty-five in his hand.

His voice carried up to the bridge against the wind.

"Get outa that goddamned boat or I'll blow your heads

off!" he shouted. "Nobody gets off this ship until I say so."

He turned and then angrily yelled at men trying to operate the falls and lower the boat even further.

"Get away from these ropes, goddamn you. If that boat hits the sea it's lost!" he raged.

On the bridge, Mitchell turned to Walsh.

"Let's give them a little surprise," he said.

Walsh followed Mitchell back inside the wheelhouse and stopped just inside the door.

"What do you have in mind, Second Mate?" he asked.

Mitchell pointed to a key-protected button located nine inches from the jamb of the door to the chart-room. A plate above the red-painted button held the warning: FAM. DANGER. DO NOT TOUCH."

Walsh gave a low amused whistle.

"Have you ever fired that thing?"

"Only once – in practice. It blew everything off the boat-deck that wasn't bolted down."

The FAM was yet another of the *Fort Harrison*'s anti-aircraft devices – a big brother of the PAC rocket on the top bridge which Mitchell had partially dismantled to use as a club. The initials stood for Fast Aerial Mine.

The massive sixteen-foot rocket was housed in a launcher situated on the port boat-deck just abaft the funnel. It pointed vertically upwards and was attached to a 600-foot coil of steel wire in an open canister. The wire, in turn, was attached to a metal container holding – amongst other things – five pounds of high explosive.

This was the mine attachment. Like the PAC, the FAM was designed to be launched in the path of low-flying air-craft. Again, the theory was that the aircraft's propellors would entangle the wire cable with a winding motion and draw in the wire until the mine attachment hit the aircraft and was detonated. Like an ancient blunderbuss, however, the FAM represented as much danger to those whom it was designed to defend as those whom it was intended to harm.

The back blast from the rocket was formidable and as often as not the mine would explode as it left the canister and not at the intended altitude of several hundred feet.

Mitchell moved the protective key which prevented the electronic firing-button of the FAM from being fired inadvertently. By moving the lever key through an arc of about thirty degrees, a metal disc which prevented the button being depressed was removed.

At that moment the telephone shrilled from the wall at the other side of the wheel.

"Answer it, Walshie," said Mitchell.

The AB crossed and lifted the phone.

"Wheelhouse. Walsh here."

Mitchell waited.

"It's the Fourth Engineer, asking for you," said Walsh. "He says he's in position and he's got Park, the donkey-greaser, with him."

"Good," said Mitchell. "Tell him to stand by. That the fun's just about to start. Tell him to keep his eyes on the port boat-deck and wait for the bang."

Walsh repeated Mitchell's message and hung up.

"Have a look out of the door or you'll miss it," said Mitchell. "Port side."

Walsh recrossed to the port-side door and looked aft.

"There's still a lot of commotion on the boat-deck," he reported.

"Good," said Mitchell. And pressed the red button.

19
Out of Captivity

O'KEEFE AND COLMAN had wrenched one of the mess-table benches from the floor of number four tween-deck. They held it now like a battering ram beneath the double doors of the wooden hatchway which led to the deck. Beside them on the stairs were the rest of "O'Keefe's Cough-drops", the men who made up the guard squad.

Loxton, the Chief Engineer, had tried to talk them out of it when he divined that the Americans were intent on breaking out of the hold. He had begged them to wait until midnight at least, when Mitchell was supposed to come off watch.

"He asked for a few hours," said O'Keefe. "That was nearly four hours ago. We ain't waiting any longer."

Colin Durham, too, had tried to intervene. But O'Keefe was having no more argument.

"These guys are Americans up there. It ain't a British fight," he said. "So you might as well stand back."

Durham and Loxton had capitulated. O'Keefe and his Coughdrops were finished with talking. Now they found themselves quietly joined by gunners and seamen from little encampments in the tween-deck.

"Where do you guys think you're going?" asked O'Keefe. He looked round uncertainly as he saw some of the British seamen lifting down big timber battens from the wall of the hold and wielding them like oversized baseball bats.

"Now, wait a minute," said O'Keefe, "we ain't got any argument with you guys. You ain't gonna try to stop us."

"We're not going to stop you," said a burly seaman. "We're going to be right behind you. There's about thirty of them and they've got guns. Well maybe they might get off a few shots and one or two may be hit – but they won't get us all. You don't mind if we join in?"

O'Keefe felt emotion rise in him like a flooding tide. Pride and affection washed through him. He could have hugged the big seaman.

"You're a bunch of crazy bastards," he said to the gathering throng, "a bunch of crazy twenty-four carat marvellous bastards. Okay, let's take those renegades up there apart. Colman and me will hit the door. When it gives, we're gonna make straight for the guy who's covering from the end of the hatch with the Lewis. We'll try to rush ..."

His words died in mid-sentence as an ear-shattering explosion, followed by a strange swooshing rush of sound, seemed to lift the hatch covers above their heads and lift the cross-beams in their sockets.

"Christ, what was that?" said a voice.

"Seemed to come from the engine-room," said another.

"Whatever it was, let's use it," said O'Keefe. "Let's get out of this hold!"

He nodded to Colman and, together, they swung the bench in a ramming motion at the hatch doors.

That one furious blow sent the doors banging outwards.

O'Keefe and Colman spilled on the deck. O'Keefe balanced momentarily on the tips of his toes at the extremity of his outward rush, then he was throwing himself left, and dashing in a straight line for the gun-nest which Quilley's men had rudely put together to house the Lewis gun below the ladder to the PO's accommodation. It was mounted to cover the doors of the hatchway.

Its custodian, startled by the explosion, was on his feet trying to find out what had happened. The sound had come from the port side beyond the cabin-housing above his position, in the area of the engine-room skylights.

From the corner of his eye, he saw the hatch-door to the tween-deck burst open and two men emerge as if shot from a cannon.

He was reaching down for the machine-gun as O'Keefe pirouetted in flight like a ballet-dancer and came straight for him. His finger touched the trigger, but only long enough to release a single shot, when O'Keefe was on him, falling on him like a door.

The bullet went clean through O'Keefe's thigh but only turned him slightly in course as the full weight of his body fell on the man, knocking him backwards. The gunner's head cracked against the steel bulkhead behind his position with a noise that echoed like a rifle shot. O'Keefe lay on top of the inert body, his breath coming in mighty gasps. He felt no pain from the gaping hole in his leg, but was aware of the warm stickiness of blood spreading above his knee. He tried to rise, but couldn't.

He was aware of Colman moving him over unceremoniously and extracting the Lewis gun from somewhere underneath him. Then Colman was firing from the hip and there was a scream from the far side of the deck.

After the single burst, Colman lowered the gun to the level of the coaming and crouched behind it peering through the sights. Now there was a lot of movement as more and more men emerged from the hatch and crouched as Colman was doing below the level of the coaming.

"You all right, Sergeant?" muttered Colman.

"I've been hit in the leg, I think. But don't mind me. Get after them bastards. You got the Lewis?"

"I've got the Lewis," said Colman. "I'm not sure what's happening over there. They're shouting and cussing something dreadful. I saw two guys pointing guns over here and hit one of them. They're keeping outa sight now – in the alleyway on the far side."

"Watch the alleyway on this side, too, Colman. They may try to circle. You got to get hold of more guns."

"The guy I hit dropped his on the deck. Reckon I'll go and get it."

Holding the Lewis at his hip, Colman stood up and advanced across the passage at the forward end of number four hold. Protected by the steel bulk of the midships housing, he moved quickly to the port side. He nimbly hopped over the steam-pipe casing which projected from the port coaming and took a right-angle turn along the after end of the Engineer Officer's accommodation.

A Lee-Enfield rifle lay on the deck beside the sprawled body of a man. Bending and keeping the Lewis pointed towards the alleyway which ran under the boat-deck, he lifted the rifle in his left hand and threw it back on the hatch-top.

"Somebody take that and cover my back," he called. He found himself joined by the burly seaman from the hold.

The man threw away the timber batten with which he had been armed and picked up the Lee-Enfield.

"It's one of the ship's rifles," he said. "Okay, soldier, I'll see that nobody takes you from behind. Let's see if we can get some more of these peashooters."

Neither man saw the stealthy movement above their heads. But Jim Roberts, who had witnessed the breakout from the hold with surprise and delight from his observation point high above the poop on the pillarbox platform, did.

Roberts had seen Colman disappear for a moment from sight and had crossed to the port side in time to see the figure with the Lewis gun also re-emerge into view. He watched the recovery of the rifle, certain that the man who now held it was one of the *Fort Harrison*'s deck crew. The white floppy hat which the man wore stood out like a beacon. It had to be Henderson, one of the ABs.

Then Roberts saw the movement at the after end of the boat-deck where, some moments before, so many of Quilley's men had been. The man on the boat-deck seemed intent on the two figures beneath him. Roberts caught a gleam in the darkness as the man appeared in silhouette against the sky as the ship rolled sharply to starboard. It could be knife or gun. Roberts did not wait to find out.

Squinting along the barrel of his own gun, he fired at the centre of the silhouette.

The shot rang out. Colman and Henderson, the AB, ducked instinctively. In the next instant a body seemed to fall out of the sky and land at their feet.

"That shot came from above the poop," hissed Henderson.

"Then it was fired by a friend," said Colman who – still half crouched – pushed the body beside him over on its back with an outstretched foot. "I know this guy. Name's Cordoba – one of the prisoners. He must have been up on the boat-deck ... and just about to jump us."

Colman moved the body further and retrieved the forty-five revolver which had fallen from Cordoba's hand.

"One more for our collection," he murmured. But Henderson was not paying attention. He had moved close to the outside alleyway without exposing himself to anyone who might be lurking along its length and was now staring and trying to identify the source of a knocking sound.

"The boat's gone!" he said, with the air of one who can't believe what he is actually seeing. "The bloody boat has gone!"

And it was true. The swinging movement of the lowered after-fall had caught Henderson's eye and it dawned on him that the knocking sound was the noise of the big four-sheave block at the lower end of the fall banging forlornly against the hull of the ship.

The boat which normally hung from the now-empty davit was nowhere to be seen.

* * *

When Quilley had left the bridge, he had by no means finally decided that the best plan was to abandon the *Fort Harrison*. There was no doubt, however, that about a dozen or so of the men who had willingly accepted his command had made this decision for themselves.

They were the men who were "off-watch", that is those without duties allotted to them by Quilley as watchdogs of the ship's watchkeeping personnel and the others imprisoned in number four tween-deck.

Alarmed by the effect of the rising storm on the ship's stability, panic had spread amongst them at the way the *Fort Harrison* had keeled over more and more to starboard as the night wore on. They had become convinced that the ship was doomed.

This placed them in a frightening dilemma. The alternative to staying on the seemingly stricken ship was to brave the angry sea in a thirty-foot lifeboat. They had argued amongst themselves. For some, taking to a small open boat represented far greater dangers than staying where they were. Then, the *Fort Harrison* would make one of its terrifying lurches to starboard until the ship seemed to be permanently lying sideways in the water. She would not swing back to the upright position, but would hang there, threatening to go further over still to a point at which she must surely capsize.

Agonising doubt would then eat at the men reluctant to risk their lives in an open boat. Legend of the unsinkable qualities of ships' lifeboats was what tipped the scales.

One man, as a result of a conversation on lifeboats which he'd had with a British sailor *en route* to Salerno, was their most eager advocate. He told how the buoyancy tanks of these small boats were packed with kapok so that, even when the tanks were holed in several places, the boats remained afloat like life-jackets. The boats were designed, he said, to ride and survive the worst Western Atlantic storms and were safer than ships one hundred times their size.

His listeners — fearstruck with each shuddering lurch of the *Fort Harrison* — came closer to his way of thinking.

Danovich was, if anything, in tune with the general idea that there was no future for any of them by remaining aboard the ship. But he had cautioned the men about the need for consultation with Quilley.

But the panic was by now too feverish for that. What Quilley thought or did not think about their intention to get off the ship was a matter of complete indifference to them.

Most of them had found themselves on disciplinary charges — and subsequently on the *Fort Harrison* — as a result of indifference to authority in matters where their own survival was at stake. They were not now, like leopards, about to change their spots and be governed by an authority which they had acknowledged briefly because it was expedient but which had no other claim on their allegiance.

The result was that when Quilley had arrived on the port boat-deck, primarily to make an assessment on the wisdom of abandoning ship, he was met by a situation which he had as much chance of arresting as stopping an Alpine avalanche once the snows had started moving.

Quilley had detoured by way of Pendlebury's former cabin. There, he had removed from the settee locker the haversacks containing his small fortune in US currency. He had previously re-united himself with his hoard soon after hearing from Pendlebury that it was safe. With a glow of well-being he had counted the money and neatly repacked it. Then he had replaced the haversacks in the locker to await the moment when he wanted to retrieve them.

That moment had come with the solidification in his mind of the idea that the *Fort Harrison* would have to be abandoned. There still lingered the thought that abandonment might not be necessary, but he accepted that it was now likely to be the lesser of the two evils from which he must choose. Thus, he prepared for it by attaching his two haversacks of money firmly about his body. Whatever happened, nothing would now separate him from his wealth.

The haversacks hung like hot-water bottles about him, warming him with feelings of power and confidence. They represented his ability to do anything in a greedy world. When all else had failed, money could achieve what brute force and guns could not. It could corrode the scruples of honest men like acid, buy the most chaste of women, open the most solidly barred doors.

But currency in a canvas bag was as useful as last year's newspapers on the boat-deck of the *Fort Harrison*. Before Quilley reached it, his "crew" of rogues and deserters had knocked away the clamps on the belly-bands which held the outswung boat secure against its boom. And they had started to lower the boat, halting it at deck level so that it could be boarded from the alleyway skirting the engineers' cabins.

Even a non-seaman like Quilley quickly realised that launching the boat was going to be impossible in the conditions. Because the ship was listing to starboard, vertical descent for the boat to the water was out of the question. All that would happen would be that the boat would ride down the side of the *Fort Harrison* and very probably tip over. Certainly if the side of the ship took the boat's weight at any point, the weight would go off the falls holding the boat, the blocks holding the boat would become unhooked, and the boat would fall into the sea.

Quilley screamed with rage as he tried to warn of the danger. Waving his forty-five and threatening to shoot if they didn't do as they were told, he ordered his erstwhile supporters away from the boat. Some ignored him. Cursing Quilley as volubly as he cursed them, they clambered into the boat, making sure that when it was finally lowered into the water their places would be secure.

The men holding the ropes to lower the boat had secured them temporarily with extra turns round the cleets of the squat mooring-pillars. They had the dismay and uncertainty on their faces of men who had made a bad decision. By taking on the task of lowering the boat, they had – it seemed to them – deprived themselves of booking a seat in it.

Pritchard was manning the after-fall with another man. To his surprise, his companion dropped the rope and ran to the edge of the boat-deck. Ignoring shouts from Quilley, he seized a lifeline which had snagged near the davit. He swung himself out between the davits as the snagged end cleared itself and he lowered himself into the boat.

His final jump into the boat was sufficient to cause the rope in Pritchard's hand to move and drag him nearer to the tethering cleet. The rope burned round the cleet until Pritchard threw on yet another turn to hold it.

It was at that precise moment that Mitchell, on the bridge, pressed the firing-button of the FAM.

Pritchard was aware of a rushing sound in his ears. It reached him almost simultaneously with a wall of fiery air. This invisible wall struck him with the speed of an express train, forcing him ahead of it and throwing him against the angled frames of the boat-deck gun-nest's pillars and folding him through them. His spine and both legs were broken with the first impact. His body hung, tangled for a moment among the metal supports, then as the ship came from the depths of its starboard roll to upright, the rag-doll which was Pritchard was catapulted in a slow arc out over the port side.

The fall which Pritchard had been holding had instantly dropped from his hand. Freed from the tension between the cleet and that exercised by Pritchard's weight, the rope shed two turns from the cleet and began to jump round the squat mooring-pillar.

The after end of the partially lowered lifeboat dropped only slightly more slowly than if the fall rope had been cut with an axe. It crashed with a splintering thud against the *Fort Harrison*'s exposed port hull.

The men in the lifeboat were pitched somersaulting over the stern sheets of the lifeboat into the sea. Oars and other equipment, which they had unlashed, followed them while, for the space of perhaps a minute, the boat hung by its forward davit only.

The two men holding the boat's forward-fall suffered a fate similar to Pritchard's, only there were no gun-nest supports to trammel their flight. Both men were hurled over the forward end of the boat-deck and fell twisted and broken against the coaming of the side bunker-hatches. The blast in itself did not injure them, but the force with which they hit the solid coaming of the bunker-hatch did. They were to survive – but never to walk again.

It took just under sixty seconds for the rope of the more securely tethered forward-fall to begin working its way round the cleets of its mooring-pillar. The single fall now held her entire weight of the upended boat.

As the dangling boat's stern crashed against the ship's

hull for the third time, the ship's side took the weight of the boat for a fraction of a second. This was long enough for the tension on the forward-fall to be relaxed in that flash of time. When the boat's weight re-asserted itself against the forward-fall, there was a slight jerk which began to work its way back through the block sheaves to the single rope bent round the cleets of the mooring-pillar. The tug was enough to start the manila jerking round the pillar, slowly at first, then running beyond control.

The boat fell from the remaining davit which held it, struck the ship's side and then, freed forever from its parent, arched over and splashed upside down into the sea.

The single catalyst to these events was Mitchell's firing of the button on the bridge. Current had flowed into the detonating-chamber which launched the FAM rocket from its steel stand on the boat-deck. It had started with a sudden hiss as twenty-eight pounds of explosive packed into the long snub head of the rocket had begun to force the air away from its tail-jet.

The hissing had intensified as the force of burning gases had thrust downwards in a searing wave, been turned laterally by the solid steel deck and finally achieved the powering force which lifted the rocket clear of its launcher and pillaring up into the night sky.

As the downward thrust of gases had built up and pushed air before them, the blast had followed the lines of least resistance. Encountering steel deck or superstructure of any substance, the rushing air was not great enough to go through them so it simply spread along their surfaces building above itself a cloud as it went and as the explosive build-up behind intensified and multiplied in force.

The timber chocks on which the lifeboat had rested demonstrated the strength of this rush of air. The bases of the chocks were welded to the deck in angle-irons and the timber bolted through these angle-irons. The blast passed over these bases, unable to move them. The top halves of the chocks, however, were fixed to the bases simply by metal hinges screwed into the timber. These hinges were nothing against the rushing force. The blast tore the top halves of the chocks away from their bases like paper caught in a wind and threw them far out to sea.

Similarly, anything with no firm support to the deck was borne away before the rushing air like pieces wiped from a chess board by a sweep of the arm.

Pritchard and the men on the forward-fall were swept away like rag-dolls. The mighty frame of Danovich was propelled far out over the top of the lifeboat like a ball of tumbleweed. Not a man on the boat-deck escaped the wall of air as it funnelled out from the base of the rocket.

Quilley was nearest to the rocket.

He was supporting himself against the roll of the ship by holding the handrails of a short ladder giving access from the boat-deck to the skylighted roof of the engine-room. His revolver, in his right hand, hampered the firmness of his hold on the rail with that hand. His left-hand grip on the rail was firm.

As the blast rushed at him, he had instinctively dropped the revolver and clung to the ladder-rails with all the strength he possessed. The breath seemed to be sucked from his body. A solid wall seemed to be pressing at every part of his anatomy, squashing him into the rungs of the ladder and against the raised platform of the engine-room's roof. Still he clung on.

The air tore at his clothing. The haversacks lifted, tearing to be free. His clothing shredded and whipped away. The stitching of the straps of the haversacks ripped itself out as if lanced by invisible razor-blades. The bags themselves flew off like missiles and thousands of dollar notes filled the air like confetti.

The rocket lifted from the launcher only a few feet away. Behind it, in whipping arcs of flashing steel, writhed the steel wire — six hundred feet of it — leaping at a speed of ten feet per second from its canister home. The wire cascaded from the canister in tangled arcs which widened before the soaring rocket's flight whipped them straight.

One spinning arc lashed across the ladder to which

Quilley hung, severing two of his fingers and his hold. He felt himself buffeted against the ladder. But now the source of that terrible blast had moved away.

He fell forward. His body sprawled momentarily close to the canister from which the wire was still snaking. A section looped out, throwing a half-hitch over Quilley's body. Still flying upwards, the wire tightened round him below the armpits. It cut through clothing and flesh. It encountered the bone of Quilley's rib-cage and gripped.

Quilley was jerked upwards by the rocket, plucked clear of the boat-deck like a marionette on a string. His boot struck the top of the launcher-stand with sufficient strength to slacken the welded frame of the base. Then he was clear above the engine-room skylight before the motive power of the rocket found itself unequal to the task of carrying the unscheduled cargo of one hundred and eighty pounds of man. Somewhere high above the *Fort Harrison* the wire broke.

Quilley's brief flight ended as quickly as it had begun. His snared body fell back to the ship some twenty or thirty feet distant from the point of take-off and on to a section of superstructure fifteen feet above the boat-deck. It was a miraculously soft landing, considering the hideous possibilities available.

Abaft the engine-room skylights – over which Quilley had hovered – was the housing of the POs' accommodation. The ship's four petty officers used the roof of their quarters as their own private lounge-deck. It was covered by a canvas awning. This roof-deck also housed two large cylindrical tanks – the fresh-water reservoirs for all the midships living accommodation.

The rocket had lifted Quilley a good height and distance away from the boat-deck but, at the moment his flight ended, his dangling heels were barely inches above the awning atop the POs' housing.

His body thudded down on to the awning, carrying part of it away but breaking his fall as gently as if he had been caught in a fireman's blanket. He slid gently from the broken awning, whose ties had remained secure on three sides, and slid from its fold on to the top of a fresh-water tank. From the top of the tank his body slithered to the deckhead of the POs' Mess.

Alternate waves of red and blackness seemed to come and go before Quilley's eyes. His brain told him he was alive but it seemed incapable of registering more than that. Precisely what had happened to him and what was the source of the tidal waves of pain washing over him with every heartbeat was lost somewhere in the ascending and descending curtains of black and red mist.

He found he could move his arms ... and his legs. But movement caused blood to bubble up into his mouth, choking him. He coughed. It enveloped his chest in a pinion of pain.

He forced the fingers of his good hand to search for and find the wire which circled his chest. It was grooved into him. He tried to unwind it away from him. Pain blanketed his mind. The curtain of blackness descended again.

When consciousness returned, it brought with it only one burning thought ... to get free from that wire. Quilley's fingers worked a turn of the wire holding him around a hand valve of the water tank. Securing it there, he rolled his body away. The effort brought more blood bubbling up from his lungs into his mouth ... but he was free. He cried out as his own weight unwound along the groove in his flesh and released him from the wiry stranglehold.

He lay on his chest, tears of pain streaming from his eyes. He felt the tug of death inviting him to surrender to its sweet oblivion, but he raged against it, clinging to the shredded strand of life still within reach.

A terrible fury made Quilley hang on. At the front of his tortured mind was the instinctive knowledge that, somehow, one man had caused the loss of his money and reduced him to this tenuous finger-hold on life. And that man was Andrew Mitchell.

Vivid in Quilley's darkness was the image of Mitchell's face thrust defiantly before him. Was it only yesterday?

He recalled striking the face with a hate that had its roots in fear. The eyes blazing in that face seemed to taunt Quilley now, and fan the flickering flame of his last mortal strength.

It was as if, from the very first, Quilley had glimpsed in Mitchell the face of his own executioner. Well, he wasn't finished yet. He would cling tenaciously to that fraying strand of life long enough to destroy the instrument of his own destruction. He would cheat death long enough to perform this one final act.

Fed by his hate, the spark of life left in Quilley glowed.

He knew he was dying. Every hissing breath that issued from him proclaimed the fact. He could identify in a sea of pain the place where rib had pierced the sighing bladder of lung.

But he was not going to die alone. All that mattered now was that he took his executioner with him.

Using the pipes from the fresh-water tank as support, he fought bayonets of pain and hauled himself to his feet. He clung to the tank, blind with the cost to his body and breath. He wavered close to unconsciousness, aware dimly of a movement on the boat-deck below him. He did not recognise Cordoba, his one remaining ally. Nor did Cordoba see him.

Cordoba had been in the deck alleyway beside the engineers' accommodation when the lifeboat had plunged from its davits. He had not panicked like his companions. Nor had it occurred to him that there had taken place in that moment a dramatic change in the balance of power aboard the ship.

What did occur to him was that some of the ship's crew had somehow shown fight. Cordoba had no intention of letting it go at that. Whatever had caused the loss of the lifeboat and the men in it, Cordoba was steelily determined that the ship's crew should not be allowed to use the catastrophe to regain control of the vessel.

Armed with the other of the two forty-fives, he had

shaken himself away from the men in the alleyway and gone forward. Beside the side bunker-hatch he had found the two severely injured men who had been manning the forward lifeboat fall. He could not understand how they had come to be injured although he did connect the fact of their injuries with the hissing explosion he had heard shortly before the lifeboat fell.

He had reasoned that the answer lay on the boat-deck. Abandoning the wounded men, he had mounted the ladder. But there was nothing and no one on the boat-deck. He was alerted by a single shot.

It had seemed to come from the direction of the hold where the ship's crew were being held. Even nearer. He moved silently aft along the deserted and devastated boat-deck, stopping when he heard voices from beyond and below.

Then he heard a burst of fire, most certainly from the Lewis gun. From a vantage position he had watched Colman retrieve a rifle from the deck and toss it to a crew-man. Colman – whom Cordoba recognised immediately as one of O'Keefe's guards – had the Lewis gun.

Cordoba decided that this was a state of affairs which he must reverse. Whoever had the Lewis gun had the most effective means of controlling the ship.

Unaware of how close he was passing to the injured Quilley, Cordoba climbed stealthily through the framework of gun-nest supports outside the POs' Mess at the after end of the boat-deck. There was only one way to get the Lewis gun – and that was to kill the man who had it. He aimed the forty-five until it was pointing down at Colman's unsuspecting face. Cordoba wondered why people seldom noticed danger from above them.

They would look right, left and centre in anticipation of danger – but they hardly ever looked upwards.

Cordoba began to tighten the pressure on the trigger. That was the instant in which the bullet fired by Jim Roberts hit him. It was perhaps ironic that if Cordoba had looked aft and upwards towards the pillarbox platform high above the poop, he would have seen his executioner's silhouette clearly against the night sky.

* * *

The taste of victory was sweet in Andrew Mitchell's mouth when he emerged from the wheelhouse to see the devastating results of firing the FAM rocket. He did not immediately leave the bridge. He was in no doubt that at least half of Quilley's men were out of action but that left a sizeable strength still to be accounted for. He had no way of knowing what was happening on the afterdeck.

The sound of shooting – there was the unmistakable chatter of the Lewis gun – turned his blood to ice. His first thought was that it had been used against Roberts on the poop or that it had been turned on the men who were still prisoner in number four hold. Then Roberts rang the bridge to tell Mitchell of the breakout from the hold.

Conscious of the need to hold the bridge at all costs, Mitchell posted Walsh on one ladder with a carbine and the Carpenter, similarly armed, on the other. He, himself, would investigate what was happening below without arms. He made his way towards the deck.

He was making his way aft, taking advantage of every shadow, when a group of Quilley's men emerged from the alleyway beneath the boat-deck, their hands held high. Behind them, covering them with the Lewis gun, came Colman and Henderson, the AB, with a carbine.

Mitchell stepped from the cover of the timber-built ablutions hut which had been erected in the deck space forward of the side bunker-hatch – and came close to being blasted by the Lewis. Colman stopped himself from firing just in time.

"Real sorry about that," he apologised. "Ah thought ah'd flushed another o' them skunks. They said some of their friends ran up thisways."

Colman regaled Mitchell with details of the breakout

from the hold. He was appalled at the folly of it and yet elated by the desperate courage shown by O'Keefe's men and the imprisoned crew.

All fight had gone from the renegades. Several, having seen or heard what had happened to the lifeboat, had taken refuge in the ship's saloon. They surrendered meekly.

Mitchell's first thought – when it was apparent that the battle for the ship was over – was for the wounded. He instructed the Chief Steward to organise the saloon as a temporary hospital. He found Colin Durham administering first-aid to the severely wounded O'Keefe.

"What happened to the German prisoners?" Mitchell asked Durham.

"I've no idea," said the Third Officer. "They were down number four with the rest of us. I suppose they must still be there."

They were not in the hold. They were on deck, standing in a group near the mast-house. As Mitchell approached, Willi Klemper moved out of the group and came to meet him.

"I am pleased to see you are still alive, Herr Second Officer."

Mitchell studied the sardonic smile on the other's face, not quite sure if Klemper was being sincere or sarcastic.

"I am equally pleased to see that you and your compatriots are all in one piece," said Mitchell.

"We have been having a debate. We were left unguarded. The suggestion was made that while our enemies fought amongst themselves, the opportunity might occur to take advantage of the situation ... Perhaps even take control of the ship and sail it to Sardinia."

"What decision did you reach?"

"Most were in favour of the Swiss decision."

"Swiss decision? I don't understand."

"To remain rigidly neutral ... And do nothing. Of course, I reminded them that as German officers it was our duty to try to escape."

"Did you now?" said Mitchell. "And they agreed?"

"Yes. They also agreed that it must be done without dishonour ... Without unnecessary loss of life."

Mitchell's eyes glinted.

"Without German loss of life?"

Klemper stiffened.

"Without loss of life to your crew," he said. "You and your crew are civilians, are you not? You are not trained to kill like military people – only to defend yourselves and your ships. Our political masters might say that our drawing of this distinction contained an element of treason – that you are all enemies of the Reich. But then our political masters are not in our situation ... And political actions are not always governed by what is honourable and what is dishonourable. We were prepared to have ... how do you say? ... a gentleman's agreement? To help you fight the murderers."

"Is that true?"

Their eyes met.

"Do you need to ask?" said Klemper.

"No," said Mitchell. "You're like me, Willi Klemper – an old-fashioned son of the sea, an honest sailorman who doesn't know how to lie. I believe you."

"Blood has been shed," said Willi Klemper, "perhaps for us. We are convinced that there would have been no mercy for us from the traitor soldier." He shrugged. "You and your men fought to save your ship, I know. But you will have no trouble from us while there is storm at sea. We are in same ship and it is, in sailor words ... All hands to the pumps, eh?"

Mitchell smiled.

"Why did you come up on deck?"

"To smell the air again, not to make trouble. And we were ... we *are* ... ready to help you. If you reject our help and lock us up again, we shall understand. That will free us from any obligation to you to be good boys."

Mitchell made an instinctive decision.

"There are several badly injured men who will need care night and day until we reach port. One of them is the

American Sergeant who led the escape from the hold. I am prepared to let you and your men have freedom of the deck if they will give their word as officers to make no attempt to escape or overthrow the security of the ship. There is only one condition – that you and your men become responsible for the care of the wounded until we reach port."

Klemper spoke to the Germans and returned to Mitchell.

"We agree to your terms, Herr Second Officer. We are at your service. But only until we reach port."

"Good," said Mitchell. "I'll pass the word to our people and get somebody to take you to the saloon. We're using it as a dressing-station."

Mitchell sought out Durham, returned briefly to the bridge with him, but stayed only long enough to get the ship under way again and restore normal watchkeeping procedures.

He went below to the saloon to find that the German prisoners were already helping the Chief Steward with the casualties.

Five of Quilley's men had been injured. There were the two who had been blown off the boat-deck by the back blast from the rocket. Two more had been wounded by Colman's blast from the Lewis gun. Still unconscious with a possible skull fracture was the man who had been manning the Lewis gun when O'Keefe had led the breakout from the hold.

Then, of course, there was O'Keefe. Mitchell ordered his removal to the relative comfort of the ship's hospital. The hole in his thigh had been cleaned, plugged and dressed and he had been given a morphia injection by the Chief Steward. No more could be done for him meantime.

Mitchell cursed the limitations of his scanty medical training when he surveyed the five injured men in the saloon. They had between them a variety of wounds so numerous and complex that he scarcely knew where to begin.

The suspected skull fracture was the easiest. His wound

was bound and he was lain flat to sleep. The Chief Steward attended to him. Then he departed to the galley to boil up a tray of knives and other instruments which, Mitchell decided reluctantly, would be needed to patch up the other four casualties.

Assisted by Willi Klemper, Mitchell started by giving the four men shots of morphia. Then, using Klemper as interpreter, he instructed the German prisoners to prepare each of the men for treatment by undressing them as far as was possible and seeing that the field dressings which had been used to contain bleeding were held firmly in place.

The main saloon table was to be used as the treatment table. Mitchell mentally rejected the term "operating table". He was hollow-eyed with fatigue and strain and he prayed like Christ before the cross for the cup to be taken away from him.

But it was his duty, and no other's, to drink the unpleasant cup to the dregs.

He signalled that the first man be put up on the table. The man had a hideous abdominal wound. Mitchell peered under the field dressing and felt nausea rise inside him. He turned away.

"I'll have to wash my hands," he mumbled to Klemper.

The German flashed him a look of compassion.

"Of course."

Mitchell stumbled across the passage to the pantry. He splashed cold water over his face, then scrubbed his hands.

He was returning to the saloon when the Chief Steward came into the passage with a steaming tray of instruments.

"They've found the one called Quilley," said the Steward. "He's still alive. They're bringing him here."

"I was told he went over the side with the lifeboat," said Mitchell. "Where was he?"

"I dunno — on top of the Chippy's cabin, I think."

Mitchell strode into the saloon. The Steward followed him, placing the tray down at the end of the long table on which the wounded man lay.

Klemper gave him a nod of encouragement.

"You are ready?"

"Yes."

At that moment Quilley, carried by Colman and one of O'Keefe's GIs, was supported into the room.

His mouth and lips were flecked with blood, his eyes wild and staring. They focused on Mitchell.

He shook off Colman and the other man.

"I can stand on my own feet. Leave me alone!"

"It's your funeral," said Colman.

The effort of speaking brought another foam of blood and spittle from Quilley's mouth. He stood there, his breath coming in great hissing gasps. His eyes never left Mitchell's face.

"It was you, wasn't it? That rocket ... It was you?"

"On the boat-deck? Yes, I fired the rocket, Quilley."

"I knew it! I knew you were the bastard that did for me!"

"It's all over now, Quilley," said Mitchell without emotion. "All over. Look, you're hurt ... You're going to need attention ..."

Quilley coughed and staggered.

"I'm dying, Mr Second Officer Mitchell," he grated out. "There ain't nothing that you or anybody else can do for me now."

He stood swaying.

"There's just one thing ... You're gonna die, too."

His hand flew to the tray of instruments. When it rose, it was gripping a narrow-handled knife with a five-inch blade – a replacement from the galley for the scalpels which the Chief Steward had been unable to find in the ship's hospital. Spewing blood from mouth and nostrils, Quilley lunged at Mitchell.

Mitchell never moved. He stood rooted to the spot, seemingly mesmerised by the flash of steel above his head. It was Willi Klemper who moved.

With arm upflung, he threw himself bodily in front of Mitchell. The knife sliced into Klemper's shoulder but he seized and held Quilley's wrist. Using all his strength, he turned the wrist. Suddenly Quilley sagged. The instant that he ceased to struggle, all Klemper's weight thrust forward and the knife plunged to the hilt into Quilley's stomach.

Quilley slumped to the deck and lay there, eyes staring. Klemper stood back. His face was ashen and he was trembling.

"I never killed a man before," he said softly. He put a hand to his shoulder, then withdrew it and looked in surprise at the blood staining his fingers.

Mitchell emerged from his bewildered trance in time to support Klemper as he staggered.

"You could have got yourself killed," he whispered, but there was concern in his voice, not reproach. He lowered Willi Klemper to a sitting position.

"You saved my life," he said softly. "Thanks, Willi."

"You would have done the same for me," said the German. And passed out.

20

Landfall

THE *Fort Harrison* limped through the Straits of Messina at first light. More than forty-eight hours had passed since Quilley's death. Mitchell had not slept throughout that time. He had been wholly occupied restoring the routine of the ship, moving from one to the next of the hundred and one responsibilities which seemed to have been thrust upon his shoulders. He was aware, however, of a massive reaction striking at his physical and mental strength.

He felt like an Olympic marathon runner who had gone off course and who then, after pounding an additional ten miles, had rediscovered the point of departure from his original route. Physically spent and emotionally sapped, he now kept his legs going in rubbery movements, no longer interested in winning but kept mobile by some inner force which demanded that he must finish the course.

From some source, he found the strength to be surgeon to the wounded, organiser, watchkeeper and navigator. He had worked out a course to take the ship through the Lipari Islands to the west of Stromboli and south-east to Messina.

For part of a day and most of a night, the beacon of Stromboli had been in sight. Wreathed in smoke by daylight, flaming like a giant torch after dark, the 3,000-feet-high volcano had finally faded from sight in the dawn of a new day. And the new day had brought them into sight of a higher and equally angry volcano. A frown of smoke had wreathed the brow of Etna, hiding its summit, as the *Fort Harrison* had limped through placid water towards the neck of sea which ran between the Sicilian and Calabrian shores.

The second dawn had seen the crippled ship through the Straits. A sleek corvette with a bow like a racing yacht came

283

with a bone in her teeth to meet the merchantman.

Mitchell and Durham were both on the bridge. Mitchell had decided to put into Augusta and had set a course direct from the Straits. With luck they would be in port by evening.

Durham studied the newcomer through glasses.

"She has a lovely line," he said. "Don't recognise the class though. What do you make of her?"

Mitchell took the glasses and raised them to his eyes, which were puffed and reddened with strain and lack of sleep.

He focused the glasses with difficulty.

"French," he said. "She's flying the tricolour. No ... wait. That's the bloody Italian flag!"

It gave him an uncomfortable feeling to see an enemy warship steaming towards him like that. Then he remembered that Italy was no longer at war with the Allies.

"Wasn't there something on the news about the Italian navy being instructed to surrender?" he asked Durham.

"Yes, but she's obviously come out from Catania or somewhere. You don't think she's going to surrender to us?"

Mitchell laughed weakly.

"That would be a bloody joke. No, I don't think that's what she wants. Hey, she's flashing. Where's the Aldis?"

Durham ran into the wheelhouse for the Aldis lamp. He acknowledged the warship's call signals. As the light flashed from the bridge of the Italian corvette, he called out each word. Mitchell, with signal pad and pencil, read the Morse, too, and wrote down the message.

"ARE YOU FORT HARRISON?"

"Signal yes," said Mitchell, and Durham began to waggle the trigger of his lamp.

The second message from the warship read:

"YOU ARE OVERDUE. SENIOR NAVAL OFFICER AUGUSTA EXPECTED YOU IN THIS AREA THIRTY-SIX HOURS AGO. HAVE BEEN ORDERED ESCORT YOU TO AUGUSTA. WHAT SPEED CAN YOU MAKE?"

"I'll dictate if you send," said Mitchell to Durham. "Tell him: 'Sorry we were delayed. Can only make four knots.'

284

Oh, and add: 'Have you British naval officers on board?'"

The reply came:

"COMMANDER PIETRO SENNA SENDS COMPLIMENTS. THIS VESSEL IS MANNED BY ITALIAN NAVAL PERSONNEL ONLY. DO NOT BE ALARMED. WE ARE ON YOUR SIDE. WE ARE PART OF ESCORT FLOTILLA ZEBRA NOW ATTACHED 'H' FORCE, ROYAL NAVY, AUGUSTA."

"What's the Italian for welcome?" said Mitchell.

"Ben venuto, I think," said Durham.

"Send it then," said Mitchell.

Durham flashed the words. The Italian warship immediately replied.

"What was that?" asked Mitchell. "I'm still trying to work out the first word. I didn't write it down."

"Felicitations and thanks," said Durham. "But he didn't spell felicitations right."

"I can't even say it," said Mitchell.

The corvette circled the *Fort Harrison* and then took up station ahead of it.

"Looks like our former enemy is going to walk us home," said Durham.

"Funny thing, war." mused Mitchell. "A couple of weeks ago she would have blown us out of the water. Now she's our very own guardian angel. A couple of days ago we were prisoners in our own ship being kicked around by people who spoke our language and were supposed to be our greatest friends."

"Don't say that to Sergeant O'Keefe," said Durham. "He wouldn't care to be lumped in with Quilley and his goons just because they happened to be Yanks."

"Oh, I wouldn't offend O'Keefe. You know what I mean. It's the irony of the whole bloody mess of war that makes an obscene joke of it. The Americans have guys you would give your life for ... Like O'Keefe and that Colman and Jim Holcroft who was killed at Salerno ... and that captain with the dried-up face, Diamond. And thousands of others just like them. But no side has a monopoly of the good guys or the bad guys. You get them in every kind of uniform and out of it, too. It just happens to be an accident, or something

285

like an accident, on who is running the show on any side at any one time ... whether there are more good guys making the decisions or more bad guys.

"Quilley was American but he probably would have made a bloody good Nazi. That E-boat commander, Klemper, was fighting for the Nazis because he was born German, but I'd take him for a shipmate any day of the week before I'd ship out with somebody like the late-lamented Pendlebury."

He paused and stared at the horizon. God, he was tired. He had never felt a weariness like this.

"You should get some sleep," said Durham gently.

Mitchell smiled.

"I'll sleep tonight, Colin. When we're safely in port."

"Your trouble is that you think about things too much. You analyse them and try to take them apart. You do the same with people, always wondering what makes them tick."

"What you're saying is that I take a bit of trouble to try to understand people. Well, what's wrong with that? We're all born with an intelligence that makes us ask questions, makes us search for answers. We hope to find some of the answers to give meaning to our lives ... and our deaths. We can't just fill in time mindlessly between the day we're born and the day we die." He grinned at the younger man. "You're gaping at me, Colin. I was running off at the mouth like the oracle of the mountain – and you should have seen your face. You should have reminded me of the first rule of Mitchell's Law."

"And what the hell is that?"

"Take life seriously, but never the sounds that come from your own mouth."

Durham smiled.

"I'll remember that and use it in evidence against you."

"If I forget it," said Mitchell, "please do. In the meantime, it's your turn to push the cigarettes. There are times, Colin, when that memory of yours isn't worth a damn."

The smell of frying bacon was coming from the galley when Mitchell came down from the bridge. It played around his nostrils, tantalising him. I must be alive and well, he thought ... I'm hungry.

*   *   *

About a hundred ¬iles north and west from the *Fort Harrison*'s position   lone seagull wheeled in the sky above the Tyrrhenian Sea. It dived towards a small patch of flotsam. The water was covered with small green pulpy rectangles, some of which were adhering to each other in bundles. The seagull raised a splash of spray as its beak cleaved the water and scooped a bundle of disintegrating pulp from the sea. The seabird soared upwards, swallowing into its gullet the saturated tasteless remains of a hundred American dollars in ten-dollar bills.

Bestselling Thriller/Suspense

☐ Hell is Always Today	Jack Higgins	£2.50
☐ Brought in Dead	Harry Patterson	£1.99
☐ Russian Spring	Dennis Jones	£2.50
☐ Fletch	Gregory Mcdonald	£1.95
☐ Black Ice	Colin Dunne	£2.50
☐ Blind Run	Brian Freemantle	£2.50
☐ The Proteus Operation	James P. Hogan	£3.50
☐ Miami One Way	Mike Winters	£2.50
☐ Skydancer	Geoffrey Archer	£2.50
☐ Hour of the Lily	John Kruse	£3.50
☐ The Tunnel	Stanley Johnson	£2.50
☐ The Albatross Run	Douglas Scott	£2.50
☐ Dragonfire	Andrew Kaplan	£2.99

Prices and other details are liable to change

ARROW BOOKS, BOOKSERVICE BY POST, PO BOX 29, DOUGLAS, ISLE OF MAN, BRITISH ISLES

NAME..

ADDRESS..

....

....

Please enclose a cheque or postal order made out to Arrow Books Ltd. for the amount due and allow the following for postage and packing.

U.K. CUSTOMERS: Please allow 22p per book to a maximum of £3.00.

B.F.P.O. & EIRE: Please allow 22p per book to a maximum of £3.00

OVERSEAS CUSTOMERS: Please allow 22p per book.

Whilst every effort is made to keep prices low it is sometimes necessary to increase cover prices at short notice. Arrow Books reserve the right to show new retail prices on covers which may differ from those previously advertised in the text or elsewhere.

Bestselling War Fiction and Non-Fiction

☐ Passage to Mutiny	Alexander Kent	£2.95
☐ Colours Aloft	Alexander Kent	£2.95
☐ Winged Escort	Douglas Reeman	£2.95
☐ Army of Shadows	John Harris	£2.50
☐ Decoy	Dudley Pope	£2.95
☐ Gestapo	Rupert Butler	£4.50
☐ Johnny Gurkha	E.D. Smith	£2.95
☐ Typhoon Pilot	Desmond Scott	£2.95
☐ The Rommel Papers	B.H. Liddel Hart	£5.95
☐ Hour of the Lily	John Kruse	£3.50
☐ Duel in the Dark	Peter Townsend	£3.95
☐ The Spoils of War	Douglas Scott	£2.99
☐ The Wild Blue	Walter J. Boyne & Steven L. Thompson	£3.95
☐ The Bombers	Norman Longmate	£4.99

Prices and other details are liable to change

ARROW BOOKS, BOOKSERVICE BY POST, PO BOX 29, DOUGLAS, ISLE OF MAN, BRITISH ISLES

NAME. . . . .

ADDRESS. . . . .

. . . .

. . . .

Please enclose a cheque or postal order made out to Arrow Books Ltd. for the amount due and allow the following for postage and packing.

U.K. CUSTOMERS: Please allow 22p per book to a maximum of £3.00.

B.F.P.O. & EIRE: Please allow 22p per book to a maximum of £3.00

OVERSEAS CUSTOMERS: Please allow 22p per book.

Whilst every effort is made to keep prices low it is sometimes necessary to increase cover prices at short notice. Arrow Books reserve the right to show new retail prices on covers which may differ from those previously advertised in the text or elsewhere.